ROMANTIC TIMES PRAISES CONNIE MASON, WINNER OF THE STORYTELLER OF THE YEAR AWARD!

LION'S BRIDE

"This wondrous tale is a must-read for the medieval fan and Ms. Mason's legion of fans!"

SIERRA

"Ms. Mason has written a definite winner!"

WIND RIDER

"A delightful, action-packed love story!"

TEARS LIKE RAIN

"Vivid...strongly written!"

TREASURES OF THE HEART

"Connie Mason adds sizzling sensuality and a cast of unique characters to turn *Treasures Of The Heart* into another winner."

A PROMISE OF THUNDER

"Once you pick up *A Promise of Thunder* you won't want to put it down."

ICE & RAPTURE

"*Ice & Rapture* is filled with one rip-roaring escapade following on the heels of another wild adventure.... A delightful love story!"

BRAVE LAND, BRAVE LOVE

"*Brave Land, Brave Love* is an utter delight from first page to last—funny, tender, adventurous, and highly romantic!"

GENTLE PERSUASION

"I'm not going to hurt you," Jack said, sensing her fear. "This isn't new to you; you've been loved before."

"No...I..." What could Moira say? That she'd lied to him from the moment she awakened in his bed? It was long past the time for confessions.

The moment for truth had passed as Jack lowered his head and kissed her eyelids, feathering them gently. His mouth moved down to brush her lips, nibbling lightly, delicately, stroking his tongue against the seam before urging them open so he could taste more fully of her sweetness. When her tongue touched his, his body tightened painfully, less willing to accept being patient than his mind.

Connie Mason

Pure Temptation

LEISURE BOOKS **NEW YORK CITY**

A LEISURE BOOK®

July 1996

Published by

Dorchester Publishing Co., Inc.
276 Fifth Avenue
New York, NY 10001

Printed in the United States of America.

Chapter One

London, 1795

Ghosts were so bloody unpredictable.

During his youthful years, Jackson Graystoke had searched every nook and cranny of the crumbling stone mansion that he had inherited, looking for Lady Amelia's ghost, and he came up empty-handed. When he was a stripling he would have given his eyeteeth for a glimpse of the elusive lady who occasionally haunted the halls of Graystoke Manor. But certainly not now, not when he no longer believed that ghosts existed.

During the two hundred-odd years following the death of Lady Amelia, who according to legend appeared only to those male Graystokes who walked the path to perdition, she had appeared infrequently, since few of her upstanding descendants throughout the years were debauched enough to need her help.

Until Black Jack Graystoke. The black sheep of the Graystoke family, a man dedicated to dissipation.

Rogue, bounder, rapscallion, rake, seducer of women. Men liked him, women loved him. And Lady Amelia, who hovered over his bed like an avenging angel, glared down upon him with obvious displeasure.

"Go away," Jack said irritably. He had just gotten to bed after a night at the gaming tables and had no time for an apparition who could or could not be a figment of his imagination. He knew he'd had too much to drink, but didn't think he was *that* foxed.

Clothed in shimmering light and flowing garments, the ghost shook her head.

"What in the devil do you want?"

Lady Amelia merely stared at him through hollow eyes.

"Why now? Why have you chosen this time to appear when there was a day I would have welcomed a glimpse of you?" Jack was familiar with the legend of the family ghost, having heard it many, many times. "I'm too steeped in sin; nothing you can do will save me from perdition."

Lady Amelia floated away, toward the door. Jack raised up on his elbow and saw that she was motioning to him. He groaned in dismay and fell back against the pillow, squeezing his eyes shut. When he opened them, Lady Amelia was still there.

"Where am I to go? 'Tis raining out, for God's sake!" The windows rattled, confirming his words. Unfortunately, the rain had turned to pelting sleet, driven against the house by ice-laden wind. "Can't it wait till morning?"

Lady Amelia wrung her hands and appeared agitated. Obviously she wasn't going to go away. She shook her head and pointed toward the door again, even more determined that Jack should rouse himself and plunge into the blustery night.

"Bloody hell, is there no compromise?" Lady Amelia shook her head. "Very well, my lady, you win. Take me where you will—I can see there is no sleep for me this night."

The light surrounding Lady Amelia flickered as if in agreement, then, before Jack's very eyes, the apparition evaporated through the closed door. Muttering an oath, Jack flung aside the covers and threw on his recently discarded clothes, taking particular care with his neck cloth. He never appeared anywhere less than impeccably attired.

Still grumbling, Jack strode from the room, not surprised when he saw Lady Amelia waiting for him at the head of the stairs.

"Where in bloody hell am I supposed to go?" His handsome features, which women loved to distraction, bore a decidedly annoyed look.

Lady Amelia merely bowed her head and crooked her finger. He followed her floating figure down the stairs. She led him to the front door.

He hesitated. "Do you realize what it's like out there? 'Tisn't fit for man or beast. Do you expect me to awaken my coachman on a night such as this?" Lady Amelia merely stared at him, as if to suggest he lacked a sense of adventure. Jack spit out an oath. "Oh, what the hell! I'll drive the carriage myself, if it will make you happy. All I ask is that you give me some idea where I am to go."

Lady Amelia seemed disinclined to offer further information as she backed away from the door. Her shimmering light dimmed, then went out.

"Wait! Don't go! You haven't told me . . ." It was too late. Lady Amelia had already disappeared in a wisp of smoke.

Thunderstruck, Jack stared at the empty space where Lady Amelia had stood just moments before. Had he imagined it all? Was Lady Amelia a figment of his rather fertile imagination? Perhaps, he thought ruefully, he was more foxed than he thought. He paused with his hand on the doorknob. What to do? If he were smart, he'd go back to bed and treat this as a bad dream. Or he could accept the challenge and brave the inclement weather.

Black Jack Graystoke had yet to turn down a challenge. Ghost or dream, he was already awake and dressed. If nothing else, he could go to White's Club and drink with his friends, some of whom would likely be out and about despite the weather. He wouldn't have returned home so early himself if he hadn't had the world's worst luck at cards tonight.

Needles of icy sleet blasted him as he opened the door and stepped outside. Bowing his head against the howling wind, Jack walked briskly to the carriage house and harnessed the handsome pair of grays he'd won in a card game to the shabby carriage, his only conveyance. Nearly everything Jack owned had been either won or lost at cards. His family, impoverished relatives of the young Earl of Ailesbury on his mother's side, had left him nothing but an inherited baronetcy, a pile of debts and a crumbling mansion located in the heart of London's Hanover Square that had been in the family for over two hundred years. The mansion demanded so much of his resources that just the upkeep emptied his pockets.

Marriage to an heiress was Jack's only recourse, and he was seriously thinking about ending his bachelorhood soon by marrying Lady Victoria Greene, a wealthy widow he'd been dallying with. A love match was out of the question. Everyone knew Black Jack Graystoke was too much of a rogue to offer undying love to any one woman.

Jack struck a light to the side lamps of the carriage, leaped up onto the box, took up the ribbons and guided the reluctant grays out of the gate. The sleet struck him forcefully, and he buried his face in his collar, cursing Lady Amelia for his misery. He hadn't the foggiest idea why the ghost had sent him abroad on a night such as this, and he longed for a bracing brandy or something equally fortifying. Until he learned Lady Amelia's intention, he might as well make the best of it. Jack drove through deserted, windswept streets to White's Club and parked at the curb.

The warmth inside the club was inviting as Jack relinquished his cape to the doorman and strode into the brightly lit room. He was immediately greeted by his good friend, Lord Spencer Fenwick, heir to a dukedom.

"Jack, you old dog, I thought you'd gone home hours ago. What brings you out again in such foul weather? Do you anticipate a change of luck? Shall we find room at one of the gaming tables?"

"If my luck has changed, it's for the worse," Jack complained, thinking of Lady Amelia's unexpected haunting. "I'm in desperate need of a drink, Spence, old chap," he said, placing an arm around his friend's padded shoulders.

On the way to the refreshment room, Jack found himself surrounded by simpering females, all eager for his attention. A tall man, muscular and lithe as a stalking tiger, Black Jack was pure temptation to women of all ages. Wavy dark hair surrounding a bold masculine face, and full tempting lips gave hint to his sensual nature, but it was his wicked gray eyes that captured the ladies' fancy. Once Black Jack aimed his potent gaze at a woman, she was lost. The problem was that Jack saw no reason to focus those incredibly sexy eyes on any one woman.

"Drink up, Jack," Spence urged when they finally had drinks in hand. Jack needed no inducement to drown the memory of Lady Amelia in strong liquor. He must have been mad to have conjured up the family ghost he had all but forgotten years ago.

Hours later, both Spence and Jack were deep into their cups, nearly staggering, in fact. Spence had the rare good sense to suggest they call it a night, and Jack agreed. Nothing good could come of this night, Jack decided, still annoyed at Lady Amelia for sending him out in such miserable weather. Whatever did she have in mind for him? Probably mischief, he thought glumly, as if he needed any more mischief in his life. He was more than capable of dredging up enough of that on his own.

"Wise of you to bring the carriage," Spence drawled as he reeled from the club on rubbery legs and spied Jack's team and carriage standing at the curb. "I walked, myself. How about a lift? Bloody raw night to be afoot."

None too steady himself, Jack wove an erratic path to the carriage. "Climb aboard, old chap. Glad to give you a lift."

"Damned if I ain't tempted to walk," Spence grumbled when he noted Jack's unsteady gait.

"Drunk or sober, I can handle a carriage and team as well or better than any man alive," Jack boasted as he picked up the ribbons.

Spence had barely settled beside his companion when Jack slapped the reins against the horses' rumps and the carriage rattled off down the icy road with a jolt that shook Spence to the core.

"Bloody hell, Jack, are you trying to kill us?"

Jack laughed uproariously, until a barrage of icy pellets brought a measure of sobriety, making him realize that his recklessness could endanger not only himself but his good friend. He struggled to control the unruly grays now that they had their head, and he'd nearly succeeded when he felt a jolt.

"My God, what's that? Stop, Jack, we hit something!" Hanging on for dear life, Spence peered over the side into the dark street while Jack fought the prancing grays. With great effort, he brought the carriage to a screeching halt.

Jack's sodden brain had registered the small bump but had thought nothing of it until Spence had cried out a warning. Had he hit something? Or someone? God forbid! Leaping down from the box, he felt sober as a judge as he frantically searched the rain-slicked street for a . . . body? He certainly hoped not.

The night was so dark and the carriage lamps so dim that Jack stumbled over the woman before he saw her. "Bloody hell!"

"What is it?" Spence called from his perch on the box. "Did you find something?"

"Not something, someone," Jack said, dropping to his knees to examine the body. Searching frantically for injuries, his hands encountered two gently rounded mounds of woman's flesh. He inhaled sharply and removed his hands as if burned. "God's nightgown, a woman!"

Spence appeared at his elbow, staring in horror at the body lying in the gutter. "Is she dead?"

Jack's hands returned to the woman's chest. The faint but steady cadence of her heart told him she still lived. "She's alive, thank God."

"What do you suppose she's doing out on a night like this?" Spence wondered aloud.

"Plying her trade," Jack opined. "Only a whore would be out this late. What in the hell are we going to do with her?"

"We could leave her," Spence offered lamely.

"Not bloody likely," Jack responded, manfully accepting responsibility for the accident and any injuries the woman sustained.

"What do you suggest?"

"You could take her to Fenwick Hall, Spence, and see that her injuries are treated," Jack offered hopefully.

"Are you mad? My parents would skin me alive if I brought a whore into their home. I'm in line to inherit, for God's sake!"

"Thank God I am no one of importance," Jack drawled with studied indifference.

Spence flushed, glad for the darkness that hid his stained cheeks. "I didn't mean that, old boy. But you aren't anyone's heir. You have no parents to tell you what to do. You don't give a fig about propriety. You're a free agent, Jack. You're the notorious Black Jack. Bringing a whore into your home would cause no raised eyebrows and only moderate scandal."

"Rightly so," Jack said with a hint of irritation. His reputation was already black—what was one more mark against him? "Damn you, Lady Amelia," he muttered beneath his breath. "If this is your idea of a joke, I don't appreciate your humor."

Spence looked at him curiously. "Who is Lady Amelia?"

"What? Oh, I didn't realize I'd spoken aloud. Lady Amelia is the family ghost. I think I've mentioned her on occasion."

"What has she to do with this?" Spence asked curiously.

Just then the woman groaned and began to shiver uncontrollably, bringing the men's attention back to her.

"We'd best get her off this icy street," Jack said, regaining his sense of chivalry. He'd never made a woman suffer in his life, no matter what her calling. "Help me lift her into the carriage. Careful," Jack chided when Spence staggered sideways. "Never mind, I'll do it myself." He pushed Spence aside and lifted the woman carefully, surprised that she weighed so little. In his arms, cradled against the broad expanse of his muscular chest, she seemed little more than a fragile child.

"Get inside," Jack ordered as he placed the injured woman in the carriage and stepped aside so Spence could enter. "Try to keep her comfortable until we reach Graystoke Manor."

Jack drove with more care than was his normal custom. His irresponsible behavior weighed heavily upon him. He'd often been criticized for his reckless ways, but somehow this incident emphasized his impulsive rush toward perdition. Not even Lady Amelia could save him from the course his life was taking.

The carriage entered the gates of Graystoke Manor just as a gray dawn lifted the night sky. The driving sleet had turned into gentle rain, and mauve streaks coloring the horizon gave hint of better weather in the coming days. The moment the carriage clattered to a halt, Jack leaped from the box and flung open the door.

"How is the woman?"

"Still unconscious."

"I'll carry her inside while you go for the doctor. I hope you have coin on you; I'm temporarily out of funds.

If not, I'll figure out something. I don't care what it takes, just get the doctor here.''

Jack took the woman into his arms and banged on the front door with his foot. In due time, a gaunt, sleepy-eyed servant wearing a hastily tied robe answered. He seemed not at all alarmed to see his employer return home at dawn carrying an unconscious woman.

''Bring hot water and towels to my chamber, Pettibone,'' Jack ordered crisply. ''There's been an unfortunate accident. Lord Fenwick has gone for the doctor.''

''Right away, sir.'' Pettibone shuffled off, the hem of his robe trailing the ground.

Once in his chamber, Jack carefully placed the woman in the center of his bed, then stood back to take his first good look at her. He was more than a little disturbed to see that she was young and not the slattern he expected. Her patrician features and dainty body belied her profession. Had she newly taken up whoring? he wondered as his gaze roved over her petite form. Jack was no stranger to women of all kinds, and he thought he knew everything about them there was to know, but this woman—no, not woman, for she was no more than a girl—defied definition.

A mop of glorious dark red hair covered her shapely head and fell in a tangled mass about her narrow shoulders. Her features were finely wrought, and he was surprised to find himself contemplating the color of her eyes. Beneath her wet clothing, her body appeared slim and shapely. Though her face was bruised and swollen, which was his fault, he suspected, she was lovelier than he would have guessed at first glance.

''I suppose I'd best rid you of these soaking clothes,''

Jack said to the unconscious figure as he lifted her slightly and removed her wet cloak.

The dress beneath was no less dry, and Jack was startled to see she was modestly robed in a demure woolen dress of inferior quality, sporting no ornament whatever. He'd never known a whore to dress in such drab clothing. One would expect to see women of her sort garbed in flaming scarlet with most of her bosom exposed. Turning her slightly, he unfastened the row of buttons marching down her back and pulled the dress away from her body. The pervading dampness had rendered her chemise all but transparent, revealing lush breasts topped with ripe, cherry-red nipples. When he heard Pettibone open the bedroom door, he quickly slid back the quilt and pulled it over her.

"The water, sir," Pettibone said, presenting a steaming pitcher and a stack of towels. "Will you be needing anything else, sir?"

"You're completely unflappable, aren't you, Pettibone?" Jack said with a hint of amusement. "I knew I acted wisely when I kept you on. Though I can little afford servants, I don't regret retaining your services."

Pettibone looked enormously pleased. "Living with you has taught me to expect anything, so nothing you do surprises me, sir. Will the lady be all right?"

"We won't know until the doctor examines her. Send him up the moment he arrives. Tell Fenwick to await me in the library. We would appreciate something to eat later."

Pettibone left the room, and Jack turned back to the woman occupying his bed. She was shivering, and he placed another blanket over her, wondering how long she had been out in the brutal weather. Did she have no sense at all? Didn't she know she'd find little business on a night like this?

The disgruntled doctor, perturbed at being routed out of bed at such an ungodly hour, arrived a few moments later and shooed Jack out of the room. Jack joined Spence in the library.

"Well, how is she?" Spence asked, smothering a yawn behind a lace-edged handkerchief.

"Still unconscious," Jack said, frowning. "I fear I may have done the woman irreparable harm. She's my responsibility now, though Lord only knows what I'm going to do with the wench once she's recovered. It would be a travesty to send her back out on the streets. She's younger than we thought, Spence, and probably new at her trade. I may be a black-hearted rogue, but I'm not a devil."

"Hire her on as a maid," Spence said, wagging his eyebrows suggestively. "Or keep her to warm your bed."

Jack sent him a black look. "As you well know, I can't afford a maid. As for warming my bed, I have no problems on that score. My tastes are rather discerning. I prefer women who don't ply their trade on the streets."

"Lud, Jack, I think you're stuck with the woman until she recuperates and you can send her on her way."

"The woman upstairs in that bed isn't going anywhere for a while, gentlemen."

The doctor entered the library and plopped into an overstuffed chair that had seen better days.

"What's wrong with her, Doctor . . . I'm sorry, I didn't catch your name."

"Dudley. For starters, her left arm is broken. She has numerous bruises and most likely will develop pneumonia, which can be quite serious. Pretty little thing. Who is she, and how did she get hurt?"

Jack hesitated, suddenly at a loss for words. For some obscure reason, he didn't want to reveal the fact that the woman was quite likely a whore.

"She's a distant relative of Jack's, from the Irish side of the family. Her father is a baron. He sent his daughter to London to be introduced to society," Spence said, warming to the subject. "She's Jack's ward. She was injured when her coach overturned on the outskirts of London. She lay out in the rain several hours before help arrived and she was brought here."

Jack groaned in dismay. Spence's fertile imagination would be the death of him one day.

Enormously pleased with his quick thinking, Spence sent Jack a smug grin. Jack's virulent scowl was anything but amused.

"That would explain the injuries," Dr. Dudley said. "I'll leave medicine and return tomorrow to put a cast on her arm. By then the swelling should recede. She's likely to be in considerable pain, but laudanum should ease her. Barring unforeseen setbacks, Lady Moira should be right as rain in four to six weeks."

"You know her name?" Jack asked, sending Spence a fulminating look. "I don't recall mentioning it." He could cheerfully strangle his friend for getting him into this muddle. Relative, indeed.

"She awoke briefly while I was treating her. When I asked her name, she told me it was Moira. Her Irish brogue is delightful. Since she is in no condition to answer questions, I decided get them from you instead."

Spence had had no idea Moira was really Irish when he'd woven his tale, and he was now enormously pleased that his story at least held a thread of truth. On the other hand, Jack appeared ready to explode. Not only was Jack

21

saddled with an injured whore, but he had claimed her as a relative, thanks to Spencer Fenwick and his wicked sense of humor. Jack hoped Dr. Dudley would be discreet but feared the old man was inclined to gossip.

"Will you stay for breakfast, Doctor?" Jack invited courteously. He hoped the doctor would refuse, for he couldn't wait to get Spence alone and berate him soundly.

"No time," Dudley said, levering his bulk from the chair. "Office hours start early. I'll be back tomorrow evening to look in on the patient."

Pettibone appeared with a breakfast tray, which he set down on a table with a flourish. Sensing the doctor was ready to leave, he bowed and escorted him to the door, leaving Spence and Jack alone.

"You wretched oaf, you really threw the fat into the fire," Jack thundered. "Relative, indeed. Whatever possessed you to tell that old gossip that the whore upstairs is related to me?"

His mouth full of food, Spence grinned. " 'Tis a grand joke, eh, Jack? I outdid myself this time. What a hoot. How many whores can you claim in your family?"

"None that I know of," Jack replied soberly. "And I'm not about to claim any now. Especially not for your amusement. One day your pranks are going to backfire."

Jack ate in silence. When he finished, he threw his napkin down and rose abruptly.

"Where are you going?" Spence asked, setting down his fork.

"Upstairs to see the patient."

"Wait, I'm coming with you."

Moira looked to be sleeping as innocently as a babe when the two men tiptoed into the bedchamber. But evidently she wasn't sleeping as soundly as they thought, for she opened her eyes and gazed up at them.

Rich, warm honey, Jack decided as he stared into her eyes. Not brown, not hazel, but pure amber with gold flecks.

"Who are you? What happened?" Her lilting voice was as enchanting as the doctor had indicated. "Where am I?"

Mesmerized, Jack had to clear his throat twice before he could answer. "You are in my home. Do you recall what happened, Moira?"

Moira's gaze turned inward, then grew murky. She recalled very well what had happened, but it was nothing she wanted to tell these two strange men. "How do you know my name?" She tried to sit up, grasped her splinted arm and groaned. "Blessed Mother, I hurt."

"Don't move. Your arm is broken," Jack said. "Can you remember anything?" Moira shook her head. "My carriage ran you down last night. 'Twas a most unfortunate accident. I learned your name from Dr. Dudley. I'm Sir Jackson Graystoke, and this is Lord Spencer Fenwick."

"Black Jack?" Moira asked, her eyes widening.

Jack's gray eyes sparkled with amusement. "I see you've heard of me."

Moira swallowed convulsively. "Aye. Though I believe none of the gossip, sir."

Jack tilted his head back and laughed. "You should. You had no identification on you," he continued, "so I brought you to my home and summoned a doctor to treat your injuries. I'm sorry about the accident. If you have relatives in town, I'll gladly contact them for you."

"There's no one in England. My brother and his family live in Ireland. He has three small children and a wife to support. I left home some weeks ago to find work in London and ease his burden.''

"Is there anyone who should know about your accident?'' Jack asked, skirting the issue of her obvious occupation. "An employer, perhaps?''

"I'm an unemployed domestic servant, sir,'' Moira replied.

"Unemployed?'' Spence asked. "How have you been supporting yourself?''

"Just recently unemployed,'' Moira amended. "I haven't had time yet to look for work. I have no money, sir. I fear I can't pay for the doctor.''

For some reason her remark made Jack angry. "Have I asked you for money? Until you're well, you're my responsibility.'' Deliberately, he picked up a small bottle from the night table and poured a measure into a glass. "Dr. Dudley left laudanum for your pain. Drink,'' he ordered gruffly, holding the glass to her lips.

Moira sipped gingerly, made a face at the bitter taste and refused to take more. "Thank you. You're very kind.''

"The soul of kindness is Black Jack,'' Spence said, smothering a laugh. "You're in good hands, my dear.''

When Moira's lids dropped over her incredible amber eyes, Jack pushed Spence out the door and followed him into the hall, closing the door firmly behind them.

"Do you believe her?'' Spence asked, openly skeptical. "What would a decent woman be doing out late at night? Why do you think her employer fired her? She'll be a proper beauty once all that swelling goes down. Do you suppose she was diddling the master or his sons?''

"I'm not about to speculate, Spence. What concerns me more is what I'm going to do with her once she recovers. Perhaps I should send her back to Ireland.''

"Lud, she'd probably starve to death if conditions are as bad there as we've been led to believe. Famine, disease and crop failure have decimated the population.''

"Confound it, Spence, must you be so damn practical? What do you suggest?''

A mischievous gleam came into Spence's blue eyes. He didn't envy his friend's predicament, but what a grand opportunity for a little devilment! Life had been bloody boring lately. Like most of his rich and idle friends, Spence loved harmless mischief. That's why he and Black Jack were such fast friends. Both men possessed a perverse sense of humor.

"Very well, I do have an idea, though I guarantee you won't like it.''

Jack's handsome features grew wary. "Spit it out, Spence.''

"Little Moira may be a prostitute, but she isn't your ordinary one. She is daintily fashioned, well-spoken and not in the least coarse. Her features, even swollen as they are, are refined and almost genteel. I've already planted the seed that she is a distant relative of yours.'' He paused for effect.

"Continue," Jack said, almost certain he wasn't going to like what Spence had to say.

"Why not pass Moira off as a lady?'' Spence eagerly suggested. "Introduce her to society and find her a husband. What jolly good fun we'd have. You never did have any use for those macaroni dandies who mince about London wearing high heels and makeup. Why not introduce 'Lady' Moira to society and marry her off to one of those fancy puppies?''

At first Jack looked astounded. Then he began to laugh

uproariously. "Your wicked sense of humor leaves me speechless, Spence. But your idea does have merit." He grew thoughtful, toying with the notion. "She will need substantial polishing."

"Remember, 'tis already established that she's a country girl. No one will expect her to be too accomplished."

"Granted she is surprisingly well-spoken for a commoner, but making her into a lady will require time and energy. I'm not certain I wish to devote so much effort to the task."

Admittedly the notion of making a silk purse from a sow's ear piqued Black Jack's sense of the outrageous, and Spence knew it. Not only was Jack intrigued with the endless possibilities such a challenge presented, but the gambler in Jack saw a way to enrich his coffers.

"How about sweetening the stakes?" Jack proposed.

"I thought you'd come around." Spence chortled, slapping Jack's back jovially. "What an adventure, eh? One of us will be the richer for it; you'll get rid of the Irish baggage, and we'll both be able to sit back and spin tales about this for years to come. I'll put up two thousand pounds against your matched pair of grays that you can't pass the girl off as gentry and get her engaged within . . . oh . . . say three months."

"Three months," Jack repeated, rubbing his stubbly chin thoughtfully. Two thousand pounds was a lot of money. Then again, his grays were the only thing of value he possessed. "I don't know. It will be at least four weeks before she is capable of moving about in public."

"You can use the time to groom her," Spence suggested eagerly. "You're a sporting man, Jack. What do you say? Are you up to the challenge?"

Spence's good-natured goading made it impossible for

Jack to refuse. "With one exception. The girl has to agree to our proposal. Otherwise the bet is off."

"Agreed," Spence said gleefully. "I have every confidence you can charm the girl into falling in with our harmless little charade. Returning to the streets cannot possibly compare to what can ultimately be hers if she marries well."

Chapter Two

Moira O'Toole did not drop off to sleep easily. She worried excessively about the kind of trouble she had gotten herself into this time. From the moment she had flung herself from Lord Roger Mayhew's moving coach and struck her head, she recalled nothing. From what she knew of men, which was blessed little, they were egotistical, lust-crazed wretches who demanded their way with helpless women. If they didn't get what they wanted, they found ways to make women suffer. Did Jackson Graystoke live up to his nickname? she wondered bleakly as she pictured the man whose bed she occupied. He pretended to be a gentleman, but his intense gray eyes held the weariness of a man who had indulged freely and frequently in every vice known to man.

Was Black Jack—the very name made her shudder—a disciple of the infamous Hellfire Club like Lord Roger? She must be extremely careful, Moira told herself, or she'd find herself in another dangerous situation. Black Jack and his friend must never know her shameful secret.

Moira had expected life in London to be difficult for a poor Irish immigrant, but never did she expect to encounter such unmitigated evil.

Clutching the gold locket circling her neck on its delicate chain, Moira thought of her sainted mother and how she would have despaired to see her daughter in such desperate straits. The locket was a cherished heirloom, a legacy from Moira's grandmother, who had died giving birth to Mary, Moira's mother. Mary had always cherished the locket, for it bore the tiny faded likeness of a young man in uniform who Mary had always assumed was her father, Moira's grandfather.

Haunted by her illegitimacy, Mary had given the locket to her daughter, Moira, explaining that it contained proof that she and Kevin had noble blood flowing through their veins. Moira's mother had been told by the nuns who raised her that her father was an English nobleman who had deserted Mary's pregnant mother.

"Mother, what am I to do?" Moira asked despondently, expecting no answer and getting none. Her cheeks wet with tears, she closed her eyes and slipped effortlessly toward sleep. She did not see Lady Amelia's ghost hovering above the bed, but a tentative smile stretched Moira's lips as a comforting warmth engulfed her, wrapping her in protective arms.

* * *

Jack awoke long after the sun made a belated appearance in an overcast sky. He stretched and yawned, disoriented at finding himself lying in a guest bed. Total recall came instantly. At this very moment, his bed was occupied by a woman he had run down in his carriage. He groaned in dismay. He could hardly afford to support himself, let alone assume responsibility for another human

29

being. Yet what could he do? He had caused her injuries and couldn't in all conscience throw her out on the street.

He rose quickly and rang for Pettibone. The servant, dressed somberly in unrelieved black, appeared almost immediately, bearing a tray containing a teapot and cup.

"Ah, Pettibone, you always seem to know just what I need. Though truth to tell a stiff brandy would serve me better. Something tells me I'm going to need fortifying today."

"Are you referring to the young woman, sir?"

"Then I wasn't dreaming." Jack sighed. "I was hoping . . . Never mind. Is the woman awake?"

"Aye, Miss Moira is indeed awake. I took her up a tray just moments ago. If I may be so bold, sir, you should engage a woman to see to her needs."

"How in bloody hell am I supposed to pay for the services of a maid?" Jack wanted to know.

Pettibone did not offer a solution to Jack's dilemma as he helped Jack dress and prepare for the day. By the time he finished eating his breakfast, Jack was ready to confront Moira about the idea he and Spence had hatched the day before. He knew it was a harebrained scheme, but the longer he thought about it the more the idea of passing off a woman of questionable virtue as a lady appealed to him. Making bloody fools of his peers filled him with wicked delight. And it did offer a solution to the perplexing problem concerning the future of the woman he had run down. The sooner he rid himself of the unwelcome burden, the better.

Struggling from bed, Moira used the chamber pot behind the screen and then returned to bed just moments before Jack rapped lightly on the door and barged into the room. He stood at the foot of the bed, legs spread wide, hands clasped behind his back, staring at her. Looking into his keenly intelligent gray eyes, Moira felt as if she had inadvertently dropped into the turbulent depths of a violent storm.

There was inherent strength in the bold lines of his face, she thought as her gaze settled on his lips. They were firm and sensual, set above a square chin that suggested a stubborn nature. He was a compelling, self-confident presence, one Moira had learned to fear from her dealings with Lord Roger.

Jack unclasped his hands and stood with his arms akimbo.

"How are you feeling, Miss O'Toole?"

"Better, thank you. I'll be on my way in a day or two."

Jack's lips curled in amusement. "And just where do you think you're going?"

Moira's chin rose fractionally. "I won't impose on you any longer than necessary or accept charity. You've been very kind, but I must find work."

"With a broken arm? There is still the possibility of pneumonia. You don't even have a place to live, do you?"

Moira bit the soft underside of her lip. Everything Jack Graystoke said was true. Her life was in a shambles. Moreover, once she left the safety of Black Jack's house, she'd likely find herself imprisoned in Newgate. But even that was preferable to being forced to participate in vile, heathenish rites.

Jack stared at Moira, enthralled by the silky-soft texture of her bright hair, so rich and heavy and lush it almost seemed alive. He couldn't recall ever seeing hair that exact shade of red before. Not exactly auburn, not really red, more like burnished copper. When she returned his gaze with mock bravado, her eyes reminded him of sweet, wild honey.

"Most domestics live in," she informed him. "I had no need for separate quarters."

Jack eyed her narrowly. "Except for a delightful lilt, you speak flawless English. One could almost deduce that you have been educated beyond your station."

Moira hung on to her temper by a slim thread. She thought his lazy drawl sounded somewhat condescending. "My mother insisted that my brother and I be educated. She taught us at home, and when she and my father could afford it, they hired a tutor."

"I'm surprised they saw the need to educate you and your brother. It isn't as if you're gentry."

Refusing to be goaded, Moira's hand closed convulsively on her locket. She had only her mother's fanciful notion that she came from noble stock. "My family are poor dirt farmers. Kevin is trying to eke a living for his wife and children out of the drought-ravished land left to him by our parents. Mama and Da died of typhus five years ago."

"Who was your last employer?" Jack inquired. "Why were you let go? What aren't you telling me? Perhaps I should speak with him . . ."

Moira blanched. "No! Don't bother, sir. I'll be gone soon."

Jack shifted uncomfortably. "You may have forgotten that it was my carriage that ran you down, but I haven't. I intend to take care of you until you're on your feet again."

Moira gulped nervously. "Take care of me?" She didn't even want to guess what he meant by that remark.

"I can take care of myself." It was shameless of her to let him go on thinking he was responsible for her injuries, but she had no choice.

"That's all well and good, but I owe you my protection. If I hadn't been foxed and hell-bent on driving at breakneck speed last night, I wouldn't have run you down. Do you have any plans for your future? A promise of employment, perhaps?"

Though his question was innocent enough, Moira suspected an ulterior motive. It was with good reason that this man was called Black Jack. "I left Ireland to find work and earn money to help out my brother. He's barely scraping by on the farm. My first employment didn't work out, but I'll find something soon."

What Moira didn't say was that it was unlikely she'd ever work as a servant again. Lord Roger had seen to that. Her only recourse was to return to Ireland and become another dependent on her poor brother, not that Kevin would mind. He'd welcome her with open arms, and so would his wife, Katie.

"Your meager servant's pay isn't enough to help your brother substantially," Jack said, choosing his words carefully. Nor would a streetwalker's earnings, he thought to himself. "Perhaps I can be of service."

Moira sent him a wary look. "How so, sir?" Her gaze lifted to the faded wallpaper, continuing on to the worn draperies and threadbare carpet. It appeared as if Jackson Graystoke wasn't well-heeled enough to take care of his own affairs, let alone hers.

Noting the direction of her gaze, Jack shrugged philosophically. "I know what you're thinking, Miss O'Toole, and you're right. I'm nothing but an impoverished baronet who can't even see to the upkeep of his own home. My main source of income arrives via the gaming table, and I must marry money soon or see my ancestral home fall down around my ears. But I'm not powerless to help you.''

''Why do you care?''

''I have accepted responsibility for your injuries. What in God's name were you doing out so late on a raw night like last night?'' He searched her face. ''Were you meeting a lover?''

''What!'' Her eyes blazed with outrage. ''What makes you think that? I'm not like that. I thank you for your concern, but I'd rather not say.''

Jack mulled over her words, deciding there was more to Moira O'Toole than met the eye. She claimed to be from the serving class, but she neither talked nor acted like any servant he knew.

''Dr. Dudley said you'd be unable to use your arm for at least four weeks, so you may as well content yourself to remain here until you're able to function on your own. Meanwhile, I'll hire a maid to see to your needs.''

''There is no need. I'll . . .''

''It's all settled, Miss O'Toole.''

Before Moira could offer further protest, the jangle of a bell coming from somewhere in the far reaches of the old house caught her attention. She looked askance at Jack.

''Someone is at the door,'' Jack said in response to her unasked question. ''Pettibone will see to it. He's the jack-of-all-trades around here. Couldn't exist without him. Now, where were we? Ah, yes, I was about to ask if you have any preferences as to a maid.''

Moira was on the verge of denying her need for a maid when Lord Fenwick burst into the chamber unannounced.

"Ah, I see our little patient is alert this morning. Have you told her yet, Jack?"

Spence looked like a cat who had just swallowed a canary.

"Tell me what?" Moira asked sharply. Just what did Black Jack and his friend have in mind for her? Judging from the guilty expression on Jack's face, it had to be something devious.

Jack sent Spence a blistering look. "Bloody hell, Spence, do you always speak without thinking? I haven't said a word yet to Miss O'Toole, but I would have come around to it eventually."

Moira certainly didn't like the sound of *that*. "I don't believe I'll stay after all." Had she jumped from the frying pan into the fire? She started to climb out of bed but remembered she was wearing naught but a threadbare shift. It suddenly occurred to her that if Jack Graystoke had no maid, then he must have undressed her himself. Her face flamed scarlet and she jerked the covers up to her neck.

"We mean you no harm, Miss O'Toole," Jack assured her, though he could see she wasn't convinced. "What my precipitous friend here wanted to know was did I mention to you a plan we had discussed concerning your future."

"Plan? Why should you care about my future? I'm not . . ." she gulped, unwilling to say the word aloud, "what you think." Moira could tell by the way Jack talked that he thought her a fallen woman.

"It matters not one whit what you are, Miss O'Toole. As for your future, I told you I have assumed full responsibility for your accident. I merely want to right a wrong. There is nothing evil in my intent, so don't reject

35

something that could benefit you greatly. Hear me out."

What choice did she have? Moira wondered. She was injured and helpless in a strange bed, in a strange house, wearing naught but her shift. She had no money, nowhere to live and no one to turn to for help. So far, Sir Jack Graystoke had made no demands on her, had in fact accepted full responsibility for her "accident" and offered amends. The least she could do was listen with an open mind.

"Very well, Sir Graystoke, what is this plan you and Lord Fenwick have devised for me?"

"First let me explain. Spence is in line for a dukedom and will do nothing to damage his reputation. He's a marquess in his own right. Thank God I do not aspire to so noble a rank. My young cousin, Ailesbury, is welcome to the title."

"Get on with it, Jack," Spence nagged. "I'm sure Miss O'Toole has no interest in my family tree or your lack of title."

"Sorry. I merely wanted to impress upon Miss O'Toole that we mean her no harm." He turned to Moira, impaling her with the gray intensity of his eyes. "Since you are temporarily unemployable, Miss O'Toole, with no prospects of future work, Spence and I have come up with a solution to your dilemma."

Moira's warm golden gaze settled disconcertingly on Jack, making him decidedly uncomfortable. "I refuse to be used for vile purposes. Others have tried and failed."

Jack stared at her through narrowed lids. What in bloody hell did she mean by that remark? What vile purposes was she referring to? "My dear Miss O'Toole, Spence and I have no designs on your person. You are perfectly safe with us."

Moira looked skeptical but gave him the benefit of the doubt. "Go on, sir, I'm listening."

"If you agree to the little escapade Spence and I propose, I can promise you a grand adventure. Moreover, if it works out as we expect, you will never have to worry about money again. You'll be able to better your own lot and provide for your brother's family."

Moira's eyes widened in disbelief. "How do you propose to do that?"

Jack perched on the edge of the bed, his eyes crinkling with amusement. "Have you ever wondered what it would be like to be a lady? To belong to the gentry?"

Moira stiffened indignantly, taking his words as an insult. "I *am* a lady! I may not be gentry, but that doesn't make me any less a lady."

The corner of Jack's mouth lifted upward. He had her now. "Prove it. Let's see if you've got what it takes to be accepted by London society."

Forgetting that she was scantily clad in a threadbare shift, Moira jerked upright, wincing in pain when her injured arm protested the sudden jolt. "Are you daft, sir? 'Tis highly unlikely I'll be accepted by society, let alone mistaken for gentry."

Jack gave her a lazy grin. "Spence and I intend to prove you wrong. You *will* be accepted, Miss O'Toole. We'll coach you in etiquette, and when the time is right, you'll be introduced as my ward, a distant relative from Ireland. We'll make your father a baron, which will make you a lady. Lady Moira. How does that sound?"

"Outrageous."

"Spence and I will do our level best to see you married to an upstanding member of London society, one wealthy enough to keep you in grand style and provide funds for your brother. If that isn't enough inducement, just consider the endless hours of entertainment Spence and I will derive from our little charade.''

Moira's thoughts scattered. What Sir Graystoke suggested was ludicrous. No wonder he was called Black Jack. His warped sense of humor would get them all in trouble. Pass her off as a relative, indeed. How could anyone believe she was gentry? Her mother had told her many times that her grandfather was highborn, but there was no proof to substantiate her claim. That kind of thinking was dangerous. But so were the alternatives, which were definitely unpalatable. Finding another job without references was next to impossible. She had no funds with which to purchase passage to Ireland, even if she decided to burden her poor brother with another mouth to feed.

Actually, after careful consideration, Moira thought the idea that the two gentlemen proposed had some merit. The idea of marrying money had much to commend it. One possible drawback was having to deal with Black Jack on a daily basis until she left. The man was too arrogant, too handsome and too damn male!

"Well, what do you think of the idea?" Spence asked excitedly. He was literally hopping from foot to foot, waiting for Moira's decision.

"Why would you go to the trouble? There is more to this than an escape from boredom. What do you have to gain by passing me off as a lady?"

"A pair of . . ."

"Nothing," Jack interjected, abruptly cutting off Spence's response. He thought it best not to mention the wager he and Spence had agreed upon. His pair of grays against two thousand pounds. "We have your best interests at heart. The diversion your entry into society will provide will give us endless hours of amusement.''

Jack's eyes roved over the upper part of Moira's body, bared when the blanket dropped to her waist. Her breasts were round and full, though not particularly large; he could see the darker aureoles push impudently against the thin material of her shift. A jolt of blatant lust made him want to reach out and encircle the fleshy mounds with his large hands. His fingers tingled, imagining the warmth of her flesh against his palm. He blinked and looked away, surprised at the direction of his thoughts. Moira recognized the look in his eyes and yanked the covers up to her chin with her uninjured arm. She neither needed nor wanted *that* kind of attention.

''Amusement,'' Moira said bitterly. ''Do the gentry think of naught else?''

Spence grinned. ''What else is there?''

''Come now, Miss O'Toole, what do you say?'' Jack asked with gruff impatience. ''You've nothing to lose and everything to gain.''

What did she have to lose? Moira wondered. What if she chanced to meet her former employers while she was out and about in society? What if she met Lord Roger at some social function or other? Perhaps he wouldn't recognize her dressed as a lady, she reflected hopefully. Due to their age, the elderly Mayhews attended few social events, and as for Roger, tame amusements did not interest him. But there was always a possibility of their paths crossing. She'd just have to cross that bridge when she came to it.

''Very well,'' Moira reluctantly agreed. ''Your scheme has some merit. I will do it to prove to you that I *am* a lady, that I'm as good as any woman born to the gentry.

And to help my brother. But mostly because I do not wish to remain a burden to you.''

Jack sent her a dark look. ''I must marry money myself if I am to survive, but I will fulfill my responsibility where you're concerned. If not for me, you would be hale and hearty today instead of recovering from injuries.''

''Good show, Miss O'Toole!'' Spence enthused, sending Moira a pleased look. ''When you're ready, Jack will introduce you as a distant relative and let nature take its course. You're a beauty, Miss O'Toole. There is nothing coarse or common about you. If Jack wins, we'll be toasting your engagement inside three months. But if I'm victorious . . .''

''That's enough, Spence!'' Jack warned. ''We've tired Miss O'Toole. I suggest we repair to the study and let her rest. We've plans to make.''

''Don't we though,'' Spence said as Jack hustled him out the door.

Moira cradled her injured arm and pondered Jack's outrageous plan. She'd been a fool to agree, but what choice did she have? Despite Jack's argument to the contrary, clearly he did not want the added responsibility she represented. He thought he had run her down with his carriage, but she knew for a fact he couldn't have hurt her much more than she'd already been when she'd flung herself from Lord Roger's coach. She felt guilty about lying to Jack about his involvement in her ''accident,'' but she feared that telling the truth presented a far greater risk.

She was in so deep that Moira saw no way to extricate herself gracefully from this muddle. She'd see this through and prove to Black Jack Graystoke that being a lady did not depend upon one's birth.

Moira's thoughts scattered when she heard a discreet

knock on the door. Moments later Pettibone poked his head into the room.

"Come in, Mr. Pettibone."

He stepped inside. "Can I get you anything, miss?"

"No, thank you. You've been more than kind. Have you been with Sir Graystoke long?"

"Aye, miss, a very long time."

Moira bit her lip, then blurted out, "Is he as black-hearted as his name implies?"

For a moment Pettibone looked rattled, then he quickly recovered his dignity. "Not at all, miss. You mustn't believe everything you hear. I'll admit he can be a bit of a rogue at times, but I've never known him to hurt anyone knowingly, particularly a woman."

"Does he truly earn his living at the gaming tables?"

"True enough, miss. His folks left him little beyond this haunted mansion. And as you can see, it's in a pitiful state of disrepair."

Moira's eyes grew round. "Haunted?"

"Indeed, miss. 'Tis said Lady Amelia Graystoke wanders the halls at night, so don't be alarmed if you see or hear anything out of the ordinary."

"Have you ever seen her?"

" 'Tis said Lady Amelia appears only to family members in desperate need of her help. 'Tis rumored she has saved more than one rakehell of the family. In recent years she's had little reason to appear and no one to redeem, until Black Jack, that is. But alas," the old man sighed, "as far as I know, Lady Amelia has yet to appear to her wayward great-great-grandson."

"Why does Lady Amelia haunt the Graystokes?" Moira asked curiously. Being Irish, ghosts and such had always intrigued her.

41

" 'Tis a sad story, miss," Pettibone said, warming to the subject. He enjoyed nothing better than displaying his knowledge of Graystoke family lore. "Lady Amelia's only son was a wastrel of the worst sort. He spent his days drinking, gambling, dueling and ... er ... visiting ladies of ill repute. 'Twas he who lost the family fortune. Lady Amelia finally managed to get him married to a lovely girl, but it didn't change his dissolute ways. He was killed in a duel days before the Graystoke heir was born."

"How sad." Moira sighed.

"Upon her death some years after that of her son, Lady Amelia made a deathbed promise. She vowed that no Graystoke heir would walk the same path as her wastrel son, even if she had to haunt future generations of Graystokes to accomplish it. And the story goes that she has kept her vow, appearing only to those male Graystoke heirs who led debauched lives and were well on the road to perdition."

"Do you believe that tale?" Moira asked, thoroughly intrigued by Lady Amelia and her pledge to the future generations of Graystokes.

Pettibone shrugged. "Aye. There have been no wastrel males in the Graystoke family for several generations. Like as not it could be the result of Lady Amelia's intervention."

What he left unsaid was that Black Jack Graystoke surely qualified for Lady Amelia's help, and if Lady Amelia didn't intervene soon, it would be too late for his rakehell master.

"Thank you for telling me, Mr. Pettibone."

"If there is nothing you wish, miss, I'll continue with my chores."

"I was wondering what happened to my clothing. I don't see them anywhere."

"They are being cleaned and mended. They'll be returned when the doctor says it's all right for you to leave your bed. He'll be here later today to place a cast on your arm."

After Pettibone left, Moira had much to think about, not the least of which was her handsome benefactor. Just how well-meaning was Jack Graystoke? she wondered. She wasn't so naive as to think that men did good deeds without expecting some kind of reward. Jack didn't strike her as an altruistic man. Pleasure-seeking, self-indulgent, arrogant came to mind. Was amusement his only reason for wanting to pass her off as a lady and find her a husband?

Sweet Blessed Mother! Moira found it impossible to think of anything but Black Jack's sensual gray eyes—eyes that held a tempting touch of wildness, of vital energy almost mesmerizing in its intensity. She was grateful for the lesson Lord Roger had taught her. No man was worthy of trust. She vowed to remember that lesson in her dealings with Black Jack Graystoke.

Chapter Three

Jack did not let his houseguest interfere with his normal habit of visiting his usual haunts that night. After a solitary dinner, he dressed carefully and left the house at nine after first stopping by to bid Moira good night. He hoped to win enough at the gaming tables to pay off a few pressing debts. Tomorrow would be time enough to begin the task of turning a little Irish nobody into a lady of quality.

White's was crowded. Jack was greeted by numerous friends as he threaded his way to the gaming room. More than one lady smiled coyly at him, while others openly ogled the infamous Black Jack Graystoke. A beautiful, sophisticated woman boldly approached Jack and took his arm in a possessive manner that bespoke of familiarity.

"Jack, you rogue!" She tapped his arm playfully with her fan. "How naughty of you to keep me waiting."

"Had I known you were waiting, Lady Victoria, I would have made haste," Jack returned gallantly.

Lady Victoria Greene's keen blue eyes hinted of unbridled passion and promised much more. She knew Jack needed to marry money, and since she was immensely rich, she considered herself perfect for a rogue like Jack. She wasn't concerned that Jack was merely a baronet, as was her dead husband, for Jack gave her something quite extraordinary. His passion was stunning; no man of her acquaintance came close to giving her what Jack had in abundance. In bed together, they approached perfection. She wanted Black Jack Graystoke, wanted him desperately. And not for a tumble or two. She wanted him exclusively, forever. She counted on her vast wealth to keep him in line once they were wed.

Victoria licked her full lips and smiled fetchingly at Jack. " 'Tis so noisy in here, Jackson, dear. Why don't we seek more private environs? Your house would be best since my servants love to gossip, and your man is the soul of discretion.''

Jack's gray eyes narrowed. There was nothing discreet about Victoria, but then he'd always known that. They were great in bed and he loved her money. But truth to tell, he'd rather be the instigator in affairs of the heart. Victoria was aggressive in bed and made no bones about her desire to become his wife. Jack was well aware that one day soon she would have her wish.

"I thought to try my luck at the tables first," Jack said smoothly. "I feel lucky tonight."

"I'd say you already got lucky," Victoria said, smiling at her double entendre. "I'll wait for you, so don't be too late." She gave him another playful tap with her fan and strolled off into the crowd.

Jack frowned as he watched her hips twitch bewitchingly beneath the expensive material of her skirts. Jack had always enjoyed as well as appreciated Victoria's unrestrained sexuality and derived great pleasure from the uninhibited bed sport they shared together. Why should she seem so bold and brash all of a sudden? Why did her overblown charms appear well used and faded? He shook his head in an effort to clear it of such foolish thoughts. Lady Victoria Greene was a perfect choice for his needs—rich beyond his wildest dreams. He'd never have to worry about money again.

Jack knew Victoria expected to curb his excesses once they married, but no one knew better than he that it wouldn't work. It would take a far better woman than Lady Victoria to cure him of his wild streak. Regardless of decorum, Black Jack Graystoke did as he pleased. Heedless, rash, direct were words used to describe him, and most of them were true.

Jack enjoyed incredible luck at the gaming table. He couldn't seem to lose no matter what he did. For the first time in weeks, he felt as if Lady Luck was smiling at him. His pockets were bulging with several hundred pounds and his head spinning from one drink too many when he rose and excused himself. The hour was late, but he found Victoria still waiting. She joined him in the vestibule when he retrieved his cloak, her red lips curved downward in mock anger.

"You've kept me waiting a long time, love."

Jack leered at her. "I'm ready now. More than ready."

She grinned back in eager invitation. "So am I." She took his arm, nearly dragging him from the club. "Hurry, darling, I'm dying to feel you inside me. Waiting has sharpened my appetite."

He handed Victoria into his carriage, gave instructions to his coachman, then vaulted in beside her. His pockets were full, he had a willing woman to warm his bed, he was pleasantly foxed and everything was right with the world. Or nearly right. He tried not to dwell on his injured guest, or the wager he had made with Spence.

Jack still hadn't decided whether Miss O'Toole was a domestic servant or a whore. She seemed so vague about her former employment that Jack had grave doubts concerning her true occupation. Not that it mattered. The wager he and Spence had made could line his pockets, provide amusement and rid him of his responsibility to Moira O'Toole. At risk was the one possession he truly valued—his matched pair of grays.

"You're quiet tonight, darling," Victoria purred as they rode through the gates of Graystoke Manor. Her hand stole to his leg, boldly massaging the bulging muscles of his thigh beneath the fine material of his tight trousers. He stiffened and groaned when her hand suddenly dipped to cup him between the legs.

"Greedy bitch," Jack muttered, meaning no disrespect.

Leaping from the carriage the moment it rolled to a stop, he came around and lifted Victoria into his arms, striding purposely toward the house. Lust and driving need thrust all thought from his mind, his energy focused on filling Victoria with his hard erection.

Jack kicked the door with his foot, summoning Pettibone, who shuffled up to answer it, obviously roused from his sleep. The old man's eyebrows rose several inches when he saw Jack push past him with Lady Victoria in his arms.

"My word, another one, Sir Jack?" Pettibone asked dryly. "I would think you learned your lesson last night."

"Go to bed, Pettibone," Jack said with gruff impatience. "I'll see to myself tonight."

"As you wish," Pettibone said in a long-suffering tone.

"Good night, sir. Do be careful of the stairs; you look none too steady."

"Good night, Pettibone," Jack said tautly.

Victoria buried her head in Jack's shoulder and giggled. "What a horrid old man. Once we are wed, he'll have to go."

Jack kissed her into silence as he took the steps two at a time. He was so hot, so damn hard he felt the buttons on his trousers popping open. Perhaps, he thought dully, being married to Victoria wouldn't prove too difficult. There were compensations as well as drawbacks.

Driven by lust, by the time Jack opened his chamber door he'd forgotten his room was being occupied by someone other than himself. Charging through the door, he made directly for the bed, eager to thrust himself inside Victoria and stroke them both to blinding ecstasy. The few glowing embers remaining in the hearth were too dim to reveal the slight figure lying in the bed.

Moira awoke to the sound of voices as someone burst through the door. She rolled to the opposite edge of the bed moments before a crushing weight came down beside her. She heard a woman squeal and a man's answering groan before she came to her senses and screamed.

Jack spit out a curse and jerked upright, his fuzzy mind belatedly recalling that he had given up his room to Moira. Victoria was too stunned to move. Jack's hand shook as he struck a light to a branch of candles on the nightstand beside the bed. Victoria stared at Moira in horror, ignoring Jack's groan of dismay.

"Who are you?" Victoria asked in a voice shrill enough to raise the dead. "What are you doing in Jack's bed?"

Moira pulled the covers up to her neck with her uninjured arm and shrank away from Victoria's unremitting anger. She had no idea who Victoria was, but it wasn't difficult to guess Jack's reason for bringing the woman into his house, womanizer that he was.

"Bloody hell," Jack said, dragging his fingers through his unruly hair. "I completely forgot about Moira."

"That's obvious." Victoria's voice dripped with venom. "I suggest you keep your women straight, darling. Or did you intend to please both of us tonight?"

"Lady Moira is my ward, Victoria," Jack said, using the story he and Spence had agreed upon. "She is the daughter of a distant relative on my father's side of the family. She met with an unfortunate accident en route from Ireland, and I'd forgotten I'd given her my room."

He turned to Moira. "Lady Moira, this is Lady Victoria Greene. Moira is here for the season," Jack explained to Victoria.

"This is the first I've heard of a ward. Is Lady Moira husband hunting?" Victoria asked, giving Moira a haughty stare. "You're Irish." She made it sound like an insult.

Moira opened her mouth to answer, but Jack forestalled her. "Lady Moira is indeed Irish. Her father is a baron who prefers the country to city life. You might say that Moira is husband hunting," Jack allowed.

"I am acquainted with nearly all the likely prospects this season. I'll see that you're introduced," Victoria said.

"It will be several weeks before Moira's arm is healed enough to appear in public," Jack said. "But this is neither the time nor place for small talk. Come along, Victoria, Moira needs her sleep."

Jack all but pulled Victoria from the room, angry at himself for making such a disastrous blunder. He should have known better than to drink too much. Liquor had already gotten him into trouble the night before, and he should have learned his lesson. As he dragged Victoria out the door, he vowed to avoid all hard liquor in the future. Had Lady Amelia heard his vow, she would have smiled.

"Where are you taking me?" Victoria asked as Jack shoved her toward an unoccupied chamber.

"There's more than one bed in this pile of stone," Jack told her.

Victoria dug in her heels. "I'm no longer in the mood." Her lips turned downward in displeasure. "Your little ward took me by surprise. What kind of accident was she involved in? Her face is still swollen and bruised."

"Carriage accident," Jack explained succinctly. "Are you going to beg off? 'Tis not like you, Victoria."

"I'm displeased with you, Jack. I'm not even sure I believe you. Ward, indeed! You're a first-class rake, Jackson Graystoke. Lord knows why I stand for your nonsense. Take me home."

Jack shrugged with easy grace. "Very well, my dear. I'll instruct my coachman to take you home. I'll see you at the Whitcombs tomorrow night. I hope you'll be over your pique by then."

"Perhaps," Victoria replied sulkily, "and perhaps not."

With mixed emotions, Jack watched the carriage carrying Victoria drive off. Truth to tell, his own ardor had cooled considerably after bursting in on Moira. That wasn't to say he didn't still need Victoria and her money. Nevertheless, the moment the carriage disappeared from sight, Victoria was relegated to the far reaches of Jack's mind as Moira occupied her place.

Without conscious thought, Jack's steps slowed as he passed Moira's room—his room, really. He should apologize, he supposed, though he owed Moira no explanation. Moira had burst into his life uninvited, and he strongly suspected Lady Amelia was behind the entire fiasco. If not for the family ghost, he would have been snug in his bed last night and someone else would have run Moira down. He had no idea what Lady Amelia had in mind for him, but he felt certain it wasn't nearly killing an Irish whore.

Some perverse imp inside Jack made him knock softly on Moira's door and call out her name. If she didn't answer, he would go on to his own bed, he decided, and put off explaining until another time.

Sleep was out of the question for Moira. She shuddered to think how close she came to witnessing Jack Graystoke making love to his mistress. The man was an incorrigible womanizer. Did he have no scruples?

"Moira, it's Jack. Are you awake?"

Moira hesitated for the space of a heartbeat before answering. "Aye, I'm awake."

"May I come in for a moment? I owe you an explanation."

"Come in, Sir Jack, though you owe me nothing. I'm merely a guest in your home. You may do as you please."

Jack stepped inside the room and crossed to the bed. He stood over her, looking much like a naughty child, Moira thought, with one side of his mouth turned up into a lopsided smile. If excessive vice had ruined him, it did not show in his face.

"I'm sorry this happened, Moira. As usual, I had too much to drink and forgot I'd given you my chamber."

"I'm an intruder in your home, Sir Jack. I absolve you of all responsibility where I'm concerned. I'll leave in a day or two, so you may have your privacy once again."

Jack heaved a weary sigh and sank down on the edge of the bed, being careful of Moira's injured arm. "You're not going anywhere. 'Tis my fault you were injured and up to me to see to your welfare."

Candlelight bathed Moira's face, and Jack was struck anew by Moira's beauty. Even with her face swollen and bruised, one could see she was no ordinary beauty. Her facial bones were delicately sculpted, her mouth full, her nose exquisitely dainty. There was both delicacy and strength in her face. The rich, glowing auburn of her hair gleamed with shadows ranging from deep gold to dark copper. Yet beyond the delectable fragility of her features, Jack saw a strength that did not lessen her femininity.

Confused by the warm glow in Jack's eyes, Moira started violently when he raised his hand to her cheek, tenderly grazing the bruised flesh with his knuckles. "I think your beauty is going to surprise us all, Moira, once your face is back to normal." His finger traced the outline of her lips, acutely aware of their lush fullness and his uncontrollable urge to taste them. "You're going to make some lucky man happy."

Without warning, he gently grasped her face between his hands, lowered his head and kissed her. The kiss was slow, thoughtful, tentative, as he moved his mouth over hers in gentle exploration. Her eyes closed. Strength, warmth. For the first time in weeks she felt safe. Yet she knew better than to trust a man like Black Jack. She sighed in pleasure. How wonderful it would be if she could confide in him.

A subtle eroticism heated her body and rattled her

senses. She opened her lips to the gentle probing of Jack's tongue, and it slid unhindered into the sweet cavern of her mouth. Pleasure radiated outward as Moira's emotions whirled and skidded. She had no idea a simple kiss could make one so giddy. Slowly her body softened and melted to his, wringing a groan from Jack as he responded by wrapping her in his arms and pulling her tightly against him.

His kiss deepened. Blood pounded in her brain, leapt from her heart and made her body weak. Moira felt transported on a spiraling, dizzying journey. Her first experience with passion was a heady adventure into an unknown realm, and she reeled under the soul-reaching expertise of Jack's mouth.

She groaned in disappointment when Jack's lips left hers. But the groan quickly turned into a strangled sigh as he showered soft, tingling kisses around her lips and along her jaw, her brow, against her earlobe. She moaned as his lips followed the slope of her slender neck to the hollow between her breasts, all but exposed beneath the threadbare shift she wore. A startled gasp left her lips when Jack's mouth covered one of her nipples, thoroughly soaking it with his tongue through the thin material, and his hand somehow found the shape of her other breast.

Moira closed her eyes, but brilliant lights of desire still flashed behind her lids, blinding her to all but the sweet torment of Jack's mouth and hands.

''Blessed Mother!'' she cried, feeling her flesh pucker as it reacted to Jack's talented mouth. What was this scoundrel doing to her? Did he want the same thing from her that Roger Mayhew had wanted? Did he intend for her to take Lady Victoria's place in his bed? She tried to push him away, but her broken arm protested and she cried out in real pain.

Jack reared back instantly, his face taut with disbelief. What in bloody hell was he doing? The Irish wench had bewitched him. He couldn't ever recall losing control like that. No matter what her occupation, whore or servant, he had no business treating her so callously after assuming responsibility for her welfare. The sweet seductive promise of her kisses had momentarily blinded him to his obligation where Moira was concerned. For one tormented moment, he wanted to bare her sweet body and thrust himself inside her.

"I'm sorry, Moira. Did I hurt you? You shouldn't have tempted me. I'm accustomed to taking what a woman offers."

Moira's temper exploded. "Tempt you! I did no such thing. I offered you nothing." Not only was Moira angry at Jack for forcing his attentions on her, but she was livid at herself for enjoying them. She'd allowed him to go too far. No one had ever touched her body in such an intimate manner. Moira wasn't ignorant of what went on between a man and woman, having lived in close quarters with her brother and his wife, but until now she'd never been enticed to passion.

Jack's steady gaze bore into her in silent contemplation. "Do you think I was born yesterday? You were quite eager until I inadvertently hurt your arm."

"You took advantage of me!" Moira raged. "I have no experience with men."

Jack's arched brows lifted in obvious disbelief. "If you say so. It's late, Moira. I won't dispute your claim. I came to apologize for blundering into your room, not to seduce you. The kiss meant nothing. Forget it ever happened.

Sleep well, Moira. Victoria is gone—you won't be bothered again tonight.''

Moira's gaze followed Jack as he stormed from the room. The tingling sensation in the pit of her stomach abated somewhat after he left, but it didn't entirely disappear. In her estimation, Black Jack Graystoke lived up to his reputation as a rogue and womanizer. If she had any sense at all, she'd leave the moment she was able and run for her life. Unfortunately, though, there were some things more dangerous than Black Jack Graystoke.

All things considered, Jack Graystoke offered the least peril. She felt capable of fending off his advances, and he did offer her the opportunity to escape a worse fate. If she married money and position, many of her problems would disappear.

Jack threw himself down on the bed without bothering to undress. He had no idea what had come over him in Moira's bedroom. Had his encounter with Victoria so aroused him that no woman was safe with him? It wasn't like him to force himself on a defenseless woman—not even one of questionable virtue. Willing women could be had anywhere. Most women of his acquaintance made themselves available to Black Jack Graystoke. He'd been a bloody fool, Jack decided irritably. And it wouldn't happen again.

Punching his pillow in a show of annoyance, he turned on his side and closed his eyes. He'd had damn little sleep in the past several nights, and he faced a daunting task. He had to turn Moira O'Toole into a lady and marry her off to the highest bidder. Sighing wearily, he tried to think of anything but Moira's wide golden eyes, pink-tipped breasts and smooth white flesh. Not an easy task for a man in a painful state of arousal.

A bright light shimmering against Jack's closed eyelids brought him into blinking awareness, and he raised his arm to cover his eyes, hoping the light would go away. If anything it grew brighter, and Jack spit out a curse, wondering if Pettibone had come into the room and lit a lamp or started a fire in the grate. Curiosity got the better of him, and he slowly opened his eyes. What he saw made him wish he'd kept them closed.

The ghost of Lady Amelia hovered over the bed, nodding her head and looking quite pleased with herself.

"What in bloody hell is the matter now?" Jack bellowed. "You sent me on a wild goose chase in foul weather, and look what happened! There's a strange female sleeping in my bed, and I'm not even in it with her!"

Lady Amelia did not seem at all daunted by Jack's outburst. In fact, if it could be said that ghosts smiled, then that's what Lady Amelia was now doing.

"There's no way you're sending me out tonight, milady," Jack said grumpily. "I've had damn little sleep lately, thanks to you."

Lady Amelia shook her head, as if to say there was no need for Jack to leave his bed.

"Can you tell me why you're here, milady?" Jack asked courteously. "What is it you want of me? Can't you speak? I told you before that the Devil has already laid claim to my soul. I'm beyond redemption. Let me walk the path to perdition in peace."

Lady Amelia drifted closer, so close Jack could feel the warmth of her brilliant light. He stiffened slightly when she bent toward him, not knowing what to expect. He felt a heat against his ear, and a rasp of sound so low he thought he imagined the words.

She will save you.

"What? What did you say? Who are you talking about?"

If there was an answer, it was lost in the far reaches of the room. The light dimmed, and Lady Amelia was gone. Jack groaned and closed his eyes. Sleep came instantly. When he woke the next morning, he recalled Lady Amelia's words and wondered what they meant. The pesky ghost was fast becoming a bloody nuisance.

Moira awakened late. Having had her rest rudely interrupted the night before, it was close to dawn before she'd finally fallen asleep.

"Are you awake, miss?" The question followed a timid rap on the door.

Moira smiled when she recognized Pettibone's voice. "I'm awake, Mr. Pettibone. Come in."

Pettibone entered, bearing a tray of steaming tea and tempting biscuits. "Are you hungry, miss? I'll have something more substantial later."

"Do you cook, too, Mr. Pettibone?" Moira asked of the erect old man.

"I do, indeed, miss. A woman comes in twice weekly to clean and wash, but I do whatever needs doing in between."

"You're a gem, Mr. Pettibone. I hope Sir Jack appreciates you. Perhaps when my arm heals, I can help."

Pettibone beamed, smoothing the lines in his weathered face. "Oh, no, miss, Sir Jack wouldn't allow it." He flushed and looked away in embarrassment. He wondered how Moira would react to the news that Jack had confided to his valet his plans to pass her off as a lady.

Unaware of his thoughts, Moira continued brightly,

"I'd like to get up today. My arm feels much better."

"Sir Jack will tell you when you may leave the bed."

"Please tell Sir Jack I'd like to speak with him," Moira requested.

"Certainly, miss, as soon as he returns. He's gone to call on young Lord Fenwick."

Jack faced Spence over the breakfast table. None of the other Fenwicks had arisen yet, and Spence would still be abed if Jack hadn't pounded at the door at the ungodly hour of nine in the morning.

"What can I do for you, Jack?" Spence asked, yawning hugely. "Rumor has it you and Lady Victoria left White's together last night. I arrived shortly after you left. Have you proposed yet?"

"Forget Victoria, Spence. That's not why I'm here."

"Why in the deuce *are* you here at this early hour? Are you having problems with the Irish lass?"

"I wish it were that simple," Jack muttered, recalling the kiss that had nearly led to something more and how it had affected him. "My problem concerns my lack of blunt. 'Twas not my intention, but Victoria met Moira last night, and I had to introduce the wench as my ward. In order to keep this all circumspect and avoid nasty gossip, I must hire a maid to act as chaperon. Otherwise we'll find suitors few and far between. The girl has no fortune to commend her."

"I concur wholeheartedly, but I'm slightly bent myself until my next quarterly allowance. I'd hate for my parents to know I've gambled away my last quarterly. I don't come into my own fortune for two more years."

"Bloody hell, what a sad state of affairs when neither of us can afford the price of a maid. I won several hundred pounds at the tables last night, but I gave it all to Pettibone to settle some of the more pressing debts I've run up.''

''I've got an idea,'' Spence said brightly. ''There are so many maids in this house, my mother can't keep track of them. I'll simply go to the kitchen, select one of the kitchen helpers and loan her to you for a few months. No one will be the wiser, and she can remain on the Fenwick payroll.''

''You expect a scullery maid to act as maid to Moira?''

''Do you have a better solution?'' Spence asked, pleased at having solved the problem so handily. ''Let's go and see who's available now, before my parents are up and about.''

The young girl they chose to be Moira's maid had potential despite her shyness and youth, Jack thought as Spence explained what was required of her.

''A lady's maid, my lord?'' young Jilly Scranton asked when informed of her temporary employment with Sir Jack Graystoke. ''I'm to care for a lady recovering from injuries she got in a carriage accident? I ain't never been a lady's maid.'' A comely girl of sixteen, Jilly was a sweet-faced blonde with guileless blue eyes and an engaging smile. And she was as innocent a girl as Jack had ever seen.

''You'll learn, Jilly,'' Spence said confidently. ''You must tell no one about this temporary employment. I'll arrange it through the housekeeper so that no questions will be asked when you return. I'll see that you're paid a bit extra out of my next quarterly.''

''Are you certain you can clear it with the housekeeper?'' Jack wondered.

Spence sent him a confident smile. ''The old bird has a soft spot for me. If I butter her up a bit, she'll agree to anything.'' He turned to Jilly. ''Go along with Sir Jack, Jilly. It will be all right.''

Jilly sent Jack a skeptical glance. She'd heard about the scandalous Black Jack Graystoke. Who hadn't? She wondered if she was doing the right thing, but only for a moment. Anything was better than scrubbing pots and pans from morn to night and getting cuffed by Cook for not doing it fast enough. Well, almost anything. At the first hint of impropriety on Black Jack's part, she'd be out of there faster than you could shake a stick.

''Come along, child,'' Jack said, annoyed at the way Jilly was staring at him. ''I won't eat you. I prefer more worldly women. I have grave doubts about all this, but you seem intelligent enough to learn what's expected of you.''

''Oh, yes, sir. I catch on fast, I do. I'll gather my things and be back before you know it.''

''You've been a great help, Spence. I hope this works out like we planned. Moira isn't exactly your meek miss. I made a terrible blunder when I brought Victoria home last night.''

Spence swallowed a grin. ''I would have liked to see that. What happened? Did your—er—ward catch you in a compromising situation?''

''Something like that,'' Jack said dryly, recalling the pure temptation of Moira's sweet mouth and soft flesh. ''But that's neither here nor there. I just hope I can placate Victoria enough to convince her to marry me.''

''I doubt she'll need much convincing,'' Spence said blandly. ''By the way, did you hear the latest gossip?''

''What gossip? Rumors abound in London Town.''

''This rumor is genuine. It involves Lord Roger Mayhew, the old Earl of Montclair's heir.''

"What did Mayhew do now? Nothing would surprise me where that scoundrel is concerned. Did you know that he's a member of the Hellfire Club? He and his friends tried to get me to join, you know."

"Thank God you resisted. 'Tis rumored he bought passage to the Continent in the dead of night," Spence confided. "It was all very mysterious. His friends denied prior knowledge of his departure. Seems he left a score or more gambling debts behind. His parents are furious."

"Good riddance," Jack said succinctly.

Chapter Four

Jack arrived back at Graystoke Manor just as Moira was finishing breakfast. Eating was rather awkward without the use of her right arm, but she managed to get enough food to her mouth to satisfy her hunger. She was grateful for the interruption when Jack knocked, then entered the room with Jilly in tow. Lying about in bed was beginning to bore her.

"Good morning," Jack greeted her gruffly. Recalling the sweet temptation of Moira's pouting nipple in his mouth, Jack found it difficult not to stare at the steady rise and fall of her breasts beneath the sheet. "This is Jilly," he said, bringing the girl forward. "Your new maid."

Round-eyed, Jilly stared at Moira's battered face, bobbing a curtsy only after a nudge from Jack. "Good morning, milady. I'll do my best to please you. Sir Jack said you'd been in an accident."

Moira sent Jack a startled look. He knew she was no

"milady." But his warning glance told her to dispute nothing he did.

"Aye, a carriage accident," Moira said truthfully. "I'm sure we'll get along fine, Jilly."

"Is there anything you'd like, milady?"

"A bath," Moira requested. "If that's possible," she added, sending an inquiring glance at Jack.

" 'Tis indeed possible. Find Pettibone, Jilly. He'll carry up the tub and show you where things are kept. It will take a few days to learn your way around this pile of stone. Go along with you now, and take the empty tray with you to the kitchen."

Jilly bobbed another curtsy, took the tray from Moira's lap and all but ran from the room in her anxiety to please.

"If you don't like her, we'll find someone else," Jack said.

"Jilly will do fine. I'm uncomfortable being waited upon. If not for my injury, I'd not even need a maid."

"A maid is necessary for propriety's sake," Jack intoned dryly. "In case you've forgotten, I'm responsible for your broken arm and sundry bruises. Now, is there anything else you'd like?"

"Aye. When can I get out of bed? I'm unaccustomed to lying about. I'd like my clothing back."

He sent her an assessing glance. She did look better, he conceded. Her bruises were fading, and the swelling about her face was receding. "Did Dr. Dudley stop by yesterday?"

"Aye. He said things were progressing nicely and that the pneumonia he feared hasn't materialized. He put a cast on my arm and said it could come off in four weeks."

"Then I suppose you could get up and move about for

short intervals, but don't tire yourself. I'll instruct Petti-bone to return your clothing. I believe he had them cleaned and mended. Which leads to another problem. You're going to need clothes in keeping with your new station in life.''

''My station?'' Moira asked tartly. ''I assume you're referring to the station you and Lord Fenwick created.''

''Aye, milady,'' Jack said, sending her a mocking grin. ''Henceforth you are to be addressed as Lady Moira Gree-ley. O'Toole is too common a name. Since we are to work together closely, I will call you Moira and you may call me Jack. Now that that's settled, I'll summon a mantua maker to measure you for an appropriate wardrobe.''

''I don't like this. Can't you get into trouble?''

Jack gave a shout of laughter. ''Who is there to refute my claim that you are a distant relative? Unless,'' he added ominously, ''there is something you're not telling me. What about your former employers? Will they rec-ognize you if you meet them at a social function?''

''My former employers are elderly and rarely attend social functions,'' Moira said. ''Even if they did, they might not recognize me dressed in fancy clothing.'' She thought it best not to mention Lord Roger, since in all likelihood he was still abroad.

''Then I see nothing to hinder our plans. Once you're properly dressed and versed in the finer points of etiquette, I'll introduce you to society. If you're up to it, we'll start tomorrow on your lessons. Can you play an instrument? Or sing? Or dance?''

''I play the harpsichord and sing,'' Moira said with pride. ''But I never learned to dance.''

Jack was stunned. Not only did Moira speak like gen-try, but she was taught to play an instrument and sing.

Why had her parents educated her beyond her station? There was a mystery here somewhere; he just had to figure it out. "I'll teach you to dance myself."

Their conversation came to a halt when Pettibone arrived with the tub. "I'll bring hot water directly, milady."

"I'll leave you to your bath," Jack said, turning away. Just the thought of Moira in her bath made him break out in a cold sweat. This wasn't like him, not like him at all. Women were necessary to his well-being, but this pressing need Moira aroused in him confused him. She exuded a lavish sensuality that she wasn't even aware of. It shouldn't bother a profligate rogue like him, but it did.

Whitcomb's rout was a bore, Jack thought as he made his way to the gaming room. He abhorred the crush of people, but the gaming tables looked promising. Most of the men engaged in gambling were playing for high stakes and could afford it. If his luck held, and he felt it would, he would go home tonight with enough blunt to pay for Moira's wardrobe.

"I decided to forgive you."

Jack turned at the sound of Victoria's voice, composing his face into a smile. "I'm forever grateful." His mocking tone went over Victoria's head.

"Did you doubt it? No one can hold a candle to you in bed. Shall we go to my house tonight so I can show you how well you please me?"

"I'll come to you after I finish at the gaming tables," Jack said. "Leave the servants' entry unlocked. I can see myself up to your room."

"I'll be waiting," Victoria purred throatily. "Don't be late."

For some unexplained reason, Jack could muster scant enthusiasm for Victoria's bold invitation. A few days ago he would have welcomed with eagerness a few scintillating hours in Victoria's bed. Now he hoped he could rise to the occasion.

The play proved lucrative and Jack won several hundred pounds. He couldn't recall when he'd been so successful at gambling—he'd never won enough to live comfortably. Perhaps he wasn't cut out to be a gambler, he thought as he pocketed his winnings and excused himself. For the second time in as many days, Black Jack Graystoke admitted to excesses in both drink and gambling and thought seriously about giving them up, which frightened the hell out of him. Something was happening to him and he didn't like it, not one damn bit.

Was this Lady Amelia's doing? he wondered as he collected his cape and walked out into the raw night. Since that fateful day the family ghost had chosen to haunt him, his life hadn't been the same. Didn't Lady Amelia know it was much too late to redeem him? He had already ransomed his soul to the Devil.

Deciding he needed to clear his head, Jack sent his coachman home and walked the short distance to Victoria's house, the invigorating air making him see things precisely as they were. He needed Victoria's money, yet the thought of having Victoria as a wife chilled him as effectively as the cold night air. Jack wasn't certain he believed in love, but there should be more to a relationship than lust. And lust was all he felt for Victoria, though truth to tell even that was beginning to pall. What would it be like after a few years of marriage to her?

Marriage wouldn't change him, Jack decided. He'd still have a mistress or two, still gamble, still drink, still find amusement in unlikely places. And Victoria would discreetly carry on her own affairs of the heart once their passion cooled, which it undoubtedly would. The picture was unappetizing, yet Jack could find no alternative to his pressing need of money.

All that thinking gave Jack a massive headache and an aversion to bedding Victoria tonight. If he went to her now, in this state of mind, he would do neither of them justice. Hoping she would forgive him his lapse, Jack turned back in the direction of Graystoke Manor.

Moira felt well enough to go downstairs and explore the house the following day. With Jilly's help, she dressed in her plain dark serge and walked from room to room, discovering the charm and faded grandeur of the run-down mansion. At one time it must have been spectacular, she reflected. It could still be dazzling once restored to its former elegance. But of course that would take a considerable fortune, which Jack did not possess.

Jack discovered Moira in the reception hall perusing the paintings decorating the walls. ''I've been looking for you. How are you feeling?''

''Well enough, thank you, Sir Jack.''

''Just call me Jack. My title is a minor one; I rarely use it. Only Pettibone insists on calling me Sir Jack. I thought we might engage in conversation so I might judge your ability to speak intelligently on various subjects.''

''My first lesson, Jack?'' Moira asked tartly, displaying some of her old mettle.

Jack grinned. ''You're not short on wit—that's a good sign. Let's go to the study; it's less intimidating than the drawing room. I met Jilly in the hall and asked her to bring refreshments.''

"First tell me about the people in these paintings. Who are they?"

"Various ancestors," Jack said. "Lord, I haven't looked at these pictures in years."

"That must be your father," Moira said, pointing to a dignified man standing stiffly at attention. "You resemble him."

"He died when I was twelve. My mother is on his right."

"She's beautiful. You have her eyes. Who is the other lady?"

"Lady Amelia, my great-great-grandmother. This house was built for her."

"She looks sad."

"She had good reason. Her only son died a wastrel. 'Tis said she haunts the manor from time to time, trying to save others from her son's fate."

Moira's eyes grew round. "Have you seen her?"

"I don't believe in ghosts," Jack said abruptly. "Come along. Our refreshments will be arriving soon."

A few minutes later, they were seated in the study, basking in the warmth of the hearth. Jilly brought tea, then promptly left to assist Pettibone with dinner.

"What should we talk about?" Moira asked, sipping delicately from the cup. Jack watched her closely, studying her manners and deportment. What he saw seemed to please him.

"I must say your parents did well by you. Are you certain neither of them were gentry? It isn't unusual for a woman of gentle birth and breeding to fall in love and marry a man far beneath her in station. Or perhaps it was your father who married beneath him."

"Da owned a small farm. Mama was an orphan. She

was raised by nuns after her mother died birthing her. Her mother was an innkeeper's daughter, but Mama never knew the name of her father. Being illegitimate always bothered Mama, but Da loved her dearly, never questioning her reasons for educating my brother and me above our stations.''

"Strange," Jack mused thoughtfully. "Why would a farmer's daughter need an education? You certainly can't claim to be a lady. There are things you've neglected to tell me, Moira. Such as why you were walking the streets late at night in a blinding storm. Did your lover abandon you? Are you a prostitute?''

Moira rose clumsily to her feet, sheltering her injured arm. Anger and outrage stiffened her petite form and brought a dangerous glitter to her golden eyes. "You, sir, are no gentleman! Strictly speaking I may not be a lady, but I am not a prostitute!''

The corners of Jack's lips lifted upward. "Strictly speaking," he mocked, "I am no gentleman.''

"You owe me an apology, sir.''

"Sit down, Moira. I'll apologize after I hear your explanation.''

God, she was splendid when roused to anger, Jack thought. Full-lipped and provocative, she tantalized with an intense eroticism that enticed and enthralled him. He envied her lover, if indeed she had one.

"I owe you no explanation," Moira insisted, too upset to sit down. "As long as we're airing our grievances, I may as well tell you I do not trust you, and your grand plan for my future is suspect. Why should you care what happens to me? My problems are none of your concern.''

Jack unfolded his lanky length from the chair. "I'm making it my business. You're my responsibility, and I'd rather find you a husband than have you interfering with my own marriage plans. You saw Lady Victoria's reaction to you. It wouldn't do to have a beautiful ward underfoot when I bring her home as my bride."

"I'll get by," Moira returned.

"I don't doubt it. I want the truth, Moira. What were you doing out the night my carriage ran you down?"

Moira turned away, unwilling to divulge the truth for fear of ending up in Newgate. Much to her dismay, she realized she needed Jack's protection. Since he seemed inclined to believe her earlier lies, she decided to invent another. "Very well. I was meeting my—my lover. I told him that my employers were letting me go because their son fancied me." Almost true. "I begged my lover to marry me, and he became angry because I had lost my source of income. He broke off our relationship. I was running after him, to beg him to reconsider, when your carriage hit me." There, she hoped the lie would please him and he would stop hounding her.

"I thought so," Jack said with a hint of disappointment. He had hoped—ah, well, he should have known better. A beauty like Moira was bound to have lovers. He wondered if Moira had deliberately enticed her employer's son. "Your choice of lovers leaves much to be desired."

Moira had no answer.

"No matter." Jack shrugged. "Needless to say, were I your lover I wouldn't be so inconsiderate."

He grasped her chin, raising her face so he could look into her eyes. "Forget the past, Moira. Think only of the future. You're bright enough to convince any man you're an innocent virgin. You almost had me convinced." His smile did not quite reach his eyes.

A flash of pain dimmed Moira's golden eyes as she stared back at Jack. She didn't deserve his scorn, yet that was exactly what she got. A man as roguishly handsome and virile as Jackson Graystoke could have any woman he wanted. Why should she believe his interest in her was other than what he'd claimed? Jack felt a certain responsibility for her, nothing more.

"What are you thinking, Moira?" Jack drawled when he saw her eyes turn dark. "Are you wondering if I'm a better lover than your last one?" His hand dropped away from her chin, landing on her shoulder before trailing down to her breast. Jack knew he was treading on dangerous ground but couldn't help himself. Moira might be experienced, but she had a look of sweet innocence about her that intrigued him. Sweet innocence and pure temptation—what an explosive combination!

Moira held her breath as she felt the heated path of his gaze follow his hand. Her breasts tingled beneath the intensity of his look and intimate caress, and a spark of desire settled in her center and began to grow as she reacted to his touch. She felt her nipple harden against his palm and drew back in alarm.

"Stop it!"

Jack sighed regretfully and removed his hand. "You're right. As much as I'd like to continue this, I fear you're not up to it yet. Besides, I'd rather not get involved intimately. 'Tis best we keep this on a purely impersonal level. At least until we find you a husband. After you're safely wed, we can explore this attraction we have for one another more fully."

"You think I'd be unfaithful?" Moira gasped in outrage.

"What I think doesn't matter."

"I'm not attracted to you. You're a profligate rake and scoundrel. I find little about you to admire."

"Don't you?" he drawled lazily.

Jack couldn't ignore the challenge. Reaching out, he pulled her close and kissed her long and thoroughly, thrusting his tongue past her open lips, plunging her into sweet perdition. He tasted spicy and hot and delicious. Before she realized what she was doing, she began kissing him back.

Jack was enjoying the kiss too much. He pulled away with effort. The pure wonder of Moira's response inflamed him beyond repair. Mesmerized, he watched the pulse throbbing in her white throat and fought the urge to place his lips there.

"I didn't mean for that to happen." His voice held a strange hoarseness and he cleared his throat noisily. "I think we've conversed enough for one day. You're tired. You should rest and get your strength back. You'll need it when I introduce you to society. I predict you'll be an instant success. An original. We'll have you married in no time. Tomorrow we'll discuss current events and literature. A woman should know just how far to go before a suitor is turned off by her intelligence."

Moira turned and fled. It was a long, long time before breath and awareness returned. By that time she was safely in her chamber, where Jack's magnetic presence could not tempt her. Jack Graystoke was too intense, too bold, too handsome. She was no match for him.

During the following days, Moira was put through a test of sorts by Jack and Lord Fenwick. She was brought abreast of current affairs, practiced pouring tea, grilled on etiquette and proper behavior with the ton. To Jack's delight, he found her well-versed on a variety of subjects and intelligent enough to pick up quickly on those she was not familiar with.

During this period, a dressmaker had been engaged to sew Moira a complete wardrobe. Two day dresses arrived within a week, with the promise of three ball gowns to be delivered in time for Moira's introduction into society. The day dresses were lovelier than any Moira had ever owned, and she wondered where Jack got the money to pay for them. She hoped it wasn't from Lady Victoria.

To Moira's vast relief, she and Jack were seldom alone. If Spencer Fenwick wasn't with them, either Pettibone or Jilly was in attendance. Two weeks after she arrived at Graystoke Manor, Jack announced that she was ready for dancing lessons. When Moira arrived in the drawing room for the first lesson, she was surprised to see Pettibone seated at the out-of-tune pianoforte and the rug rolled back.

The first lesson was a disaster. With Jack's strong arms around her and the heat of his body assaulting her, Moira couldn't concentrate on the steps. Even when the dance steps parted them, she could still feel the warmth where his hands had rested on her body. When he introduced her to the waltz, she became so rattled that Jack threw up his hands in despair.

"What's gotten into you, Moira? A graceful creature like you should be able to pick up the steps without difficulty."

"Don't scold her, Jack," Spence chided. "Moira's done better than either of us has a right to expect. She's a country girl, not gentry."

Jack stared at Moira, seeing much more than a simple country girl. Her beauty outshone the brightest star, and her intelligence was as keen as his. Moira puzzled him. She was like no poor farmer's daughter he had ever seen. He was convinced she could hold her own with any high-born lady of his acquaintance. Moira was an enigma, Jack decided, and he envied her former lovers.

Moira's heart beat a rapid tattoo as Jack continued to stare at her. What was he thinking? she wondered. Wasn't she proving amusing enough? The thought that he was grooming her for another man made her strangely uncomfortable.

"Can we continue tomorrow?" she asked, shaken by her thoughts. "I've had enough lessons for one day."

"Of course," Jack agreed, "we'll continue tomorrow. Dancing will be easier once the cast is removed from your arm."

He watched her walk away, struck anew by her beauty. It occurred to him that he should be grateful to Lady Amelia for throwing Moira into his path. He was enjoying this little charade immensely. Spence's two thousand pounds were as good as in his pocket.

"You seem quite taken with Moira," Spence said, watching Jack closely. "Beware, Jack, the lady has a way about her."

Dragging his thoughts back to his friend, Jack sent Spence an amused look. "Don't worry about me, Spence. Moira represents two thousand pounds, the exact amount you'll owe me when she bags a rich husband. She will, you know. With our backing and her natural beauty, how can she miss?"

"I fear you may be right." Spence heaved a regretful sigh. "I was counting on those grays. They'd look magnificent hitched to my coach. But she isn't engaged yet, old boy. And if you aren't careful, she might bag *you*."

Strangely uncomfortable with that remark, Jack released a nervous laugh. "I need to marry money, not some little Irish baggage who's had too many lovers for my taste."

"You're sure of that? Has she told you she's had lovers? She looks so innocent."

"That's what I'm counting on, Spence. I don't want her prospective suitors questioning her innocence, or lack of it. Moira admitted she was meeting a lover the night I struck her down."

Spence's disappointment was obvious. "Ah, well, so much for fantasies. I'd imagined many different scenarios, most involving our timely rescue of a damsel in distress."

"You're a dreamer, Spence." Jack's voice held a hard edge that made his friend fondly recall the Black Jack of old. "We both knew what Moira was from the beginning and were willing to play out our little game. We're doing this for amusement, remember, and to rid me of an unwanted responsibility. After all, it *was* my carriage that ran her down."

He should have known Jack wouldn't allow a woman to become important to him, Spence reflected upon hearing Jack's remarks concerning Moira. Still, he couldn't help thinking there was more between Jack and Moira than met the eye. The air around them vibrated with awareness when they were together. Spence could almost feel the tension between them. He thought this whole business was growing more interesting by the minute and couldn't wait for the final outcome.

"Are you sure you're not attracted to Moira?" Spence wanted to know.

"I'm a man, Spence. Does that answer your question?

What man wouldn't be? But I'm not about to lose my head over her."

Jack's answer seemed to satisfy Spence. "When do you think Moira will be ready to enter into society?"

"By the time the cast is removed from her arm, she should be groomed and ready to meet the ton. I think the Griswald rout will be a perfect time to bring her out. I received my invitation just yesterday."

"Have you proposed to Lady Victoria yet?"

Jack shifted uneasily, recalling the countless excuses he'd given Victoria lately to explain his inattention. She hadn't been happy about it, especially after he failed to show up at her house after the Whitcomb rout. In fact, Jack found himself avoiding her whenever possible.

"Not yet, but soon. I'm aiming for a spring wedding."

"Invite me to the ceremony," Spence said. "Well, I must be off. Will I see you tonight at White's?"

"Perhaps," Jack said noncommittally. He wasn't going to admit to Spence that gaming no longer held the same appeal for him it previously had. Nor did drinking to excess. Lady Amelia's appearance had turned his life awry, and he hoped she was happy.

Two weeks later, the cast was removed from Moira's arm. She flexed it gingerly and smiled at the doctor when no pain resulted.

"Good as new," the doctor said, beaming. "I wouldn't lift anything heavy for a while, though I doubt Sir Jack would allow it. I understand you're his ward."

Moira could tell by the doctor's tone of voice that he didn't believe the story they had concocted. "Aye. We're distantly related."

"Of course," the doctor said without conviction.

"Well, young lady, the best of luck to you. I hope you'll have no further need of my services."

"Kind of mouthy, ain't he?" Jilly said once the doctor left. "He was hinting at something improper. Why, from what I've seen, Sir Jack has been nothing but a gentleman."

"Thank you, Jilly, but I fear you don't know me very well. Few people would call me a gentleman."

Moira's eyes's widened when she saw Jack filling the doorway, looking magnificent in tight gray trousers and a black jacket molded perfectly to his broad shoulders. His powerful presence was intimidating—just the sight of him was enough to send blood pounding through her veins. He stepped away from the door and crossed the room to where Moira was sitting.

"The doctor said your arm is good as new. How does it feel?"

"Well enough," Moira replied, flexing her healed limb.

"I'm glad." Suddenly aware of Jilly staring curiously at them, Jack said, "You may go, Jilly, I wish to speak to your mistress in private."

"What do you wish to say to me that demands privacy?" Moira wanted to know once Jilly was out of hearing.

"I didn't think you wanted Jilly to know we're not really related. Are you satisfied with your new clothes?"

"They're lovely," Moira admitted. "I've never had anything so grand."

"Wait until you see the ball gowns. I chose styles that will be flattering to your figure and coloring. I think you'll be pleased."

"My dancing has improved," Moira said, fishing for Jack's approval.

"So it has. No one will find fault with your dancing. You've exceeded my fondest hopes in every way. You'll take London by storm. I predict you'll be married before spring."

The warm glow from Jack's compliments faded abruptly when Moira pictured herself married to a man she had yet to meet. A man other than Jack. Lord, where did that thought come from? She wouldn't have a man like Jackson Graystoke if he was served to her on a silver platter. A disreputable rake like him would abandon the marriage bed before it was cold.

"Doesn't that please you?" Jack asked, puzzled by her silence. "You'll be able to bring your family to London. Or help them financially if they wish to remain in Ireland."

"Of course that pleases me," Moira snapped. "Anything is better than being dependent on you. What about your own wedding plans? Has Lady Victoria accepted your proposal?"

Jack looked away. "I haven't proposed yet. Been too busy grooming you for your introduction to society. I don't anticipate any problems. Marrying money is as necessary to me as it is to you. I suppose I could ask my cousin for money, but I'm not the sort to go begging."

"Your cousin?"

"Aye, the Duke of Ailesbury. Though we're not close, he's a likable sort and we respect one another. His father and my mother were siblings. Mother married beneath her, but it never bothered her. Young William is to marry soon, and I expect an heir will follow in short order. Will and I have no other living relatives."

"Your cousin is a duke? I didn't know you had relatives so highly placed."

"Titles do not impress me, nor do macaroni dandies. Young William is welcome to the dukedom; I never aspired to the title and he knows it. The title is entailed; that's why I urged him to marry and produce an heir. I'm perfectly content with being the black sheep of the family."

Moira's golden eyes twinkled mischievously. "Black suits you, Sir Jack. You wear it well."

Jack threw back his head and gave a shout of laughter. "And you, Lady Moira, will set London on its ear with your wit and beauty. I wish . . ."

Moira's attention sharpened. "What do you wish, Jack?"

He drew her to her feet and into his arms. "I wish I had been the man you were meeting that night. I wish I had been your lover."

Chapter Five

"I wish I had been your lover," Jack repeated when Moira appeared dazed by his admission. "You're pure temptation, do you know that?"

Their eyes met, and in the taut, vibrating silence that followed, Moira realized she was completely out of her element. Her body felt heavy with yearning, her heated center liquid with anticipation and throbbing with a craving she didn't fully understand. She tried to deny the feelings Jack's volatile presence evoked in her, but all she could think of was the searing heat of his evocative gaze and the warmth of his hard body.

When Moira tried to summon an answer, Jack's mouth came down on hers—hard, ruthlessly compelling. All semblance of control fled and her knees went weak. An audible sigh gurgled in her throat. His mouth opened wide over hers, his tongue thrusting past her lips and teeth, drinking, tasting, withdrawing and thrusting again in imitation of what his nether parts would like to do. She felt the hardness of his loins pressing against her soft belly, felt his hands kneading her breasts, and untrammeled rapture, pure and sharp, raced through her veins. His mouth on hers felt wonderful. She had never known anything to compare with the bone-deep pleasure of his touch and taste. It was gloriously decadent.

Instinct ruled her brain as she brought her arms around his neck and sighed against his mouth. Her pleasure intensified his wild hunger and he drew her closer, filling the heat of her mouth with his taste even as he consumed hers. When he started to drag her toward the bed, Moira's senses quickened, warning of danger. With strength born of desperation, she pulled away from him, breathing hard, her eyes wary.

"You set me afire," Jack confessed hoarsely. "The thought of making love to you intrigues me. When I'm with you I can think of nothing else. You're a mystery, Moira O'Toole, a tantalizing mystery." He fingered the locket suspended around her neck on a gold chain, wondering not for the first time why she seemed so fond of it. "Where did you get this locket? Did one of your lovers give it to you?"

"There is nothing mysterious about me, sir. And if you must know, the locket belonged to my grandmother and then to my mother. Now it is mine."

"What are we going to do about this attraction that exists between us?" Jack asked softly, the locket forgotten as he bent to nibble at the pulse throbbing in her neck. Moira's world spun dizzily. "Keeping our association on a strictly impersonal level is too bloody difficult for a rake like me."

" 'Tis for the best," Moira said, backing away.

"Damn it, Moira, you've had lovers before. What difference will one more make?"

Moira's cheeks pinkened. She supposed she deserved that for lying to Jack about her nonexistent lover. "What about Lady Victoria? I doubt she's the forgiving kind. Nor one to share her men."

Jack gave a hoot of laughter. "Surely you're not so naive as to think I'll remain faithful to Victoria after we're married, are you? Why do you think they call me Black Jack? I'm no saint, Moira. I'm beyond even Lady Amelia's help."

Moira sent him a puzzled look. "Lady Amelia? Are you referring to the family ghost? The one whose portrait I saw in the hall?"

"Lady Amelia be damned! 'Tis you I wish to discuss. I want you, Moira, and I always get what I want."

"Until now," Moira said with asperity. She pitied the woman who married Black Jack Graystoke. He was too handsome and too arrogant and too damn sure of himself. She didn't know him well enough to trust him.

"Are you going to deny me? Deny us? I can tell when a woman wants to be bedded, and your kisses tell me you're as eager as I to consummate our mutual attraction."

Moira's golden eyes blazed with fury. "You're an arrogant, conceited reprobate, Sir Jack! I could walk out of this charade you and Lord Fenwick hatched right now and look back with no regrets."

Jack's brow turned upward. "Could you? Where would you go? You have no money that I know of. You don't even have a promise of employment. By your own admission, your lover wants nothing more to do with you. You need me, Moira O'Toole. I'd say we have a mutual need of one another." His eyes smiled at her, one corner of his mouth turned up, and he looked so cocky Moira wanted to slap the smirk from his face.

"You can't possibly know what I need," Moira observed. "Save your ardor for your fiancée and mistresses. I don't want it. You promised me a rich husband, and that's all I want."

If Moira sounded mercenary, it was because she was desperate. Her brother's last letter had hinted at his dire straits, and the sooner she sent financial support, the better.

The light in Jack's gray eyes dimmed, and he stepped away from her. "Have it your way, Moira. I've never forced a woman in my life, not even a whore. . . ." He left his sentence dangling, but Moira knew he was referring to her. What else could he think when she had led him to believe she was a streetwalker instead of an innocent virgin?

"We'll find you a rich husband and you can go on your merry way. Passing off a woman of your . . . er . . . calling as a lady of quality will be vastly amusing." And lucrative to the tune of two thousand pounds, Jack thought but did not say. "There's a ball on Saturday night. 'Tis a perfect time to introduce you to society. Now, if you'll excuse me, I'm to call on Lady Victoria this afternoon. 'Tis a perfect time to propose. We will both have rich spouses by spring. Good day, Moira. I won't be joining you for supper tonight. 'Tis likely Lady Victoria will have appropriate entertainment planned to celebrate our engagement."

"Good day, Sir Jack," Moira returned coolly, knowing full well the kind of entertainment Lady Victoria would provide for her virile fiancé. She had no idea why, but the thought of Jack and Victoria together intimately made her physically ill.

*   *   *

Jack slammed out the door in a fine rage. It wasn't as if he was asking something of Moira she hadn't already given to others. He knew the attraction between them was perilous to his future plans with Victoria, but he couldn't help himself. He seemed to be racing toward some unknown destination, guided by an unseen hand. He'd be damned if he'd permit it to ruin his plans! His life was his own, to live as he bloody well pleased. Until he'd gotten foxed and run down an Irish serving wench who'd been ditched by her lover, he'd been perfectly content with his life. Keeping himself amused and bagging a wealthy wife had been his only goals in life. He couldn't wait until he found an unsuspecting husband for the woman of questionable virtue he'd brought into his home. It couldn't be too soon to suit him.

"Oh, milady, you look like a princess." Jilly sighed wistfully. "Sir Jack is going to be so pleased. Why, I'll bet you'll outshine every woman at the ball tonight. You'll nab a husband in no time at all."

Moira stared, entranced, into the pier glass, unable to believe the reflected image was her own. The ball gown had been delivered just this afternoon. The silver tissue, shimmering with iridescent hues of violet, hugged her breasts and cinched her waist most becomingly, then belled out in regal splendor. The neckline dipped enticingly to reveal the upper curves of her breasts without appearing overly daring, while the long fitted sleeves gave the appearance of demure elegance.

Her hair had been lovingly groomed by Jilly, who piled her gleaming tresses atop her head in a spill of curls that provided an enchanting frame for her delicate features. If

Moira wasn't looking at herself in the glass, she would have sworn such a transformation was impossible. Yet the living proof was staring back at her.

"You flatter me, Jilly," Moira demurred modestly. "Bring my wrap. It wouldn't do to keep Sir Jack waiting."

Jack was growing impatient, pacing the hall and pausing every few seconds at the foot of the stairs to glance upward. He was as nervous as a mother about to present her daughter to society. So much depended upon Moira's acceptance by the gentry. He needed Spence's two thousand pounds to finance his wedding to Victoria, and Moira required a rich husband to take her off his hands.

His marriage proposal had gone off without a hitch until Victoria had placed a stipulation upon their engagement. She refused to marry him until his ward was established in a household of her own. Damn! If he didn't have funds soon to restore Graystoke Manor, it would fall down around him. Jack had been relieved to find that Victoria's mother had arrived unexpectedly for a visit, thus enabling him to make a graceful exit without making up excuses to Victoria for not bedding her, as she would have expected had she been alone. His reluctance puzzled him. Not too long ago, bedding Victoria had been more pleasure than chore.

His empty pockets should have made Jack more than eager to placate Victoria in any way he could. Like finding Moira a husband. On the other hand, imagining Moira making love with another man made him physically uncomfortable. He supposed that feeling would pass once they were both safely wed.

Pausing at the foot of the stairs, Jack glanced upward again, stunned by the vision before him. Resplendent in shimmering silver, looking like an angel, Moira seemed to float down the stairs. Her feet must have sprouted wings, for it seemed to Jack that she barely touched the steps as she approached the bottom, where he stood waiting. Jack was scarcely aware that he had stopped breathing until a gasp of air exploded from his chest. When Moira reached the landing, he gallantly offered his arm and guided her into the foyer, where he stepped back to scan her critically.

His searing gaze dropped from her eyes to her shoulders, then slowly and seductively upward to her breasts, his stare bold and assessing. Moira's whole being seemed to be filled with waiting; the prolonged anticipation was almost unbearable.

"Do you approve, sir?"

Approve? Jack more than approved—he was overwhelmed. Never in his wildest imagination did he think the pitiful creature he had brought home over a month ago could be transformed into this glorious woman standing before him. The pit of his stomach churned and he had to force himself into calmness, repeating to himself that he couldn't afford to become involved with a penniless waif who was most likely a whore. And Moira couldn't afford to marry anyone without blunt if she wished to help her relatives. They were a fine pair, he thought dimly. He was a disreputable scoundrel willing to swap affection for money, and she was a woman with deplorable taste in lovers.

He considered her a moment, then shrugged. "My approval isn't the one we're seeking. 'Tis your prospective suitors you need to impress. But 'tis my opinion you'll do very well. Just remember your lessons and be mindful of your dance steps, and I predict you'll have swains aplenty. One would hardly think from looking at you that you're . . ." he halted in mid-sentence, then said after a dramatic pause, "from the serving class."

Moira didn't need second sight to know what Jack had started to say; his awkward pause said it all. Since she had nothing to add to alter his opinion of her, she said, "Shall we go?"

Jilly appeared with Moira's new fur-lined cape, and Jack draped it over her shoulders. His hands lingered a moment too long, and the heat from his touch warmed her all the way to the Griswald mansion in Mayfair. Why did Black Jack Graystoke disturb her so much? Moira wondered dismally. How could she concentrate on another man when Jack's virile appeal assaulted every sense she possessed?

"We're here," Jack said as the carriage rolled to a stop before a huge stone edifice whose tall windows spilled light into the street. People were leaving their carriages and strolling toward the entrance in droves. The driver lowered the step and Jack exited first. He offered a helping hand to Moira.

Moira's hand shook as she placed it in his. Jack covered her fingers with his and patted them reassuringly. "Just be yourself and remember the story we concocted to explain your appearance in London. I'll keep an eye on you."

"I'm not sure that's wise. Won't Lady Victoria be upset if you watch me too closely?"

"Perhaps, but you're my ward, and I'm expected to keep tabs on you. Besides," he added dryly, "the sooner we find you a husband, the happier Victoria will be."

The staircase leading to the second-floor ballroom was teeming with people going in either direction. Jack greeted several by name while merely nodding to others. Most seemed startled to see him with a woman other than Victoria, since rumor had it that Jack and Victoria were all but engaged. When they were announced, all heads turned in their direction as the majordomo called out, "Sir Jackson Graystoke and his ward, Lady Moira Greeley."

What followed was a general stampede to be introduced to Moira. Jack led her to the host and hostess first, explaining Moira's identity with a few succinct words. Since no one refuted his claim or questioned Moira's right to attend the rout, she allowed herself a shaky breath of heartfelt relief. Jack squeezed her arm and whispered, "You're launched. The rest is up to you."

Spence came up to join them, eyeing Moira with open admiration. "You look like an angel, Moira. I can almost guarantee your success." He sent Jack a meaningful look. "I reckon I can buy my own grays." He walked away, chuckling to himself. "Watching this unfold is worth the loss."

Moira looked at Jack askance. "What is he talking about?"

"Pay him no heed. Spence often talks in riddles."

Further explanation was forgotten as she and Jack were immediately surrounded by young gentlemen demanding to be introduced to Moira. There were so many, Moira could hardly keep them straight, let alone settle on anyone who caught her fancy. So she danced with them all, batting her eyes coyly, which was totally out of character. Flirtation was new to Moira; so was the kind of deception she was involved in.

When midnight arrived, both Lord Harrington and Lord Renfrew asked to partner her for supper. When she looked to Jack for guidance, she saw that he was paying rapt attention to Lady Victoria and was unaware of her dilemma. Using her own judgment, she smiled beguilingly at both men and accepted an arm from each, allowing the eager swains to lead her in to supper together.

"Your little ward appears to have made some rather important conquests," Victoria said with a smirk. "Both Harrington and Renfrew seem quite taken with her."

Jack's head snapped around sharply. "Renfrew? The man's an arrogant bastard. A rake of the worst sort and definitely not the marrying kind. Excuse me while I rescue Moira."

Clinging to Jack's arm, Victoria refused to release him. "Leave her alone, darling. Perhaps the chit will reform him. His parents have been after him for ages to marry and produce an heir. They've threatened to disinherit him if he doesn't change his wicked ways. They fear he's involved with the Hellfire Club."

"Moira has led a sheltered life," Jack said blandly. "She isn't equipped to handle a man of Renfrew's ilk. Both Renfrew and Harrington are macaroni dandies. I heard Harrington got a girl pregnant, and she killed herself when he wouldn't marry her."

"Idle gossip," Victoria alleged. "Both men are imminently suitable for a country girl with no fortune to commend her. They are both wealthy enough to marry whomever they want without benefit of a dowry. Renfrew's parents will be so happy to marry him off, her lack of fortune won't matter as long as her bloodlines are good. You did say her father is a baron, did you not?"

"Aye, a baron," Jack replied, distracted when he saw Renfrew bend to whisper intimately into Moira's ear. "The horny bastard is staring down her cleavage!" he spat between clenched teeth. "Can't he see Moira's an innocent?"

His words gave him pause for thought. An innocent? What in God's name made him say that? Moira was anything but innocent, despite her virginal appearance. She was undoubtedly more than capable of handling reprobates like Renfrew and Harrington. Nevertheless, he decided to have a private word with both suitors sometime during the evening—and with any other man he deemed unsuitable husband material.

"Take me in to supper, darling," Victoria said. "You've been neglecting me of late, and I don't like it."

" 'Tis all but impossible to find you alone since your mother came to visit." Truth to tell, her mother's visit gave him a perfect excuse not to bed Victoria. He would have been forced to do so had she demanded it of him, but it wouldn't have been proper with her mother in the house, and she knew it. Strange as it may seem, since Moira's arrival in his life, making love to his intended bride held little appeal.

"I'm as disappointed as you," Victoria purred throatily. "Perhaps a short period of celibacy will make you an eager bridegroom. Just remember, darling, keep your trousers buttoned in the meantime. Everything you have is mine."

Jack stiffened with resentment. His lack of money was demeaning and embarrassing, and he didn't enjoy being dictated to by Victoria, but losing Graystoke Manor was a thought he didn't relish. Should that happen, *all* of his ancestors would surely haunt him. He already had Lady Amelia to contend with. Somewhere down the line, if his situation didn't improve soon, debtor's prison loomed before him. The picture was not a pretty one. But he'd be damned if he'd put up with Victoria's possessiveness.

"Go in to supper alone. I'll join you directly. I wish to speak with my ward first." Victoria's protest sputtered and died as Jack wheeled on his heel and left.

Moira smiled beguilingly at the two men dancing attendance on her, feeling more at ease as the evening progressed. When she heard Jack call out her name, she stopped and waited for him to approach. His brows were furrowed, and she wondered what she had done to displease him. Victoria had claimed his entire evening, allowing him not even a single dance with her.

"I'd like a private word with my ward," Jack said, dismissing Renfrew and Harrington with a curt nod. "She'll join you directly." Both men moved off to wait a short distance away.

Moira looked at Jack askance. "Have I done something wrong?"

"Not yet," Jack said tersely. "I wanted to warn you about Renfrew and Harrington. I know them, and they aren't what you're looking for in a husband. Both are notorious rakes and definitely not husband material."

"Just what am I looking for?" Moira wanted to know.

"Bloody hell, Moira, you're not dumb. You know what they're after. I'd advise you to take no lovers until after you have a husband."

Moira's eyes flared angrily. "I know you have a low opinion of me, but this is appalling. Isn't that Lady Victoria marching toward us, looking as if she could strike me dead? You'd best be on your good behavior or risk losing her wealth."

Jack's gray eyes turned cold as stone, his voice low and strident. "There are other heiresses where she came from."

"I suppose there are always women vying for Black Jack Graystoke's attention. Have women always come easily for you?"

He gave her an irresistibly devastating grin. "Always, but that's besides the point. I merely wished to warn you about Renfrew and Harrington."

"Darling, we'll be late for supper," Victoria said, sailing up to them. "Can't you see you're keeping Moira from her admirers? Aren't you happy she's such an overwhelming success?"

"Very happy," Jack said, turning the full force of his potent smile on Victoria, obtaining the result he sought when she nearly melted on the spot.

Good grief, Moira thought as she turned away in disgust. Did the man have no pride? He'd do anything, say anything, to get what he wanted. But who was she to judge when she was no better than he? She was willing to take a husband without benefit of love as long as he possessed wealth. The need to clear her name and help her brother were more crucial than her happiness.

Renfrew and Harrington appeared at her side again, and they proceeded into supper. Throughout the interminable meal, Moira felt the heat of Jack's gaze resting on her as she conversed in an animated manner with her two supper companions. Jack sat across from her, making his displeasure known by clearing his throat noisily whenever one of the men bent too close or she flirted too gaily. When supper ended, they filed from the dining room back into the ballroom to resume the dancing. Lord Merriweather came to claim her for the next dance, arriving at the same time as Jack, who took her arm and dragged her away from the young man.

"I'm sorry, Merriweather, this dance is mine." The

band struck up a wicked, scandalous waltz, and without another word, Jack spun Moira into his arms and onto the dance floor. Their bodies molded in perfect union as he held her indecently close.

"What do you think you're doing?" Moira charged.

"Watch out for Merriweather. He was looking down the front of your dress without a morsel of shame. 'Tis easy to see what he's after."

"It's only a dance, Jack. You're acting as if I really were your ward."

Startled, Jack realized the truth of Moira's words. What in hell was he about anyway? He was acting like a jealous fool when he had absolutely nothing to be jealous about. Things were working exactly as he and Spence intended, but somehow he wasn't amused. The only thing that kept him from spiriting Moira away from the crush of people was the two thousand pounds he'd win when Moira landed a husband. The strange thing was that Jack craved neither wealth nor title. Money came and went with the success of the game. It wasn't until his losing streak threatened the loss of Graystoke Manor that he realized he had to marry money.

"You're absolutely right, Moira. I have no right to be . . ." He hesitated, "—judgmental. I don't even have the right to dictate your life, for we aren't even lovers." He sent her a hungry look. "Though 'tis not from lack of desire." Jack had almost said jealous instead of judgmental, but at the last minute sanity returned. "I should congratulate you. You've done exceptionally well tonight. No one has the remotest idea you're not what you pretend to be."

"What am I, Jack?" Moira asked, searching his face.

Jack gave her a mocking grin. "A lady, of course."

Moira flushed and looked away. She wished she had never asked.

"Spence is spreading the rumor that your father is an Irish baron, distantly related to me on my father's side," Jack continued blithely. "He's telling everyone that your father placed you in my care with instructions to launch you into society."

The dance ended and Jack escorted her off the floor. When Moira was besieged by a deluge of admirers, Jack melted away to find Victoria, who was still fuming at Jack's desertion. Two hours later, Moira was ready to drop from exhaustion but was spared that indignation when Jack approached with her wrap.

" 'Tis time to leave, Moira. Bid your admirers good night."

A clamor of protests rose up around her, but Moira deftly fended them off, leaving a gaggle of disappointed swains behind.

"Thank you for rescuing me," Moira said once they were seated in the carriage. "I'm exhausted. It must be close to dawn. My duties as maid were easier than being on display all evening."

"If things work out, you'll never have to work for anyone again. Or depend on a fickle lover like the one who abandoned you."

Moira flushed guiltily. She was aware that her lie had branded her a fallen woman and was sorry she'd had to resort to such desperate measures. She fell silent, too tired to interpret the unsettling look leveled at her from beneath the heavy lids of Jack's storm-gray eyes. Once in the safety of her own room, though, his heated look came back to haunt her, rousing feelings she neither wanted nor understood.

Undressing quickly, Moira slid into bed and closed her eyes. Exhausted, she fell asleep. Her dreams took her across time and space to the weeks preceding the night Jack Graystoke found her lying in the gutter.

Chapter Six

Prelude to Disaster: Lord Mayhew's home, six months earlier

Moira entered Lord Roger Mayhew's rooms with trepidation. Since the day she'd taken employment with the Mayhews, she'd had to fend off the earl's son and heir, whose uninvited attention filled her with loathing. His pursuit of her had become so intense that she made a point of staying out of his way when he was home, which thankfully wasn't often. Debauched and morally dissolute, his dark vices made him utterly destestable. If Roger knew she had inadvertently learned he was a disciple of the wicked Hellfire Club, her life would be in danger, she was sure of it.

Quickly stripping the soiled linen from Lord Roger's bed, Moira was unaware that her nemesis had entered his room and quietly closed the door behind him. The barely audible click of the door latch sent her spinning around to face the man she had come to fear.

"Ah, Moira, how convenient to find you in my bed-chamber."

"Lord Roger. I thought you'd left. I'll come back at a more convenient time to finish cleaning your room."

Tall and lean to the point of gauntness, his long aristocratic face and colorless eyes gave hint to his cruel nature. Not unhandsome, Roger Mayhew had been spoiled and indulged most his life. He did not tolerate rejection well. For a man of wealth and breeding, gratification of his every whim was a duty—nay, a pleasurable goal. And Roger Mayhew indulged himself to the fullest.

"No need to leave, Moira. I propose we put the bed to good use while you're here. I've been waiting to get you alone for a very long time. Finding you in my chamber is a stroke of luck I hadn't anticipated."

Moira stepped back in fear. "I'm a good girl, milord." She tried to walk past him, but he deliberately placed himself in her path.

"You always did put on airs above your station, Moira. You should be more appreciative of my attentions. Most women in your situation would be eager to accommodate me. You won't find me ungrateful."

"I'm not most women."

When she tried to sidle around him, he laughed cruelly and grasped her upper arms, dragging her against him forcibly. "You aren't going anywhere. You're nothing but a sluttish Irish tease. You know what I want, and I aim to have it. Don't pretend innocence with me."

"Let me go!" Moira struggled furiously, but despite his leanness, Roger was surprisingly strong. Grasping her head between his hands, he slammed his mouth down on hers, biting her bottom lip viciously. Moira tasted blood and struggled violently to escape.

Her strength was meager compared to Roger's. In a shockingly short time, he had her pinned beneath him on the bed, his sloppy kisses and wet, thrusting tongue making her gag. She felt his hand sliding beneath her skirts, shoving them upward, baring her legs and thighs. Her scream was aborted when Roger placed a hand over her mouth.

"What are you trying to do, raise the household?"

Moira nodded her head vigorously. That was exactly what she wished to do.

"You want this, Moira. You're just being stubborn. At heart you're a whore. All women are whores."

Suddenly Moira went limp beneath him, leading him to believe she was submitting willingly.

"That's better," he said with a leering grin. "I knew you'd see reason."

He removed his hand from her mouth so he could kiss her, and summoning every bit of breath available, Moira screamed at the top of her lungs. Enraged, Roger slapped her with the flat of his hand, then covered her mouth with his. Pain exploded inside her head. Roger took advantage of her dazed condition to flip her dress up to her waist and thrust her legs apart. Desperate now, Moira bit down hard on Roger's lip. Roger yelped in pain and slapped her again.

Suddenly the door was flung open and Lord and Lady Mayhew spilled into the room. Lady Mayhew put her hand to her mouth and would have swooned if Lord Mayhew hadn't steadied her.

"What is going on here?" the old man thundered. Though long past his prime, Lord Mayhew was still an impressive man. Moral, stern and honest, he was the complete opposite of his sadistic son and heir.

Roger leaped to his feet. He couldn't afford to anger his father, who had been threatening for years to disinherit him in favor of his younger brother. Malcolm was trustworthy and dependable, everything Roger wasn't. Thus Roger was obliged to hide his cruel nature in order to placate his parents. If they ever found out about his involvement with the Hellfire Club, or looked into his gambling debts, there would be hell to pay.

"The Irish whore has been toying with me since she arrived," Roger lied. "I'm just giving her what she wants."

Moira flipped down her skirts to cover her legs and pushed herself up on her elbows. "That's not true, milord. I was minding my own business when Lord Roger accosted me. I'm a good girl, I don't want . . ." she gestured toward the bed and grimaced, ". . . this."

"Oh, Roger, how could you?" Lady Mayhew lamented. "Why can't you be more like your father? Or your brother Malcolm?"

"I can't believe you'd take a whore's side. I'm your son, for God's sake!"

Though Lord Justin wasn't cognizant of every aspect of Roger's debauchery, he'd heard rumors of his son's vices. And he'd seen nothing in Moira's behavior to suggest she was a wanton out to entrap his son.

"I don't believe Moira's to blame," Lord Justin concluded. "I'm giving you fair warning, Roger. This is never to happen again, do you understand? In the future, leave the servants alone. I know you have a mistress tucked away somewhere, so go to her when you feel the need. If you persist in mistreating the servants, I might find it necessary to strike you from my will in favor of your brother."

Roger stiffened. He was counting on inheriting his father's title and estate, and no one was going to cheat him out of it.

"I understand, Father. It won't happen again." Contriteness galled him and he vowed to make Moira pay for embarrassing him before his parents.

Lord Justin nodded, satisfied with Roger's response. Obviously he didn't know his son very well. "You may leave, Moira. I'm sure you have duties to perform."

Moira rose shakily from the bed and shook out her skirts. When she moved past Roger, he lowered his voice and said for her ears alone, "I'm not through with you, bitch. I'll have you yet—on your knees begging for my attention."

Swallowing convulsively, Moira fled the room.

A few days later, Moira learned how truly evil Roger was when Lady Mayhew called all the servants to the hall long after they had retired. They filed in in various stages of undress and looked in bewilderment at one another when informed that a valuable diamond-and-emerald necklace was missing from Lady Mayhew's jewelry case. Since no one admitted to the theft, Roger suggested that all the servants' rooms be searched. They were sent to their rooms shortly afterward to wait for Lord Roger and his father to conduct the search.

Moira waited on pins and needles. She wasn't really worried, knowing that she wasn't guilty, but this whole matter made her distinctly uneasy. She recalled Lord Roger's threat and feared his reprisal.

Lord Roger and his father arrived in due time. They searched through her meager belongings first and found nothing. Then Roger sent her a smug look and turned back her thin straw mattress. Beneath it he found the necklace still encased in its velvet bag. Moira let out a cry of dismay.

"It can't be! I swear I didn't steal the necklace."

Saddened, Lord Justin looked at Moira and shook his head. "I'm disappointed in you, Moira. Perhaps I've been wrong about you all along and owe my son an apology."

Roger said nothing. He didn't need to. His gloating expression spoke volumes.

"I don't know what I'm going to do about this," Lord Justin said. "I can't condone this kind of behavior in my household. 'Tis best I call the watch and let the authorities deal with you, Moira. You're confined to your room until they arrive."

"I'll guard the door to make sure Moira doesn't escape, Father," Roger offered.

"I doubt she'll go anywhere on a blustery night like this," Lord Justin said, "but perhaps you're right. It will take considerable time to summon the watch in this kind of weather, if they can be roused at all."

After his father left, Roger shut the door and turned the key in the lock. "I told you I'd have you." He sneered viciously.

"You planted your mother's necklace in my room!" Moira accused, stunned at the lengths to which Roger was willing to go to get what he wanted.

"Of course. Did you doubt it?" Roger admitted remorselessly. He shoved her backward onto the bed. "On your back, wench. I'll wager you've not spread your legs for an heir to an earldom. Accommodating me will be a treat from the usual riffraff you've bedded."

Moira made a disgusted sound deep in her throat. "Don't touch me! I'll scream the house down if you do."

"Don't be foolish." Roger snarled. "If you please me,

I'll persuade Father to drop the charges against you."

"I'd rather go to prison," Moira declared, scrambling off the bed to the other side.

Roger, disagreeable even in the best of times, turned downright ugly. "Do you think you're too good for me? You've always put on airs above your station." He grabbed for her. "Women are good for only one thing."

She twisted out of his grasp. "If you don't leave me alone, I'll tell your father about your involvement with the Hellfire Club!"

Roger went still, his eyes as cold as death. "What do you know about the Hellfire Club?" His voice held a hint of menace, but Moira had gone too far to stop now.

"I know you're a disciple of debauchery. I overheard you and a fellow member bragging about throwing some poor girl in the Thames after you'd kidnapped her off the street and used her in your evil rituals."

Roger's face twisted into a vengeful grimace. "You were eavesdropping!"

Moira's chin rose fractionally. "I was cleaning outside the room. You didn't know I was there. I overheard every word. And I'll tell anyone who will listen about your depravities. Your reputation, such as it is, will be torn to shreds. Your entire family will be cut by society once your evil deeds are brought to light."

"Too bad you'll not get the chance to tell anyone," Roger said, lunging for her. His move came so unexpectedly that Moira had scant time to elude him. He covered her mouth with one hand while pinning her arms to her sides with the other.

"Do you think I'll let you go free now, when you know so much about my activities? Father would disinherit me for sure. You sealed your own fate, slut." He pulled her toward the door. "I'll tell Father I felt sorry for you and let you go. He'll be angry and will probably file charges anyway, but no one will find you."

Fear turned Moira's eyes to luminous gold. Why had she goaded Roger with her knowledge of his secret activities? she lamented. Because he had driven her to it, she thought, answering her own question. She'd known the information was dangerous when she'd heard it and had not breathed a word of it to anyone. What a muddle she'd gotten herself into. If only she had held her tongue. She should have realized that threatening Roger was a foolish and dangerous thing to do.

Grabbing her cape from the nail, Roger tossed it over her head and dragged her from the room. No one was in the hallway, and he pushed her toward the backstairs leading down to the kitchen. The servants were all abed this time of night, and they passed through the kitchen unseen. Roger's strength was relentless as he wrestled Moira through the rear entrance and into the rain-drenched night.

Kicking and struggling furiously, Moira was dragged to the carriage house and tossed into the coach. Roger followed close behind, bellowing for the coachman, who came stumbling from his warm bed above the carriage house.

"Are you going abroad, milord?" the man asked sleepily. "'Tis a raw night."

"Hitch the horses to the coach, Stiles," Roger ordered brusquely. "I'll be going to the Dashwood estate tonight."

As the man moved around to do Roger's bidding, he caught sight of Moira, struggling inside the coach. "What's amiss, milord?"

"Nothing, Stiles. You saw nothing, understand? If you

value your position, you'll mention this to no one.''

Stiles was no fool. He had a cushy position, a warm bed and an extra coin or two for a willing wench. He'd driven Lord Roger on more than one occasion to the Dashwood estate and was aware of the evil doings that took place in limestone caves on the grounds, but since he valued his life, he had kept the knowledge to himself. Besides, Lord Roger made it worth his while. If Lord Roger wanted this incident forgotten, then he'd forget it, although he couldn't help feeling a twinge of pity for the poor Irish lass being abducted for illicit purposes.

''Aye, milord, as ye wish. Give me a minute to dress and I'll be with ye.''

''Help me!'' Moira cried when she found her mouth free of Roger's hand.

''He'll not help you,'' Roger growled, turning on her. ''Go ahead and scream—no one will hear you above the pounding rain.''

''Where are you taking me?''

''Since you profess to know so much about the Hellfire Club, I thought I'd take you to our ceremony tonight and let you experience firsthand what goes on during our rituals.'' He laughed nastily. ''You're going to be our sacrificial virgin, whether you're virgin or not. The disciples will be delighted, though 'tis unlikely you'll recognize any of them. We all wear monk's robes and hoods over our heads.''

''I want nothing to do with your debauchery!'' Moira cried. ''Let me go. I won't tell a soul what I overheard. I'll disappear. I'll go back to Ireland.''

''Too late,'' Roger said as the coach rattled down the driveway. ''Sit back and enjoy the ride. You may even like what's going to happen to you tonight, though I doubt it. You will make yourself accessible to all or any of the disciples who desire you. Be assured I'll be the first in line to sample your wares.''

Moira closed her eyes and shuddered. Would her ravaged body be found floating in the Thames tomorrow? she wondered dully.

''After tonight's ceremony, I know of a dockside brothel that will be happy to take you off my hands. I vow you'll not see the light of day once you're locked inside.''

Moira drew her cape around her chilled body and huddled in the farthest corner of the coach. The night was raw and blustery but could not compare with the coldness inside her soul. She would rather die than be used and abused by Lord Roger and his evil cohorts. Moira had always considered herself a resourceful woman, and becoming someone's victim did not appeal to her. Her mind raced furiously, searching for a way to escape.

When Roger sat back and leaned his head against the backrest of the speeding coach, Moira shifted her gaze past his relaxed body to the door handle, so close yet so far. If she lunged past Roger when he least expected it, was it possible to plunge down the door handle and leap through the opening before he could stop her? She would likely suffer a small injury, but if luck was with her, she'd be up and away before Lord Roger gained his wits.

Moira's chance came when the coach skidded around a corner, throwing Roger off balance. In that split second Moira made her move. Lunging past Roger's knees, she pushed down on the door handle and hurled herself through the opening. She hit the ground with a resounding thud, crying out in pain when she struck her head a stunning blow. Rolling head over heels in the dirt and mud, she came to rest in the filth-strewn gutter. Stunned, she lay still as death, every muscle wrenched, every bone jarred, unable to breathe, let alone move, her head pounding.

The coach clattered to a halt a few yards down the deserted street. Roger was out the door before it came to a full stop. A few seconds later, the coachman joined him. Together they ran to the place where Moira had fallen.

"Is she dead, milord?" Stiles asked fearfully as he peered into Moira's white face.

"See if she's breathing," Roger ordered, too fastidious to touch the lifeless bundle lying at his feet in the filthy gutter.

Stiles knelt and placed his ear on Moira's chest. "I don't hear a heartbeat, milord."

"Bloody hell. Let's get out of here before someone happens along. My father will have a fit if my name is linked to Moira's death. Take me to the Renfrew mansion. I need blunt to buy passage to France, and Renfrew owes me a favor. I'll return when all this blows over. I'll make up some story for you to tell my father. If you value your life, I suggest you forget tonight ever happened."

Stiles blanched. "Ye can trust me, milord. Nary a peep will leave me lips."

Moira drew in a shuddering breath when Roger hauled himself back to the coach. When she fell the breath had been knocked from her lungs, and she had deliberately withheld air in order to convince Roger she was dead. Lord knows she felt dead. When she tried to rise, her body refused to obey, and she lay unmoving in the freezing rain, thinking she'd probably freeze to death before someone happened along. Marshaling her meager strength, she tried to stand by bracing herself on her arms. Debilitating, excruciating pain shattered through her. She screamed and sank into oblivion.

The Present

Moira was still screaming when she awakened from her terrifying dream. She would have died from exposure if Jack hadn't found her. She owed him her life and deeply regretted the fact that she couldn't tell him he hadn't been the cause of her injuries.

Suddenly the bedroom door burst inward and she saw Jack's tall, muscular form outlined against the gray dawn. He wore only his breeches, left gaping open in his haste to slay the dragons attacking Moira.

"What's wrong? Are you ill?"

Moira sat up, hugging the sheet to her breasts. "Nothing is wrong."

Jack crossed to the bed, stopping along the way to light a candle.

"Something is wrong. You screamed. I heard your cry clear down to the guest room. Look at you, your cheeks are wet. Have you been crying? You're white as a ghost." His eyes narrowed thoughtfully. "Don't tell me Lady Amelia paid you a visit. I thought she only haunted family."

"Lady Amelia?" Comprehension dawned. "The ghost? No, nothing like that. I hadn't realized I cried out. It must have been a nightmare," she said, unwilling to disclose the details of her disturbing flashback.

Jack perched on the edge of the bed, taking her trembling hands in his. "Do you want to tell me about it?"

Moira shook her head. "I can't."

"Don't you trust me?" Tenderly, he brushed a stray tear from her cheek. "Why were you crying?"

"I hadn't realized I was. 'Tis nothing, truly. I'm sorry I awakened you."

"Bloody hell," Jack cursed, rising abruptly. He ached to stay with her but knew what it would lead to. "Get some sleep. We're to attend a ball at Vauxhall tonight, and I want you at your best."

Sleep, Moira thought bleakly. Would she ever sleep again? What would happen to her when Roger returned from France and they chanced to meet at a party? After careful consideration, she decided her safest course was to marry well and let her husband's name protect her. With those thoughts in mind, she finally drifted off to sleep.

Jack knew the moment he entered his room that he wasn't alone. He groaned in dismay when the shrouded figure of Lady Amelia's ghost pulsed with eerie light.

"What do you want now?" Jack asked irritably. "I'm in no mood for your haunting."

Lady Amelia's celestial light dimmed a bit as Jack threw himself down on the bed and flung an arm over his eyes.

"Why are you doing this to me?" he challenged. "My life was carefree and untroubled until you threw Miss Moira O'Toole into my path. What in bloody hell did you hope to gain? I was more than content to spend my nights drinking, gambling and carousing. I'm marrying money; that aught to make you happy, since the house will now stay in the family and you can continue to haunt future Graystokes, should I produce an heir. Which is highly unlikely, knowing Victoria."

Lady Amelia floated across the room to hover beside the bed. She looked down at Jack and shook her head.

Sensing her nearness, Jack removed his arm from his eyes and stared back at her.

"You don't talk much, do you? For God's sake, listen to me. I'm talking to a ghost! Ah, well, what does it matter since you can't repeat what I say.

"I don't know what to make of Moira, or my feelings where she's concerned," Jack continued, as if talking to a ghost was a natural occurrence. "Damned if I don't find myself wanting the sensuous Irish light-skirt. I can't recall when I've been so bewitched by a woman. Granted she's not your usual Irish servant, but that's no reason for me to wish for things that can never be. I *need* to marry money."

Lady Amelia leaned closer, so close that Jack felt the heat of her brilliant light warm his body. She shook her finger at him, as if scolding him for something he'd said.

"This is your doing, isn't it?" Jack accused. "If not for you, I wouldn't be hot to bed a woman who's had one too many lovers. My emotions where Moira is concerned are tautly drawn and at odds with what I know about her. I've accepted responsibility for her injuries and am doing my level best to see to her future, but perversely, I don't want another man involved in her life. What in the hell is wrong with me? Is Moira a witch as well as a whore? If you think Moira will somehow redeem my soul, you're wrong as hell. Perdition has already claimed me."

Lady Amelia seemed upset by Jack's outburst. With a toss of her head, she began fading away into a pinpoint of light, finally disappearing completely, leaving Jack with a strange emptiness that had nothing to do with his meddling ancestor or her obvious disapproval of him.

Chapter Seven

Moira felt the effects of attending three balls in a row in her aching feet, slumping shoulders and tired facial muscles, stretched unnaturally into a perpetual smile. And next week would be just as busy. Invitations arrived daily for one society function or another. For the past two weeks she had laughed, danced and eaten her way through countless parties with countless men paying her court.

Following the first ball, Lords Harrington, Renfrew and Merriweather had called upon her at Graystoke Manor in fashionable Hanover Square, bearing gifts and flowers. She had been invited for drives through the park and various other activities, earning Jack's displeasure. No matter which suitor she saw, Jack disapproved. In truth, Moira found little to admire in her suitors except for their wealth.

Soon her three admirers were joined by yet another ardent swain, Viscount Peabody, somewhat older than the others but just as rich and in line for a dukedom. Moira was bewildered by Jack's response to her popularity. As the number of her suitors increased, Jack became more disgruntled.

"I don't want you going out alone with any of those men," Jack told her after a visit from Lord Renfrew. "Be sure and take Jilly with you. They are all notorious rakes and womanizers. When I see them posturing and preening for your benefit, I thank God I am neither titled nor a macaroni dandy."

"You're a baronet," Moira reminded him.

"Ah, but baronets are not peers. I may travel in the same circles, but I am just a cut above a commoner."

Moira thought Jack anything but common. "Do none of my suitors please you?"

Jack frowned, wondering the same thing. "I am responsible for you. I'd not like to see you make a disastrous marriage. Surely you can't be serious about either Harrington, Renfrew, Merriweather or Peabody, can you? Have they dazzled you with their gifts and compliments? Do you fancy any of them?" His voice had a hard edge to it that betrayed his annoyance.

"Lord Peabody seems very nice, not like the others who are vying with one another for my favors."

"Peabody has already done in two wives. Do you want to be his third victim?" Jack asked tightly.

"He killed them?"

"Well, no," Jack admitted, "but he left his first wife in the country to bear their child alone. 'Tis rumored she died of heartbreak due to her husband's neglect, though the doctor said she expired from an illness brought on by complications of childbirth. The second was killed in an accident."

"Jack Graystoke, you know better than to listen to gossip! Lord Peabody seems too nice to be guilty of the things you're suggesting."

"Nevertheless, he's not good enough for you. We've got time. Someone I approve of is bound to come along."

Moira seriously doubted Jack would find anyone he approved of, and she couldn't imagine why. He'd told her Victoria wouldn't marry him until Moira was established in her own household, so why was he being so obstinate about this?

"I'll make up my own mind, thank you. Where are we going tonight?"

"We're going to the Duke of Marlboro's reception for a visiting dignitary from Russia. Prince Gregor Vasilov is in London with his retinue, and I was lucky enough to wrangle an invitation. Everyone who is anyone will be there."

The opulence of Lord Marlboro's house was staggering. The ballroom was twice—nay, three times—the size of their entire cottage in Ireland. The rooms were ablaze with thousands of candles, and the buffet set up in the dining room contained food she was unfamiliar with, prepared by chefs with culinary expertise beyond her imagination. Moira was so in awe of her surroundings that she felt woefully inadequate and out of place.

She was grateful for her four swains, who rarely left her side, and for Jack, who maintained watch over her. The highlight of the evening came when Jack presented her to Prince Vasilov, who had begged for an introduction. The prince was an impressive blond giant dressed in a dazzling white uniform embellished with shiny gold braid. In contrast to his fairness, his eyes were as black as sin, their lively twinkle making his handsome features come alive. His smile, as he bent over Moira's hand, was capable of chasing away the darkest gloom.

"You are enchanting, mademoiselle," the prince said in French-accented English. French was the language of the Russian court, and all noblemen spoke it fluently. "I am Prince Gregor Vasilov. Will you honor me with a dance?"

"I'd be delighted," Moira said, returning the prince's smile. The dance happened to be a waltz, and he swept her away, leaving a scowling Jack in his wake.

"Moira's made another conquest," Spence said as he came up beside Jack. "I hadn't counted on a Russian prince, but he'll serve if he wants her badly enough."

"He can't have her!" Jack thundered ominously. Those close enough to hear looked at him curiously.

"Not so loud," Spence warned. "What in the devil is the matter with you? We wanted a little diversion from boredom, and that's what we're getting. 'Tis amusing the way Renfrew, Harrington, Merriweather and Peabody are fawning over Moira, thinking her a lady. And now the prince. 'Tis well worth the two thousand pounds if she bags royalty. Ah, there's Lady Gwen. I've been looking for her. Tell Moira I said she's doing splendidly."

Jack's fingers raked through his hair, becoming more discomfited by the minute as the prince held Moira much too close for his liking. He was on the verge of rushing to the dance floor and tearing her from the prince's arms when Victoria approached, clearly annoyed.

"Well, who would have thought your penniless Irish ward would attract a prince?" Victoria sounded more jealous than surprised. "I hear he's unmarried. Do you suppose she has a chance with him?"

"Not if I have anything to say about it," Jack bit out. "She's reaching too far above her. I had thought a viscount or marquess, even a duke, but a prince is out of the question."

Victoria yawned, bored with the subject. "I'm dying of thirst, darling. Would you get me something to drink from the refreshment room?"

"Of course," Jack said with a hint of impatience. He stalked off, but instead of going to the refreshment room, he waited at the edge of the dance floor for the music to end so he could drag Moira off for a private word.

Moira was enjoying herself immensely with the prince, who seemed utterly taken with her. She saw Jack glowering at her from the corner of her eye and briefly thought she detected a hint of jealousy in his fulminating glare. Grasping for rationality, she chided herself for a fool and turned her attention back to Prince Gregor. Jack's only interest in her was finding her a husband so he could transfer responsibility to another.

"Will you honor me with another dance later?" Prince Vasilov asked as the dance ended. "I find you fascinating, mademoiselle. Are all Irish women as enchanting as you?"

"You flatter me, Prince," Moira said coyly. "There are women here tonight who far outshine me."

"Not in my eyes, *ma petite*. Will you allow me to call on you tomorrow?"

They had reached the edge of the floor where Jack stood waiting. "Lady Moira isn't receiving tomorrow," he said bluntly as he snatched her away before either Moira or the prince could protest.

"What's the matter with you?" Moira hissed, her displeasure obvious.

"We need to talk."

Moira sighed in resignation as she followed him from the ballroom into a small unoccupied anteroom nearby. "What is it now, Jack? Are you going to tell me that Prince Vasilov is a lecher?"

"You're enamored with him," Jack accused. "Set your sights elsewhere, Moira. The prince must marry royalty; you can reach no higher than his mistress."

"Why won't you let him call on me?"

"Bloody hell! It's bad enough having those four rakes drooling over you. I refuse to endure a love-struck prince who can offer you nothing honorable."

Moira stifled a smile. Instinct told her that Jack was jealous, and her heart soared in unrestrained joy. The moment men had started courting her, he began acting strangely. Daring to hope that he cared for her was almost too much to ask.

"If I didn't know better, I'd think you were jealous, Jack."

There was an explosive silence. Jealous? Jack's thoughts scattered. Is that what was wrong with him? That revelation was definitely annoying . . . and probably true. "Damn right I'm jealous!" he all but shouted. His admission shocked them both. "I made you what you are. No one has more right than I to become your lover. I don't understand your rejection. Or perhaps I do," he amended bitterly. "There is no way I can compete with wealth or title."

"This charade was your doing," Moira reminded him. "I wanted to leave Graystoke Manor after I recovered from my injuries."

"Injuries I was responsible for," Jack returned, suddenly realizing how unreasonable he had been acting.

"Forgive me for interfering. Go back to your swains." He turned away with visible regret.

Moira wanted to call him back but knew she had no right. Jack belonged to Lady Victoria. He needed to marry money even more than she did. She watched him leave, biting her tongue lest she cry out his name as she sank down into the nearest chair.

"Here you are, my dear. I saw Sir Jack leaving a moment ago and hoped I'd find you alone. I have something important to ask you."

Moira watched warily as Lord Percy Renfrew seated himself on a stool at her feet.

"How long have we known one another? Three, four weeks?" Renfrew asked, taking her small hand in his. "No matter, 'tis long enough to know you're the woman I want to spend the rest of my life with. Will you do me the honor of becoming my wife, Lady Moira?"

Renfrew hoped he'd used the right note of sincerity. His parents were breathing down his neck to marry, and Moira seemed to have no inkling of his affiliation with the Hellfire Club. Most of the disciples went to great lengths to conceal their identities, and he was no different.

Moira stared at Renfrew, thinking this proposal was exactly what Jack had been grooming her for. "I'm honored, Lord Renfrew, but . . ."

"But what? If you're worried about Sir Jack, I assure you he'll be delighted. My lineage is impeccable."

"I have no fortune and no dowry," Moira said evasively. "My family is an old one, but we have no wealth to speak of." At least part of her statement was true. If there was nobility in her family, she had yet to discover it.

"I'm rich enough to marry whomever I please. I can't

recall when I've been so taken with a woman." True enough. "My parents will be delighted that I am finally taking a wife and will offer no objections when they learn your family is suitable."

In his exuberance, Renfrew dropped to his knees before Moira and raised her hand to his lips. "Say yes, my dear, and we'll announce our engagement tonight."

"I need Sir Jack's consent," Moira temporized. "Give me time to consider."

Percy frowned, thinking Moira was holding out for higher stakes. "If you think Prince Vasilov will offer for you, you're mistaken. He needs to marry royalty. I know he seems taken with you, and he's handsome as sin, but he can only set you up as his mistress. I offer my name and respectability."

"I know. And I assure you Prince Vasilov has made no such offer."

"Very well. A week, no longer. Meanwhile, don't let the others talk you into anything. They all have designs on you, not all of them honorable."

"You'll have my answer at the end of the week, milord," Moira said demurely.

Renfrew gave her a dazzling smile, rose to his feet and pulled Moira with him. "Since we are all but engaged, I think a kiss is in order."

He pulled her close, molding her body to his. She felt the leashed passion coiled inside him and shuddered delicately. The thought of giving her body to Lord Renfrew made her physically ill. Had Jack been holding her instead of Lord Renfrew, she was certain she'd feel no such revulsion. Then Renfrew kissed her, his mouth wet and hot, his tongue a revolting spear of flesh that sought more intimacy than she was willing to give. When his hands brushed the undersides of her breasts, Moira knew real panic. How could she ever marry a man she didn't love—didn't even like—and submit to all the intimacies marriage demanded?

"Sorry, I didn't know this room was occupied." Jack stood in the doorway with Lady Victoria. His gaze was riveted on Moira, his eyes a turbulent gray that reminded her of a violent storm-tossed sea.

Renfrew stepped away from Moira with reluctance, but not before Jack saw where his hands had been. Jack's eyes narrowed when he noted what appeared to be Moira's aroused state. Her breath escaped her parted lips in rapid puffs of air, and her eyes were glazed with what he mistakenly thought was passion.

"Damn, Graystoke, you could have knocked," Renfrew said mulishly.

"Let's find another room, darling," Victoria urged. "Can't you see these lovers want to be alone?"

That's exactly what worried Jack.

Moira closed her eyes, her expression stark with relief. "No need to leave on our account," she said in a rush. "I was just leaving. I promised another dance to Prince Gregor, and I'd hate to disappoint him."

When she rushed from the room, Renfrew threw up his hands in disgust and rushed after her.

"It looks as if we burst in on a private moment." Victoria giggled. "I don't think your ward is as innocent as she pretends. After that little seduction scene, perhaps you can convince Renfrew to offer for her. The situation looked compromising to me."

"Perhaps you're right," Jack said, not at all amused. "I had no idea Renfrew would attempt seduction this soon, though he's a notorious rake and I should have expected it. And here I was worried about Prince Vasilov. Nevertheless, I think we should return to the ballroom where I can keep an eye on my ward. She has a way of inviting trouble.''

"What about the privacy we sought for ourselves?" Victoria asked, pouting. She didn't like having her own plans for Jack thwarted. She and Jack hadn't had a private moment in weeks, and she was aching for him.

"Another time," Jack promised, chafing to return to the ballroom where he could keep an eye on Moira. He all but pulled Victoria from the room.

He spotted Moira immediately, in the arms of the tall, resplendent Russian prince. They complemented each other perfectly, Jack thought jealously as he watched them whirl about the floor. Suddenly the prince waltzed Moira out onto the balcony, and Jack felt the hackles rise on the back of his neck. Did the little fool have no sense at all? Was it up to him to save her from her own passionate nature? How did she expect to land a husband if she insisted upon behaving shamelessly?

Jack noted that Victoria was speaking with another woman and took advantage of her momentary distraction to hurry after Moira and the prince.

"Are you cold, mademoiselle?" Prince Gregor asked as he gallantly removed his jacket and placed it over Moira's shoulders. "In Russia, this is mild weather. You would love Russia, and I would love to show it to you."

"I doubt I will ever see your country, Prince Gregor," Moira said wistfully. "Though I am certain I would like it."

"Then we will see that you are given the opportunity to visit," Gregor said with feeling. "As my . . . special guest, of course."

Moira had an inkling of what he intended to say and sought to turn his mind in another direction. "Have you ever been to Ireland, Prince Gregor?"

"Never, but perhaps we could go together one day."

Moira groaned in dismay. How did one gracefully refuse what she knew the prince was going to offer? "That is unlikely."

Not one to be denied, Gregor turned Moira to face him. Then, placing a finger beneath her chin, he lowered his mouth and kissed her with an expertise that left her breathless. It was nothing like Lord Renfrew's sloppy kisses, or the mesmerizing, soul-destroying ones Jack gave her, but Gregor's kiss was rather pleasant in an unexciting sort of way.

"I fear my ward is unfamiliar with the rules of propriety, having been born and raised in the country. Please forgive her for acting improperly."

Moira groaned in dismay. For the second time tonight, Jack had caught her in a compromising position. And neither time had the man's attentions been invited.

Prince Gregor did not look at all embarrassed, which sent Jack's temper soaring. "Your ward is delightful. Again I ask your permission to call on her tomorrow."

Jack sent Moira a piercing look. "Permission denied. We both know nothing can come of it. Come, Moira, 'tis time we left."

Prince Gregor took Moira's hand and brought it to his lips. "I deeply regret your guardian's decision."

Jack's tightly clenched fists were the only signs of his anger. That and the hard glint in his eyes. Aware of Jack's annoyance, a small rebellious thought took flight in Moira's mind. Jack was becoming entirely too protective. Not one of her suitors pleased him. He wanted her to marry, yet he found fault with every man who expressed interest in her. What did he want from her?

Tearing her gaze from Jack, Moira smiled at Prince Gregor and said, "Thank you for the dance, Prince. It was most enjoyable."

The prince sent Jack a fulminating glance as he kissed Moira's hand again, then reluctantly released it. "The pleasure was all mine." He nodded to Jack and said, "I congratulate you on the charm and beauty of your ward."

"Don't forget your jacket, Prince Gregor," Jack said as he whisked the garment from Moira's shoulders and thrust it at the prince.

A tense silence ensued after the prince's departure. The silence between them lengthened, until suddenly Jack let out an explosive breath, grasped Moira's shoulders and gave her an angry shake.

"What in the hell is the matter with you? Are you deliberately trying to destroy your reputation? Two men in one night is too much. Have a little regard for propriety. I know you've been indiscreet in the past, taking lovers indiscriminately, but that was before you made your debut as a lady. The least you can do is act with decorum until you land a husband."

Moira's Irish temper exploded. "The hell with you, Jack Graystoke! I don't need a keeper. The only reason I went along with this harebrained scheme was because . . . because . . ." Her words skidded to an abrupt halt. She didn't trust Jack enough to tell him that she was a candidate for Newgate prison.

"Because what, Moira? I always suspected you were hiding something from me. What is it?"

Her lips clamped together stubbornly. "Nothing. I went along with your scheme merely to prove to you that I am capable of acting like a lady. And . . . and marrying a rich man appealed to me.''

"As well it should,'' Jack said sourly. "More the reason for you to act with proper decorum until you land the right man.'' He grasped her arm, escorting her back to the ballroom. "Come along. I think it's time we left. I've had enough of these macaroni dandies for one night.''

As luck would have it, Victoria was dancing with Spence and did not see him leave. Jack left a message with the footman for her and hustled Moira out to his carriage.

Huddled inside, Moira fumed in impotent rage. She had no idea what was wrong with Jack, or why he seemed so upset with her. She was doing what he wanted, wasn't she? What more did he want from her?

"Stop pouting, Moira,'' Jack said, still irritated over the kisses Moira had shared with Renfrew and the prince. He should have known an immoral creature like Moira would enjoy enticing men until they were wild for her. Who knew better than he? He could still taste her kisses. The memory of them was as vivid as heaven's brightest star.

"I'm not pouting,'' Moira declared. "I'm angry. You have no right to treat me like chattel. I'm through with this charade. I'm tired of you telling me what to do, how to act, whom to offer friendship. You're not responsible for me, Jack. I can take care of myself.''

Jack spit out a string of oaths that stung her ears. "Oh, you can, can you? If I hadn't walked in on you and Renfrew, you'd have found yourself on your back with your skirts over your head and your legs spread.'' His eyes narrowed. "Perhaps that's what you wanted.''

His brutal accusation stunned her. "For your information, Lord Percy offered for me tonight.''

Jack went still. *"He offered you marriage?"*

"Isn't that what you and Lord Spencer were hoping for? Are you suitably amused? Passing me off as a lady and watching your dandified friends vie for my attention must have given you hours of entertainment at my expense."

"Did you accept?" Jack asked tightly, unable to think of anything but that bounder Renfrew taking from Moira what he'd dreamed of taking for himself.

After a long, drawn-out pause, Moira said, "Not yet. I'm to give him my answer next week. But I see no reason to refuse. His offer is an honorable one. He's in line for a dukedom, and I'll be a countess one day. I'll have the means to help Kevin and his family."

"Which is more than I can give you," Jack returned shortly. "What about the prince? Do you intend playing one man against the other?"

A slow heat crept up Moira's neck. He was accusing her unjustly. "Prince Gregor is a charming man, but I know better than to expect an honorable proposal from him. 'Tis best I marry Lord Renfrew."

"Like hell!" Jack thundered. "Percy Renfrew isn't the right man for you. He pretends to be a gentleman, and few people are aware of his true nature. You're marrying no one without my consent."

"I don't understand you, Jack. I thought you'd be happy to be rid of me so you can wed Lady Victoria."

"The hell with Victoria!" Jack ground out harshly.

Jack lapsed into a moody silence. Damn Lady Amelia for her interference, damn Spence for suggesting this charade, and damn him for going along with it! What had at first promised to be an amusing venture had turned into a debacle. If he'd had the slightest inkling he would find the Irish wench so bloody irresistible, he would have left her lying in the gutter.

Wanting Moira had turned his life upside down. He ached with the need to make love to her. She filled his senses; the sound, the touch and the scent of her fed his hunger. Since meeting Moira, he'd lost all interest in gambling and drinking, and Lord knows he had no desire to bed Victoria, his intended bride. Moira's entrance into his life made him question his own sanity.

He'd been foolish not to partake of her charms, he reflected. He should have taken what he wanted when the need was upon him instead of denying himself. Had he done so, she would be out of his system by now and he could get on with his life. It wasn't as if Moira was an innocent. She'd freely confessed to having at least one lover, and only the good Lord knew how many others there had been. What would one more hurt?

When the carriage rattled to a halt before Graystoke Manor a few minutes later, Jack was still in a fine fury. He climbed down and reached for Moira. But instead of helping her alight, he whisked her up into his arms and carried her to the house. Pettibone opened the door before they reached it.

"I told you not to wait up, Pettibone," Jack said as he swept past the flabbergasted servant. "Go to bed. I've no further need of you tonight."

"Are you sure you know what you're doing?" Pettibone asked with quiet dignity. "Perhaps I should see Lady Moira to her room."

"Stop meddling, Pettibone," Jack said from between clenched teeth. "I'm quite aware of what I'm doing."

"Well, I'm not!" Moira countered. "Put me down. I'm perfectly capable of walking."

Jack's eyes glittered dangerously. "Our argument is far from finished."

"It is as far as I'm concerned," Moira said with rising panic. What did Jack intend? He appeared too angry to listen to reason.

He took the stairs two at a time, unaware that Pettibone was following close behind until the man said, "You're angry, Sir Jack, and you know how your temper can get you into trouble. Let me call Jilly to see to Lady Moira."

"Go to bed, Pettibone," Jack repeated. "Moira doesn't need Jilly tonight. If you're worried about Moira, don't be. I won't hurt her."

"Very good, sir," Pettibone said, flapping his hands helplessly as he cast one last glance at Moira. He was gone by the time Jack reached Moira's room.

The door to Moira's chamber was open, and a branch of candles lit all but the darkest corners of the room. A cheery blaze in the grate chased away the chill. Jilly's doing, Moira supposed as Jack slammed the door behind him and set her on her feet.

If Moira expected Jack to turn and leave she was mistaken. "What are you going to do?" She was trembling, and not from cold. Could it be from anticipation?

Jack gave her a wicked grin, nearly stopping her heart. "First I'm going to help you undress, then I'm going to make love to you." In spite of his earlier anger, his voice held a note of sensuality that sent shivers down her spine.

Flustered, Moira retreated several steps. Jack stalked her relentlessly. "It isn't as if you haven't done this before. For weeks I've watched you flirting with different men, tempting them with your siren's smile. I'm a man, Moira. I can take only so much. I've wanted you from the moment I first set eyes on you, all bruised and battered and covered in gutter filth. I promise I'll be a patient lover. Your pleasure is as important to me as mine. You'll have no complaint about my handling of you.''

Moira gulped noisily. ''I thought we decided not to become intimately involved. Becoming lovers would only complicate our relationship.'' She feared that if she told him she was a virgin he'd know she'd been lying from the beginning. She wasn't ready to tell the truth, for she wasn't sure she could trust him. Newgate prison did not appeal to her.

''Ah, love, you talk too much.''

Still grinning, he reached out, pulled her into his arms and kissed her. His lips were softly seductive, tenderly persuasive, wonderfully warm. With a small cry of surrender, Moira surged against him. His arms offered a safe haven against the cruel world, his mouth and teasing tongue an invitation to sinful pleasures she could only imagine. He was pure temptation. When his hands moved over her body, Moira felt she would melt into a puddle.

Chapter Eight

For a long time, Jack simply held and kissed Moira, until the tension in her taut muscles and tendons began to relax. His warmth and desire surrounded her, slowly allowing her temperature to heat to match his. His kisses were more dangerous than she realized, for he made her long to trust and confide. It seemed so natural to be in his arms that she paid little heed to the slither of her dress as it slid down her hips to pool at her feet.

The urge to pour out her fears and soak up his strength was so strong that she nearly forgot that Black Jack Graystoke was a man known to take his pleasure where he found it. The thought jarred her out of her contentment. She broke off the kiss, shaken, and tried to escape his arms.

"This is wrong."

Jack sent her a lazy grin. "Feels right to me." His mouth clamped over hers, effectively silencing her protests. The velvet stroke of his tongue made it difficult to recall why she shouldn't be allowing this kind of intimacy. Her dim pleasure thickened to sharp craving when he cupped her breast and stroked her nipple with his thumb.

His kiss grew bolder, deeper, evocative. He slid the straps of her chemise from her shoulders and untied the laces of her corset, pushing both down past her hips to join her dress and petticoats at her feet. He bent his head and pressed the moist heat of his mouth to her breast, the pounding of her blood matching the rhythmic lapping of his tongue. Her body arched and she pushed upward, guiltily aware that she was offering him free access to the forbidden fruits of her body.

Jack moaned, sucking her nipple into his mouth and tonguing it to erectness. Moira's knees buckled. Jack made a growling sound deep in his throat, swept her up in his arms and carried her to the bed. He laid her full length on the soft surface, pausing to remove her shoes and stockings before leaning back to admire her.

"You're perfect," he whispered as he gazed down at her. "But you've probably been told that before."

He cupped her breasts in his warm hands, then leaned forward to suckle them. A deluge of delicious new sensations made her whimper and jerk involuntarily. His hands skimmed her limbs and torso, taking untold pleasure in the fragile flesh beneath his fingertips, so warm, so silken, so utterly enthralling. She couldn't be called voluptuous, but she possessed more than her share of womanly attributes, Jack thought as his lips and tongue memorized the ripe curves of her breasts.

"Blessed Virgin, what are you doing to me?" Moira gasped, alarmed by her eagerness to participate in Jack's depravities. Something dark and consuming clawed its way through her fear, heated her blood, sped her heart and speared her body with strange, aching desire for that which she had never known before.

"Making love to you," Jack whispered huskily. "I don't want you thinking of any other man while I'm loving you."

How could she think of another man, Moira wondered distractedly, when Jack was doing such incredible things to her body? Before she knew what he was doing, he stripped off his trousers, hose, jacket, shirt, shoes and small clothes, and was pressing his nakedness against her in fervid longing. Moira made a sound of strangled delight as she felt her muscles surrendering to the melting warmth of his body.

"This is a mistake!" Moira cried out, gathering the last vestiges of her control. "Don't do this to me."

He gave her a wicked chuckle. "I wanted to kill Prince Gregor tonight, not to mention Renfrew. Seeing you in their arms drove me wild with jealousy, and I don't like the feeling. Once I satisfy this craving for you, I'll know peace again." For some reason unbeknownst to him, he wanted her with a strong, irrational longing that exceeded his good sense.

She lifted her head to stare at him in unguarded surprise. That a womanizer like Jack Graystoke should express jealousy on her account was curious indeed. More than curious—downright strange. But before she had time to explore the possibilities, his hand slid down between her legs, rubbing the heel of his palm against her, slowly, erotically, until her hips arched against his hand seemingly out of instinct and she felt a liquid heat bathe her there.

Dismayed, she cried out, and his eyes seemed to glow pure silver as he watched her, a dark, hungry expression on his face. He was resting against her hipbones, the hard ridge of his flesh gently prodding her between the legs. She closed her eyes, suddenly wanting what Jack was offering though she knew it was wrong, that he was merely using her to assuage his lust. He would add her to his list of conquests and blithely go on to the next, forgetting she ever existed.

"I'm not going to hurt you," Jack said, sensing her fear. "This isn't new to you; you've been loved before."

"No . . . I . . ." What could she say? That she'd lied to him from the moment she awakened in his bed? It was long past the time for confession.

The moment for truth had passed as Jack lowered his head and kissed her eyelids, feathering them gently. His mouth moved down to brush her lips, nibbling lightly, delicately, stroking his tongue against the seam before urging them open so he could taste more fully of her sweetness. When her tongue touched his, his body tightened painfully, less willing to accept being patient than his mind.

His fingers delved into her slick, hot interior and found her wet and ready. He probed more deeply, encountering folds of delicate flesh that pulsed against his fingertips, lavishly moist and surprisingly tight. Moira gave a startled cry and buried her face in his shoulder, lost in a haze of raw sensation.

"Oh, sweetheart," Jack groaned in a strangled voice that bore little resemblance to his usual resonant tones, "don't hold back. Tonight is ours to explore all the ways to make you happy. Just tell me what you like. You'll find me a generous lover."

Thrusting again and again, his fingers set up a clamoring in her that built to a shattering crescendo. When he bent his head and licked her nipples, every muscle in her body tightened and she climaxed abruptly, crying out his name in shock and fear. Never had she felt anything so intensely gratifying or frightening in her life! It was almost as if Jack had torn out a little piece of her, a piece that could never be replaced.

She had barely revived from the shock of her very first climax when he grasped her hips to raise her a little as he began to move into her. She felt herself fill and stretch; it was not yet painful, but very close. She grasped his sleek, powerful shoulders to push him away.

"No!"

Jack went still. "No?"

"I . . . It won't work. You're too . . . too . . . It won't fit."

Jack let out a bark of laughter. "Your other lovers must have been woefully lacking, sweetheart. I'll admit it's a tight fit, but you'll adjust."

Holding her hips at an angle, he pushed farther into her. He was perspiring heavily from unaccustomed restraint, wondering why he didn't just thrust himself to the hilt like he wanted instead of taking precious time with a woman who was probably as experienced as he. Truth to tell, he was beginning to grow uneasy at the tightness he was encountering. Suddenly the tip of his staff butted against a barrier that wasn't supposed to be there. He paused and frowned, noting that Moira's eyes were closed tightly and she was biting her bottom lip as if in pain.

"Damn you! You lied!"

But it was too late to pull back now. He was so hard he ached. His body was drawn taut as a bowstring, and if he didn't find release soon, he'd explode. Still, he didn't want to hurt Moira unnecessarily. Grasping her legs, he pushed them as far apart as they would go and wedged himself against her.

"I'll try not to hurt you. You're very tight, but you're also very wet."

Moira held her breath. Jack's face was stark with need and taut with self-imposed restraint. Looking into her eyes, he drew back and surged into her in one powerful stroke. Shock and surprise slammed through Moira, and she screamed as pain ripped through her. She felt suddenly too full, too tight, too consumed by Jack. *He was all the way inside her.*

"Hush, sweetheart," Jack crooned into her ear. "The pain will last but a moment."

Just when she thought she couldn't bear the pain a moment longer, Jack rocked gently back and forth, creating a delicious sensation that sent Moira's blood singing through her veins and soothing the hurt he'd created moments before. She dug her fingers into the firm muscles of his shoulders and waited for the pain to return. When it did not, she moved tentatively to meet his downward strokes. Jack groaned in delight and urged her on with words of praise. When he grasped her legs and wrapped them around his waist, Moira's thighs gripped him tightly, rocking with him as he began moving more forcefully, thrusting and withdrawing in a vigorous, jerking motion that sent her senses reeling.

The intimacy was shattering as he moved forcefully within her, his lips capturing hers in a drowning kiss, smothering the cries she wasn't aware of making, his hands caressing her breasts, her hips, her thighs, as if he couldn't get enough of touching her.

"Relax, sweetheart," Jack urged. "You're doing beautifully." She arched against him, bringing him even deeper into her tight sheath. "That's it, arch your lovely body, give all of yourself to me."

Moira couldn't have held back even if she wanted to. Her body no longer worked in accordance with her wishes. It was attuned to Jack and the incredible things he was doing to her. When she began to shudder and gyrate in a frenzy of need, Jack groaned, grasped her buttocks and drove powerfully, embedding himself to the hilt. To Moira it seemed as if he had been holding himself in check until her own climax began, for the moment she cried out and burst into flames, Jack drove into her once, twice, stiffened and gave a hoarse shout. Then he collapsed against her, breathing hard, his chest pumping furiously.

After a few moments, he pushed himself away and settled down beside her, one arm flung across his eyes. "Are you all right? I didn't hurt you, did I?"

"You didn't hurt me," Moira said, waiting expectantly for the explosion she knew would surely come. She didn't have long to wait.

Raising himself up on one elbow, Jack nailed her with his silver gaze. "What else did you lie about? Have you told me the truth about anything? Damn you! Didn't you think I'd know a virgin when I encountered one?"

Moira flinched beneath the fury of Jack's implacable anger. She deserved it, she supposed, but she owed him no explanation. Since there was nothing she could say, she remained mute.

Her silence only served to fuel Jack's rage. "Well, have you nothing to say for yourself? You've never had a lover, have you?"

When she refused to look at him, he jerked her upright to face him. Moira looked into the silver inferno of his eyes and knew a moment of panic. "I never had a lover, and I never wanted you to find out this way."

He gave her an angry shake. "Damn you! Who are you? What were you doing out on the street that night I ran you down?"

"I told you, my name is Moira O'Toole. I'm a domestic servant. I didn't want to lie, but I was desperate."

"Obviously," Jack said with scathing contempt. "Had I known you were a virgin, I would never have touched you." That wasn't entirely true, Jack allowed as he silently contemplated his hunger for her. He seriously doubted Moira's virginity would have made the slightest difference in what happened tonight. This precise moment had been preordained since the day he'd brought Moira into his home. "You owe me an explanation, Moira."

"I don't owe you a thing, Jack Graystoke! I told you long ago I absolved you of all responsibility for me. I should have never agreed to stay and engage in this charade."

" 'Tis too late now to change what happened. What's done is done. Since marrying you myself is out of the question, and I can't afford a mistress, 'tis my duty to see you properly wed. And that doesn't mean to Percy Renfrew."

"His offer was honorable," Moira spat out indignantly.

"That's how much you know! His parents gave him an ultimatum: He either had to marry or be disinherited. His reputation is so disreputable that no respectable woman would have him. He was growing desperate until you came along."

"There are other men," Moira reminded him.

"Ah, yes, your other suitors. None of them will do. While you remain in my care, you'll marry someone I approve of. The season is far from over, and there are better prospects than those macaroni dandies.''

Moira stared at him, wondering if he was being obstinate because he genuinely cared what happened to her or for some ulterior motive she knew nothing about. After what happened between them tonight, she'd be wise to leave this house as fast as her legs could carry her. But where would she go? She'd need to steal money to get back to Ireland, and after her experience with the Mayhews, stealing held no appeal for her. She was already a wanted woman.

Suddenly Moira became aware that Jack's attention was focused on her breasts and she tried to cover herself with her hands, realizing she was fully exposed and vulnerable to his inspection. Jack stared at her, arrested, his searing gaze shifting downward from her breasts over the gentle rise of her hips to the tangled triangle of red curls between her legs. His breath caught in his throat and his shaft hardened instantly, rising in splendid erection.

Moira couldn't tear her eyes from that male part of him as she recalled the pleasure it had given her short moments ago. When he reached out and pulled her against him, she felt brittle enough to shatter. She knew what he wanted—and what she wanted as well—and feared she was following Jack to perdition.

''Sweet Virgin Mary,'' Moira cried out, swept into the turbulence of his passion.

A bubble of laughter gurgled from Jack's throat as he bore her down on the bed, covering her with his body. But laughter fled abruptly as his face grew stark and tense with hunger and his eyes became shards of pure silver. ''I want you again, Moira.''

Before Moira could form an answer, he rose gracefully,

dipped a cloth into the water pitcher resting on a nearby table and returned swiftly to her side. Moira gave a gasp of shock as he spread her legs and proceeded to wash away traces of blood and seed. When he finished, he tossed the cloth aside, lay down beside her and kneaded her breast gently with his palm. Before leaning over to kiss her, he whispered, "You have the kind of beauty that leads men to madness. I knew you were pure temptation the moment I laid eyes on you."

His lips teased her mouth with soft brushing kisses, then moved down her neck and over her tender breasts until he found the crests he sought. His mouth hungrily began to caress the pouting tips, coaxing them to stiff points of raw pleasure. With a will of their own, her fingers grasped his dark head, holding it closer, so she could experience more of those exquisite sensations coursing through her. All concern that he was using her to assuage his lust was momentarily forgotten. Gone were her maidenly objections; shyness had fled the instant he touched her intimately. She wanted his kisses, needed his caresses, craved his hands and lips on her body.

"I don't care who or what you are, sweetheart," Jack groaned against her mouth. "The need to be inside you is a sickness that only your sweet flesh can heal."

A slow, deep yearning began to creep through her, forcing her to acknowledge her own growing need. And when Jack's mouth began a trail of fire down her body, she trembled in anticipation and arched into him, feeling his heat, savoring the hot, pungent scent of his arousal. His mouth continued its downward path and Moira gasped in dismay when she realized where he was headed. She tried to push him away, but he held her hips in place as he lowered his mouth to taste her honeyed sweetness.

Moira jerked reflexively, shocked to the core. "Jack! Don't!"

Reluctantly, Jack desisted, realizing she was much too innocent to enjoy the more intimate loving he sought. "Very well, but one day you'll let me love you this way."

"Never!" Moira vowed.

Jack gave her a cheeky grin and rose above her, but instead of covering her with his body as he did before, he abruptly changed positions and lifted her atop him. Moira uttered a strangled gasp as he slowly lowered her onto his erection.

"Am I hurting you?" Jack asked, his restraint slowly unraveling. In his memory Moira was the only woman who made a mockery of his reserve. He'd always prided himself on his ability to maintain control at all times, but with Moira he was like an eager boy with his first woman.

Moira felt herself stretching, filling, but there was no pain, only a feeling of being possessed more fully than she ever thought possible. "You're not hurting me."

Her words seemed to release a demon inside him as he flexed his hips and thrust sharply upward. He took her hard and fast, swift and deep, loving her with the fury of one driven by desperation—the desperation of knowing their paths were never meant to cross. That they had met at all was due to a meddling ghost.

Moira felt a melting sensation deep inside her. Her own body was beyond her control, she reflected with one of the few rational thoughts left to her. Then all rationality fled as her head jerked forward and the air left her lungs on a low keening wail. Jack continued to move inside her while she felt herself begin to tremble, the shattering sensation spreading upward and outward from the point of his deepest penetration. Jack waited until her chin dropped to her chest before giving free rein to his own explosive climax.

An unknown space of time passed. Seconds, perhaps minutes; she did not know. But when awareness slowly returned, Moira found herself stretched full length atop Jack, her legs lying between his outstretched limbs, her cheek resting against his bare chest. They were still joined, but she could feel him slowly receding. When she tried to rise, he held her firmly in place.

"Go to sleep, Moira. I need time to think about what happened between us tonight. I never expected to find a virgin in my bed. I don't know why you lied, but I intend to get to the bottom of it."

Moira heard nothing past "go to sleep." Her eyelids fluttered shut, and she slid effortlessly into sleep. Jack heard her even breathing and sighed, frustration keeping his own slumber at bay. Shock was too mild a word to describe how he felt when he discovered that Moira was a virgin. There was simply no feasible explanation for her lie. What did she hope to gain by letting him think she was a woman of questionable virtue? There was a mystery here somewhere, and he hated mysteries, especially ones he couldn't solve. He had treated Moira like a whore, and she had no one to blame but herself.

But even as the thought formed in his mind, his arms pulled her closer, strangely reluctant to admit how good she felt in his arms, how wonderfully well her supple body had pleased him, how extraordinarily beautiful she looked sleeping on his chest. Just then the candles sputtered and went out one by one, plunging the room into darkness. Jack realized the fire in the grate had burned to gray ash, adding to the impenetrable gloom. Carefully shifting Moira onto the bed, Jack pulled the blanket over her and started to rise in order to rekindle the fire.

His feet had barely touched the floor when a hazy light formed near the door. He lay back on the bed and looked away. When he returned his gaze to the light, it had intensified. Jack groaned aloud as an inner brilliance within the light took shape.

Lady Amelia.

"Good evening, milady," Jack said dryly as he hastily pulled the blanket over his naked loins. "To what do I owe the pleasure tonight?"

Lady Amelia floated closer. She appeared to be frowning, if that was possible. With slow deliberation, she lifted one arm and pointed a bony finger at Moira.

Jack turned and gazed at Moira, still sleeping soundly and looking like an innocent child. "I know what you're thinking," Jack said, speaking low so as not to awaken Moira. "I warned you I was beyond help. Aye, I seduced her, but if you hadn't placed her in my path, she wouldn't be in my bed now." Lady Amelia shook her head, clearly distraught. "I'm headed straight to perdition and there's not a damn thing you can do about it. Did you ever consider that perdition is exactly where I want to be? Go back where you came from, milady. Perhaps a future generation of Graystokes will have need of your services."

Lady Amelia floated toward Jack on a carpet of mist, coming so close that Jack swore he could feel her cold fingers graze his cheek. He flinched, then touched his cheek, feeling the icy flesh left in the wake of her touch. She spoke then, and though her words had no substance, they reverberated loudly in Jack's head.

"She will save you."

"Excuse me? What did you say? Who will save me?

139

And why in the devil do I need saving when I'm perfectly happy the way I am?''

Jack imagined he saw Lady Amelia smiling. But it was so fleeting he could not attest to it. He darted a glance at Moira and thanked God she was still sleeping, for she'd find this hard to believe. He could scarcely credit it himself. When he turned back to confront his meddling ancestor, Lady Amelia was gone.

''Milady, wake up. 'Tis time to rise.''

Moira groaned and turned over. Surely it wasn't time to get up so soon. She had just gotten to sleep after Jack . . . My God! Jack! She opened her eyes slowly, fearful of what she'd see. If Jack was still in bed with her, she'd die of embarrassment. She trembled with relief when she realized she was alone.

Moira started to rise, saw she was naked and scooted back down beneath the covers. Jilly paid her little heed as she picked up Moira's hastily discarded clothing from the floor. ''Would you fetch me some tea from the kitchen, Jilly?'' Moira asked, refusing to budge until the maid had left.

''Right away, milady,'' Jilly said agreeably. ''You'd best hop into the tub. I filled it in your dressing room while you were still sleeping.''

The moment the door closed behind Jilly, Moira eased herself from the bed and walked to the dressing room, every bone in her body protesting. She ached in places she never knew existed. The hot water felt wonderfully soothing to her bruised flesh, not that Jack hadn't been gentle last night, especially after he discovered she'd been untouched. After the wanton way she'd acted, she dreaded the thought of facing Jack. Not only that, but she knew he'd demand an explanation of her virginal state after she'd told that outlandish lie about being abandoned by a lover.

"Are you finished, milady?" Jilly asked as she brought Moira's tea into the dressing room.

Moira stepped out of the tub and into the fluffy bath sheet Jilly held out for her. She dressed with little enthusiasm and allowed Jilly to style her hair into a charming array of tumbling curls atop her head. By the time Moira finished her tea and toast, she was ready to greet the day and whatever it brought.

Jack was standing beside the hearth with his back to her when Moira entered the parlor a few minutes later. He turned when he heard her and gave her an inscrutable look.

"I took the liberty of turning Merriweather and Peabody away this morning."

"You're taking this guardianship far too seriously, Jack. I am my own woman, capable of making my own decisions." Did he think he owned her now that he'd bedded her?

"You are an innocent, being pursued by a pack of wolves. I have no idea why you saw fit to lie to me. I no longer know what is the truth and what is not. As long as you're under my roof, you will abide by my rules. You will *not* marry a bounder like Percy Renfrew."

"What would you have me do," Moira asked, thoroughly incensed, "become your mistress? You had no qualms about . . . about making love to me last night."

Jack's silver eyes glittered dangerously. "That was your fault. Had I known you were an innocent, I would not have touched you."

The lie nearly choked him. Wanting Moira had become

an obsession. He feared he would have taken her even if he'd known she was a virgin.

Moira glared at him. "It won't happen again. It *can't* happen again. I won't allow it. From now on I will make my own decisions about my future. We both know what we have to do. You must marry Lady Victoria, and I will marry advantageously so I can help my brother. I'll always be grateful to you for this opportunity, but you are *not* my guardian."

"Damn it, Moira, I'm only thinking of your welfare."

"*My* welfare! Pray tell how bedding me helped me in any way?" she challenged.

Jack had the grace to flush. "I take full responsibility for my lack of control, but I'll be damned if you're going to marry Renfrew, or any other man of his ilk. Is that clear?"

"You've made yourself perfectly clear," Moira retorted. "And now I shall make myself clear. I appreciate your saving my life, but I shall be leaving as soon as I gather my things. When I find employment, I'll repay you for everything you've done for me."

She turned to leave. "Bloody hell!" Jack growled, grasping her arm and bringing her around to face him. "You're not going anywhere."

They glared at one another, and in the taut, vibrating silence, the heat emanating from their bodies was hot enough to scorch the air around them. His piercing look was so devastating that Moira felt the need to escape lest she be devoured by Jack's hunger. She inhaled sharply as Jack reached for her, shattering the tension that had built to towering proportions. His touch was like fire. Then he kissed her, paralyzing her body and mind.

She was trembling like a leaf in the wind when he

finally released her. She stepped away, her eyes as wide as a frightened doe's. There was a hint of devilry in the slant of his full mouth, in the glint of his silver eyes. Sexual tension oozed from his pores, melting her bones. She had never felt more helpless or confused. Turning abruptly, she fled as if Satan himself was after her.

Chapter Nine

Moira kept out of Jack's way the rest of that day. Falling into his arms like a ripe plum had been a terrible mistake, albeit one she had no control over. But now that she knew the danger of his touch and its effect upon her, she intended to make damn certain she wouldn't fall victim to his fatal charm again. To that end she took pains to avoid him. She briefly considered leaving as she had threatened, but after careful reconsideration, she decided Jack was right. Where would she go? She had no money, no friends, no promise of employment. Her situation, her very well-being depended on Jack and that god-awful charade he and Lord Fenwick had hatched to pass her off as a lady. Unfortunately, after last night, she was convinced she could not marry for the sake of money, no matter how desperate she was to help her brother. After having tasted love, she would be satisfied with nothing less.

Jack's thoughts paralled Moira's. He was sorry he'd ever made that absurd bet with Spence. If Moira had been a whore as he'd assumed, he'd have no qualms about

144

bedding her—or relieving Spence of two thousand pounds. And he would allow her to marry whomever she pleased, even Renfrew. Discovering that Moira was innocent had changed everything. He hated to admit it, but he was jealous of every man who sniffed at her skirts. To make matters worse, his obsession with the Irish beauty had led him straight to her bed.

And she'd been a damn virgin!

He still couldn't get over the fact that he'd been the first with her. The best thing he could do for her now was permit her to marry Renfrew, or whomever she pleased. It wasn't, God forbid, as if she loved Renfrew. And she needed Renfrew's blunt as much as he needed Lady Victoria's. Yet the thought of Moira in another man's bed drove him wild with jealousy. Perversely, if he couldn't have her, he didn't want any other man to have her. If this jealous rage was the result of Lady Amelia's meddling, he wished her straight to Hell.

It suddenly occurred to Jack that he still had no idea why Moira had lied to him, and all kinds of implications ran the gamut of his thoughts, some not so pleasant. From whom was she hiding? Obviously she had been running from someone that night his carriage ran her down. Who or what was she afraid of? His questions were so pressing—he wanted answers and he wanted them now. And he needed to tell Moira of a decision he had made.

After her sleepless night, Moira decided to take a nap, telling Jilly she didn't wish to be disturbed. But Jack paid little heed to Jilly's pleas as he burst in on Moira, awakening her from a sound sleep.

"Jack, what is it?" Moira asked, brushing sleep from her eyes. "Can't it wait?"

"No, it can't wait." He sat down on the edge of the

bed, frowning when she cautiously backed away from him. He supposed he had earned her distrust, but it rankled nonetheless. "It isn't my place to tell you what to do or who to see. You're free to marry Renfrew, if that's what you want. After all, it *was* my plan to find you a husband. You need to marry a wealthy man just as I need to marry a wealthy woman." The words nearly choked him, but his decision best for all concerned. He was becoming far too involved with Moira for his own well-being.

"You want me to marry Lord Percy?" His words offered little comfort.

"He wouldn't be my choice, but it isn't my place to dictate to you. I've heard rumors about him but nothing that can be proved. He has money, and in your situation one man is as good as another." He watched her through narrowed lids. "You *don't* love him, do you?" There was a strong hint of male arrogance in his words.

"No, of course not," Moira answered hastily.

"Good. Since that is out of the way, we can now concentrate on your reason for lying to me. What are you frightened of, Moira? Or rather, who are you frightened of? You're hiding from someone. Who is it? Whoever or whatever it is, you can tell me."

Moira blinked and looked away. Jack was too astute not to realize she was hiding something from him. Unfortunately, it was nothing he could fix. This dilemma was hers to solve; no one could help her. Bringing Jack into it would only confuse matters.

"I'm sorry to disappoint you, but I'm not hiding from anyone or anything." The stubborn tilt of her chin warned Jack that dragging information from Moira wasn't going to be easy.

"You owe me an explanation, Moira."

"Perhaps I do, and maybe one day you'll get it, but not now. It's nothing you can help me with."

"Who were you running from the night my carriage ran you down?" Jack persisted. No answer was forthcoming. "Are you frightened of someone?" Silence. "Damn it, Moira, you're the most aggravating female I've ever come across. I want to help you."

"No one can help me."

"Let me try. I don't blame you for not trusting me, and I can assure you I won't interfere in your life again."

"I'm sure Victoria will be pleased to hear that," Moira said tartly. "Do you love her, Jack?" Moira knew the question was none of her business, but she couldn't help asking it.

"Good Lord, no! But we suit. I suppose we'll go our own ways after the newness of marriage wears off. Victoria isn't known for her fidelity to her lovers. Heaven only knows why she wants me."

Heaven might not know, but Moira did. If Jack made love to Victoria with the same fervor and expertise with which he made love to her, Moira knew exactly why Victoria wanted Jack. What woman wouldn't? She wondered what it would be like to be his wife, to experience passion and intimacy with him again and again. It was a recklessly seductive thought, one she didn't dare entertain. She wondered how Victoria would handle passion without emotion. Passion would certainly satisfy the body, but once pleasure was spent only emptiness remained. This thought led to another. After Jack had made love to her last night, why had she felt fulfilled instead of empty? She had been exhilarated and content beyond bearing. What did that say about her emotions? The answer to those questions teased the borders of her mind, but she deliberately thrust it aside. Those sentiments were too dangerous to contemplate. Admitting she had feelings for Black Jack Graystoke would only lead to heartbreak.

"Please leave, Jack. I'll be in no shape for Vauxhall tonight if I don't get some rest."

"Is that your final word, Moira? I realize I can't force you to divulge your secrets, but I'm not about to let this go. Rest; we'll discuss it another time. I've arranged for Spence to take you to Vauxhall tonight since I'm escorting Lady Victoria."

Moira did manage to find sleep, but only after clearing thoughts of Jack from her mind, which wasn't an easy task given the way he dominated every aspect of her life. Lately, even her dreams were filled with his vital presence. After last night, she had but to close her eyes and recall the feel of his weight pressing down on her, the arch of her body meeting his, the plunging of his hard flesh into hers. She wondered if he was remembering the same thing.

Moira awoke from her nap refreshed but no less troubled. Jilly brought a tray up to her while she dressed for Vauxhall, and Moira managed to gulp down enough food to stave off hunger until the midnight buffet was set out for the guests. She wore the second of the three gowns Jack had ordered made for her—a green velvet with low square neckline, puff sleeves that clung to her upper arms and a skirt that fell from just below her breasts in shimmering folds. She refused to have her hair powdered and wore her own auburn curls atop her head in an elaborate confection of spirals and poufs.

"Lord Fenwick is here, milady," Jilly said as she entered the bedchamber with Moira's wrap. "He's in the library with Sir Jack."

"I'll be ready in a moment," Moira said. Truthfully, she didn't care one way or another if she went to Vauxhall. She was sick and tired of this whole charade. It may be a game to Jack and Lord Spencer, but to her it was an abomination. She didn't like lying. Unfortunately, fate had given her little choice. Lady Victoria would not marry Jack until Moira was gone from his home, and Jack was desperate for her fortune. She didn't want to stand in the way of Jack's future.

Moira heard male voices coming from the study when she reached the bottom of the staircase. Her attention sharpened when she heard her name mentioned. She moved toward the door and paused to listen, aware that she was eavesdropping but too curious to turn away.

Jack raised the glass in his hand to the light, admiring the clear amber color of his last good bottle of brandy. He took a sip, sighed in appreciation and turned toward Spence, who lounged carelessly in a worn leather chair.

"Fine brandy is like a willing woman," Jack mused. "They are both best when savored slowly. Proper care enhances their flavor. One must appreciate the subtle nuances of their character to enjoy them." He took another sip, rolled it on his tongue and swallowed. "Moira is somewhat like this brandy," he continued blandly. "She has all its fine flavor, but unfortunately none of its character."

Spence stared at him curiously. "What in the hell is that supposed to mean?"

"Simply said, Spence, I find Moira's character lacking. She is a liar. She wouldn't know the truth if it stared her in the face."

"Would you care to elaborate?"

"No."

Spence gave a careless shrug. "Damn fine brandy, Jack." He sent Jack a piercing look. "But I can't rightly compare its flavor to Moira, not having tasted the lady's charms. Clearly you're an expert on both fine brandy and Moira. I have to hand it to you, old boy, you sure didn't waste any time. You've had her, I presume?"

Jack frowned, realizing he had spoken out of turn. He hadn't meant to divulge his intimate relationship with Moira. "No such thing, Spence. Moira is merely a responsibility I'm anxious to be rid of." He took another deep drag from his glass. "Percy Renfrew offered for her. Looks like I won the bet."

"I never doubted it for a minute, though I did so covet your grays." Spence grinned. "I suspected Renfrew might be the first since his parents gave him an ultimatum to marry or else, and he's had the devil's own time finding a woman who wasn't aware of his sordid reputation. Rumors are rife about his participation in the Hellfire Club. Personally I don't think he has the balls for it."

Jack's eyes darkened and his frown turned into a ferocious scowl. "It's probably all too true."

"Do you think Moira will marry him?"

"Probably."

"I'll bring your two thousand around tomorrow."

Moira's gasp echoed loudly in the room, bringing the men's attention to the door, where she stood poised in the doorway. Her face was ashen; she felt cold and hot at the same time.

"Moira. How long have you been standing there?"

"Long enough to know that passing me off as a lady

and finding me a husband is more than just a game to you.''

"Don't be angry, Moira," Spence pleaded. "Placing a monetary value on the outcome of our charade made it more interesting. Amusement is well and good, but a small wager added zest to the game."

"Spence is right, Moira," Jack said, dredging up a smile. "I made a tidy bundle off Renfrew's proposal. It's what we were all aiming for, wasn't it?"

"I learned the hard way what *you* were aiming for, Jack," Moira said bitterly. "Your honor is sadly lacking."

Jack's expression hardened. "What happened last night . . ." He flushed and looked at Spence, who was listening raptly to every word that passed between him and Moira. His mouth tightened. Revealing his personal life to his nosy friend simply would not do. "Your welfare is important to me, Moira. Think what you want—you will anyway—but don't forget I'm making it possible for you to help your brother. You needn't marry Renfrew; 'tis best if you don't. Someone more suitable will come along, and then you'll thank me for bringing it all about. Right now you need me, Moira. I don't know what or who you're hiding from, but you need my protection."

"I can do without your brand of protection," Moira charged, unwilling to divulge how close she had come to loving Jack Graystoke. Being loved by Jack had been the most incredible experience of her life, and he had turned it into something tawdry. To Jack, bedding her had been but a passing incident to be savored and forgotten.

"You're being too hard on Jack," Spence protested. "You've provided us with an escape from boredom while earning Jack some needed blunt. Had I won, Jack's grays would now be mine.''

Jack saw the anger in Moira's eyes fade to hurt and disillusionment, and his heart contracted painfully. How could a simple bet end with such disastrous results? He'd never meant to hurt Moira. He had no idea the injured woman he'd dragged from the gutter would change the course of his life. He'd resisted her for as long as he could. Who would have thought jealousy would be the cause of his downfall? He couldn't ever recall being jealous of a woman in his life.

Despite Moira's blatant lies, Jack still wanted her. Just looking at her now sent hot blood racing through his veins and brought certain parts of his body to attention. Bloody hell! *She'd been a virgin!* That alone should have kept him away from her, but no, last night he'd gloried in her innocence and lost himself in her sweet flesh not once, but twice. And he'd do it again unless he learned to control his unbridled lust for the wench.

''Jack can go to hell for all I care,'' Moira told Spence. ''I've decided to marry Lord Renfrew so Jack will be free to wed Lady Victoria.'' She squared her shoulders. ''I'm ready to go to Vauxhall, Lord Spencer.''

''At your service, milady,'' Spence said, executing a gentlemanly bow. He followed Moira out the door, sending an abashed look at Jack over his shoulder. The situation was becoming more complicated by the minute. He'd never seen Jack so taken with a woman. And obviously Moira returned his regard.

Sometime over the past weeks, Jack and Moira had become lovers—any fool could see that. Unfortunately, Jack needed to marry money, and Moira was a simple farm girl from Ireland with beauty and little else to commend her. An interesting situation, one that would bear watching.

Moira did not lack for dancing partners that night, though Jack was not among them. Victoria kept him on a tight leash, barely letting him out of her sight. But Moira could still feel the heat of his gaze on her when he thought she wasn't looking. Each time she turned to meet his gaze, her heart began thumping wildly, unable to deny the feelings he roused in her. It hurt to think she was merely a pawn to Jack. Obviously she was nothing to him except a means to fill his purse. He'd taken her virginity with callous disregard, then gave his permission to marry Lord Renfrew, or someone like him. Her emotions were so raw she was eaten up inside with despair.

"Ah, there you are, Lady Moira. An admirer would like to meet you."

Pasting a smile on her face, Moira turned to acknowledge Lord Peabody. But when she saw who was with Peabody, her smile wobbled dangerously and she nearly collapsed. Strict control was all that kept her knees from buckling when Lord Roger Mayhew took her hand and raised it to his lips.

"Dear lady, I just had to make your acquaintance. I am Lord Roger Mayhew. Perhaps you've heard of me." The malevolent glitter in his colorless eyes told Moira that he remembered her, and not fondly. "I understand you're Black Jack Graystoke's ward." The corners of his mouth curled upward into a parody of a smile. "How extraordinary."

"Sir Jack is a distant relative," Moira endeavored to explain. She knew he didn't believe her, but for appearance's sake she had to play the game out to the bitter end—which was approaching sooner than she'd like.

"So I understand. Would you honor me with a dance?"

"No, I'm tired and . . ."

Roger wasn't about to take no for an answer. He grasped her elbow and led her out onto the dance floor. Moira stumbled over the steps, wanting desperately to flee in panic. Had she known Lord Roger would return from the Continent so soon, she would have fled London weeks ago. She had hoped to be married and out of his reach long before he returned.

"I need to talk to you alone," Roger whispered into her ear. "I could unmask your little masquerade right now if I've a mind to, but I'm curious to learn what Graystoke's stake is in this game. I thought you were dead, you know." He squeezed her waist so hard she winced in pain. "Meet me in the summer house in fifteen minutes."

Moira blanched. "I can't. Jack would notice my absence and come looking for me."

"Very well, I'll play along with your game until I learn more about it. Plead a headache and go home. My carriage will be in the alley behind Graystoke Manor. Sneak out at midnight. I'll be waiting."

"No!"

"Do it or I'll announce to one and all that you are a fraud and your lover has made fools of his peers. Do you want to see Graystoke ruined?"

Moira blanched. She didn't want that at all. "I don't know what you're talking about."

"I'm not stupid. You and Black Jack are lovers."

The dance ended. Roger escorted Moira off the floor, bowed gallantly and left after imparting one last word. "Tonight." She was shaking uncontrollably as she watched him walk out the door.

"What's wrong, Moira? Did that bastard insult you? Roger Mayhew doesn't ordinarily attend tame functions like this. I'd heard he was abroad. A pity he returned. England doesn't need his kind."

Moira was so glad to see Jack she could have kissed him. As it was, she clutched his arm with a desperation that both pleased and astonished him.

Jack's brows furrowed. "Something *is* wrong. What in the hell did Mayhew say to you?"

"N—nothing. I have a terrible headache. I wish to go home."

Jack expressed immediate concern. "I'll take you."

"No! I don't want to cause a fuss. I'll hire a hackney and . . ."

"Damn it, Moira, I said I'll take you home and I meant it."

"But Lady Victoria . . ."

"The hell with Victoria. She can entertain herself until I return. I'll let her know I'm leaving for a bit and retrieve your wrap. Meet me in the foyer."

Moira didn't wait around to watch Victoria's reaction to Jack's announcement that he was leaving. She left the room immediately and headed directly for the foyer. Five minutes later, Jack arrived with her wrap. She could tell by the look on his face that it hadn't gone well with Victoria.

"This really isn't necessary, Jack. I can get home on my own. Lady Victoria is important to you; you shouldn't upset her."

Jack searched her face. "I fear she's been upset since the day I brought you home. She'll get over it. Besides, I'll be back in time to escort her to the midnight buffet and take her home." What he didn't say was that Victoria's mother had finally left and Victoria expected him to spend the night in her bed.

Both Jack and Moira were somewhat subdued during the ride home. Had Moira been privy to Jack's thoughts, she would have been surprised. Jack was thinking how tiresome Victoria was becoming with her demands. Because she knew he needed her money, she expected him to dance to her tune. During the past weeks, Jack had decided that her demands had become excessive. True, he needed blunt, but he was too proud to be dictated to by a woman. It occurred to him that he had no desire to make love to Victoria. The only woman he wanted to make love to was sitting beside him. What in the hell was wrong with him? he wondered distractedly. Gambling no longer appealed to him, drinking himself into a stupor seemed a waste of time, and other women paled in comparison to Moira. If he wasn't careful, he'd be mending his wicked ways and destroying a legend.

Lord, wouldn't Lady Amelia be pleased!

Intuition warned Jack that everything that had happened was the result of Lady Amelia's meddling. He wished he knew what she had planned for him. He could see no way out of marrying Victoria or someone like her, unless he wished to end his days in debtor's prison.

All too soon the carriage rolled to a stop before Graystoke Manor. When Jack prepared to step down, Moira placed a restraining hand on his sleeve. "Don't bother, I can see myself in the house. Lady Victoria is expecting you."

Jack's eyes narrowed suspiciously. "Are you trying to get rid of me?"

Moira's gaze met his and skittered away. Did Jack suspect anything? No matter how much she dreaded meeting

Lord Roger, it had to be done. She'd do anything to keep from hurting Jack and ruining his plans to marry wealth. "No, it's nothing like that. Why would I wish to get rid of you?"

"I don't know. Ever since you danced with Mayhew, you've been acting strangely. The man is debauched and unfit for polite society. But for his family name he would be blackballed. His family is a very old and powerful one. I know things about Mayhew that would shock you."

He helped her down from the carriage and walked her to the door. But instead of leaving her as she hoped, he followed her inside. "Moira, what *did* Mayhew say to upset you?"

"Please, Jack, I have a splitting headache. I don't want to talk about Lord Mayhew. Go back to Lady Victoria; she's waiting for you." She turned abruptly and walked briskly toward the stairs. Jack sprinted after her, grasping her arm and turning her to face him.

"Damn it, Moira, Victoria can wait forever as far as I'm concerned. I'm tired of being dictated to. She doesn't own me, and I don't like the feeling of being led around by the nose. As for her money, I'd rather ask Ailesbury for a loan. William is a good sort; he wouldn't turn me down."

"You don't need to explain a thing to me," Moira said, still upset over the wager Jack and Spence had engaged in at her expense. "After I marry Lord Renfrew, perhaps I can convince him to discharge your debts."

Her words sent Jack into a fine rage. Moira belonged to *him*. He'd been the first with her, and the thought of her in another man's bed sent his temper into orbit. He couldn't ever recall feeling so strongly about a woman. The turmoil in his heart played havoc with his emotions.

His feelings were in direct opposition to the way he'd lived his life up until Moira O'Toole entered it. Black Jack the rogue, the hard-drinking womanizer, the gambler—where had that man disappeared to? And why?

"Let me go. I told you I had a headache." Moira didn't want him to touch her. One touch was all it would take for her to recall in vivid detail everything that had happened between them last night, each arousing caress, every provocative word and intimate look from his smoldering gray eyes.

But Jack did more than merely look at her—much, much more. Pulling her into his arms, he lowered his head and kissed her. His kiss had no boundaries. It was hungry, open-mouthed and intimate. It was bruising and possessive. He tasted all of her, plumbing her mouth until she had no control over her body's response. It thrilled and terrified her. Never had she felt so out of her depth. Never had she wanted a man like she wanted Jack Graystoke. She let his kiss carry her away, let his hands roam freely over her body, let him pick her up and carry her up the stairs to her room, let him lay her down on the bed.

Mesmerized, Moira watched as Jack tore off his clothes, his piercing gray gaze never leaving hers. When every glorious inch of him was finally revealed, her mouth went dry and she licked moisture onto her lips. She tried but couldn't resist looking at him, fascinated beyond her ability to control her reaction. Last night she'd been too embarrassed to really look at him, but tonight she wanted to see him, all of him. She knew this was wrong, knew allowing Jack to make love to her again would complicate her life, but God forgive her, she wanted to feel him inside her, wanted him even knowing that she was merely a pawn in his wicked game. With Roger Mayhew threatening her, this might be the last time she'd be with Jack like this.

His shoulders were broad; his chest and arms rippled with supple muscles. The strong columns of his legs rose to meet lean hips, and at their juncture rose a rigid column of flesh that pulsed with a life of its own. She stared, impressed and a little frightened by his maleness.

"God, Moira, don't stare at me like that. 'Tis hard enough to maintain control without you devouring me with those golden cat's eyes." He lowered himself to the bed and kissed her, carefully working the fastenings on her dress loose so he could push it down past her shoulders.

"This shouldn't be happening." Moira gasped, annoyed by her failure to discipline her emotions. So much for her resolve not to let Jack take advantage of her again. "I told you I wouldn't be your mistress. I swore I wouldn't allow you to take advantage of me, but it's happening again. What am I going to do?"

"Let me love you," Jack said, "that's what you're going to do. I've never felt like this before, never wanted a woman like I want you. This is pure madness, and you're pure temptation."

Suddenly Moira recalled Roger's words about meeting him at midnight, and she went still beneath's Jack's roving hands. "What time is it?"

"Does it matter?"

Moira swallowed her rising panic. "It matters a lot. Please, what time is it?"

Jack sighed, reached across the bed to his discarded jacket and pulled his pocket watch out. "Ten-thirty. Can we continue now?"

"We shouldn't. I'm still angry over that ill-advised wager you made with Spence. I'm not a possession you can manipulate at will. I'm a flesh-and-blood woman.''

Jack nailed her with a piercing look. ''God, don't you think I know that? You shouldn't have lied to me about something as important as your virginity.''

''It's too late for recriminations. What about Victoria?''

''What about her?''

''She's expecting you.''

''Not until later. Besides, I'm having second thoughts about marrying her. She won't be too disappointed; she already suspects I'm losing interest.''

''But you need her,'' Moira persisted. ''What about Graystoke Manor?''

''I'll survive, and so will Graystoke Manor.'' He continued to undress her, making short work of her dress, petticoats and underclothes.

''Wait!'' She rolled away, emerging from the opposite side of the bed. ''I'm not a whore, Jack. I can't do this. We settled that last night. Go back to Vauxhall. Make amends with Lady Victoria. If you care about me . . .'' She choked back the rest of her sentence. It was ridiculous to think that Jack had feelings for her. Even if he did, those sentiments would do neither of them any good. She still had Roger Mayhew and her past to contend with, and Jack needed Lady Victoria's wealth. The last thing she wanted was for Lord Roger to hurt Jack's chances for a prosperous marriage.

Jack looked stunned as Moira tore the sheet from the bed and wrapped it around her. ''I thought you wanted me. You let me kiss you, you kissed me back.''

''You don't understand, do you?'' Moira said softly. ''Kissing and making love mean nothing to you except pleasure.''

Jack sent her a mocking grin. "Are you telling me you didn't enjoy it?"

"I enjoyed it so much I lost sight of my principles. You have a way of distracting me, of making me forget the morals I learned at my mother's knee. I can't do this; it isn't right. I'm going to try to forget last night ever happened."

"You little tease!" He reached for his trousers, pulling them on in angry jerks. "I've never taken an unwilling woman, and I never will." Frustration and disappointment churned inside him. He regretted the wager he'd made with Spence, regretted trying to find Moira a husband, regretted everything but making love to her. He could make love to her every night for the rest of his life and not regret it. But he was smart enough to know he was no good for Moira. She needed someone who could provide for her and her family, and he wasn't that man.

He slammed out the door carrying his boots, pulling them on as he raced down the stairs. When Moira heard the carriage roll down the gravel drive, she collapsed on the bed, aching for Jack's touch and knowing she could never have him. Even if she dared think of Jack and love in the same breath, it would be wishful thinking. She had no idea what evil Lord Roger planned for her now that he was back in London. Whatever befell her, she had to protect Jack at all costs.

Chapter Ten

The clock on the mantel struck midnight as Moira eased out the kitchen door. Jack hadn't returned yet from Vauxhall, and she supposed Lady Victoria would keep him occupied until dawn. Though it pained her to think of him with another woman, it was for the best, Moira thought as she crept toward the back gate leading into the alley where Lord Roger had said to meet him. No matter how frightened she was, she had to find out what he wanted from her. She feared he would use his knowledge of her past to ruin Jack, and she couldn't allow that to happen.

The hackney was waiting just beyond the back gate. Moira approached it with trepidation, noting that the driver was hunched over the reins, looking neither right nor left. Lord Roger must be paying him well to mind his own business, Moira thought dimly. The last thing she wanted was to be alone with Roger, and she had no intention of entering the hackney, but the choice was taken from her when the door swung open and a hand reached out, hauling her inside. Moira cried out in dismay as she sprawled across the seat in a flurry of swirling skirts. The door slammed shut and the hackney rattled off. Moira righted herself with difficulty, pushed down her skirts and glared at the man lounging in the opposite seat. Neither Moira nor Roger saw Jilly watching from the rear door. The little maid couldn't sleep and had gone to the kitchen for a snack when she saw Moira creeping out the back door. Jilly stared in disbelief when she saw the dim outline of a man's face through the window of the hackney.

"You were wise to show up," Lord Roger said with quiet menace.

"Where are we going?" Panic gnawed at the edges of Moira's control. She recalled with rising panic what had happened the last time she was alone with Lord Roger. She had nearly been killed jumping from his coach.

"To rooms I keep for occasions like this. Don't worry, I won't do anything you haven't allowed your lover to do. And I'm not taking you to Newgate. I have other plans for you."

"You're despicable. You know I didn't steal that necklace. Why don't you tell your parents the truth?"

"Not bloody likely. They're already angry with me for letting you go and for leaving London without a word of explanation. I had to borrow passage money to France. I won't come into my inheritance for another fortnight, and my father keeps me on a tight budget. Damn bloody sod."

They had gone but a short distance when the coach rolled to a stop. "We're here. Come along. We'll continue this conversation inside." Grasping her arm, he hauled her from the coach, instructing the hackney to wait. A frisson of fear slithered down Moira's spine when she realized Roger intended taking her into the most disreputable inn she had ever seen. A weathered sign hung askew over the door, and despite the late hour, boisterous laughter could be heard coming from within the dimly lit interior.

Moira balked when Roger tried to drag her inside. "I'm not going in there."

"You will if you know what's good for you. Pull your hood over your head. You're not the first whore I've brought to my rooms at the Hen and Rooster, and you won't be the last. The riffraff that frequents this place pays little heed to a doxy plying her trade."

When Moira continued to resist, Roger jerked viciously on her arm and hauled her through the door. The sound of ribald revelry assaulted her ears. The nauseating odors of stale liquor and unwashed flesh gagged her. She flinched away from curiosity seekers and burrowed deep within her hood as Roger pulled her up the rickety stairs.

"Here we are," Roger said, opening a door and pushing her inside. "Take off your cloak and make yourself at home."

"No, thank you," Moira demurred as she gave the dingy room a cursory glance. "I'm not staying long. What did you wish to discuss?"

"You know damn well what I want. What happened to you after you jumped from my coach? I was certain you were dead; that's why I fled London. You can't imagine how shocked I was when I saw you at Vauxhall tonight. When I was told you were the daughter of an Irish baron, I was nearly overcome with laughter. Then I learned that you were Jackson Graystoke's ward, and I wanted to expose you for a felon immediately. But after considering the situation, I changed my mind. I decided that keeping your little secret might better serve my purposes. I still want you. Seeing you in the trappings of a lady tonight whet my appetite for a taste of what you denied me weeks ago."

Moira sent him a scathing glance. "You disgust me."

Roger laughed nastily. "Unless you wish to be jailed for theft and Jack Graystoke reviled and ostracized by his peers, you'll do exactly as I say. Rumor has it that Graystoke needs to marry money and he's set his sights on Lady Victoria Greene. I've had her. She's a hot little piece," Roger observed. "What do you think will happen when Lady Victoria learns you're no more Graystoke's ward than you are mine? She'll think the worst, of course. Marriage to an heiress will be out of the question for Graystoke once society learns how he hoodwinked them. Is that what you want for the man who saved your life? He did save your life, didn't he?"

"He didn't leave me lying at the side of the road to freeze to death or die of injuries," Moira charged. "He has compassion, something you lack."

Roger sneered derisively. "Whose idea was it to pass you off as a lady? Sounds like one of Graystoke's brilliant ideas."

"That's none of your business."

"I'm making it my business. If you don't do as I say, I'll ruin Graystoke. Society has little use for him anyway. He's called Black Jack with good reason."

"What do you want from me?" Moira asked, rounding on him in fury. "Whatever it is, leave Jack out of it."

Roger gave her a sly grin. "Perhaps. If you do as I say. I think you know well enough what I want. You cheated the disciples once, but you shan't again."

The Hellfire Club. The man was truly evil. "No! I'll never agree."

"Wait, I'm not finished. If you refuse, I'll turn you over

to the magistrate and inform him that Graystoke was your accomplice in the theft. Did you know there's a reward for your capture? Your choices are limited. It's either Newgate or the Hellfire Club.''

Never had Moira hated a man more. Rage scorched the edges of her temper. ''I'd rather die than be debauched by you and your vile friends. I've heard that few women survive a night with those Satan worshipers. If I live through the ordeal, I swear I'll go straight to your parents and expose you as a member of the Hellfire Club.''

''Oh, you'll survive. I'll see to it. Afterward, arrangements will be made to place you in a brothel. You may even like what the disciples do to you. Most prostitutes we hire seem to enjoy it. Graystoke has been a member for some time. I'm surprised he didn't bring you to our rituals before this. The bloody bastard probably wanted to save you for himself.''

''Blessed Virgin help me!'' Moira cried. ''You're lying. Jack would never become a member of a vile organization like the Hellfire Club.''

''Pray all you want, sweet Moira, it will change nothing.'' Roger congratulated himself for his cleverness. Planting seeds of doubt in Moira's mind about Black Jack's involvement with the Hellfire Club was a stroke of genius, even if it was a lie. ''Newgate is an unpleasant place, I'm told. Disease, pestilence, filth, starvation—you'll experience all of those and more. It won't be difficult to name Black Jack your accomplice. I could easily get someone to swear that he talked you into stealing Mother's necklace. 'Tis common knowledge he is always in need of blunt.''

Moira blanched. ''Not even you could be that reprehensible.'' Was he lying about Jack? Her mind said he was not, but her heart utterly denied that Jack could be involved with a group dedicated to evil. Yet it made sense. No doubt he had earned his nickname.

Roger smiled thinly. "I could and I am. As a disciple of the Hellfire Club, I learned that nothing is more important than gratification of all the senses. Whatever it takes to get what we want is acceptable. Evil is exciting. Ask Black Jack if you doubt me. Or Lord Renfrew. They are all disciples. All dedicated to pleasure."

Color leeched from Moira's face. Lord Renfrew, too? "If your parents knew the kind of man you were, they'd disown you."

"Father is a pompous ass who constantly berates me for my wicked ways, though he doesn't know the half of it. He's threatened to disinherit me in favor of my younger brother, a self-righteous twit if I ever saw one. No one will cheat me out of my inheritance. The title belongs to me."

There was so much evil in his voice that Moira feared for the life of his father and brother. Revulsion speared through her. Corruption of this sort frightened her. "I can't do what you ask, no matter the consequences."

"I'm giving you no choice. Take off your clothes. I have a yen to sample you before the others take their turns with you."

Moira took a step backward. "No."

Roger reached for her, pulling her against him roughly. "I'm not a patient man."

He bore her backward onto the bed. Panic raced through Moira, imbuing her with courage beyond her meager strength. She felt his hands on her breasts, felt him searching beneath her skirts, felt his hot tongue probing against her closed lips. She gagged and swallowed

Connie Mason

bitter bile. She couldn't allow this abomination.

Roger's lean, wiry body was hard as steel as he pinned her to the bed and ground his loins into her. His slobbering kisses tasted of sin and corruption. She fought valiantly, but when she realized Roger was enjoying the struggle, she went limp beneath him. Then she saw it, the crockery water pitcher sitting on the decrepit nightstand, barely within reach.

Roger had her skirts to her waist now and was momentarily distracted with the fastenings on his trousers and by the mesmerizing sight of the shimmering copper curls between her thighs. Driven by desperation, Moira stretched out her arm, offering a heartfelt prayer of thanks when her fingers curled around the pitcher's handle.

Aroused to the point of madness, Roger grasped the obscenity between his legs and positioned it at the portal of Moira's delicate petals. "Prepare yourself for a real man between your white thighs," he said hoarsely as he flexed his hips for the plunge to sweet rapture.

Moira had other ideas. Even as Roger tightened his buttocks and flexed his hips, she lifted the pitcher and brought it crashing down on his head. He reared up, stared at her in disbelief, then slumped heavily against her as his eyes rolled upward in his head. Moira scrambled from beneath him, still holding the severed handle of the pitcher. She looked at it in horror, then let it drop from her nerveless fingers. Roger lay face down on the bed, utterly still, and she pushed him away from her. Sparing him but a single glance, she straightened her clothes, donned her cloak and ran from the room.

She thanked God that the inn was emptying for the night as she raced down the stairs and out the door. The hackney stood at the curb. Moira had nearly forgotten that

Roger had told the driver to wait. Gathering her courage, she called to the driver in an authoritive voice, "Take me back to Hanover Square."

The driver shook himself awake and peered down at Moira through bleary eyes. "Where's the gent?"

"He decided to stay. You're to take me home."

The man scratched his head. "I don't know, miss. I was paid to wait."

"And so you did," Moira said curtly. "You have your money, now take me home to Hanover Square. No need to climb down; I can get myself into the coach."

The driver stared at her in confusion, then nodded agreement. Moira practically threw herself into the conveyance, keeping a sharp eye on the inn for any sign of Lord Roger. But she needn't have worried. No sooner had she slammed the door shut than the hackney lurched forward. Moira leaned back and closed her eyes, still shaking from her close call. When Roger awakened he'd be furious with her. She had no idea what he'd do, but she held one trump card. She knew about his involvement in the Hellfire Club and had no qualms about informing his parents.

Jack let himself into the house and trod wearily up the stairs. Getting rid of Victoria after the ball had been no easy feat. She'd been angrier than he'd ever seen her when he refused her blatant invitation to spend the night in her bed. He couldn't even recall the excuse he'd used this time, but it hadn't satisfied her. She had given him an ultimatum: Unless he proved his devotion to her, she'd take herself and her money elsewhere. She did not lack for suitors, she'd told Jack in no uncertain terms.

Jack hadn't even bothered to apologize for his lack of

passion. He'd turned abruptly on his heel and left. Not long ago, marrying Victoria had seemed a good idea, given his desperate state of finances. It shocked him no end when he came to the realization that no amount of money could make up for lack of love in a relationship. Bloody hell! He found it difficult to believe he'd changed so drastically in the past few weeks. Where had the old dissolute Black Jack disappeared to? Where was the debauched rake he knew and loved?

When Jack reached the top landing, his thoughts turned to Moira. She had claimed a headache and the need for bed, and now his brow furrowed in concern. He knew he shouldn't, but the urge to look in on her was too pressing to ignore. Pausing before her door, he turned the handle and eased it open. The dying fire in the grate spread a dull glow throughout the room, providing just enough light to see that the bed was empty. Jack went rigid. Where was she? After lighting a candle, Jack searched the room, feeling relief when he saw that all Moira's clothes were in place except for a dark cloak. The next emotion he experienced was unbridled rage. Where had she gone—and with whom?

Charging down the stairs, Jack had the front door open and was ready to rush out when he heard a noise behind him. Whirling on his heel, he saw Jilly, her cowering figure a grotesque shadow against the wall.

"For God's sake, Jilly, if you know where your mistress is, tell me!"

Jilly blanched, more frightened than she'd ever been in her life. Black Jack's fierce expression made him appear every bit as dangerous as his infamous name implied.

Jilly's fright must have gotten through to Jack, for his expression softened. "I'm not going to hurt you, Jilly. Did you speak with Moira? Did she tell you where she was going this time of night?''

''No, sir,'' Jilly said in a trembling voice. ''I saw Lady Moira leave the house through the kitchen door, but I don't know where she went or who the man was in the hackney.'' Jilly's single sentence told Jack everything he wanted to know. He looked away, his silver eyes glowing with menace.

''Man?'' That thought sent rage pounding through him. ''Moira met a man and went off with him in a hackney?''

''Aye.''

''Who?'' Jack asked tersely.

''I don't know, sir. It was dark. I didn't get a good look at his face. If it helps any, I don't think Lady Moira went willingly.''

Jack's features took on the consistency of granite. ''Did she leave the house of her own free will?''

Jilly swallowed convulsively. She'd never willingly do a thing to hurt her mistress. If only Sir Jack wasn't so frightening. ''I . . . I don't know.''

Jack's fists clenched so tightly his knuckles turned white. ''Thank you, Jilly. You may go back to bed now.''

''But, sir,'' Jilly began timidly, ''I don't think Lady Moira would . . .''

''Go to bed, Jilly. I'll handle things.''

Unprepared to test the full extent of Black Jack's ire, Jilly turned and fled. She pitied poor Lady Moira and did not envy her the task of facing Black Jack's formidable temper.

Jack returned to his chamber to await Moira's return, his thoughts in a turmoil. Why had she sneaked off in the middle of the night, and with whom? Once again he had been lied to, and rage built inside him. Unfortunately, the long wait for Moira to return did little to improve his temper.

Two hours later, he heard the unmistakable sound of a hackney rattling down the street. Watching from the window, he saw it stop and discharge its female passenger. Moira had returned from her rendezvous, and his expression turned grim. The urge to do her bodily harm burned deeply within him as he heard Moira let herself into the house and creep up the stairs. Two angry strides took him to his chamber door, but before he could throw it open to confront Moira, an apparition appeared before him, blocking his path.

"Bloody hell!" His violent outburst gave hint to his shattered patience. "I've no time for you now, milady. Moira is going to tell me who she was meeting or I'm going to wring her lovely neck. I was right about her all along. She's nothing but a bed-hopping little tease. Once I took her virginity, she wanted to stretch her wings and try out new lovers. Damn it! I won't stand for it, do you hear?"

Lady Amelia appeared disinclined to move. She seemed aware of Jack's violent temper and wished to spare Moira the brunt of his anger.

"Go away! You're nothing but a figment of my imagination," Jack raged. "Don't try to interfere. The little tart had an assignation with a man, and I'm going to find out who he was or else."

Lady Amelia shook her head and stood firm.

"You've placed me in a hell of a fix, milady. My prospects for an advantageous marriage have flown out the window, and with it my reputation as a rake and womanizer. 'Tis your fault I no longer care to drink and gamble and chase women," he accused sullenly. "'Tis your meddling that brought Moira into my home. I haven't been the same since. Bedding the little Irish witch was a mistake. How could I know she was a virgin?''

Lady Amelia tilted her head, as if assessing every word Jack said.

''Don't you understand?'' Jack continued earnestly. ''Moira needs money as much as I do. We do not suit. I know I should let her go, but damned if I can bring myself to part with her.'' Lady Amelia nodded her head. ''I know I have nothing to offer Moira, or she me. But I'll be damned if I'll let another man corrupt her.''

Lady Amelia placed a hand over her heart, as if trying to convey a wordless message, but Jack was too incensed to figure it out. And he wasn't inclined to let a meddling ghost stop him from confronting Moira. He knew he should wait until his temper cooled, but the thought of Moira with another man had robbed him of whatever good sense he possessed. He took a step forward, as if to push past the ghost, but Lady Amelia's inner brilliance burst into a blazing halo of light, creating an intense heat that forced Jack to retreat.

''Bloody hell! What am I to do?'' Lady Amelia merely stared at Jack, but her words were somehow projected into his brain.

Don't hurt her.

''Do you really think I could hurt Moira? Even if I confronted her at the peak of my temper, I doubt I could bring myself to harm her.''

Obviously placated, Lady Amelia nodded and stepped aside, permitting Jack to leave. Jack didn't have time to figure it out as he flung open the door and strode purposely toward Moira's room.

* * *

Moira was still shaking when she'd entered her room. Had she killed Lord Roger? She doubted it. She had hit him solidly, but the blow had been blunted by the awkward angle, due to her prone position on the bed.

Moira undressed by the light of a single candle and climbed into bed in her shift, too tired to don her prim nightgown. Dawn was but a whisper away as she closed her eyes, searching for sleep. Her mind was consumed with Roger's vile plans for her. She had escaped this time, but would she again? Would he leave her alone now or consider her knowledge of his activities too dangerous for him to ignore? Leaving London seemed prudent at this time, but finding money to buy passage to Ireland created a problem. She was still contemplating her alternatives when Jack burst into the room.

"Where in the hell have you been?" His voice was harsh, his face as hard and unyielding as stone, his arms crossed over his chest. Moira darted a quick glance at his implacable expression and realized by the dark, seething look on his face that he knew she had left the house. Thank God he didn't know why or with whom she was meeting.

She could hardly bear to look at him. Imagining him participating in satanic rites with men like Lord Roger Mayhew made her visibly ill. "What are you doing home? I thought you and Lady Victoria . . ."

Jack stalked into the room and loomed over her. "You thought wrong. If you were itching to be bedded, why didn't you come to me? Why another man, for God's sake? Bloody hell, Moira, I don't know what to make of you. You continue to confound and confuse me. Until we made love, you were an innocent. Did I create a wanton?"

Though Moira seethed inwardly, she remained stubbornly mute, which sent Jack's temper soaring. "I thought I knew you, but I was wrong. You may have been a virgin when I took you, but you're a whore at heart."

"And I thought I knew you!" Moira shot back.

"Perhaps you wouldn't be looking for another man to bed had I followed my instinct earlier tonight and made love to you. But if it's a man you want, I'll gladly oblige. As you well know, I'm not lacking in that department."

Jack knew he was letting his anger rule his head, but he couldn't help himself. It hurt too damn much to think of Moira with another man. He wanted to punish her, make her pay for denying him. He removed his jacket and tossed it aside, his shirt following.

"What are you doing?"

Jack sent her a look so dark and devouring that her skin suddenly felt too tight for her body. "I'm going to make love to you. If you can accommodate others, you can accommodate me."

"Don't touch me!" The breath froze in her throat when Jack peeled his trousers down his legs and removed them along with his shoes and stockings. His stern, implacable expression was anything but comforting. But it wasn't his face she was looking at. Her eyes slid downward. He was fully erect, his body hard and unyielding, every muscle tense with seething desire.

He gave her a mocking smile that did not quite reach his eyes. She shivered and tried to look away, but couldn't. "Is your lover better endowed than I?" His arrogance unleashed Moira's Irish temper.

"You contemptible bastard! Think what you will, but I have no lover. You're the only one. Had I known the kind of man you were and the vile things you were capable of, I would have left this house before you defiled me."

"I don't know what in the hell you're talking about." He had no idea she was referring to the Hellfire Club as he lowered himself to the bed and pulled her roughly against his pulsing body, too aroused to figure out the meaning behind Moira's words. "Furthermore, I wouldn't believe anything you said."

Moira stiffened and tried to escape, but she was no match for his formidable strength as he pinned her to the bed. "Do you wish to explain?" His voice was deceptively calm, which should have warned her.

"No."

Grasping the edges of her chemise, he rent it in half, baring the supple curves of her body. "Who was the man you were with tonight?" He fondled her breast, and shards of unwelcome heat shot downward from where his hand rested.

Her mouth clamped shut. She felt as if she didn't know Jack anymore; had she known him at all?

"You're a beautiful woman, Moira. Any man would want you."

If Moira hadn't been aware of Jack's involvement with the Hellfire Club, his words would have thrilled her. It rankled to think that she had worried about ruining Jack's chances for a prosperous marriage when she should have been worrying about herself and his plans for her. Were both Jack and Lord Renfrew conspiring to place her at the mercy of the disciples of evil?

"I was with no one you know."

"You expect me to believe that?" With startling insight, Jack realized that he wanted to be the only man in Moira's life. For the first time in his life he bemoaned the fact that he wasn't born into wealth. He cared nothing for a title, but wealth would make it possible to marry a woman of his choice instead of someone like Victoria. Victoria had expressed little desire to give him an heir and would doubtlessly cuckold him the moment the newness wore off their marriage. Nor could he promise faithfulness to a woman he didn't love.

Love. Bloody hell! That exalted state had meant nothing to him in the past; why should he be contemplating it now? He gazed down at Moira, his body tense with longing. He wanted this stubborn little witch more than he'd ever wanted another woman. But he still couldn't get past the fact that Moira had met someone in the dead of night. She had denied bedding another man, and he was inclined to believe her, but that still explained nothing. He sensed something deeper, something frightening in her denial. And what in the hell was she accusing him of?

"You've consistently lied to me, from the very beginning," Jack charged. "Why can't you tell the truth for once in your life?"

Moira shook with revulsion. "Why can't you?"

"I've not lied to you. Why don't you trust me?"

"I trust no man. Not after what I learned tonight. How could you?"

Jack saw the glimmer of tears in Moira's golden eyes, and all the anger left his body, replaced by the urgent need to soothe her, to make love to her until she forgot everything but their mutual pleasure. But her last remark puzzled him too much to let slide. "How could I *what?* You're still talking in riddles."

"I know!" Moira all but shouted. "I know you're a member of the Hellfire Club."

"What? Who told you such an outrageous lie?"

177

"Are you denying it?"

"Hell, yes, I'm denying it."

She wanted to believe him. Sweet Virgin, she wanted to believe him, but she couldn't. "I'm not the only liar in this room," Moira bit out.

Shifting positions, he lifted her above him effortlessly. The muscles in his arms rippled with strength, the planes of his face sharpened with hunger. When her breasts were dangling above his face, he brought her down atop him so he could caress her nipples with his mouth and tongue. Panic seized her. She didn't want this to happen. She fought against it. Then every nerve in her body caught fire and burst into flame.

After giving each breast tender attention, he caught her mouth in a soul-destroying kiss, his tongue teasing, probing, exploring the sweet depths. He kissed her until she grew dizzy, until she gasped for breath. Then, rolling, he pressed her to her back, seeking greater access. Grasping the torn remnants of her chemise, he pulled it away and tossed it aside, wanting no barriers between them.

"Who was the man you were with tonight?" he asked with quiet determination.

"Why do you care?"

Seizing her hand by the wrist, he pressed it against the rigid length of his shaft. "Feel how hard I am, Moira. Feel what you do to me. Believe me when I say I care."

Moira's fingers curled around him. He was stiff and hard beneath her hand. Velvet-covered steel. Alive, swelling and pulsing with heat. Moira glanced up at him. In the flickering candlelight, his eyes were two silver pools, reflecting his ravening hunger. He looked feverish, as if his skin had been pulled too tightly over the sharp planes of his face. His nostrils flared with each breath he took, reminding her of a sexually aroused beast.

Jack groaned, closing his teeth around her nipple. Moira whimpered, the feeling so exquisite it lingered somewhere between ecstasy and pain. Her hand tightened around him in response.

"Sweet, sweet Jesus!" His voice was a harsh plea as tremors racked his body. He flung her hand away so violently she feared she had hurt him. "Damn it, I lose all control when I'm with you. You have no idea how close I am to spending. You were meant for pleasure, Moira, and I want to be the one to give it to you. I'm a jealous lover."

He trailed damp warm kisses along her flat belly, his tongue ringing her navel and his hands sliding into the tangled curls that guarded her sex. Spreading the petals with his fingers, he eased two of them gently inside her. "Soft, so soft," he murmured as he spread her legs wide and knelt between them. "So wet." He kissed the insides of her thighs, his fingers still pressing inside her, continuing to tease and stroke her.

She arched upward, biting her lip to keep from crying out his name. All he could manage was an answering groan as he continued to spread more soft kisses upward along her thigh, until he found the tiny pink bud of her desire and settled his mouth over the inflamed fold of sensitive flesh.

"Jack! No! What are you doing? That's wicked."

"It's not wicked," Jack murmured against her flesh. "There are many ways to love a woman." Then his tongue touched her there and the ability to speak left him. Her musky scent inflamed him, sending pure fire into his loins, making him pulse and swell with unspent passion. He felt her small body bow upward, saw her face transfix with pleasure, and replaced his fingers with the wet thrust of his tongue.

Moira screamed, clutching his shoulders in desperation. She was ablaze with need, aching and pulsing with every tortured breath. He heard her moan in her passion, felt her legs fall farther apart as he laved and tasted of her sweetness. He plundered her ruthlessly, his hands sliding beneath her, grasping her buttocks and forcing her to accept each bold stroke of his tongue. Her breathing came swift and ragged. She stiffened until he feared she would shatter. And then she did. He heard her small gasp, felt the tremors convulsing her body, and knew she had found pleasure.

Before she had fully recuperated from the incredible upward spiral, Jack eased upward between her legs. His hardness probed, found her entrance, then plunged deeply inside her.

Moira's eyes flew open and she cried out at the incredible heat and hardness of him, at the velvet thickness of his shaft and the bunching of his muscles as he strained above her. Waves of raw rapture washed over her, scorching heat suffused her and she felt herself reaching for that high plateau of erotic sensation with every relentless thrust of his body. She was on fire with pleasure so potent it threatened to consume her.

Wrapping her arms and legs around him, she clung to him fiercely.

"Jack . . ." His name was a breathless sigh as she reached her peak, her body shaking with spiraling splendor. "Oh, Jack . . ." The feel of him driving inside her intensified her pleasure as she felt him jerk violently, felt the hot rush of his seed leave his body and fill her.

The last spasms had barely passed through her when

the painful knowledge of Jack's involvement with the Hellfire Club brought her abruptly to her senses. Tears formed at the corners of her eyes and spilled in salty beads down her pale cheeks. He was cut from the same cloth as Roger Mayhew and Lord Fenwick. He had used her and she had let him. She tried to push Jack away, but he rolled to his side, pulling her against him. He felt moisture dampen his chest and reared back to look at her.

"Why are you crying?"

"I hate you." Moira sobbed.

"You could have fooled me."

"You steal my will and rob me of my senses."

"Then we have something in common." He'd bedded countless women, some whose names he couldn't even recall, but never had making love been such a moving experience. With a flash of insight, he knew he could not let another man have Moira. Not now, not ever.

"Were you with Lord Renfrew tonight? You may as well tell me, for I'll find out one way or another. What did he say to make you so angry with me?"

Moira sent him an oblique look. "I haven't seen Lord Renfrew since he proposed. Are you aware that he is a member of the Hellfire Club?"

Jack recoiled in alarm. "Who in the hell told you that? The men wear robes and hoods in order to keep their identities secret from one another. Did someone try to talk you into attending their rites tonight?"

"I'd never agree to anything like that! Not even Lord Roger . . ." Suddenly realizing what she'd said, Moira clamped a hand over her mouth.

Fear and revulsion shuddered through Jack. "You were with Roger Mayhew tonight? Are you insane? Didn't you heed my warning?"

"I agreed to meeting him for your sake, but when he told me about your involvement in the Hellfire Club, I realized what a bloody fool I'd been."

He grasped her shoulders, giving her a violent shake. "For *my* sake! What in the hell are you talking about? I know for a fact that Mayhew is a member of the club, but I certainly am not." His eyes blazed with implacable fury. "I think I'm beginning to understand. You knew Roger Mayhew before we met, didn't you? He was your employer's son, wasn't he? The one who fancied you. What did he say to talk you into meeting him tonight?"

Moira stared at him, realizing that he was too close to the truth for comfort. Yet she couldn't tell him about the theft. If he was a member of the Hellfire Club, he had no scruples. As desperately as he needed money, he'd probably turn her in for the reward.

"I owe you no explanation. I loathe him as much as I loathe you. I told you I didn't bed him, and that's all I'll say."

"We're at an impasse. Neither of us trusts the other. All we have is this." He grasped her hips and positioned her beneath him, his voice as grainy and rough-edged as his passion. Jack knew this insatiable wanting was madness but couldn't help himself. Savage tension coiled inside him as he plunged inside her and began to move, the thunder of his heartbeat escalating to match the tempo of his thrusting body.

The gripping passion of feeling her tightness surround him took over, making him oblivious to everything but the joining of their bodies, the primitive need to press himself inside her as deeply as possible. Anger leeched from him like an ebbing tide as he thrust faster, his hips grinding against hers until her body went taut and she climaxed. He gave a gritty cry, buried himself to the hilt and gave up his seed.

When she opened her eyes, Jack was staring at her strangely. The molten silver of his eyes pierced through to her innermost soul. His fiercely possessive expression sent shards of panic racing through her. She knew he'd not rest until he had the truth from her about her association with Lord Roger and resigned herself to telling it.

"Damn it, Moira, enough of your lies! I won't be played for a fool. I'm not leaving this room until you tell me what's going on."

Moira fixed her gaze on the pinkening sky outside the window. Dawn was but a dim memory as streaks of daylight lightened the eastern sky. How could her life turn into such a disaster? she wondered bleakly. All she could do now was tell the truth and pray Jack believed her. If he had a shred of decency, he'd realize she wasn't capable of deceit. She'd opened her mouth to unburden her soul when fate intervened in the form of Pettibone.

"Sir Jack! Are you in there? Wake up, sir. A messenger has arrived all the way from Cornwall. He's ridden without respite to bring you news. 'Tis most urgent, sir."

Chapter Eleven

"This better be good, Pettibone," Jack said, throwing back the covers and reaching for his trousers. "Show the man into the study. I'll be with him directly."

"Sweet Virgin, he knows you're in here with me," Moira wailed unhappily. "What must he think of me?"

"There isn't much going on in this house that Pettibone isn't aware of," Jack said dryly. "Don't worry, he's the soul of discretion and completely faithful. I'm sorry our talk was interrupted, but this doesn't let you off the hook. When I return, we will begin where we left off."

Looking as presentable as he'd ever looked at such an ungodly early hour, Jack let himself out the door and into the hallway, where Pettibone stood waiting. "You say the messenger is from Cornwall?" Jack asked as Pettibone trailed after him down the stairs.

"Aye, that's what he said. But I could get little else out of the man."

"My cousin Ailesbury is in Cornwall. Perhaps he wishes me to attend his wedding, though 'tis rather late to summon me. I hope naught is amiss with Will.''

By the time he reached the bottom landing, Jack felt vague stirrings of misgiving. He'd had premonitions at various times during his life, but nothing as strong as the vibrations he was receiving now. With trepidation, he opened the door and stepped into the study. Pettibone followed close on his heels.

The messenger jumped to his feet, and Jack could see deep lines of fatigue etched around his eyes and mouth. The man looked ready to drop from exhaustion, and Jack realized only something of grave importance could drive a man to ride without respite.

''Sit down before you fall,'' Jack said, motioning the man back into the chair he'd just vacated. ''My man said you had a message for me.'' He held out his hand. The messenger dug in his pocket and pulled out a sealed envelope, which he placed in Jack's open palm. Jack stared at it, his premonition so strong he wanted to fling the message into the fire without looking at it.

''Take the man to the kitchen, Pettibone. He must be starved. Then show him to a room where he can rest.''

The moment Pettibone and the messenger left, Jack broke the seal on the envelope, removed the single sheet of parchment and quickly read the message. When he reached the end, the paper dropped from his fingers and fluttered unheeded to the floor. He turned to stare out the window, oblivious to the glorious sunrise coloring the eastern sky.

With sudden insight, Jack realized he wasn't alone. Turning slowly, he encountered Lady Amelia. He showed no surprise, just numb acceptance. ''Did you know this would happen, milady?'' Jack couldn't be certain, but he thought he saw Lady Amelia shake her head. ''You know

I never wished for this. It was the last thing I wanted or expected.'' Lady Amelia bowed her head in commiseration.

Pettibone chose that precise moment to return. He stared in awe at the ethereal figure clothed in flowing white. He exhaled sharply, unable to believe his eyes when the apparition slowly faded away. To Pettibone's credit, he was too disciplined to mention the fact that the family ghost had visited one of the most dissolute Graystokes of all time. Pettibone thought it all quite extraordinary and happily accepted the fact that Black Jack was marked for redemption. Then he spied the letter lying at Jack's feet and bent to pick it up.

''Is aught amiss, Sir Jack? I could get little out of the messenger except that he was the bearer of sad tidings.''

Jack turned to face Pettibone, and the servant was struck by the deep lines of grief etched upon his employer's handsome face. ''It couldn't be worse, Pettibone. Ailesbury is dead. Killed on the way to his wedding. His coach was caught in a violent rainstorm. The high cliff road he was traveling gave way beneath the wheels of his vehicle, and it plunged down an embankment. Will was killed instantly.''

Jack buried his face in his hands, trying to gain his composure. When he finally looked up, Pettibone was shocked to see tears in his employer's eyes. ''It doesn't make sense, Pettibone. Will was a good man. He had a full life ahead of him. He was going to marry the woman he loved and produce heirs for the dukedom. *I* am the reprobate. Why couldn't it have been me?''

Pettibone had not seen Jack so overcome with grief since he'd lost his parents. ''You must accept young

Ailesbury's death as the will of God. Will you go to Cornwall?''

"Aye, I leave immediately to escort the body back to Dorset for proper burial. News of Ailesbury's death has been sent to his lawyer and to the king. I expect to hear from the lawyer shortly. Will you see to my packing, Pettibone?''

"Aye, milord.''

Jack gave him a startled look. Milord. He never wanted the title, never aspired to Will's position as Duke of Ailesbury, but now, by the hand of fate, it was his. Somehow it didn't seem right. It was an awesome burden, but he was duty bound to accept the responsibility. Duty. He'd given little thought to duty during his twenty-seven years. He didn't wear duty and responsibility well. Already he could feel it weighing heavily upon his shoulders. Had he been groomed for the dukedom, it would have been different, but having to assume it under tragic circumstances left him with feelings of inadequacy.

"It's going to be difficult to accustom myself to a title when I've always held nobility in scorn,'' Jack told Pettibone.

"You will manage, milord,'' Pettibone said bracingly.

"I hope so. In my absence, you are to hire any servants you deem necessary to run Graystoke Manor properly. You've managed on your own long enough. I'm counting on you to look after Moira in my absence.''

"You can trust me, milord,'' Pettibone said as he left to do Jack's bidding.

Jack paused, lost in thought. Moira. He hadn't considered what this would mean to their relationship. Not only would the title pass to him, but the entire bulk of Ailesbury's estate. There were numerous holdings, including valuable property and all the monies for rents on those estates. Not to mention the thousands of pounds in various banks and lucrative investments in shipping, mining and farming. Now they were all his. No longer did he have to marry money. He had all he needed and more. Enough to give Moira funds to help her family and protect her from whatever or whoever threatened her.

They had said things in anger last night that shouldn't have been said. He couldn't bear the thought of Moira meeting another man, and she had accused him of something vile. Unfortunately, there was no time now to clear up the misunderstanding or solve the mystery concerning her association with Mayhew.

Moira was already up and dressed when Jack returned to the bedchamber. She had worked herself into a fine rage, still incensed about his affiliation with the Hellfire Club, but one look at his face told her it was neither the time nor the place to confront him.

"Jack, what is it? Did the messenger bear bad tidings?"

"The worst," Jack said, crossing to where she stood and taking her into his arms. She stiffened but did not pull away. " 'Tis Will. He's dead. He was the only relative I had left in the world."

Compassion melted her anger. "Oh, Jack, I'm so sorry."

"I'm leaving immediately to escort Will's body to Dorset for burial. I won't be long. Two weeks at the most. Pettibone is packing for me now, and I expect Ailesbury's lawyer shortly."

"I know you were fond of your cousin."

"It was more than fondness. We respected one another. I want your promise that you will remain at Graystoke Manor until I return. I still don't know what's going on between you and Mayhew, or what makes you so ready to believe his lies about me, but we will resolve everything when I return. I don't want you leaving the house while I'm gone. Pettibone will see to your needs.''

''Not leave the house?''

''That's right. I wouldn't ask it if I didn't think it was necessary. Mayhew is dangerous; Lord knows what he's planning. I'll take care of it when I return.''

He didn't wait for a reply as he pulled her tightly against him, seeking her mouth with almost frantic desperation. He kissed her hard, almost hurtfully, leaving Moira dazed and shaken. A moment later he pushed her away and murmured, ''Don't think about leaving, sweetheart. I'll find you no matter where you go. We have some unfinished business to discuss.'' He kissed her again, hard. Moira closed her eyes to escape his piercing silver gaze. When she opened them, he was gone.

The house seemed empty without Jack. The day after he left, Lord Renfrew called, demanding an answer to his marriage proposal. Moira felt little regret at turning him down. After learning that he was a member of the Hellfire Club, she could barely stand the sight of him.

''You're turning me down?'' Renfrew said, stunned. ''You won't get a better offer.''

''I'm sorry, milord. I'm not in love with you,'' Moira demurred.

''Love is a state of mind. You can will yourself to love me if you try.''

''I'm sorry.''

Upon hearing her last word on the subject, Renfrew flew into a rage. ''You little tease! Aren't I rich enough for you? You've led me on for weeks, making me believe you'd accept my proposal. I've heard rumors about you and Black Jack but was generous enough to ignore them. You're his mistress, aren't you? Now that he's a duke, you don't *really* think he'll marry you, do you? Black Jack isn't the marrying kind.'' He eyed her narrowly. "Lord Mayhew said you're not even a lady. He said you and Black Jack hoodwinked us all. Is that true?''

"If you believe that, why did you come here expecting me to accept your proposal?'' Moira charged.

"Do you actually believe I wish to saddle myself with a wife? What an innocent you are. My parents are breathing down my neck to marry and produce an heir. I needed to find someone who knew nothing about me or my . . . er . . . escapades. Then you came along. But if Mayhew is correct about your common background, you'll no longer do. My parents are sticklers about blood-lines.'' He leered at her. "That doesn't mean I can't bed you. You must be a damn hot little piece to satisfy a man like Black Jack. Perhaps I'll get the opportunity to try you one day soon.''

Moira recoiled in revulsion. How could she have believed this man cared for her? Were all men vile and corrupt? How could she have been so misled? She knew intuitively that Lord Mayhew hadn't lied about Lord Fenwick's affiliation with the Hellfire Club. And if he had been right about Lord Fenwick, he had in all likelihood been telling the truth about Jack. All three blackguards were disciples of the Devil.

"I'll escort you to the door, Lord Renfrew.'' Pettibone appeared like magic at Moira's side, his stern countenance enough to put fear into the stoutest hearts. And Renfrew wasn't the bravest of men. "You *were* leaving, weren't you?''

Renfrew blasted Pettibone with a withering glance, then turned abruptly on his heel. "My business here is finished. Give Ailesbury my regards when he returns from Cornwall. A rare stroke of luck, him inheriting the dukedom, what?"

Moira was still shaking when Pettibone returned a few minutes later to announce Lord Spence. Spence rushed into the room, clearly distraught. "The jig's up, Moira. Lud, what I wouldn't give to have Black Jack here now."

"Whatever are you talking about, milord?"

"We've been undone. 'Tis all over London that you and Jack made fools of the gentry. Lady Victoria is furious, and she isn't the only one."

"Who told them?" Moira knew the answer; Spence could only confirm it.

"Lord Mayhew. The bastard is telling anyone who will listen that you were a maidservant in his house, and that you seduced him and then talked Jack into passing you off as a lady."

"Be grateful that Lord Mayhew doesn't know you're involved. Do you think the gossip will hurt Jack?"

"It might. He's titled now. He has to maintain a certain standard. Is there anything I can do? I fear you're the one who will suffer most for our misguided plan."

That's not the half of it, Moira thought but did not say. Lord Mayhew must be furious with her for bashing him. She feared she hadn't heard the last from him. There was only one thing to do now, and that was flee for her life.

"Thank you for your concern, Lord Spencer."

"Lud, Moira, I feel rotten about this. It was my idea to pass you off as a lady. Why didn't you tell us that Mayhew could identify you?"

"It's a long story, milord. Lord Mayhew was abroad.

191

I didn't think he'd return anytime soon. Besides, I didn't have many options.''

"Thank God, Jack will return soon. He'll put a stop to this gossip and set things right. Well, I must be off. If you need me, don't hesitate to send word around.''

Moira saw Spence to the door and returned to her room. Jilly was waiting for her. "Pettibone is hiring new servants, milady. Will I be sent back to the Fenwicks? I'd rather stay here with you.''

"I'm sure something can be worked out, Jilly. I'm perfectly satisfied with you, but I may not be here much longer. Speak to Pettibone; he'll take care of everything.''

Jilly beamed from ear to ear. "Thank you, milady. I'm ever so grateful. I'd hate to go back to scrubbing pots.'' Suddenly her smile wavered. "Are you going somewhere, milady?''

"I'm not sure,'' Moira said uncertainly. She hadn't the slightest idea what the future held for her, but she felt herself being squeezed between two evils: Lord Mayhew on one side and Jack on the other. Lord Mayhew wanted her to participate in unholy orgies, and for all she knew so did Jack. Were there no honorable men in this world, except for her brother? Even her poor grandmother, who had been abandoned by a lover of noble birth, learned the hard way that men couldn't be trusted.

Moira had just packed two of her most durable dresses, appropriate underwear and personal belongings in a large carpetbag she found in the attic when Pettibone appeared at her door, wringing his hands and clearly distraught.

"What is it, Mr. Pettibone? Has something happened? It isn't Jack, is it? He's all right, isn't he?'' She didn't know why she should worry about Jack. Men like him always landed on their feet.

"I haven't heard from His Lordship, milady, but Lord Mayhew is downstairs demanding to see you. I fear there may be trouble. He's brought two constables with him." For the first time since she'd known him, the unflappable Pettibone seemed to unravel.

Moira squared her narrow shoulders, knowing full well what Lord Mayhew wanted. He was getting even. It was too late to run now. She had to face the music and pray for a sympathetic judge. "I'll be right down, Mr. Pettibone. Would you tell Jilly to unpack my bag? I won't be going anywhere now." Except to prison, she silently ruminated.

Pettibone kept Lord Mayhew and the constables cooling their heels in the foyer. As Moira came down the stairs, all four men turned to watch her. Of them all, only Mayhew looked at her with anything but appreciation. He still bore the knot on his head where the little hellion had bashed him, and he wasn't one to forget or forgive. He had contemplated his revenge while he spread the rumor that Moira was not who his peers thought she was. He had hoped to ruin Black Jack at the same time, but fate had intervened and placed a dukedom in his hands.

While society might look down their collective noses at Moira, they would be more forgiving of a duke. When Mayhew learned that Jack had made posthaste for Cornwall, he decided to strike while Moira was temporarily without a protector. After careful consideration, Mayhew had confided his plan to Lord Renfrew, who had complained bitterly and with resentment at the way Moira had scorned his well-intentioned proposal of marriage.

"It's about time," Mayhew sneered when Moira

reached the bottom landing. "Did you think you could commit theft and not be caught?" Moira remained mute. "I've brought two constables with me. Once I identify you as the thief who purloined my mother's valuable necklace, you'll be arrested and taken to Newgate to await trial."

"I'm sure there is some mistake," Pettibone intervened. "Lady Moira is no thief."

"*Lady* Moira is no lady at all. She's a common strumpet who worked in my home as a maidservant. She tried to seduce me but failed." He turned to the constables, who were looking profoundly uncomfortable. "This is the woman, all right. Arrest her."

Loyal to the bone, Pettibone stepped in front of Moira, trying to protect her with his skinny frame.

"Out of the way," one of the constables ordered. "Interfering with the law is a crime."

"It's all right, Mr. Pettibone," Moira said, stepping around him. The last thing she wanted was to make trouble for Jack's faithful servant. Pettibone was so loyal, he'd probably expire when he learned that Black Jack was cut from the same cloth as Lords Mayhew and Renfrew.

"But milady," Pettibone protested, "His Lordship isn't going to like this. I promised to look after you."

"*His Lordship* can go straight to hell." Mayhew laughed as he grasped Moira's arm and hustled her out the door.

If Lord Mayhew hadn't brought the law, Moira wouldn't have gone without a struggle. But she knew defeat when it stared her in the face. She turned back to look at Pettibone, who stood in the doorway looking profoundly stricken.

* * *

The dark, clammy passages of Newgate stank of urine, feces and mildew. Moira shook like a leaf, cold, miserable and frightened.

"This is it," the turnkey said as he stopped before a sturdy oak door and fit a large key into the lock. "It ain't exactly plush accommodations, but the straw gets changed every six months and the slop buckets emptied every other day."

Moira cried out in panic when he opened the door and pushed her into a dark, dank cell lit by a single candle. She watched in horror as wraithlike figures detached themselves from the shadows and moved toward her. Before the door closed behind her, Moira sent Mayhew a pleading look. As he turned away from her, he sent her a malicious smile.

To Moira's dismay, her cloak was wrested from her by one of the dark shadows that had materialized from the dim recesses of the cell. "That's mine!" Moira cried as a pock-faced slattern with lank hair and wild eyes placed the cloak around the tattered remnants of her clothes.

"It's mine now," the slattern cackled. "Look at me! I'm a bleedin' lady." She pranced around the cell, lording it over the other occupants.

"You'll never be a lady, Birdie." Moira watched in alarm as another woman sashayed into the circle of light.

"Aw, hell, Min, jest because yer prettier than me and get special treatment fer playin' whore don't make ya a lady," Birdie said plaintively.

Moira stared at Min, acknowledging the woman's beauty despite the dirt and grime befouling her face and body. Her rags were somewhat less tattered than Birdie's, and at one time might have been considered flamboyant. Suddenly a woman she hadn't noticed before crept out from the shadows, eyeing her dress greedily. Divining her purpose, Moira backed away. But there was nowhere to go, no place to hide. Birdie and Min stood aside as the large, rawboned woman advanced on Moira.

Suddenly Moira had had enough. If this woman wanted her dress, she would have to fight for it. She braced herself as the woman fell upon her. In the end it was no contest at all. Outweighed and inexperienced, she was soon overpowered and stripped to her shift. When the women would have removed her shift, Min stepped forward.

"Ya gonna strip her naked, Alice? Ya know damn well the dress ain't gonna fit ya. Ya aughta at least leave her shift."

Alice sat back on her heels. "Damn it, Min, I can trade the dress and shift fer a blanket if they don't fit me."

"Leave her shift," Min repeated. "It ain't right to strip a body naked. And give her back her cloak, Birdie. Ya want her to freeze to death?"

To Moira's surprise, Alice desisted immediately, complaining bitterly as she crept back to her moldy pile of straw, hugging the dress to her sagging breasts. Even Birdie complied as she returned the cloak to Moira, albeit somewhat less than charitably. Moira pulled it around her, sending Min a grateful look.

"Thank you," Moira said. It was obvious the other women considered Min their leader.

"Don't thank me, honey, I'm merely protectin' myself. One look at you in yer shift and the guards will stop askin' for my favors and look to you for easin'. I ain't about to give up the privileges I earn on my back, so don't get no ideas about cozying up to the guards."

Moira recoiled in horror. "I would never do such a thing!"

Birdie laughed derisively. "Wait till yer here a while. Ye'll be more than happy to oblige a randy guard if it gets ya a warm blanket or extra food. I'd do it, only I ain't pretty like you or Min. Even Alice earns a few extra privileges when the guards are horny enough and there ain't no one else available."

"What's yer name?" Min asked.

"Moira O'Toole."

"Irish. I thought so. What's yer crime?"

"Theft, but I didn't do it."

Alice hooted with laughter. " 'Course not, none of us are guilty."

Min ignored her. "Ya already know our names. When's yer trial?"

"I don't know. This is all new to me. Have you been here long?"

"Long enough to give ya a word of warnin'. Don't cross Alice or Birdie—they're dangerous. Both women have killed and would do so again without remorse. If one of the guards want ya, oblige 'em. Life is a hell of a lot more comfortable if ya know when to spread yer legs. Just don't take any of my personal favorites or ya'll be sorry."

"I don't want any men," Moira said with feeling. "There's not a man in this world save for my brother who is worth a fig."

Moira thought of Jack and how completely he had fooled her. She suspected from the beginning that he was debauched, but his charm and guile had seduced her into believing that he cared, as she was beginning to care for him. Actually, "care for" were mild words compared to how she really felt about Black Jack Graystoke. But after learning he was a disciple of the Hellfire Club, she would never trust him again.

Conditions at Newgate were deplorable. Everything Moira had heard about it was true. The food was barely edible, the dank, cold cells cesspools of pestilence and disease, and the sadistic guards the dregs of humanity. The foul stench of sickness and death turned her stomach. During the four days she'd resided within the walls of Newgate, Moira experienced gnawing hunger, bone-chilling cold and verbal degradation. She thanked God that she hadn't been physically abused. But in her heart she knew it was only a matter of time before the guards looked on her with lust. For some unknown reason, Moira suspected that Min was protecting her. Every time a guard looked speculatively at her, Min turned his attention to herself, flaunting her charms before him and goading him to lust.

Moira curled up in her pile of straw, sick at heart and body. Was Jack home from Cornwall? she wondered. Did he know of her fate? Did he even care? She scratched absently, recoiling in horror when she encountered a flea. What did she expect? Everything and everyone in the cell was crawling with vermin. How had she fallen so low? Housed with murderers and prostitutes, she felt as if the entire world had conspired against her.

Suddenly she heard the key turn in the lock and looked toward the door with trepidation. The turnkey, holding a light aloft, searched the room. His eyes settled on Moira with greedy anticipation.

"Come along with ye, mistress. Yer wanted."

Moira's heart beat frantically as she stared fearfully at

the turnkey. "What for?" Had the guards decided she was fair game?

"Ye've got some powerful friends, that's all I'll say."

Moira rose shakily and followed the turnkey, her heart soaring. Had Jack learned of her fate and come for her? Hope blossomed in her heart.

"Good luck," Min called softly behind her.

When Moira was called to the warden's office, she dared to hope the horror of her existence had come to an end, to believe that she had been exonerated and free to leave. She had never been more wrong.

Chapter Twelve

"In you go, missy," the turnkey said as he rapped on the warden's door, opened it and shoved Moira inside. Moira stumbled through the opening, righted herself and gaped at the two men inside the room. She groaned in dismay, seized by a sense of doom so sharp she could taste it.

"You're a lucky woman, Miss O'Toole," the warden said, frowning at Moira in disapproval. "The Mayhews have dropped the charges against you and are willing to take you back into their household. Few people are given a second chance. Use it well, though I hold out little hope. Once a thief, always a thief, I always say."

Moira looked from Lord Mayhew to the warden, too stunned to speak. As much as she wanted out of this hell-hole, she didn't trust Lord Mayhew. "The Mayhews have dropped the charges?" she repeated numbly. "Are you sure?"

"Lord Mayhew said it is what his parents wish. They no longer want to prosecute. You are free to go with Lord Mayhew."

Mayhew's smirk filled Moira with dread. She wanted nothing to do with the diabolical demon. "If I'm free to go, I prefer not leaving with Lord Mayhew."

Mayhew took a step in her direction, more menacing than friendly. "Would you prefer going back to your cell? I can always refile the charges." Moira stared at him speechlessly. "I thought not." He grasped her arm. "Come along, my dear."

Forcing herself to take that first step, Moira was pulled along in Mayhew's wake. Only when the doors of Newgate closed behind her did she resist in earnest. "I'm not going anywhere with you! Let me go!"

"Not bloody likely," Mayhew ground out as he dragged her toward his waiting coach. "I thought that after cooling your heels a few days in Newgate, you'd be more than willing to participate in one of the disciples' orgies. Clever of me, wasn't it?" His expression darkened. "Perhaps I didn't leave you there long enough."

Moira dug in her heels, resisting his efforts to place her in his coach. By dint of superior strength, he subdued her, tossing her inside like a sack of grain. He followed close behind, slamming the door as he shouted orders to his coachman. Moira slid away to the farthest corner of the vehicle, unaware that her cloak had fallen open in the struggle. Mayhew gaped at her, then gave a bark of laughter.

"I see you didn't fare too well in prison." He wrinkled his nose in distaste. "If Black Jack saw you now, I doubt he'd give you a second glance. You look like a filthy street whore. Your stench offends me. Even I wouldn't touch you in that condition."

"Where are you taking me?" Moira asked, suddenly glad of her grimy appearance and flea-infested body.

"You'll know when we get there. Relax. We've a long ride ahead of us. And don't think about throwing yourself from the coach; I'll be on my guard this time. You're not cheating me again. You deserve to be punished for what you've put me through. My parents were so upset with me for leaving London without a word or explanation that they no longer trust me."

Moira sank back against the squabs, saving her strength for what was to come.

Weary to the bone, Jack stepped from the coach bearing the Ailesbury coat of arms. It had been a long two weeks since he'd last seen Graystoke Manor. He had taken Will's body to the Ailesbury country estate in Dorset, where it was interred in the family burial plot. The service was conducted in the small chapel by the village parson. People from the village and surrounding farms filled the church to overflowing, and even Jack was impressed with the moving service. Afterward, he had stayed to greet the mourners and meet his staff.

It seemed irreverent to think of himself as the Duke of Ailesbury, but like it or not, the title was his. A great number of people now depended on him for their livelihood; the responsibility was awesome to a man who had spent his days and nights drinking, gambling, wenching. Strangely, those idle pursuits hadn't appealed to him in a very long time. Not since . . .

Moira.

Lord, he missed the little hellion. The depths of his emotions where Moira was concerned seared him. She had lied to him consistently, until he had no idea what was truth and what was fiction. It had hurt him deeply when she accused him of being a member of the Hellfire

Club. She'd acted as if she expected to be recruited by him for one of their orgies. He wondered about her association with Lord Mayhew and why she chose to believe his lies. All these questions and more ate at his conscience, strengthening his determination to learn the answers.

"Milord, thank God you're home!" Pettibone met Jack at the door, more rattled than Jack had ever seen him. Jilly hovered behind Pettibone, clearly distraught. Alarm shuddered through him.

"What's amiss, Pettibone?"

" 'Tis Miss Moira, milord. The most dreadful thing has happened."

Jack's alarm turned to panic. "Spit it out, man! What in bloody hell are you trying to tell me?"

"She's gone, milord. Taken away by force. Woe is me," the faithful servant lamented. "I promised to take care of her, but it was taken out of my hands."

Jack grasped his shoulders and gave him a gentle shake. "Stop your blubbering, man, and tell me what happened."

"Lord Mayhew came with the constabulatory and took her away," Jilly volunteered.

"Took her where?" Fear lanced through Jack. If only he had dragged the truth from Moira before he left this might have been avoided.

"To Newgate," Pettibone supplied once he gained control of his wits. It was a rare occurrence for him to become emotionally distraught, alerting Jack to the seriousness of the situation. "That cur Lord Mayhew accused her of theft, and the constables carried her off to prison."

"How long ago?" Jack asked tersely. His weariness fell away, replaced by fear and rage.

"Five days," Pettibone said. "I went to the prison with some articles of clothing and food the next day, but they turned me away. Seems Miss Moira isn't allowed visitors until after her trial. Only the good Lord knows when that will be. You have to do something, milord. How long can she survive in Newgate? She's much too fragile to endure the abysmal conditions existing in prison."

Jack's jaw firmed with grim determination. "I'll get her out, Pettibone, never doubt it."

"Bless you, milord." Jilly sniffed, wiping tears from her eyes. "I couldn't bear it if something happened to the mistress."

"Nor I," Jack allowed. "I'm off to Newgate as soon as I refresh myself and change clothes. Did you hire sufficient staff, Pettibone?"

"I've been too upset to give it my full attention. Young Colin is the new assistant coachman, and there are two new maids and a full-time cook. I've not had time to interview housekeepers yet."

"Take your time," Jack said. "I imagine we'll be living part of the time at Ailesbury Hall in Dorset. I intend to refurbish Graystoke Manor immediately. See to my bath and lay out my clothes, Pettibone. And Jilly, ask Cook to fix me something to eat."

Jack took the steps two at a time. If Moira had been in Newgate five days, there wasn't a minute to lose.

Two hours later, Jack gained entrance to Newgate and demanded to see the warden.

"I'm sorry, Lord Graystoke. The woman you're inquiring about is no longer an inmate."

Jack fixed the warden with an icy glare. "Are you telling me she's been released, or are you hinting at something else? She hasn't," he caught his breath and asked fearfully, "expired, has she?"

"No, no, nothing like that," the warden assured him. The new Duke of Ailesbury wasn't a man he cared to lie to. "The charge against her was dropped, and she was released just yesterday. Her stay with us was short, indeed."

Jack cocked an eyebrow and asked coolly, "What charge?"

"Theft. Miss O'Toole was accused of stealing a valuable piece of jewelry from her employer. Lord Mayhew came by yesterday and asked that the charges be dropped. His father the earl is a forgiving man. I released Miss O'Toole into Lord Mayhew's custody. His parents have generously offered to reinstate her in their employ."

Jack tried not to show his dismay, but it was difficult. Obviously, Moira had kept knowledge of that ridiculous theft charge from him for reasons known only to herself. He scoffed at the implication. Moira might be a liar, but she was no thief. He sensed some kind of chicanery and suspected Mayhew was the culprit. And now Moira had fallen into his unscrupulous hands. The thought was far from comforting.

"Thank you, Warden. I'll call on the Mayhews immediately. It's most urgent that I speak with the young lady."

Twenty minutes later, Jack stood in the Mayhews' foyer, awaiting the earl. He appeared ten minutes later and invited Jack into his study. The old man seated himself in a wing chair and indicated that Jack was to take the chair opposite him.

"What can I do for you, Lord Graystoke? Terribly sorry to hear about your cousin."

"Thank you," Jack said, liking the man on sight. How

could such a dignified man produce a son like Roger? He came directly to the point, finding no reason to waste time in useless chitchat. "Do you have a maid by the name of Moira O'Toole in your employ?"

The earl looked askance at Jack. "What is your interest in the girl?"

"It's personal. Is she here?"

"Not now. The girl stole a valuable piece of jewelry from my wife. After it was found in Moira's possession, she was locked in her room to await the arrival of the constable. Unfortunately, my son Roger felt sorry for her and let her go. I must say I was disturbed. That's why he left so abruptly for the Continent, I suppose, to escape my anger. Moira seemed to disappear into thin air, but I felt duty bound to file charges against her."

"Did you know Moira was arrested and taken to Newgate prison several days ago?"

The earl looked startled. "My word, no. Why wasn't I informed?"

"Your son handled the arrangements. A few days later, Lord Roger returned to the prison and asked that the charges be dropped. He told the warden that you had a change of heart and were willing to give Moira another chance."

"My word," the earl repeated. "Whatever was Roger about? I haven't seen him in days. He has taken private quarters now that he has come into his inheritance from his grandmother."

"I was hoping to find Moira here. But if you haven't seen her, then obviously Lord Roger has taken her elsewhere. Do you know where that could be?"

"I haven't the foggiest. I knew he fancied her. Perhaps he set her up someplace as his mistress, though it would surprise me. I thought about this for a long time after Moira disappeared and decided that she might be a thief, but she isn't a whore like Roger intimated.'' He shook his head sadly. ''Sometimes I don't understand my own son. There's a streak of wildness in his blood that frightens me. I hope you find the young lady. My wife has her necklace, so I suppose no harm was done. I'm willing to give her a second chance if she wishes to return to my employ.''

''That's generous of you, milord, but Moira won't be returning after I find her, and I will, you know. If you see Lord Roger tell him . . . Never mind, I'll tell him myself.''

Jack's fears piled one on top of another after he left the Mayhew townhouse. If Moira wasn't at the Mayhews, then Roger had taken her someplace for purposes he didn't even want to think about. Yet the obvious answer pounded against his brain with painful intensity.

The Hellfire Club.

Had Mayhew taken her to the Dashwood estate? Was Moira destined to become a victim to the disciples' evil appetites during their next orgy? Or had she already become a victim of their rites; an innocent among a nest of vipers?

No matter how hard she tried, Moira could not stay awake. Exhausted in mind and body, she fell asleep slumped against a far corner of the coach, as far away from Lord Mayhew as she could get. She didn't know how long she had slept, but when she awoke the coach was slowing. She jerked upright and stared out the window.

Dusk was approaching, and she could see a sliver of moon rising above a large brick manor of palatial dimensions. The dim light showing through the windows was not inviting. Something about the manor was disturbing, almost eerie.

"Where are we?" she asked as Lord Roger grasped her elbow and shoved her from the coach the moment it ground to a halt.

"I doubt you'd know if I told you. Have you ever heard of the Dashwood estate?"

Moira shook her head. " 'Tis the home of Sir Francis Dashwood of Medmenham in Buckinghamshire," Mayhew told her. "The disciples gather here in limestone caves behind the property every fortnight for their rituals. You'll be Sir Francis's guest until the next gathering two days hence. Come, he's expecting you." He pushed her toward the front entrance.

A surly servant answered Mayhew's summons. "Sir Francis is expecting you," he said, looking down his long nose at Moira. "Follow me."

Dashwood was sprawled in a wing chair, contemplating a goblet of brandy. He looked up when Mayhew entered, dragging Moira behind him. "Ah, Mayhew, is this the chit who's to provide our next entertainment? Not much to look at, is she?"

"She's not much to look at now, but after she's cleaned up you'll be well pleased. She's a damn sight better than those prostitutes we usually hire, or the timid little mice with no fight in them we steal off the streets."

Dashwood took a pinch of snuff, sneezed several times and fixed Moira with a speculative look. "Can't you talk, wench?"

"I can talk very well. I wish to leave." Her bravado was commendable but not well taken.

"I thought you said she'd be willing," Dashwood said

sourly. "We can't afford problems with the law. There's already been trouble over the women we take off the streets, even though most of them are prostitutes who enjoy a good time and the money we give them."

"Don't worry, Moira won't get a chance to talk to the law. I have plans for her after our next gathering."

"Very well," Dashwood allowed. "It will be rather refreshing to have someone other than whores to entertain us. Is she a virgin?"

Moira gasped, mortified by Sir Francis's question.

"Are you?" Mayhew asked, squeezing Moira's arm painfully.

Despite her precarious situation, anger exploded inside Moira. "None of your damn business! I want to leave, and I want to leave now!"

Dashwood chuckled, vastly amused by Moira's outburst. "I like a woman with spirit. She'll do, Mayhew. She'll do very well indeed. I'll place her in my housekeeper's capable hands until we're ready for her. Wilkes is scouring London for willing whores to join us, but little Moira will be our star attraction."

Dashwood picked up a bell that had been sitting on a side table and gave it a vigorous shake. In due time, a tall, plain-faced woman of middle years appeared in the doorway. "You rang, sir?"

"Are you deaf, Matilda? Of course I rang," Dashwood said ungraciously. "Take the wench and clean her up. She's to remain locked in the guest room until she's needed. Understand?"

"Understood," Matilda replied succinctly. "Anything else, sir?"

"That's all."

"I won't go!" Moira resisted. "You can't keep me against my will."

"You're becoming tiresome, my dear," Dashwood said, stifling a yawn. "Take her away, Matilda."

Matilda sent Dashwood a look of unbridled hatred, then grasped Moira's arm and pulled her from the room. Moira resisted to the best of her ability, but the housekeeper's strength was formidable. When Matilda called for help, the butler joined her, and together they wrestled Moira up the stairs.

Once they were gone, Dashwood made a sour face. "Matilda gets more surly every day. If I didn't trust her to do as she's told and keep her mouth shut, I'd let her go."

"How can you be sure she'll not talk about what goes on here?"

Dashwood gave a nasty laugh. "Matilda is my dead wife's cousin. Years ago I took her in when she was destitute and gave her a job as housekeeper. Without me, she would have gone to debtors' prison long ago. She owes me her loyalty and knows what will happen to her if she doesn't keep her mouth shut about our ceremonies. I need her to manage the unwilling women brought in for our pleasure. She's become quite adept at keeping them in line."

"Then I feel confident Moira won't escape me this time," Mayhew said. "I'll return in two days time for our gathering."

"I'm looking forward to it with anticipation," Dashwood said, glancing toward the stairs.

Jack paced restively. Deep shadows defied the dancing candlelight as he strode the room from end to end and back. Sleep was a luxury he couldn't afford. He hadn't the foggiest idea how to get Moira away from the disciples of Satan, if indeed she had fallen into their hands as he suspected. He stopped to stare out the window, scarcely able to see the street through the damp mist rolling in from the river. He had just whirled on his heel to return to the opposite end of the room when he saw her. Truth to tell, he was never so glad to see anyone in his life. He had come to expect Lady Amelia in times of dire need.

"What should I do, milady?" he asked. His voice was so filled with anguish that the ghost reached out to him, stopping just short of touching him.

"I can't just rush headlong into the caves and rescue Moira single-handedly. Talk to me! Bloody hell, no woman deserves being used for a man's pleasure, unless it's her decision."

Lady Amelia seemed to glow from within, conveying her agreement.

"Moira insisted she loathed Mayhew," Jack continued as the ghost cocked her head to one side and listened. " 'Tis quite obvious he planted his mother's necklace in Moira's room in order to bend her to his will. I have no idea what happened that night I found her in the gutter, but I sure as hell am going to find out. The horror of it has kept Moira from confiding in me."

Lady Amelia's hands fluttered gracefully. "Are you trying to tell me something, milady? If need be, I'll recruit a whole damn army to go out to Dashwood's and rescue Moira."

Use your head.

The words held no substance, but Jack heard them as

clearly as if the lady had spoken aloud. ''What are you talking about?''

Lady Amelia appeared perturbed at Jack's inability to comprehend.

Don't fight them, join them.

As before, the ghost's thoughts were transmitted telepathically rather than spoken aloud. But the message was clear and succinct. Jack knew exactly what he must do. His smile lit up the room as he turned to thank his ghostly visitor. Being haunted by a determined ancestor certainly made for an interesting, albeit hectic life, he decided. And for some strange reason, after each visitation, perdition seemed farther away than the last time. Perhaps he wasn't beyond redemption after all.

Alas, when Jack searched the room for Lady Amelia, she had blended into the shadows, leaving naught but a glowing ember of light in her wake. Jack sighed wearily and stretched out on the bed. There was nothing he could do until daylight except pray that Moira hadn't been harmed. But each moment's delay brought frightening pictures of Moira being forced to participate in the debauched rites practiced by the disciples of the Hellfire Club.

Jack pounded on the portal of Fenwick Hall until a disgruntled butler opened the door. It was two hours past dawn, an hour when fashionable people were still abed. ''Lord Graystoke, 'tis uncommonly early,'' the man complained. ''Lord and Lady Fenwick are in the country, and Lord Spencer is sleeping. I'll tell him you called when he awakens.''

Jack pushed past the startled man. ''Tell Spence I wish

to see him immediately. 'Tis most urgent. I'll wait in the study.''

Seeing no way to convince a determined Jack to come back at a more reasonable hour, the butler acquiesced with good grace. "Very well, milord, I'll tell Lord Spencer you're here.''

Finding the study with little trouble, Jack threw himself into a wing chair, chaffing impatiently at slothful Spence's habit of sleeping until noon or later.

"This better be good, Jack,'' Spence said as he strolled into the room, pulling the belt of his robe tightly around him. "When did you get back? I know you must be angry at all the gossip circulating about Moira. Damn Mayhew! If he hadn't returned from abroad and seen her at Vauxhall, our little prank would have succeeded. Moira should have told us about him.''

"I returned just yesterday. Did you know Moira was taken to Newgate?'' Jack said without preamble.

"What! Lud, she can't be sent to prison for the little hoax we perpetrated. We're as guilty as she. What are you going to do?''

"She wasn't taken to Newgate because of our prank, Spence. It's more serious than that. She's accused of stealing a valuable necklace from Mayhew's mother while in their employ. He brought constables to the house, and they hauled her off to prison while I was gone.''

"Moira isn't a thief,'' Spence huffed indignantly.

"Indeed not,'' Jack concurred. "I hied myself to the jail the moment I arrived in town and was told the charges had been dropped and she had gone off with Mayhew.''

Spence frowned. "She did? I find that hard to believe.''

"She loathes the man, Spence. If Mayhew took her, it was by force.''

"But why? Mayhew is . . . Good Lord, you can't mean . . . He wouldn't dare take her to the Dashwood estate, would he? You know as well as I that Mayhew is involved in the Hellfire Club and that they participate in depraved rituals every couple of weeks out there in the country."

"I think that's exactly what Mayhew had in mind when he planted the necklace in Moira's room. She refused his advances, and his revenge has taken an ugly turn."

"What can we do?"

"Are you with me?"

"Damn right. Tell me what to do."

"Nothing for the moment. I need more information. As you know, Dashwood and Wilkes have been after me for months to join the club. I've always refused, having no desire to hasten my journey to perdition by joining those scoundrels. But all of a sudden I find myself quite eager to join their ranks. I'm going to call on Dashwood and express my desire to attend their next gathering."

"What about me? How can I help?"

"You're too damn straight-laced, Spence. They'll never believe you are interested in joining the group. But your help will be appreciated when I think of a way to rescue Moira. It can be dangerous. I understand that in order to protect their identities, the disciples dress in robes and hoods that cover all but their eyes. They won't be expecting trouble. We'll be armed and hooded when we go in. I'll get you a robe, and we can decide how to proceed after I've spoken with Dashwood. I suspect that infiltrating their ranks is the only way of getting Moira out."

"Count me in, Jack. This will be an even grander adventure than passing Moira off as a lady and watching the dandies make fools of themselves over her. When will you see Dashwood?"

"The sooner the better. It will take three or four hours of hard riding to reach his estate in Buckinghamshire. I heard somewhere that he's ensconced in the country permanently, coming to London only on rare occasions. I'll contact you as soon as I return so we can make our plans. I'll do a little looking around while I'm there. Who knows what I'll find."

It was late afternoon when Jack approached the Dashwood estate. Even in the light of day, the house hinted of evil. A young servant came up immediately to take the reins from Jack's hands, offering to stable the gray if Jack wished. Jack declined; he had no intention of remaining longer than it would take to join the blasted club and inquire about their next gathering.

Dashwood and Wilkes were in the parlor when a rough-looking servant ushered Jack into the room. Dashwood looked up, astonishment clearly visible on his coarse features.

"Ailesbury, what a pleasant surprise. Did you ride all this way to see me? Did inheriting a title change your views on . . . certain things?"

"Indeed it did," Jack said, assuming a bland smile. "I'm a peer now, with sufficient funds to indulge my vices. I can understand why the Hellfire Club appeals to men of wealth and position. I recalled your efforts to recruit me into your ranks and decided to take you up on your offer. That is if it still holds."

Dashwood and Wilkes exchanged uneasy glances. "Perhaps I was indiscreet in mentioning the club. At the time, I assumed a man of Black Jack's reputation would jump at the chance to join the disciples. But now that you're a peer, you might not be so willing to participate in our ceremonies.''

"Being a peer has sharpened my appetite for deliciously immoral pursuits. The Hellfire Club sounds perfect for my . . . er . . . tastes. How about it, Dashwood. Can I join?''

"Sit down, Ailesbury. You understand that utmost secrecy is required of our members, don't you?''

Jack nodded. "I don't carry tales, Dashwood.''

"Not all our members know one another,'' Wilkes added. "We wear robes and hoods, which we don before entering our meeting place. Of course there are some who don't care if their identity is known, but we offer our members anonymity if they so desire. To join, you must be willing to participate in initiation rites.''

Jack's attention sharpened. "Initiation rites?''

"That's right,'' Dashwood attested. "All new members undergo some sort of initiation to test their loyalty.''

"Exactly what must one do to be initiated?'' Jack asked cautiously.

"Don't look so serious.'' Dashwood laughed. "We exist for pleasure. We're not evil. We're not even devil worshipers. We just arrange orgies and indulge our fantasies with willing women.''

Jack yawned, as if bored with the subject. "I've heard stories about women being abducted off the streets. It's happened enough times not to be true. But don't get me wrong. I'm not against a little innocent sport as long as no one is hurt.''

"For the most part, we use whores for our orgies and ceremonies,'' Dashwood explained. "Occasionally it becomes necessary to seek women where they are available. Surely no one could possibly miss those timid little mice we take off the streets on occasion. Usually we offer them money, and they're perfectly happy to oblige us. If not . . ." He shrugged expansively.

Jack reserved judgment, knowing full well what happened to those unwilling participants. "Tell me more about this initiation. What will be required of me?"

"In our meeting room is an elevated stone slab, or altar, if you wish, upon which we conduct our sacrifices. No one is hurt, mind you. We try to find virgins for our initiations, but that isn't always possible. When virgins are unavailable, we use real blood to simulate virginal blood. We'll see that you have a vial of it to spill when you pierce the woman's maidenhead, whether or not she has one."

Jack tried not to register his disgust. "Am I to understand that initiation consists of taking a woman upon the sacrificial altar in full view of the membership? How droll."

Dashwood and Wilkes exchanged pleased glances. "I knew you'd be agreeable once you learned what we're about," Dashwood exclaimed. "I've waited a long time to initiate you into the Hellfire Club. We live for pleasure; we exist to gratify our every fantasy, no matter how exotic. If you're agreeable, your initiation can take place at our next gathering. We meet tomorrow night at precisely midnight, when the moon is at its fullest. We even have a special woman for you."

Jack tried to hide his excitement. "Special woman? Some well-used prostitute, I expect." He yawned. "I suppose if I must . . ."

"No prostitute, Ailesbury. This woman was brought in by one of our most trusted disciples. She may even be a virgin. After you've had her, the others will be worked up to such a pitch they'll be fighting one another for her, but the privilege of taking her next belongs to the man who brought her to us.''

"The girl is willing, I assume."

Wilkes laughed nastily. "She will be." He was referring to the drugs they sometimes used to control a woman's will. Jack didn't like the sound of it.

"I don't like the idea of using force. Nor will I take a woman who's been traumatized or abused. I have to give a care to my reputation. I don't want my name linked with a woman who leaves here in questionable condition. If you want me to join your ranks, you must promise not to harm the woman in any way, and that includes abusing her physically before I take her.''

"I must admit, Ailesbury, that numbering you among our disciples can only enhance our reputation," Dashwood observed. "You have my promise that the woman will be harmed in no way. Can we count on you tomorrow night?"

"Aye. I wouldn't miss my initiation for anything. Any instructions before the ceremony?"

"You'll receive your robe and hood before you leave here tonight. I'll give you directions to the limestone caves; don them before you enter. Just follow the passageway to the large cavern where the disciples gather. You'll see the stone altar in the center. Mix with the others until the woman is brought in and I announce that the initiation rites are about to commence. When I strip the sacrifice and place her on the altar, that's your cue to take her in any way you choose. The paid whores will come in once the initiation is over, and you'll be free to take your pleasure with any of them you wish.''

Jack stretched to his feet, clenching his fists to keep

himself from smashing Dashwood in the face. "If that's all, gentlemen, I'll take my leave." He was so relieved that Dashwood seemed unaware of his association with Moira that he couldn't wait to get home and tell Spence what he'd learned.

Suddenly a commotion in the foyer captured Jack's attention. Already on his feet, he strode swiftly from the parlor and into the foyer, both Dashwood and Wilkes hard on his heels. Suddenly Dashwood pushed past Jack, shoving him aside.

"How in the hell did she get out?" Dashwood thundered when he saw Moira struggling with his butler.

Moira's heart sank. Desperate to escape, she had bolted from the chamber when the housekeeper opened the door to bring her dinner. She had shoved Matilda as hard as she could, then ran out the door and down the stairs. She heard voices coming from the parlor but paid them no heed when she noted that the front door was unguarded. But luck had deserted her. The butler came from the back of the house, saw Moira and grabbed her before she reached the door.

"Let go of me!" Moira cried. "You can't keep me here against my will. There are laws against such things."

"Good work, Plunket. Take her back upstairs," Dashwood said. "As for you, young lady, the disciples are above the law. Our members are so powerful the law will not interfere."

Struggling fiercely in Plunket's cruel grip, Moira suddenly spied Jack. The shock of seeing him at the Dashwood estate was so overwhelming she went limp.

"Sweet Virgin. *You!*"

Chapter Thirteen

Jack stared hard at Moira, his gaze flowing over her face and form with quiet desperation, seeking assurance that she was unharmed. Her face was flushed, her anger and shock at seeing him here palpable. It was all Jack could do to keep from grabbing her and fighting his way past Dashwood and Wilkes and away from this evil atmosphere. He tried to convey that message with his eyes, but Moira was beyond understanding.

"You two know each other?" Dashwood asked, suddenly wary.

Moira opened her mouth to spit out a reply but Jack's warning glance rendered her mute. "We met briefly at Vauxhall," Jack said smoothly. "She's quite a tease. Had all the young bucks fawning over her."

Jack nearly gagged on the words. Moira's eyes were desperate and wounded, so full of despair that he would rather cut out his tongue than hurt her like this.

Dashwood allowed himself to relax. "Ah, yes. Mayhew mentioned some such nonsense."

A startled catch of breath froze in Moira's throat as she stared at Jack. What was he trying to do? Why was he pretending he didn't know her? He was watching her so intently she knew he was trying to convey some message, but she had no idea what. Finding him here with Sir Dashwood confirmed her belief that he was a member of the Hellfire Club. He had misled and seduced her, lied and used her. And she had fallen in love with the worst womanizer of all time. Lord help her.

"Take her upstairs, Plunket," Dashwood ordered. "And see what the wench has done to Matilda. I want her well guarded until tomorrow night. After the ceremony, Lord Mayhew can do with her as he pleases."

Moira shot Jack a pleading glance but couldn't interpret his answering look. It seemed as if he was trying to reassure her, but that seemed unlikely. He had almost convinced her that he cared for her, that he wanted to help her with her problems. Lies, all lies. How she wished she could hate him as he deserved. Then all thought came to a halt as Plunket grasped her wrist and dragged her away.

Jack watched in helpless frustration as Moira fought the burly servant. He wanted to do murder, and would have if he thought it would help Moira. But in order to save her, he had to keep a cool head. He couldn't help her if he gave his hand away or attempted a rescue without proper preparation. Pretending indifference seemed the best course, though it nearly killed him to do so.

"Don't forget, Dashwood," Jack reminded him, "you promised no harm would come to the woman. That is, assuming she is the one to be used in the initiation rites."

"You're perceptive, Lord Graystoke. The woman is indeed intended for tomorrow's sacrifice. She'll be more than cooperative by the time she's brought to the altar, so you needn't worry about experiencing the kind of resistance you've just seen. We have ways of dealing with recalcitrant women that produce no ill effects.''

Jack's blood froze. Rendering a woman into a cooperative state meant only one thing. Drugs. "I don't mind a little resistance, Dashwood. It increases the pleasure. Pleasure is what the brotherhood is all about, isn't it?"

Dashwood smiled. "Indeed. We'll make sure there is some fight left in her for your pleasure. My housekeeper will take care of everything. Go with Wilkes—he'll find you a robe and give you directions to the caves."

It was nearly midnight when Jack returned from the Dashwood estate and located Spence in the card room at White's. Spence spied Jack the moment he strode into the crowded room. He immediately threw in his hand, excused himself and intercepted his friend.

"I've been worried sick about you, Jack. Did everything turn out all right? What did you learn?"

"Not here," Jack said, glancing at the mob of people milling about the room. "Come to Graystoke Manor. I'll tell you everything."

Jack whirled on his heel to retrace his steps to the door and found himself face-to-face with Lady Victoria. "Let me congratulate you on your rise in rank and fortune," Victoria said uncharitably. "I don't appreciate being made a fool of. Why didn't you tell me your ward was really a maidservant? What did you hope to gain by passing Moira off as a lady when in truth she was your mistress? Did you think to marry her off, then dally with her after you and I were married and my fortune safely in your pocket?"

Jack flushed angrily. "First let me say that I never aspired to my cousin's title. True, I needed to marry money, but passing Moira off as a lady started out as a prank. Something Spence and I dreamed up for amusement. I won't go into details, but I owed Moira my protection.''

''Your little tart had better not show her face around here, not after the way she hoodwinked Renfrew, Peabody and Merriweather. Don't be surprised if you are treated coolly by your peers, at least until society is distracted by a new scandal.''

''I don't give a fig about society,'' Jack said truthfully. Throughout the years, he had strived hard to conceal his few good qualities beneath the weight of his reputation as a rake, gambler and womanizer. ''I am a man of few morals. An unfortunate flaw in my character.''

''I know. That's what makes you so devilishly exciting. Your name evokes all kinds of deliciously lewd thoughts.'' She shivered delicately. ''Black Jack is a name few can live up to. If you still want me, Jack, I'm agreeable. I can think of worse things than being a duchess.''

''I'm sure you can,'' Jack said, searching for a way of escaping without offending Victoria. ''As things stand now, I'm no longer looking for a rich wife. Thanks to poor Will, I now have more funds than I'll need in this lifetime. If you'll excuse me, milady, I must leave. Spence and I have urgent business.''

''I'll bet your business involves that little whore who pretended to be a lady. You've made her your mistress, haven't you?''

''You're wrong, Victoria, Moira will never be my mistress.'' If he had his way, Moira would be his wife.

''It's time we left,'' Spence said, anxious to be off before they created a scene. The ton had enough to talk about without feeding them more gossip.

Victoria fumed in impotent rage as Jack took his leave with as much grace as he could muster. Thirty minutes later, the two men were ensconced in Jack's study. Spence was all agog as Jack related details of his meeting with Sir Dashwood.

"You actually saw Moira?" Spence asked in a hushed voice. "How did she look? Is she well? Lud, she must have been shocked to see you there."

"Shock is too mild a word. Moira was horrified. And angry. She thinks I'm a member of the Hellfire Club."

"What! She should know better than that. What will you do?" Spence asked when he heard about Jack's forthcoming initiation into the club. "You're not going to ... Surely you're not going to go through with the initiation. Just thinking about Moira, or any other hapless woman, stretched out on that stone altar makes me physically ill. I take my pleasure as seriously as the next person, but I'll never resort to the methods used by the disciples of Satan."

"Nor I," Jack said quietly. "I was able to purloin an extra robe and hood for you when Wilkes had his head turned. Garbed in robes and hoods, we'll be able to enter the caves tomorrow night without fear of recognition. We'll be fully armed, of course. When Moira is led into the room, we'll make our move. Be prepared to follow my lead."

"Perhaps we should inform the authorities," Spence suggested. "I don't like the odds."

"I've thought about that and decided against it. I'm sure Dashwood pays the law to protect their secrecy. If word leaks out Dashwood might cancel the meeting and give Moira to Mayhew. I can't take the chance that Mayhew won't harm her."

Spence searched Jack's face. "I never thought I'd see the day Black Jack Graystoke would put his life on the line for a woman. You've got it bad. Damned shame you can't have her, except as a mistress. Wouldn't do for the Duke of Ailesbury to marry a woman from the serving class."

"Bloody hell, Spence, do you think I care about class distinction? I'll cross that bridge when I come to it. First things first. It's imperative we get Moira out of the clutches of the Hellfire Club." He closed his eyes, recalling the bright clarity of her spirit, the beauty of her soul.

"You can count on me, Jack. You say they're meeting tomorrow night?"

"Aye. Pettibone will drive the coach. He's the only one besides you I can trust."

"Don't worry, old boy. We'll succeed," Spence said with more conviction than he felt. It sounded as if they were biting off more than they could chew, but he was game if Jack was. For Moira's sake, they couldn't fail. "Just tell me the time and I'll be ready."

Jack climbed the stairs to his room, reviewing in his mind the plans he and Spence had made for Moira's rescue. If everything went as planned, she'd be safely returned to him and he'd never let her out of his sight again. Love was a debilitating emotion, he decided. It struck powerfully. And once it penetrated the heart, it made one weak and helpless to resist its allure. It had taken him a long time to realize he loved Moira, but once he acknowledged the emotion, he knew he'd been waiting all his life for a woman to love. Moira fed his soul and nourished his body. He had difficulty accepting it, but he knew now that Lady Amelia had placed Moira into his care for a reason. Lord only knows what would have happened to

him if Moira hadn't burst into his life. She made him see
how utterly worthless his life had been. Moira had turned
him away from the path to perdition and his date with the
Devil.

Jack stopped at the top of the stairs, suddenly aware
that he wasn't alone. Glancing down the hallway, he saw
Lady Amelia standing outside Moira's empty room. Jack
approached cautiously, until he stood close enough to feel
the heat radiating from her shimmering center. What he
saw startled him. Lady Amelia's hands were crossed over
her breasts, and she was looking at him sadly. Jack's heart
sank.

"What is it?" he asked fearfully. "Is Moira in danger?" Lady Amelia merely stared at him. "Will I fail?"

Beware.

The word pounded mutely against his skull.

"Can't you tell me more?" The ghost shook her head.
"Bloody hell, milady," Jack exploded, "if you can't tell
me anything good, why pester me at all?"

Though her features were hazy and indistinct, Jack
could tell he had offended Lady Amelia. Her image
dimmed and she faded into the shadows.

"Wait, damn it, don't go! You can communicate with
me, so why can't you tell me what I'm to beware of?"

"To whom are you speaking, milord?"

Jack whirled, surprised to see Pettibone standing at his
elbow. "Did you see anything, Pettibone?"

Pettibone peered down the dimly lit hallway. "I saw
no one, milord. Are you all right?"

Jack dragged his fingers through his hair. " 'Tis nothing, Pettibone. Go to bed. Tomorrow is going to be a long
one for both of us."

"All will go well, milord," Pettibone assured him.

"Of course," Jack said with more conviction than he felt. Lady Amelia's warning bothered him more than he cared to admit.

Moira stared out the window into the black night. Never had she felt so sick at heart or disillusioned. Imprisoned with her thoughts and her privacy, no amount of logic seemed to provide a reason for Jack's betrayal. The closeness of the walls and staleness of the closed room seemed to hamper her ability to think . . . to breathe. The knowledge that Jack knew she was a virtual prisoner and had done nothing to help her had nearly destroyed her. How could she have been so wrong about him?

What small hope Moira harbored had died the moment she encountered Jack in Sir Dashwood's home. She took no solace in prayer; obviously God had abandoned her for sinning with Black Jack Graystoke.

Moira turned listlessly from the window as the door opened, admitting Matilda, balancing a tray in her hands. "I'm not hungry," Moira announced.

Matilda sent Moira a look that defied interpretation. At times Moira felt that the woman was sympathetic to her plight, but she realized it was wishful thinking. Matilda had given no indication she was anything but Sir Dashwood's loyal servant.

"Eat, milady. Sir Dashwood will be angry if you are too weak to attend the ceremony tonight."

"The hell with Sir Dashwood!" Moira spit out. From the corner of her eye, she saw Matilda stifle a smile and wondered what was so amusing.

"Do you need help?" Plunket asked as he filled the doorway with his considerable bulk. He looked more than eager to get his hands on Moira, and she shrank away from him.

"I can handle this one," Matilda assured him. "Your services are not needed."

"I'm only following the master's orders. After the wench attacked you, Dashwood asked me to stand guard."

"It won't happen again," Matilda said curtly. "She learned her lesson."

Plunket grunted out a reply and ducked out of the room. Matilda waited until he closed the door. "The man's a pig, just like his master."

Moira's head shot up, certain she was hallucinating. "What? What did you say?"

Realizing she'd said too much, Matilda bit her lip and placed the tray on the table. "Nothing." Still she did not leave, giving Moira the impression that she wanted to say more.

"What is it, Matilda?"

Matilda glanced furtively toward the door, then shook her head. " 'Tis nothing." Yet Moira knew it was something. "I had the cook prepare something special for you. 'Tis beneath the covered dish. Try it, I think you'll find it to your liking."

Suddenly the door was flung open and Plunket stuck his head inside. "What's keeping you, woman?"

Turning abruptly, Matilda hurried from the room.

Lightning slashed the black horizon, followed by a distant rumble of thunder. His senses sharpened by the approaching storm and scent of rain, Jack glanced at Spence and wondered if his friend was as nervous as he was. The coach was nearing the Dashwood estate, and Jack rapped on the roof with the butt of his dueling pistol to warn Pettibone.

"Are we there?" Spence asked, peering out the window. Trees lined the road, obscuring the house from view, but Jack knew it lay just around the next bend.

"It won't be long. You'll be able to see the house as soon as we round the curve. There's a road around to the left of the house, leading to the caves. I've instructed Pettibone to veer to the left. We'll leave the coach hidden among the trees until we're ready to enter."

"Aren't we early?" Spence asked.

"I planned it that way. I want to make sure everyone is inside before we enter. This is one time I want to be fashionably late."

"There's the house," Spence said, his voice high with excitement. "Lud, it looks haunted."

"You don't have to do this, Spence."

"Of course I do," Spence said, offended. "What are friends for if not to help one another?"

The coach slowed, then veered to the left, following a rutted road around to the rear of the estate. A flash of lightning revealed a formation of hills directly ahead. Following directions given earlier by Jack, Pettibone swerved off the road into a stand of trees. They were near enough to the caves to watch the entrance while still remaining hidden from view. The coach rolled to a stop.

"What do we do now?" Spence asked.

"We wait." Jack pulled out his pocket watch, waited until another flash of lightning lit the face and said, " 'Tis ten o'clock. Men will start arriving soon. Wilkes told me he expected a dozen or more men to attend tonight's ceremony. We'll wait until everyone has arrived. Are you armed?"

Spence grinned and opened his coat, revealing a pair of loaded dueling pistols stuck into his waistband. "I also have my short sword."

"Good man. I hope force won't be necessary, but at least we'll be prepared for any situation that arises. Most of the disciples are of noble birth and don't want their identities revealed to the public. They want to continue their orgies unhampered and pay the local magistrate to turn a blind eye to the goings-on out here. I'm of the opinion that most disciples have been duped by Dashwood and Wilkes into believing all the women brought in for their rituals are whores who are paid to pretend resistance so as to enhance the disciples' pleasure. Something Dashwood said leads me to believe unwilling women are usually drugged."

Spence wrinkled his nose. "Disgusting."

"Exactly. Ah, look—an early arrival."

A man on horseback approached the caves. After tethering his horse, he donned a black robe, pulled the hood over his head and entered the gaping hole that served as an entrance. Soon after, men arrived by ones and twos, some on horseback, some by conveyance and others on foot, having come by way of the house.

" 'Tis time," Jack said after he had counted more than a dozen men passing into the caves.

He handed Spence a robe and hood and tapped on the roof. Pettibone guided the horses from the woods toward the caves. When the coach halted at the entrance, Jack and Spence had already shrugged into the kimonolike robes and belted them loosely around their waists in such a way as to disguise the bulge of pistols beneath.

"Be ready for anything, Pettibone," Jack called up to the man sitting in the driver's box.

"Be careful, milord."

Jack nodded. "Let's go." Taking a deep breath, he strode purposefully through the entrance into a long passageway lit at intervals by torches. Spence followed close on his heels. Eerie shadows danced upon the walls in a surrealistic dance of demons. Though he tried not to dwell on Lady Amelia's warning, it was all Jack could think about. For Moira's sake, he could not afford to fail. He *would not* fail.

Jack's heart was beating like a trip-hammer when at length they came to a cavernous chamber ablaze with torchlight. The breath froze in his throat when he saw the stone altar described by Dashwood at one end of the chamber. The disciples appeared preoccupied as Jack and Spence blended unobtrusively into their midst while remaining as close as possible to the exit. The disciples were staring at the altar with an air of expectancy. The atmosphere was heavy with the scent of male lust, and Jack braced himself for the confrontation he expected momentarily.

Chapter Fourteen

Appalled, Moira stared at the transparent robe Matilda had given her. Nothing or no one could make her wear anything so blatantly sexual before a group of strange men with perverted tastes. Matilda had told her she was to wear nothing beneath the robe and that Plunket would come for her shortly after midnight. Panic filled her veins with a desperation she'd not known before. How could Jack allow this to happen to her? Damn his black heart! Seizing the robe in both hands, she ripped the fragile material to shreds and tossed them to the floor. Then she stomped on them in a futile act of defiance.

Moira started violently at the sound of the key turning in the lock. She stared at the door in trepidation. Was it time already? The door opened and Matilda stepped inside. She held a tray supporting a glass filled with a murky white liquid. She set the tray down carefully. Moira thought the woman wore a strange expression and was both puzzled and alarmed by it. Matilda's eyes conveyed a warning, and her face showed the same kind of desperation Moira was feeling. Rooted to the spot, Moira waited with bated breath for her jailer to speak.

"Hurry, there's no time to lose." Fear and impatience made Matilda's voice shrill.

"It's going to take more than you to subdue me," Moira declared with admirable courage. "I won't go willingly to your vile master. Nor will I wear that disgusting robe."

"Forget the robe," Matilda hissed, glancing nervously toward the door. "When Plunket doesn't bring you to the caves in a reasonable length of time, Dashwood will come looking for you."

Hope soared in Moira's breast, then quickly sank. Why would Dashwood's lackey deliberately betray her employer? It didn't make sense.

"Please, miss, we haven't much time. You'll need your cloak. It's going to storm."

"Where are we going?" Moira asked suspiciously.

"As far away as we can get."

"We?" Moira hadn't missed the plural.

"If I let you go, you can be certain Sir Dashwood will want revenge for my betrayal. You must promise to take me with you."

"Why would you do this? You've been Sir Dashwood's loyal employee for many years."

"And hated every minute of it. When I think of all the helpless young women that passed through these portals, it makes me ill. At first I had no choice but to do Dashwood's bidding. He took me in at my sister's request when I was destitute, but my sister is dead and I have no reason to stay. I'm through with this whole sordid mess."

"Sweet Virgin, you're serious, aren't you?"

"Aye. I have money saved. Enough for both of us to

go wherever we choose. I can't remain here where Sir Francis will find me. I know too much.''

"Ireland," Moira said. "We can go to my brother's farm near the small village of Kilkenny. Oh, Matilda, I don't know what to say. You've saved my life.''

"Not yet," Matilda said succinctly. "And not at all if you don't hurry. I was instructed to prepare a drink containing a drug supposed to render you pliable. They will expect you soon.''

"What about Plunket?"

Matilda smiled, completely transforming her plain features. She was no beauty, but her smile made her face almost pretty. "I drugged his soup. Right now he's snoring over the empty bowl. Enough talk, miss. We'll have to steal horses from the stable. We can book passage to Ireland from London.''

"Thank you, Matilda. I'll be forever in your debt," Moira said as she took her cloak from the hook on the wall and flung it over her shoulders.

Matilda eased open the door, peered into the hallway, found it empty and motioned for Moira to follow. They negotiated the stairs without mishap. Matilda retrieved her wrap from the foyer where she had left it in preparation for her departure and opened the door. The well-oiled hinges gave without protest, and within minutes they were outside, dashing between flashes of lightning to the stables behind the house.

Jack kept his eyes trained on the single entrance to the chamber, waiting for Moira to appear. His nerves were stretched taut; the waiting was unbearable. His fingers hovered close to his belt, ready to fling aside his robe to reach his pistols if the need arose. He hoped to God it wouldn't be necessary. Suddenly there was a commotion as a man staggered into the chamber. Jack recognized him immediately as the brute who had manhandled Moira inside Dashwood's mansion. A hooded disciple whom Jack assumed was Dashwood strode forward to speak to the servant. After a heated exchange, the servant hurried off. Dashwood returned to the dais, where the altar gave mute testimony to the depravities practiced there. He raised his hands for silence.

The cacophony of raised voices dropped to a mere buzz of sound, then stopped altogether.

"Brothers united for pleasure," Dashwood said, addressing the crowd. "There's a small change in tonight's agenda. The initiation ceremony will have to be rescheduled for another time. The ladybird has flown." Groans of disappointment filled the chamber, and once again Dashwood signaled for quiet. "But we can't let one woman spoil our pursuit of pleasure. There are women aplenty to satisfy our every whim."

At Dashwood's signal, a group of women entered the chamber. As if on cue, they dropped their cloaks, revealing their scantily clad—and in some cases totally nude—bodies. The sight was met with loud cheers and a general stampede to claim one of the whores.

"She's gone," Jack whispered to Spence. "Somehow Moira managed to escape. Let's go. We have to find her." As unobtrusively as possible, they sidled toward the entrance and ducked through.

Unfortunately, one man saw them leave, a man so upset by Moira's escape he was literally shaking with rage. Roger Mayhew rounded on Dashwood. "How could this happen? This night had been planned a long time. I agreed to let you use Moira for the initiation against my better judgment; afterward she was to be exclusively mine.''

"Even you will agree that using the woman for our initiation rites was a good idea when I tell you who was to be initiated into our ranks tonight," Dashwood said in an attempt to placate Mayhew. "Black Jack Graystoke finally agreed to join the brotherhood and was to be initiated at tonight's rites. I hope the unfortunate delay won't change his mind."

"You stupid fool!" Mayhew all but shouted. "Graystoke is here tonight? Bloody hell, he's Moira's protector! If I'm not mistaken, he and his friend left the moment you announced that Moira had escaped. I'm going after them."

"Let them go, Mayhew. There are plenty of women where Moira came from. I want no trouble over this. You should have told me about the woman's relationship to Lord Graystoke. If you had, this would never have happened."

Mayhew was in no mood to listen to reason. He was armed, and he wasn't going to let anyone cheat him out of his due. He had waited too long for Moira. And he hadn't forgotten that she had bashed him on the head. Moira couldn't have gotten far. Of one thing he was certain. If he couldn't have her, no one else would. Throwing off his hood, he raced from the chamber, Dashwood hard on his heels, pleading for restraint.

Moira and Matilda reached the stables without mishap. Because of the secret gathering tonight, both the stableboy and coachman had been given the night off. Matilda went directly to a stall and led out two horses.

"Can you ride?" Matilda asked as she dragged two saddles from the rack.

"I've ridden farm horses all my life, but I don't know much about saddles. I've always ridden bareback."

"I've never saddled a horse either, but it shouldn't be too difficult."

Afraid to strike a light, they worked in darkness. Moira was sadly afraid she was botching the job, for the horse skittered and danced about nervously as she struggled with straps and buckles. They led the horses out of the stable just as the skies convulsed with thunder and rain poured down upon them in dense sheets. Lightning split the heavens, and the very foundations of the earth shook. Moira turned to help the older woman mount, then climbed clumsily aboard her own horse, already drenched to the bone.

Matilda led the way, hunched against the stinging rain. Moira followed close behind, gladly enduring the discomfort as long as it meant freedom.

Jack and Spence sprinted from the cave, searching for Pettibone and their coach. They spied Pettibone a short distance away. He had climbed down from the driver's box to calm the horses, who had been spooked by the brilliant display of lightning and rolling bursts of thunder. Pettibone saw them immediately and knew something was amiss.

"What is it, milord? Where is Miss Moira?"

Before Jack could answer, Roger Mayhew burst from the mouth of the cave, brandishing a pistol. Pettibone saw him, but Jack and Spence did not. "Behind you, milord!"

The warning came too late. Mayhew aimed the pistol and, aided by a flash of lightning that lit up the field, fired. The bullet found its mark in Jack's back. Jack made a gurgling sound deep in his throat, staggered and fell.

"Are you mad, Mayhew?" Dashwood charged, wresting the gun from Mayhew's hand. "We don't need this kind of notoriety. Do you realize what a man like Ailesbury can do to us if he chooses? He's a duke, for God's sake! Get out of here and don't come back. We're going to have to disband for a while. If and when we reconvene, hotheads like you will not be welcome."

"Give me the pistol," Mayhew snarled, struggling with Dashwood for the weapon. "I'll kill every one of those conniving bastards."

Oblivious to the struggle between Dashwood and Mayhew, Spence stared at Jack in horror. "The bloody bastard shot Jack!" Thanks to the brilliant display of heavenly fireworks, Spence had easily identified Mayhew as the gunman.

Pettibone was the first to gain his wits. He had watched in dismay as Mayhew shot Jack in the back, and he feared the shot had been fatal. Kneeling beside Jack, he noted with relief that his master's chest rose and fell in steady, albeit shallow, rhythm.

"We must get him to a doctor," Pettibone told Spence. "Help me lift him into the coach, milord."

Jack stirred and opened his eyes. "Have to ... find Moira." He fought to dispel the debilitating pain and thick blackness that threatened to claim him.

"We will," Spence assured him, "but first things first. You won't do Moira any good dead. You need a doctor."

The situation was complicated when icy needles of drenching rain pounded them. "Hurry," Pettibone urged, "before His Lordship catches pneumonia. I think we should take him directly to London. I don't trust these country doctors. Pray that he survives the trip."

"I agree," Spence said as he helped Pettibone place

Jack into the coach. The pain proved too much for Jack. He cried out once and went limp. Spence climbed in beside him while Pettibone leaped onto the box and set the whip to the horses' rumps. The coach jerked forward as Spence struggled to shut the door. Meanwhile, Mayhew managed to wrest the pistol from Dashwood and squeeze off another shot. The bullet plowed harmlessly into the coach door just as Spence slammed it shut.

Moira had maintained her seat on the horse with great difficulty. Due to her lack of experience, the saddle slipped precariously from the horse's back, and the muddy road made traveling slow and hazardous. Moira shivered beneath her wet cloak, praying that the disciples were disinclined to brave the elements and give chase. Her heart plummeted to her toes when she heard the sound of gunfire above the rumble of thunder. Matilda must have heard it too, for she glanced furtively over her shoulder, her face a mask of terror.

A few minutes later, a second report cut through the darkness, and Moira knew real panic. The sound of wheels plowing down the muddy road at breakneck speed nearly stopped her heart. Someone was coming! Had they discovered her escape so soon? Had all Matilda's planning been for naught?

"They're coming!" she screamed to Matilda.

Then the coach was upon them, beside them, their horses running neck and neck.

"Moira! Stop!"

Moira turned her head, stunned to see Spence, clad in a black robe, leaning out the window and gesturing to her frantically.

She was appalled and disappointed in Spence, assuming

that he was a member of the Hellfire Club. "No! I won't go back!"

"Miss Moira, no one here is going to hurt you!" This from Pettibone, who had slowed the coach in order to keep abreast of her horse.

Moira pulled back on the reins, stunned to see Pettibone driving the coach. Surely he wasn't involved in the Hellfire Club, was he? "You too, Mr. Pettibone? You and Lord Spencer aught to be ashamed of yourselves."

"It's not what you think," Spence called through the window. "Jack's been shot. He might die."

Jack shot? What kind of a trick was that to play on a person? Moira wondered. What if it wasn't a trick? What if Jack really was in danger of dying? Frightened at the thought of Jack's imminent death, she reined in sharply. Pettibone managed to bring the coach to a stop and hopped down from the box. Spence poked his head out of the window, his expression grave.

"Who shot Jack, and why?" Moira wanted to know.

"Come inside, out of the rain," Spence said, holding open the door.

Moira raised her chin belligerently. "I'm not going back to the Hellfire Club."

"Good God, no! We came to rescue you, not hurt you. Jack was shot while leaving the caves. We came away as soon as we learned you had somehow managed to escape. Unfortunately, Mayhew followed us."

Moira bit her lip. "How do I know you're telling the truth?"

"Look inside, miss," Pettibone urged, "and see for yourself."

Moira peered inside, seeing nothing but blackness. "I see nothing." Just then a flash of lightning split the skies, revealing more than she was prepared for. Jack lay sprawled on the seat. His face was white, his eyes were closed. She saw the splotch of blood growing ever wider on the black robe he still wore and cried out in dismay.

"I speak the truth, Moira," Spence said. "Please get inside. Jack needs a doctor. He could bleed to death if he isn't treated soon."

Moira dismounted, started to climb inside, then remembered Matilda. Searching the road, she saw the woman slouched over her horse a short distance away. Moira called to her. Matilda hesitated, then kneed her horse forward.

"Get inside the coach, Matilda. It's all right. No harm will come to us."

"Are you sure, miss?"

"Who's the woman?" Spence asked warily.

"This is Matilda, Sir Dashwood's housekeeper," Moira explained. "She helped me escape. I won't leave without her."

"Very well," Spence acquiesced, "get in. Hurry, there's no time to lose."

Pettibone moved with alacrity, helping Matilda dismount and handing her into the coach. Moira followed, and Spence closed the door behind them. With a jerk, the coach rattled off down the rutted road. Moira fell to her knees and placed a hand against Jack's heart, relieved to find the beat steady.

"Is he going to be all right?" Anxiety rose like a specter to haunt her. She understood nothing of what had happened, or why Jack had been among the disciples tonight, except for what Spence told her. Had he really come to rescue her?

"Only a doctor can tell us that," Spence said.

Suddenly the coach wheel hit a pothole, jostling the occupants. Jack groaned and would have toppled to the floor if Moira hadn't moved to sit beside him, holding him in place. With one hand, she pushed a lock of hair away from his eyes. Her fingers were cool on his forehead. Jack felt them and opened his eyes. He tried to smile, but it dissolved into a grimace of pain.

"Moira."

"Don't talk."

"What happened?"

"You've been shot. We're taking you to a doctor." He started to rise, gritting his teeth against the pain. "No, don't move." She parted the robe and tried to hide her dismay when she saw the copious amount of blood staining his waistcoat. Turning him slightly, she tore off a piece of her petticoat, made a pad from the material and pressed it against the wound.

"Shot," Jack repeated weakly. "Are you all right?"

Moira smiled through her tears. "I'm fine."

Jack grasped her hand, his grip surprisingly strong after having lost so much blood. "I was so damn worried. Joining the Hellfire Club was the only way I could think of to find out what had happened to you. I went to Newgate looking for you after I returned from Cornwall and learned that Mayhew had taken you away. I even questioned Mayhew's father. I learned nothing from him. The Dashwood estate was the only place I knew of where Mayhew might have taken you. Spence and I were planning to rescue you by force, if necessary. I don't really belong to the Hellfire Club."

"Don't talk," Moira urged. "Rest." Her words were unnecessary. Jack lost his tenuous hold on reality as he drifted into a bottomless void.

"Where are we going, miss?" Matilda dared to ask. "Sir Dashwood must surely know by now that I was the one who let you escape. Plunket will make certain of it. That man never did like me."

"We're going to Graystoke Manor," Spence supplied. "Pettibone and I agree that we should proceed directly to the city. Dr. Dudley is an excellent doctor and Jack trusts him."

"I thought we were going to Ireland," Matilda said, confused.

"We will, Matilda, but not until Lord Graystoke is out of danger. I . . . Lord Graystoke helped me once, and I can't leave him like this. Don't worry, you'll be safe enough at Graystoke Manor."

"Not if his lordship belongs to the Hellfire Club," Matilda insisted grimly. "The whole lot of them are evil."

"Now see here, my good woman," Spence said huffily. "Both Jack and I abhor what the Hellfire Club stands for. Jack pretended to join for Moira's sake. He brought me and Pettibone along to help with the rescue."

Matilda didn't look at all convinced, but at the moment no other option was available. "If you say so, milord."

The storm abated shortly before they reached London. Their mad dash from Dashwood's estate brought them to the city in the wee hours of morning. The streets were wet and deserted as they proceeded directly to Graystoke Manor. Pettibone pulled the coach to a stop before the front door, then hurried off to rouse the coachman and his assistant from their beds. Colin was sent immediately to summon Dr. Dudley, while the coachman helped to carry Jack to his room. Matilda stood aside, wringing her hands and worrying over what was to become of her.

"Mistress Matilda?" Matilda gasped and whirled, surprised to find Pettibone standing at her elbow. "I'm Pettibone. Lord Spence told me about what you did for Miss Moira. If you'll follow me, I'll show you to your room. It's on the first floor; you'll find it quite comfortable." His friendly smile gave her a small measure of confidence, and she smiled back.

"I'm not fussy, sir. Any room will do."

"Just call me Pettibone. I'm Lord Graystoke's right-hand man. We're all grateful for what you did for Miss Moira. Lord Graystoke is uncommonly fond of the lass." Fond wasn't a strong-enough word in Pettibone's opinion, but it wasn't his place to presume.

"I did what my conscience directed, Mr. Pettibone. I'm ashamed of the years I did nothing for those poor girls brought in for the disciples' pleasure. Granted most of them were ... er ... soiled ladies, but some were not. When I saw that Miss Moira was an unwilling victim, I knew something had to be done."

"You did the right thing," Pettibone said, awkwardly patting the woman's rough hand. "Lord Graystoke will wish to reward you."

Matilda's blush was her first since she had been a very young girl with stars in her eyes and dreams of a happy future.

Moira set to work the moment Jack lay stretched out on his bed. First she removed the black robe and then his jacket, instructing Spence to hold him steady while she pulled off his muddy boots. Rolling him on his stomach, Moira saw that the pad she had placed over his wound was saturated with blood.

"Tell Mr. Pettibone we'll need lots of hot water and clean cloths when the doctor arrives, Lord Spencer."

"Lud, Moira, all that blood! It doesn't look good."

"He'll be fine. Just do as I say." Her voice was sharp and fierce. Spence gave her a strange look, then hurried off to do her bidding.

Choking down a sob, Moira looked into Jack's ashen face and willed life into him. "Don't you dare die, Black Jack Graystoke!"

It was her fault he lay injured and perhaps dying. She hadn't wanted to involve Jack in her problems; that's why she had lied to him from the start. But the more lies she told, the more enmeshed their lives became. Then she had lost control of her senses and had allowed Jack to make love to her. But she had fallen in love with Black Jack Graystoke long before that memorable night.

Moira was attempting to remove Jack's shirt when he opened his eyes and groaned. Moira went still, disconcerted to find Jack's gray gaze steady, albeit clouded with pain. "Did I hurt you? I'm sorry."

"You could never hurt me," Jack said. "I like your hands on me."

"I'm sorry I misjudged you, Jack. I thought you were a member of the Hellfire Club. I was willing to believe Lord Mayhew instead of my heart. I should have known you weren't capable of such debauchery."

"You should have trusted me, sweetheart. I wanted you to confide in me. Did you think I'd believe that you were capable of theft?"

"You didn't know me. How could you not? You found me lying in a gutter and thought I was a . . . a prostitute. If you believed that, then you'd believe I could steal a valuable piece of jewelry."

Jack's eyes drifted shut, and Moira could tell he was having difficulty remaining lucid. Where was that doctor?

"Hang on, Jack. The doctor should be here shortly."

Jack reached for her hand, and Moira could not deny him as she placed her smaller hand in his. "Don't leave, Moira. Don't . . . leave . . ."

Suddenly the door opened and Dr. Dudley strode briskly forward, exuding confidence. Moira breathed a sigh of relief.

"Leave me with my patient," the doctor said crisply. "Pettibone can assist me." No sooner had the doctor spoken Pettibone's name than the man entered the chamber, bearing a pitcher of steaming water and clean cloths folded over his arm. With marked reluctance, Moira joined Lord Spencer in the hall.

"How long do you think the doctor will be in there?" Spence asked worriedly. "Jack will be all right, won't he? Lud, he's the best friend I ever had."

"You're the best friend *he* ever had," Moira said with conviction.

"Oh, milady, you're home! I'm ever so glad. We were all so worried when those men took you off to prison. Are you all right?"

Jilly had been awakened by the commotion and left her room to see what the fuss was about. When she saw Moira standing in the hallway, her face lit up with pleasure.

"I'm fine, Jilly, but I'm afraid Lord Graystoke isn't. He's been shot. The doctor is with him now."

Jilly's face drained of all color and her hand flew to her mouth. "Shot, milady? Oh, my."

"I'm sure he'll be fine, Jilly. Go back to bed."

"What should I tell the others?"

"Others?"

"Aye, Mr. Pettibone hired a staff of servants. There are two maids besides myself—Annie and Agnes. And Mrs.

Harcourt is the new cook. Then there is Colin, the assistant coachman.'' At the mention of Colin, Jilly's face turned a bright red. ''They're all waiting in the kitchen.''

''Do what you can to calm them, Jilly. Tell them there's been a minor mishap and that Lord Graystoke is going to be fine.''

''Aye, milady,'' Jilly said, hurrying off down the hall.

''I wonder what the doctor is doing?'' Spence said as he stopped his pacing to stare at the closed door. ''He's been in there a bloody long time.''

Just then the door opened and Pettibone flew out. ''Mr. Pettibone!'' Moira cried. ''What is it? Is Jack . . . ?''

''The doctor needs more hot water,'' Pettibone called over his shoulder.

''I'm going in there,'' Moira said determinedly. ''The doctor might need another pair of hands.''

Before Spence could stop her, she opened the door and stepped inside. ''Bring the water here, Pettibone,'' Dr. Dudley said without looking up.

''It's not Mr. Pettibone, Doctor, it's Moira. I want to help.''

The doctor peered at Moira over his spectacles. ''Does blood make you squeamish?''

Moira swallowed, then lied, ''No. What can I do?''

''Pettibone is a good man, but he's all thumbs. You can hold the retractor while I probe for the bullet. It went deep, but as far as I can tell it missed all the vital organs.''

Moira hurried forward and grasped the instrument the doctor indicated. ''Is Jack awake?''

''Thank God, no. He passed out when I started to probe. Now, miss, hold the retractor steady.''

Moira tried but could not look away as the doctor dug into Jack's flesh. Fresh blood welled up around the probe, but the doctor seemed unconcerned. Pettibone returned and set the hot water on the stand, then awaited further instructions. When none came, he backed away but did not leave the chamber. Suddenly the doctor gave an exultant cry, withdrew the bloody bullet and dropped it into a waiting basin.

" 'Tis done," he said, plucking the retractor from Moira's nerveless fingers and setting it aside. "Nothing left now but to stitch the wound."

"What about infection?" Moira asked, well aware that infection killed more people than the actual wound.

"I'm scrupulous about cleanliness. I've long believed that infection is the result of dirty instruments. I know my colleagues scoff at such nonsense, but I'll stand by my record. Few of my wound patients die of infection, and I'm conscientious when it comes to washing my hands and immersing my instruments in boiling water before and after each use. If one of those country doctors had removed the bullet, His Lordship wouldn't have had a chance."

The doctor threaded a needle and took the first stitch. Moira gasped. "He's so pale."

"He's lost a lot of blood, but I'm confident he'll recover. Feed him plenty of liquids. Lord Graystoke is strong and healthy. In due time, he'll be as good as new. There," he said, taking the last stitch and affixing a bandage, "finished. I'll leave laudanum for pain and return tomorrow to look in on him."

After he dipped his hands in the hot water Pettibone had brought, and scrubbed them with soap and dried them, Dr. Dudley took his leave. Pettibone followed him out the door. Spence entered the chamber almost immediately.

"How is he?"

"Dr. Dudley seems to think he'll be fine." She glanced at Spence, noting the fatigue lines etched around his mouth and eyes. "Why don't you get some rest? I'll sit up with Jack."

Spence hesitated. "Are you sure? You must be as exhausted as I."

"It's something I have to do," Moira said. "If not for Jack, I don't know what would have happened to me."

"Very well," Spence allowed. "I'll find an empty room and grab a few hours sleep. Wake me if you need me."

Moira pulled a chair up to the bed and sat down, too bone-weary to notice the spectacular dawn coloring the eastern sky. She stared at Jack, afraid to take her eyes off him. Though pale as death, the steady rise and fall of his chest was comforting. He was lying on his stomach, the same position in which the doctor had left him after removing the bullet.

Her thoughts scattered. She wondered if anyone had ever really known this man. They called him Black Jack, his name hinting at debauchery, dissipation and depravity. He was known as a womanizer and gambler, a man who engaged in all kinds of excesses.

Conversely, Moira found Jack to be kind and thoughtful and brave. She loved him but realized there could be no future for them. He was a duke and she a poor farmer's daughter. She had no right to aspire to anything greater than becoming Jack's mistress. She quickly discounted as fanciful the story her mother told her about her possible link to nobility. She had no concrete proof that her grandfather was of noble birth, and no matter how she wished otherwise, her chances for a life with Jack remained dim.

She closed her eyes against the pain that knowledge brought her.

"Moira."

Moira's eyes flew open to find Jack staring at her. "What is it? Would you like some water? The doctor said you're going to be just fine," she said.

"You're still here."

Moira swallowed and nodded her head. One day she wouldn't be here, but until that day arrived, she'd not leave his side. She rose and poured water from the pitcher into a glass, mixed in a generous portion of laudanum and held it to his lips. He drank greedily, then drifted off again. Moira returned to her chair and rested her head on the edge of the bed. In seconds she was asleep.

Chapter Fifteen

Jack awoke slowly, aware of pain and sunlight and more pain. He moved his hand and encountered something soft and silken. Adjusting his eyes to the light pouring in from the window, he was surprised and pleased to see Moira sleeping with her head resting on the edge of the bed. She hadn't left him. He rested his hand on her head, savoring the feel of her tousled copper curls beneath his fingers. She was safe and she was here and he was never going to let her out of his sight again.

Suddenly the door creaked open, and Pettibone poked his head into the chamber. Seeing that Moira was sleeping, he tiptoed inside so as not to disturb her.

"Is there anything I can do for you, milord? Breakfast will be up directly. Nothing substantial, mind you. The doctor left specific orders."

Jack shifted uncomfortably and glanced down at Moira, still sleeping peacefully. "I do have a rather urgent need, Pettibone. But first see to Moira. She's been here with me all night and needs bed rest. Later you can fix me more

251

of that laudanum. I fear the pain is rather unbearable.''

"Shall I wake her or will you?''

"I will,'' Jack said, gently caressing Moira's cheek. Moira sighed, murmured and pressed her cheek into his caress. Grasping her shoulders, he gently shook her. Moira jerked awake.

"Jack! What is it? Do you need something?''

Jack managed a wobbly smile. "I need for you to go to bed. Pettibone can see to my needs. You've sat up with me all night; you must rest.'' Moira started to protest, but Jack forestalled her. "No, no argument. I'm in no danger.''

"Very well,'' she reluctantly agreed. "But Pettibone must call me if I'm needed.''

"I will, Miss Moira. Indeed I will.''

After Moira left the room, Pettibone quickly and efficiently took care of Jack's personal needs. "And now the laudanum, if you please, Pettibone,'' Jack said. As badly as he wanted an explanation of Moira's escape and his shooting, he simply was in no condition to concentrate on details.

Pettibone administered the drug, then left quietly after Jack dropped off to sleep. A few minutes later, Spence slipped into the room and took the chair Moira had vacated a short time earlier.

Two days later, Jack was sleeping less, taking solid food and felt well enough to hear everything that had transpired after he had taken a bullet in his back. Spence related the details of their wild ride to London.

"Has anyone seen Mayhew after he shot me?'' Jack asked his friend.

"Not that I know of. The talk around London is still

about Moira's unsuccessful bid into society. There's even a bet on the books at White's on how long you'll keep her as your mistress. There hasn't been a whisper about what transpired at the Hellfire Club the other night.''

''And there won't be,'' Jack said. ''Dashwood and Mayhew are the only ones besides you, me, Pettibone and Moira who know about the shooting, and they aren't about to incriminate themselves.''

''There's Matilda.''

Jack grew thoughtful. ''Can the woman be trusted?''

''She helped Moira. Pettibone seems uncommonly fond of her.''

Jack raised a well-shaped brow. ''Pettibone? You mean that old reprobate finally found his match?''

Spence shrugged. ''I just mentioned it in passing.'' He rose to leave. ''Well, I'm off, old boy. Moira will have my hide if I tire you. She's a veritable dragon about your state of health.''

Jack smiled, inordinately pleased at Moira's protectiveness. ''I could use a rest. Keep your eyes and ears open; I'm not finished with this caper. I'll be up and about in a day or two, and then I'll decide what must be done, if anything, about Mayhew's unprovoked attack.''

If Moira let Jack out of bed in a day or two, he'd eat his hat, Spence thought.

An hour later, Moira peeked in on Jack on her way downstairs, saw that he was sleeping and smiled in satisfaction. He was gaining strength rapidly, and she was convinced now that he would recover with no ill effects. That meant she had decisions to make, none of them easy. She was grateful that Matilda was fitting nicely into the household. She had taken over the housekeeper's duties and seemed to get along famously with Pettibone.

Moira stepped into the parlor, surprised to find the new maids and Jilly in a huddle in the center of the room. Hands on hips, Jilly appeared to be engaged in a heated argument. Moira's entrance caused them to spring apart guiltily, and Moira realized that they had been gossiping about her. They scattered as soon as she stepped into the room, except for Jilly, who hung back with a hangdog expression on her face.

"I'm sorry, milady. I'll see that it doesn't happen again."

"I presume you were discussing me."

Jilly bowed her head. "Not I, milady. I'd never do or say anything to hurt you. You know how gossip travels among servants. I was merely setting them straight about a few things."

"First of all, you must stop calling me milady. Moira will do. I am no lady, as you must know by now. And I'm not even remotely related to Lord Graystoke. Second, I want to know the nature of the gossip circulating about me."

"I don't care what they say, mila . . . Miss Moira. They don't know you like I do."

"Thank you, Jilly," Moira said gratefully, "but I insist you tell me what is being said about me."

Jilly swallowed hard, clearly uncomfortable. "The gentry are saying that you seduced Lord Graystoke, then convinced him to pass you off to society as a lady. They say you're his mistress. Rumor has it that you also enticed Lord Roger Mayhew into your bed while in his employ before setting your sights on Lord Graystoke."

Moira's nostrils flared angrily. "Go on." She was determined to hear everything no matter how damning.

"Are you sure?"

"Aye."

"There's a bet on the books at White's concerning the date Lord Graystoke will send you packing."

Moira's face drained of all color. "What are people's feelings about Lord Graystoke?"

"They're ready to forgive him once he releases you from his protection. They think the whole prank is entirely your fault, but feelings are running against him, at least until he redeems himself in their eyes."

It never ceased to amaze Moira how fast gossip traveled from household to household among servants. It was ever so when she was employed in the Mayhew household, and it would be ever so until the end of time. Servants managed to get to the heart of the matter rather quickly.

"Thank you, Jilly. I appreciate your honesty."

"I don't care what they say, Miss Moira," Jilly declared staunchly. "You're good and kind and not capable of duplicity. "I don't even care if you're Lord Graystoke's mistress."

After Jilly left, Moira felt the weight of the world pressing down upon her. If Jack hadn't inherited the dukedom, his high jinks would have been considered normal behavior for a man with Black Jack Graystoke's unfavorable reputation. Gaining a title had changed everything. Jack now had certain standards to maintain whether he liked it or not. Instead of flouting society, he must now conform. And conforming meant marrying a woman of equal rank and position. Oh, he could still drink, gamble and womanize—most members of the gentry did—but when it came to marriage, there were strict rules to uphold. The gossip, combined with Jack's exalted rank, made her decision about her future painful but clear.

255

* * *

Within a few days, Jack was taking tentative steps around his chamber and determined to venture downstairs despite both Moira's and Pettibone's objection.

"This bloody wound is *not* going to keep me in bed," Jack said belligerently as Moira fussed over him one afternoon. "I have pressing duties and numerous responsibilities that must be attended to."

"They'll wait," Moira said, stifling a smile. Not long ago, Jack's sole responsibility had been to marry a wealthy wife, his only duty to uphold his reputation as a rake. "Has Mr. Pettibone spoken to you about Matilda?"

"Aye. I've never known Pettibone to take up a woman's cause as he has Matilda's. If I didn't know better, I'd think he was smitten."

Moira sent him a smug look. "Matilda has taken over duties as housekeeper and is doing a remarkable job. I'm beholden to her for helping me. She has no relatives and nowhere to go. I fear Sir Dashwood will find her and exact punishment for her betrayal if she's turned out on the street."

"I've already told Pettibone to put the woman on the payroll," Jack said. "I'm more than grateful for what she did for you. She has a job in my household for as long as she likes."

Moira's relief was immediate. She wanted no loose ends when she left. "Thank you. Is there anything you'd like while I'm here? Perhaps I can read to you."

Jack gave Moira an enigmatic look, then patted the bed. "Sit here beside me."

"I don't think . . . that is . . ."

"Please."

Put that way, she couldn't refuse. Perched gingerly on

the edge of the bed, she had no idea what Jack intended until he pulled her into his arms.

"God, I've missed you," he rasped breathlessly. He kissed the top of her head, inhaling deeply of the fragrant scent she used on her hair. He loved the color; more copper than red, so vibrant it had a life of its own.

Raising her chin, he lowered his mouth and kissed her, starved for the taste of her sweet mouth. Stunned by his strength after suffering so grave an injury, Moira submitted willingly to the hungry violence of Jack's mouth, parting her lips so he could deepen the kiss. His hand fell to her breast, and she leaned into the caress, loving him so extravagantly she had no control over her response. Her body burned with longing, making her forget he was recovering from a serious wound.

After several long minutes of frenzied kissing, Jack tore his mouth from hers. "I want you, Moira. It frightens the hell out of me when I think how close you came to becoming a victim to the disciples of the Hellfire Club." His hands sought the buttons on her dress. "I need you. I didn't realize how much until you were gone."

Moira went still. "You're not well enough for this, Jack." Deliberately she removed his hands from her bodice. "Besides, there are things you don't know about me." She took a deep breath. "About Lady Mayhew's necklace . . ."

"I know you didn't take it. You could never do anything dishonest."

Moira cleared her throat and said, "The night you found me lying in the gutter . . . Your carriage didn't strike me. I had jumped from Lord Mayhew's coach. He was taking me to the Hellfire Club, and I'd rather die than let that happen. He thought I was dead and left me lying in the gutter. It's a miracle you came along when you did.''

A ghost of a smile hovered at the corners of Jack's mouth. "It was no miracle. Lady Amelia knew exactly what she was doing that night."

Moira was too distraught to catch Jack's meaning. "It was wrong of me to let you think you were responsible for my injuries. I didn't know you and feared you would hand me over to the authorities if I told the truth. The Mayhews were determined to press charges. I had nowhere to go, no one to turn to. I took advantage of you, Jack. How can you forgive me?''

"It was I who took advantage of you," Jack corrected. "Spence and I had no business using you for our amusement. At the time, his two-thousand-pound wager was mighty tempting. At first, I sincerely wanted to find you a rich husband. After I came to know you, I couldn't bear the thought of another man having you. What a muddle I've made of things."

"I'm as much to blame as you. I could have told the truth any time I wished."

"It's over. I haven't decided yet what to do about Mayhew, but I swear he'll never harm you again. I want you for my wife, Moira."

"Wife? No! It's impossible. You can't. It just isn't done."

"I can do as I damn well please."

"You're a duke. I'm a farmer's daughter." She clutched the locket hanging from her neck, wishing she knew how much truth she could place in her mother's tale about noble blood flowing through her veins.

"I don't care what you are. You're the woman I want to marry, the woman I want as the mother of my children.'' Moira looked confused. ''You still don't understand, do you? I love you, Moira.''

''Oh, no, you can't!''

''And I think you love me.''

''It doesn't matter. I've heard the gossip. Society will never forgive you. Marrying me will ruin your reputation.''

Jack laughed. ''What reputation? Is that a polite way of saying you don't love me?''

Moira wanted to blurt out to the world that she loved Jack Graystoke beyond reason, beyond time and space, but she loved him too much to ruin him. ''I'm saying I can't marry you.''

Jack's face hardened. ''I can't believe you'd rather become my mistress than marry me.''

Moira blanched. ''I'm not saying that, either.''

''You're the most exasperating female I've ever known. I don't want you for a mistress.''

He gathered her close and held her tightly as he fought the fear of losing her. It seemed as if he'd waited his entire life for Moira. He kissed her tenderly. Fiercely. Ignoring the twinge in his back from his healing wound, he framed her face in his hands. He brushed his lips over her eyelids, the upward curve of her brow, down her silken cheeks. His tongue flicked over her lips, tasting them, teasing them, then parting them to explore the sweet depths within.

His hand trailed down her throat, across her breast, her stomach, continuing along her hip to the juncture of her legs. Cupping her between her thighs, he felt the incredible heat of her need seeping through her clothing. ''You want me,'' he whispered raggedly. ''You're hot and wet down there.'' He eased her down on the bed and raised her skirts with an upright sweep of his hand.

"Jack, no! Someone could come in. There is enough talk in the household without providing more fodder for the gossip mill."

Before she knew what he was about, he slid out of bed and locked the door. Moira gasped, unaware that he had been naked beneath the sheets. She had assumed he wore smallclothes on the lower part of his body. She gaped at him, mesmerized by the beautiful symmetry of his form. Except for the bandage covering his wound, he was pure perfection. Strong and virile and wickedly tempting. Because of his healing wound, his steps were slow and deliberate, but his body was strong and determined when he returned and pressed Moira down onto the mattress.

"You'll hurt yourself." Moira resisted. "Your injury . . ."

"It will hurt more if I don't love you," Jack told her as he began undressing her with firm, steady fingers. "You're mine, sweetheart. You'll always be mine. Fight it all you want, but I'll wear you down until you agree to marry me."

He dragged off her dress, then her chemise, tossing them aside. He stared at her breasts, cupping them gently and lifting them to his mouth. Her skin was warm and tempting, and Jack drank deeply of the clean, arousing scent of her. He heard the sharp intake of her breath when he drew her nipple into his mouth, suckling her. His hand moved downward over her abdomen and she arched against him, her body straining for the same kind of pleasure she'd experienced before in Jack's arms. When his fingers slid possessively into the soft triangle between her legs, sweet, sharp, almost painful sensations shot through her veins.

Wave after wave of delicious heat washed over her, until nothing but raw need remained. With a will of their own, her arms twined around his neck, pulling him closer, arching her back, offering more of herself to his mouth and hands. Jack stiffened and gasped. Realizing that she had hurt him, she started to withdraw, but Jack would not permit it.

"No. The pain is nothing compared to the agony of wanting you. The day I found you lying in the gutter was the luckiest day of my life."

Then his mouth followed the same path his hand had forged, blazing a fiery trail from the tight little buds cresting her breasts across her flat stomach into the lustrous copper curls crowning her thighs. A low scream tore from her throat and her hips surged upward.

"Jack! No, you mustn't!"

A ripple of laughter slipped past his lips as his hands caught her hips and held her fast. "Aye, sweetheart, I must. I promise you'll like it." He cupped her bottom and lifted her even higher, denying her escape from the intimate exploration of his mouth. She made a soft mewling sound deep in her throat, wanting to die from embarrassment. She never imagined men and women were capable of doing such wicked things.

Moira was amazed at the sensations she experienced, so new, but oh, so blissful. Searing flames consumed her woman's center, destroying her senses, stealing her reason. She was painfully aware of every sensation, every gasp, each moan, of his rough hands on her body, his mouth on her most intimate places. The chamber echoed with sensuous sounds of fevered lovemaking. The whisper of sheets beneath her naked back, the vibration of hot breath upon even hotter flesh, the silken slide of skin against skin. Love sounds, erotic sounds. Sounds too intimate to describe. Her moans were coming faster and her body shivered with liquid tremors as scalding heat sped through her veins.

"Jack! I can't bear it! It's too wicked."

"Aye. You taste wicked and wanton and incredibly wonderful. Sweeter than the sweetest ambrosia. I'll settle for nothing less than all of you."

Drugged by his words, Moira rocked against his mouth, her hands clinging to his shoulders, her nails digging into his back. She felt like a bowstring that was drawn to the limit of its endurance, and beyond. Suddenly the bowstring snapped, sending raw ecstasy surging through her. She cried out wordlessly, finding no words to describe the feeling. Then Jack was sliding upward along her body, finding her mouth and kissing her. She tasted herself on his lips, thinking vaguely that it wasn't at all unpleasant.

Grasping her hand, Jack brought it to his groin. "Feel what you do to me, love. I have no control where you're concerned."

He was hard and hot. Steel covered in velvet. She moved her hand experimentally up and down his throbbing length, shocked at her wantonness. Jack spit out a harsh growl and removed her hand. She expected him to roll atop her and take his own pleasure and was startled when he merely kissed and caressed her.

Her breath caught in her throat. Surely it wasn't possible to find pleasure again so soon, was it? Jack proceeded to show her how naive she was. He kissed her ravenously, until her lips were swollen and red, then lavished rapt attention to her breasts, sucking each nipple deeply into his mouth and laving the tight buds with the rough surface of his tongue. His hands worked magic on her slick, sensitive folds, thrusting his fingers into her moist crevice until she was vibrating with need.

"Take me, Moira. Take all of me," he said in a gasp. His control hung by a slim thread. If he wasn't deep inside her soon, he'd explode.

Moira hesitated but a moment, then grasped the thick root sprouting from the dark forest between his legs and guided it into her moist center. There were no words to mar the moment, just the thunder of heartbeats as he drove into her, filling her so completely she felt possessed. His mouth devoured her neck and shoulders, trailing downward until it latched onto her breast. Her back arched, taking him fully inside her, stretching her unbearably. The power of him, the utter strength of him seemed to flow into her with each thrust. She cried out from pure joy, caught in a whirlwind that transported her beyond mere pleasure to rapturous oblivion. Never had she felt so completely consumed by another human being.

It was a strange kind of helplessness, welcome yet frightening. The blinding heat building in her center moved upward and outward. Then she was falling, falling, spiraling down toward a dark, searing abyss that sucked her into a pool of pure bliss.

Spurred by Moira's savage response, Jack thrust long and deep within her tightness, wild with the sheer rapture of being where he belonged, where he wanted to be. When he heard her sobbing little cries intensify and felt her contract around him, he drove deep and held himself there, poised on the brink of ecstasy. When she arched up to meet him, he flexed his hips, impaling her, flowing onto her, into her, a moan rumbling in his heaving chest. She felt his seed splash against the walls of her womb and clasped him tightly with her arms and legs, wanting to keep him there as long as possible. He stared into her eyes, his own eyes wild, savage, intense. Satisfied. No matter who or what stood between them, they belonged together.

Jack sighed and rolled off Moira. The exertion had cost him dearly. His wound was afire and his head was throbbing, but it had been worth it. Moira watched him closely, realizing this kind of activity was definitely not recommended for a convalescent. Guilt washed over her, and she slid from bed.

''This shouldn't have happened. Let me look at your wound.''

Jack obliged, rolling over onto his stomach. Heaving a sigh of relief, Moira saw that the bandage showed no signs of renewed bleeding. The doctor was to remove the stitches tomorrow, and she'd have a difficult time explaining a recurrence of bleeding.

''Well, what's the verdict?'' Jack asked with a hint of amusement.

''I don't think you did yourself any harm, but to be on the safe side this can't happen again.''

When no reply was forthcoming, Moira's eyes settled on Jack's face. She wasn't too surprised to see that he had fallen asleep. She pulled a cover over him, donned her clothes and quietly left the chamber. She had much to think about. Jack's declaration of love and subsequent proposal had been totally unexpected. No matter what he said, she couldn't allow him to sully his title by marrying beneath him. He had just recently come into his title and wasn't thinking clearly. He had a responsibility to his peers and standards to uphold. He was no longer Black Jack Graystoke, debauched rake. He was the Duke of Ailesbury, an old and honorable title, one he could not besmirch. He owed it to his cousin's memory to conduct himself with reasonable dignity. And that meant marrying a woman of equal rank.

An hour later, a visitor arrived at Graystoke Manor. Since Pettibone had gone on some mysterious errand for Jack and the maids were nowhere in sight, she answered the door. When she saw who was calling, her mouth dropped open in surprise.

"Moira! I see Lord Graystoke found you. I never did ask how you two met, and I don't want to know, but he certainly seemed intent upon finding you when he called on me."

Lord Mayhew, the Earl of Montclaire, stood on the doorstep, his tall, dignified form only slightly bent with age. Moira blanched and would have turned and ran if she thought he would go away. "Lord Montclaire, I didn't know you and Jack were acquainted. Have you come about the necklace? I didn't steal it."

Montclaire gave her a startled look. "That's not why I'm here. It's imperative I speak to Lord Graystoke. May I come in?"

Moira remained firmly in place, refusing Montclaire entrance. "Lord Graystoke isn't receiving. He's recuperating from an injury."

The old man searched her face. "What kind of injury?"

"I'm not at liberty to say."

"See here, young lady, I carry no grudge against you. I understand my son rescinded all charges against you, and I'll not dispute him. Lady Mayhew has her necklace, and I'm not sure you stole it in the first place."

"That's good of you, milord. I didn't steal the necklace."

"Be that as it may, I'm giving you the benefit of the doubt. Now, we both know I'm not young anymore and I won't be kept standing around while you make excuses. I insist upon seeing Lord Graystoke."

Moira's temper flared. "Lord Graystoke was seriously injured. He needs rest. He hasn't awakened yet from his nap."

"Again I ask, what kind of injury did he sustain?"

"Very well, if you insist. Jack was shot by *your* son, milord. Shot in the back."

The earl staggered under the weight of Moira's words. "Surely you jest."

"I wish I did."

" 'Tis worse than I expected," he lamented. "I will wait until Lord Graystoke awakens."

"It's all right, Moira. Show Lord Montclaire upstairs. I'll see him."

Swiveling her head, Moira saw Jack standing at the top of the stairs. He had dressed himself in trousers and shirt and was leaning heavily against the banister.

"What are you doing out of bed?" Moira all but shouted. "Are you certain you're up to receiving company?"

Montclaire's sharp gaze settled on Moira, his perception keen despite his advanced age. He had assumed Moira was Jack's mistress, but realized now that it went deeper than that.

"Stop coddling me, Moira. I'm perfectly capable of dealing with this."

When Jack returned to his chamber, Moira issued a stern warning. "I'll show you to Lord Jack's chamber, milord, but you must promise not to tire him."

"I'll do my best, young lady," Montclaire said, "but

I must get to the bottom of this. It does concern my son, does it not?''

Clamping her mouth shut, Moira led the way to Jack's chamber. Jack was sitting in a wing chair by the fireplace, waiting. He indicated that Montclaire should take the chair opposite him. Moira turned to leave.

"No, Moira, don't go. This concerns you as well. I want you to stay.''

If Montclaire was startled by Jack's words, he hid it well. Moira perched gingerly at the edge of the bed, flushing when she recalled the wanton way in which she had responded to Jack's loving on this very bed not two hours ago. Her gaze flew to his face, searching for some sign that the strenuous activity had done him serious harm and noting with relief that he appeared relaxed and well.

"You wished to see me, milord?'' Jack said.

"I'm truly sorry, milord. I knew Roger had a wild streak, but I never imagined he would harm anyone.''

"You know?''

Montclaire sent Moira a speaking glance. "Moira told me. I wish to know everything, Ailesbury. Where and why did my son attack you? My reason for coming today was to inquire about the gossip I heard at my club, something about introducing Moira to society and pretending she was a lady. It seems my son was the one who unmasked her. I wanted to ask Roger about it, but I haven't seen him in days. Lady Montclaire is worried. I don't even know where he keeps rooms.''

"I don't know if you're ready to hear this, milord,'' Jack began, "but there are things you don't know about your son. Have you ever heard of the Hellfire Club?''

Montclaire paled. "Certainly, who hasn't? But what's

that got to do with . . . My God, you don't mean Roger . . . ?''

"Surely you suspected."

The earl looked pained. "I suppose, but one hopes. Especially when it concerns one's heir."

"Your son abducted Moira from your home for the purpose of offering her to the members of the Hellfire Club. Moira jumped from a moving coach to escape, and Roger mistakenly thought she was dead. That's why he left so abruptly for France. He feared involvement in her death. When he returned and found Moira alive, he renewed his efforts to use her in the club's rites."

"My God! It never occurred to me that he had become so debauched. We have indulged him sinfully, I fear. From the time he was born, his mother and I let him run wild. But for him to shoot another man in the back, 'tis something that cannot be forgiven. Why? Why did he do it?''

"I had gone to Sir Dashwood's estate, where your son had taken Moira and held her against her will. I planned to rescue her." He sent Moira a tender look. "As it turned out, Moira didn't need my help. She had already escaped on her own. When I went to her aid, your son took offense and shot me."

"I'm sincerely sorry, milord. What do you intend to do? Have you notified the authorities?"

"Not yet," Jack said. "Actually, I haven't decided what to do."

"I implore you, permit me to handle this in my own way." Montclaire looked as if he'd aged ten years since he'd first entered the chamber, and Moira's heart went out to him. "If this becomes public knowledge, my family will be dragged through the mud. The title is an old and venerable one, and it would kill me to see it besmirched.''

"What is your intention, milord?'' Jack wanted to know. "Your son could have killed me. I can't just forget it.''

"As soon as I learn where Roger keeps rooms, I will personally put him aboard the first ship leaving for America. He'll have to exist on a remittance until he reaches his majority next year. I can assure you he will never return to English shores as long as I'm alive. Furthermore, I will instruct my lawyers to draw up papers naming my younger son my heir. Since the title isn't entailed, I can do as I wish in the matter. Does that satisfy you, milord?''

"I have no desire to destroy a man as fine as you, Montclaire, or bring ruin upon your family. I will leave the matter in your hands.''

"I know where Lord Roger keeps rooms,'' Moira informed the men. "He is lodged above the Hen and Rooster.''

Jack sent her a startled look, but Montclaire merely nodded and thanked her. Then he thanked Jack profusely and rose to leave. He paused at the door.

"I will do everything within my power to squelch gossip concerning you and Moira. It's the least I can do. Forgive me, Moira, for ever doubting your honesty.''

"Within a very short time the gossip won't matter,'' Jack said. "I'm going to make Moira my wife.''

Montclaire's dismay gave Moira insight into how members of the nobility would react should she actually marry Jack. The scandal would ruin him. To his credit, Montclaire recouped nicely. "I wish you good fortune.''

Chapter Sixteen

That night, as she lay in bed, Moira's thoughts ran the gamut of her emotions. Leaving Jack was a painful decision, one she hadn't made easily. Marriage to a duke was out of the question. It just wasn't done. Spence's reaction to Jack's announcement that he was going to marry Moira had indicated the folly of Jack's decision. He had been stunned, to say the least. Spence may be her friend, but friendship extended only so far. His silent disapproval of Jack's intention to marry her spoke louder than words.

Earlier that day, Spence had paid a visit. When she'd left the room to see to refreshments, she lingered outside the door long enough to hear Spence say, "You're treading on dangerous ground, old boy. Granted Moira is a beauty, but you have a duty to society now. You haven't been wholly exonerated yet for the prank we played on them. Set Moira up as your mistress, but don't flout society by marrying beneath you. Black Jack could get away with thumbing his nose at the gentry, but the Duke of

Ailesbury must conform to certain rules.''

She hadn't heard Jack's reply, for she'd fled in tears. What Spence said was true. The longer she remained, the harder it would be to leave. She loved Jack too much to bring him down. She hadn't let on that she'd overheard Spence's remarks as she quietly made plans.

Moira was still wide awake at the stroke of midnight. Her body refused to accept what her mind knew to be the truth: She couldn't have Jack Graystoke. Unfortunately, her body remembered every magical nuance of Jack's lovemaking, every touch, each caress. She burned. So hot, so very hot. Throwing off the covers, she tried to free her mind of the intimate, wonderfully wicked things Jack had done to her, and failed dismally. Though she couldn't have him, she would never stop wanting or needing him. She would never stop loving him.

Jack paced his chamber restively. His face was fiercely feral, his body as tautly drawn as a bowstring. For some reason, Moira had avoided him since he'd proposed marriage. Thank God she hadn't heard Spence voice his disapproval of their marriage, he thought gratefully. But he was determined. He wanted Moira, and he was damn well going to have her! He wasn't sure he liked this duke business. No one gave a bloody damn what he did before a dukedom was thrust upon him. Why should it matter now? Being respectable wasn't all it was made out to be, he decided.

Had he really changed so much? Jack wondered. Drinking no longer interested him, and gambling held no appeal. Womanizing still held a certain allure, but the only woman he wished to bed was Moira. What in the hell had happened to him? Not too long ago, he had been satisfied with his existence, and then a mischievous ghost had intruded into his life. He sincerely hoped Lady Amelia was satisfied and had returned to the dark past where she belonged.

You still have need of me.

The silent words battered against the walls of his brain. He whirled on his heel, and there she was.

"I beg your pardon. I credit you with leading me to Moira, but I have no further need of you, milady. I sent Pettibone to procure a special license so Moira and I can wed. It rests in my bureau right now."

She will not have you.

"What did you say? Of course Moira will have me."

Lady Amelia's inner light flared in anger, then waned.

"Damn it, milady, if you didn't intend for me to have Moira, why did you place her in my path?"

You needed her.

The ghost tilted her head and stared at Jack. A strange sensation raised goose bumps on his flesh. "I'm not disputing that. I also love her," he admitted unashamedly.

Lady Amelia nodded in perfect understanding, then shook her head in vigorous denial.

"What in bloody hell does that mean? You're confusing me."

Tread carefully. Dark forces surround you.

Jack gave her a startled look. "Danger no longer exists. Nothing or no one will take Moira from me. Your haunting of me has its rewards. Lucifer is no longer my master, and I'll probably remain disgustingly sober for the remainder of my days. Gambling and womanizing hold little appeal—I fear perdition will no longer accept me. You may go back to wherever ghosts go when they aren't interfering in people's lives."

Don't let her go.

Jack stared at the ghost in bewilderment. He had no idea how she managed to communicate with him, but he understood every word though she made no sound. If she could transfer her thoughts to him, why couldn't she explain what she meant? When he opened his mouth to voice his complaint, Lady Amelia was slowly blending into the shadows, leaving behind a misty haze that bore no resemblance to the bright spirit of his interfering ancestor.

Jack resumed his pacing, mulling over Lady Amelia's words. What was she trying to tell him? Where was the danger? Suddenly the need to see Moira overwhelmed him. He pictured her naked—so clearly, so beautifully naked and soft, spread beneath his hard body, his dark hand resting on her white thigh. He saw her breasts and felt a jolt of heat sear him. He imagined the triangle between her thighs, crowned with red-gold curls, so tempting he would have sold his soul back to the Devil to be inside her now, to explore the secret path that gave him such unparalleled pleasure.

He was uncomfortably aware that Moira had avoided him today, and it upset him. The almost incandescent urge to see her, to reassure himself that she was still here, in his house, in his life, struck him forcefully. Clad only in skintight breeches, Jack picked up a candlestick and quietly let himself out of his chamber.

Tossing and turning sleeplessly in the rumpled bed, Moira heard the creak of door hinges and jerked upright. She gasped in dismay when she saw Jack's powerful form framed in a golden nimbus of light. She exhaled sharply as he stepped inside and closed the door behind him.

Jack held the candlestick high, easily finding Moira sitting in a puddle of moonlight on the bed, her hair falling about her shoulders like a shimmering copper cloak. He approached the bed in a trance, instantly hard, so damn needy he ached with it. He recalled vividly how it felt to be buried deep inside her, surrounded by the wet promise of her flesh. Moira stared at him, unable to speak past the lump in her throat.

Words were unnecessary as Jack carefully set the candle down and reached for her. Sliding down beside her on the bed, he took her in his arms and kissed her ravenously. Moira closed her eyes and leaned into his kiss, enjoying the pure rapture of it as languid heat coursed through her. The kiss was wondrous, filled with a kind of magic and poignancy she wanted to remember when she was gone.

"You shouldn't be here," Moira whispered when he lifted his mouth. "What if someone saw you? The servants are already gossiping about us."

"Gossip be damned! Besides, no one is about this time of night. And even if we were discovered, it would make little difference. I'm fully recovered, and we'll be married in a day or two. I took the liberty of procuring a special license. I sent Pettibone to my man of business, and he took care of all the details. You can't escape me, love."

Moira shook her head sadly. "I'd hoped by now that you'd gained your senses. I don't wish to create a bigger scandal or ruin your life."

"You talk too much. I hate sneaking into your bed. I want to make it legal. I want everyone to know that you're mine. I'm positive none of the disciples except for Mayhew, Dashwood and Wilkes knew you were at the Dashwood estate that night. None of them will talk for fear of incriminating themselves. There will be no scandal.''

''The scandal will occur when you marry a penniless Irish immigrant.''

''I don't wish to hear another word,'' Jack said with more bite to his voice than he intended. ''You may open your mouth, but only to kiss me.''

She opened her mouth to fling out a retort and Jack took advantage of her parted lips, capturing them with his and thrusting his tongue inside. His kiss was savage, possessive, his face fierce in his ardor. Feeling his ravaging mouth on hers, his tongue delving deep and bold, Moira's resistance melted like hot butter. She kissed him back, with all the love she held in her heart.

Stripping off his breeches, Jack tumbled her back on the bed. Never had he hungered so to possess a woman. He was on fire, bursting, starving. He spread her legs, knelt between them and pulled off her nightgown, running his hands and gaze over her flushed body. She was exquisite. Her face was as lovely as an angel's; her aroused breasts were full and swollen, and her supple thighs quivered with desire. His burning gaze lingered long, tense moments between her thighs as he caressed the mound of copper hair, then dipped his finger into her honeyed sweetness.

Her heard her soft gasp of arousal, at least he hoped it was arousal and not protest, and glanced downward to see her staring at him, her eyes dilated and her lips parted.

''I have no will where you're concerned,'' Moira complained with a gasping moan.

''That's exactly how I want it. You belong to me, Moira.''

He lowered himself atop her, resting on his elbows to keep from crushing her as he kissed her lips, her throat, then took her breast into his mouth, flicking his tongue over the taut nipple.

Moira moaned deliriously. He felt so wonderful straining against her, with the warm flesh of his massive chest pressing against her stomach and his mouth suckling her breast. When he raised slightly and slid his hand between her legs and inside her, the stimulation of both his hands and mouth was so acute Moira cried out and writhed wildly.

Suddenly Jack shifted positions, bringing them both to their sides and curling spoonlike behind her. "Lift your leg, sweetheart." She did so eagerly and felt him slide thick and hard inside her.

The hot, wet tightness of her sheath sent his senses spinning out of control. She was irresistible; so sweetly fashioned and all his. He devoured her like a starving man, thrusting, withdrawing, his hands teasing her breasts and nipples and his mouth showering nipping kisses upon her shoulders, neck and back.

Moira clung to the bedclothes in a frenzy of unbearable pleasure. Her heart was pounding furiously, her breathing sharp and wildly erratic. She was bursting with the heat and hardness of him. She arched fiercely backward, meeting his strokes with savage enthusiasm. Jack plunged into her repeatedly, her soft sobs of pleasure increasing his own pleasure tenfold. With quick deft strokes, he took them both to the edge, then hurled them over and beyond. Moira screamed, then went limp.

Withdrawing from her gently, Jack pulled her into his arms, smoothing tendrils of hair away from her damp forehead as he waited for her pounding heart to return to normal.

"Go to sleep, love. After we're wed, you'll sleep in my arms every night."

Moira slept. Jack stared at her flushed body, bathed in sweat and golden candlelight. I love you, he thought, and the words were as painful as they were sweet. Who would have thought a rake like him would fall in love? Well, perhaps Lady Amelia, he thought ruefully. It angered him to think that Moira's faulty judgment wouldn't permit her to marry a man so far above her in rank. He didn't like to think ill of the dead, but if his cousin hadn't died tragically, he wouldn't be saddled with a dukedom he neither wanted nor deserved. Since he had it, he could do nothing less than wear the title with dignity.

A low rumble of laughter gurgled in his chest. If anyone would have told him six months ago that Black Jack Graystoke would turn respectable, he'd have laughed in his face. His speaking acquaintance with the Devil had almost assured him of a place in perdition, and he had looked forward with relish to meeting Lucifer in person. Debauchery had become a way of life; he'd known no other. He lived for pleasure. Though he hadn't sunk as low as the disciples of the Hellfire Club, the only thing that had kept him from joining their ranks was his high regard for womanhood. In his opinion, no woman deserved defilement. Jack liked women far too much to debase them as the members of the Hellfire Club did their victims.

Jack had intended to seek his own bed after making love to Moira, but during his mental musings his body betrayed him. Or perhaps unconsciously he couldn't bear to leave Moira. Sleep claimed him suddenly and deeply. With Moira resting securely in his arms, he slid effortlessly into slumber.

* * *

Neither the metallic click of the door latch nor the patter of footsteps awakened the sleeping lovers. It wasn't until Jilly opened the curtains, saw the sleeping lovers and screamed that Jack and Moira jolted awake.

Oh, miss, milord, I'm s-s-so sorry,'' Jilly stuttered, throwing her apron over her head and wailing.

Jack gained his wits first, pulling the sheet up to cover their nakedness. "No harm done, Jilly. Stop your cater-wauling. You may leave and come back to attend your mistress in thirty minutes."

"Aye, milord," Jilly said, scooting out of the room like a frightened doe.

The moment the door closed, Moira rounded on Jack, her golden eyes blazing with fury. "What are you still doing here? Do you realize what you've done? My God, you did this on purpose, didn't you? I won't be forced into marriage no matter what you do."

"Damn it, Moira, I didn't mean for this to happen. I fully intended to be gone before the household stirred." He gave her a wry smile. "Although I can't deny I enjoyed sleeping all night with you in my arms. Now you'll have to marry me. Refusal is no longer an option."

Moira was so angry she was shaking. "You came into my room uninvited, seduced me, then deliberately allowed the servants to find us together. I don't deserve that kind of treatment from you."

Jack's temper flared. "What in bloody hell are you talking about? This wasn't deliberate."

Moira's anger simmered dangerously. "I think I should leave."

"Are you mad? Where will you go?"

"I can't live as your mistress. I want to go home, to Ireland."

"I never asked you to be my mistress." His voice was cold, his eyes dark and riveting. "You're being foolish. Bloody hell, Moira, don't make me regret asking you to marry me."

"It was a mistake," Moira argued. "You should never have proposed to me. I . . . don't love you," she lied. "I'm not prepared to handle the scandal that will result if I marry you. Sooner or later, my involvement with the Hellfire Club will become public knowledge." She hoped that wouldn't happen, but she'd already told him that marrying him would cause a scandal, and it hadn't bothered him in the least. It was up to her to save him from himself.

His expression was grim, his voice flat and emotionless. "The hell with love. You're not leaving and that's final. You've given me your virginity, you belong to me. If I can't have you, no one else will." His anger seared her. "You'll be my mistress. I'll set you up somewhere and visit you at my leisure." He could be just as cold and unfeeling as she was.

His dispassionate words chilled Moira to the bone. What had she done? Had she killed the love he bore her? Would he really make her his mistress? The closed, dark look on his face told her he was capable of anything. He looked and sounded more like the Black Jack of old, the debauched rake he'd been when they'd first met.

"I'll let you know when everything is set up. We'll be discreet about our little . . . arrangement. You'll find I'm a generous lover."

Moira's face turned several shades of red. Sweet Virgin, how could he treat her like that? She was no prostitute. So much for love, she thought wryly. She should have known Black Jack Graystoke was too steeped in debauchery to change.

"Go to hell!" Moira shouted. "I don't want anything from you."

Jack's rage erupted in a string of curses that would have singed the ears of a statue. He couldn't ever recall being so bloody angry. It appeared that Moira only wanted him for the pleasure he could give her. If that's all she wanted, he'd give her all the pleasure she could handle. He'd offered her respectability, his name, all he possessed, and she had turned him down. The more he thought about it, the angrier he became.

Jack uncoiled his long form from the bed and pulled on his breeches with angry jerks. Tears lurked behind Moira's eyes as she watched him. She tried to tell herself that her turning down his proposal was making him hateful, that he really didn't mean it. Didn't he realize how much he was hurting her? She was doing him a favor; even his best friend had urged him not to marry her.

"You have no reason to be so hateful to me. Why are you doing this?"

Something dark and dangerous passed over his handsome features. "That's a stupid question, Moira, and it doesn't deserve an answer. Think about what went on between us last night. I can only conclude from your refusal to marry me that you don't feel anything for me. You enjoy the pleasure I give you, yet you make feeble excuses to keep from making a commitment. Do you want the truth, Moira? I'd rather have a mistress than a wife. I only asked because I thought it was what you wanted." Turning abruptly, he stalked from the room.

Moira's eyes followed him. The arousing sight of the taut mounds of his buttocks and strong thighs encased in tight buckskin made her tingle and burn. Sweat popped out on her forehead when she recalled clasping his buttocks as he drove into her and feeling the long muscles of his thighs clench around her. Above his belt, his broad back rippled with ropy tendons, and when he reached out to open the door, she recalled the way his biceps bulged when he strained above her. She bit her tongue to keep from calling him back.

He might hate her now, but one day he'd thank her for her sacrifice. She had always suspected that he'd never wanted a wife, and he'd just confirmed her belief. He ought to know she'd never consent to be a kept woman, hiding her shame in a neat little house where he would come to her in the dead of night and leave before dawn's early light. No, Moira decided, she'd be gone long before "arrangements" were made.

Jilly did not mention that she found Moira and Jack in bed together, and Moira suspected Jack had spoken with her. No matter, by now the entire household knew she was Jack's mistress. Both Matilda and Pettibone were clearly upset at the gossip circulating in the household about Moira and Jack and tried to squelch it. Pettibone was convinced that Jack would do the right thing by Moira, especially after he'd gone through the trouble of procuring a special license to marry.

Pettibone had been the first to note the change in his dissolute master after Moira came into his life and was stunned this morning when Jack told Pettibone he didn't intend to use the license, that he was going to find a house for Moira. Pettibone knew what *that* meant and liked it not at all. He feared his master had reverted back into his debauched ways.

" 'Tis all such a muddle," Pettibone told Matilda.

"Any fool can see the two of them are in love. I'd like to shake some sense into His Lordship. How can he treat Moira like that? 'Tis obvious she was an innocent until she fell into his hands."

"Perhaps we don't know the whole story," Matilda suggested. "I have this feeling that things will work out. Mark my words, Mr. Pettibone, those two will fill this house with children one day."

Pettibone's eyes twinkled merrily. "You're a wise woman, Matilda. I thank God for bringing you into my life. I'm not young anymore, but you make me feel my oats, I swear it."

"And I'm neither young nor pretty. I'm a spinster, Mr. Pettibone. All I know of men is how vile and undisciplined they can be. I'm grateful for men like you and His Lordship."

"Sylvester."

"What?"

"My name is Sylvester. I'd be honored if you'd call me Sylvester when we're alone."

"Sylvester," Matilda repeated shyly. "It's . . . a handsome name. I'd be honored to call you Sylvester." Pettibone thought her smile charming and wished he could keep it there forever.

"What are you two gossiping about?" When Jack had failed to find Pettibone upstairs, he had headed for the kitchen. He wasn't surprised to find his man with Matilda.

Matilda's hands fluttered helplessly. "Oh, milord, we weren't gossiping, I swear it. Sylvester and I were merely discussing household affairs." Her flushed face told Jack that those "affairs" concerned him and Moira. He decided to let it pass without comment and concentrate on something more pleasant.

His mouth twitched with the beginning of a smile, his first since leaving Moira's bed earlier. Somehow he brought it under control. "Sylvester? Who, pray tell, is Sylvester?"

Pettibone cleared his throat and looked Jack in the eye. "I am Sylvester, milord."

"Sylvester?" Jack repeated, shaking his head in disbelief. "How have you managed to keep that hidden all these years? To my knowledge, no one has ever known your first name, or even that you had one."

" 'Tis a fine name, isn't it, milord?" Matilda said, eyeing Pettibone with uncommon fondness.

"Indeed," Jack agreed, keeping his mirth well under control. From the way Pettibone was glaring at him, he assumed the old reprobate was warning him not to repeat what he had just learned.

"Did you want me for anything in particular, milord?" Pettibone asked, mustering his dignity.

"I wanted to inform you that I'll be out most of the day, looking at houses."

Pettibone stiffened. "Very good, milord. I hope Lady Amelia understands," he mumbled as Jack left the kitchen.

When Moira learned that Jack would be gone all day, she used his absence to good advantage. As much as she hated doing it, she took enough funds from the strongbox in Jack's desk to buy passage to Ireland. Somehow she'd pay him back, she vowed as she calculated how much she'd need to see her safely home. Later, when the household was least likely to note her absence, she sneaked out of the house, hired a hackney to take her to the docks and found a ship leaving for Ireland the following day. She returned before Jack came home late that afternoon.

*   *   *

Fool!

Jack jerked upright, pulling the sheet around him as he searched the dark room for his nocturnal visitor. Lady Amelia was standing by the window, her back to him.

Fool. Why did you not heed my warning?

"Bloody hell, milady, you're not making sense. I offered for Moira and she turned me down flat. 'Tis obvious she doesn't want me for a husband. Therefore, I'll be her lover and protector. She has a crazy notion that marrying me will ruin my life. Damn! If I had remained Sir Jack instead of becoming Lord Jack, Moira wouldn't be so dead set against marrying me. On the other hand," he mused thoughtfully, "had I remained Sir Jack I might have married Lady Victoria, and what a tragedy that would have been."

Lady Amelia would not be placated. She whirled in a froth of iridescent light and disappeared in a puff of smoke.

"Damn it, just like a woman," Jack muttered, punching his pillow and settling back down.

He needed a drink but feared that if he fell back into his old dissolute ways, Lady Amelia would return and haunt him for the remainder of his days. He had enough problems without a disgruntled spirit complicating his life. He closed his eyes and tried to sleep. When that failed, he tried recalling in vivid detail every erotic aspect of Moira's luscious body and delightful curves. He was still angry at her, still enraged that she had spurned him. He wanted to charge into her chamber and shake her until she came to her senses.

But after careful consideration, he decided a mistress was far less trouble than a wife. He could well imagine

Moira's reaction when he told her he had leased a house for her. She had angered him so thoroughly that he'd gone off in a fit. But he'd lucked upon a perfect place. Fortunately, he now had the funds to keep a mistress in style. Of one thing he was certain: She wasn't going to leave him. He wanted her and he was damn well going to have her. He wanted her for a wife, but would settle for a mistress.

Moira squeezed her eyes shut to keep the tears from falling. The thought that this was the last time she'd be sleeping in this bed was an unhappy one. If only she could feel Jack's arms around her one final time, she thought with increasing sadness. Experience the wondrous joy of his lovemaking. Feel the vibrant power of his body entering hers, consuming her in flaming splendor. Unfortunately, Jack's hurtful words had erected a wall between them that seemed impossible to breach. Her own anger had been no less daunting. Whether he meant them or not, his insults had hurt her deeply.

Suddenly Moira felt an eerie presence. Her senses came alive; her nerves tingled. Her heart beat furiously, and beads of sweat popped out of her forehead. What she felt was surreal, something beyond reason or explanation. She searched the chamber, her gaze flitting from corner to corner, shadow to shadow, her heart beating like a triphammer. When she spied a figure clad in shimmering light, she gave a frightened yelp.

Lady Amelia sent Moira a searching glance, then seemed to evaporate through the closed door, leaving a trail of mist in her wake.

"Wait! Don't go. Who are you?"

Leaping from bed, Moira flung open the door, glanced

down the hall and saw the ghost pause before Jack's chamber. She watched in trepidation as the ghost disappeared into Jack's room through the closed door. Without considering the consequences, Moira burst headlong into the chamber.

"Where is she?"

Jack sat up, blinking in disbelief. Was he dreaming?

"Is that you, Moira? What's wrong? Are you ill?"

Moira's bare feet whispered against the worn carpet as she approached the bed. "I'm fine. She came in here. I saw her."

Rubbing sleep from his eyes, Jack wrapped a sheet around his middle, rose from bed and lit a candle. "Saw whom?"

Moira began trembling, afraid she was losing her mind. A glowing nimbus of candlelight revealed an empty room save for her and Jack. "She came in here; I know she did." Her voice held a hint of panic.

Moira's trembling became so pronounced that Jack placed an arm around her shoulders and led her to the bed. "You're cold. Hop in bed and tell me what you saw."

When Moira seemed reluctant, Jack swept her from her feet and carried her to his bed. Then he pulled a blanket over her and slid in beside her. "Now, tell me what frightened you so."

The welcome heat of Jack's body surrounded her, soothed her, made her feel warm and safe. She didn't need to touch him to sense the leashed strength in him.

Moira swallowed and licked her lips. "At first I thought it was merely a patch of moonlight shining through the window, but then I realized I was seeing some kind of eerie phenomenon. It was a ghost; I'm sure of it. I couldn't swear to it, but I vow the ghost was a woman.''

''A woman?'' Jack asked in dismay. Lady Amelia had never, to his knowledge of Graystoke history, appeared to anyone but family. ''What did she look like? How was she dressed? Did she frighten you?''

''I saw a light,'' Moira mused, vaguely aware that she had felt no fear, only curiosity. ''It was not threatening in any way. The figure of a woman appeared within the light, though how I knew that isn't clear.''

''Did she say anything?''

''Not a word. She left through the closed door before I got a good look at her. I rushed into the hall to follow and saw her entering your chamber, again through a closed door.'' She flushed and looked away. ''I'm sorry, I must have been dreaming. I didn't mean to disturb you. It was wrong of me to burst in on you without knocking.''

''I can't believe you saw Lady Amelia. It isn't like her to appear to anyone who isn't family.''

''Lady Amelia,'' Moira repeated, vastly relieved. ''I thought I was losing my mind. Mr. Pettibone told me her story. It's quite sad.''

Jack searched her face, gilded with candlelight and achingly beautiful. Her honey-warm eyes stared back at him, and her red lips looked sweet enough to taste. He felt a melting heat start in his loins and flow thick and hot through his veins. He wanted her. She was his mistress, and there was no reason he shouldn't avail himself of her charms, was there? She was here, in his bed, even though it was a meddling ghost who had brought her to his chamber, and he damn well was going to seize the opportunity to make love to her.

''Are you still frightened?'' Jack asked.

Moira shook her head. ''Not anymore.'' How could she

be frightened with Jack's strong arms surrounding her? She could feel the hairs on his legs prickling her skin and . . . She went still, realizing that Jack was nude beneath the covers. She exhaled raggedly, all thought skidding to a halt.

"Are you all right, Moira?" Jack said, mistaking her stillness for fright. "Personally, I don't believe in ghosts." He glanced about the chamber for his mischievous ancestor and prayed she'd forgive him. "But Lady Amelia is a well-meaning soul, if a bit meddlesome."

"I'm not frightened. I'm . . ." Her voice faltered. "Oh, God, I can't think. I shouldn't have barged in on you."

"You're my mistress, you have every right to be here in my bed." His careless words cut her to the quick.

"Regardless of all your grand plans, I'm not your mistress, nor will I ever be," Moira retorted tartly.

"You're one bloody exasperating female, Moira O'Toole," Jack said with asperity. "You refused to marry me once, and I'll not ask again. Black Jack Graystoke was never lacking in pride. Unfortunately, I can't resist you. You're pure temptation, lady."

His mouth moved over hers with slow seduction, his tongue a weapon of the Devil as it delved within and explored the sweet depths. Before she sank into an abyss of sinful pleasure, Moira convinced herself that Jack was more Devil than man. As his drugging kisses melted her bones, she wished she had the courage to remain with him and ruin his life.

"Your arms and kisses lead to perdition, Lord Graystoke," Moira said, pulling away from him though it cost her dearly. "I'm not your whore, and you can't treat me like one."

Anger lent her strength as she leaped out of bed and fled Jack's chamber.

"You're wrong, Moira," Jack called after her. "You're mine, any way I want you. You can run now, but you won't go far. I was Black Jack longer than I've been Duke of Ailesbury, and Black Jack has ways of getting what he wants."

Sweet Christ, he swore beneath his breath, how could a woman bring him so low?

Chapter Seventeen

Moira awoke to a dull gray day shrouded in misty fog that looked as dismal as she felt. Her ship sailed at noon, and come hell or high water, she was going to be on it. She couldn't marry Jack and she wouldn't be his mistress. After the way he had treated her last night, she felt as if she no longer knew him. She realized that spurning his marriage proposal had wounded his pride, but she hadn't expected him to act so hatefully. Were all men so thin-skinned, she wondered miserably, or was Jack showing his true colors? She'd never really seen the dark side of him, only the good, and she prayed his abrupt reversal would not be permanent. Loving him as she did, it was difficult to believe he had behaved so callously.

Deciding not to tempt fate by taking breakfast with Jack, Moira used the time to stuff a few belongings into a small canvas bag she had found in the closet. She feared that seeing Jack again would rob her of the courage to leave. Her relief was profound when, through the window, she saw Jack enter a coach bearing the Ailesbury crest.

The coach rattled off and disappeared into the fog. The clip-clop of horses' hooves on cobblestones resounded with a hollow, eerie finality.

By the time Jilly arrived with a tray of tea and toast, Moira had hidden the bag beneath the bed and composed herself. The little maid, still flustered over finding Jack and Moira in bed, barely looked at Moira as she set the tray down and inquired if there was anything else her mistress needed.

"As a matter of fact there is," Moira said, settling her face into a pained expression. "I have a terrible headache. Ask Matilda to fix me a headache powder, then see that no one disturbs me the rest of the day. I'll probably sleep all day. Use the time to do whatever you please; I'll have no need of you for several hours."

"Oh, Miss Moira, thank you," Jilly gushed. "Colin said he'd take me to see my family the first chance I got. Ma is doing poorly."

"Then by all means go," Moira urged. "Tell Pettibone I've given you leave to visit your family and that Colin is to take you in the carriage."

"Yes, ma'am. I'll bring your headache remedy right away. And thank you again. I've been ever so worried about Ma." She turned to leave, then paused. "I don't think any less of you for . . . I don't care what anyone says, you're a good woman." Having said her piece, she fled out the door.

Moira's expression turned solemn as she watched Jilly scoot from the chamber. The maid's words served to confirm her belief that she and Jack were the talk of London. The scandal surrounding them wasn't likely to disappear until something more noteworthy appeared to take its place. Her decision to leave Jack hadn't been lightly made, and she knew it was a good one. Last night Jack had made her feel like a whore, and she didn't like the feeling. His temper had been awesome and his words contemptible. How dare he think he could set her up as his mistress against her will!

The house was quiet. Jilly had left with Colin, and just minutes ago she heard Pettibone and Matilda leave the house to do the marketing. With Pettibone gone, the maids were probably taking their ease in the kitchen, drinking tea and gossiping. The hall clock had just struck nine o'clock, and Moira had three hours to reach London Pool to board the packet, *Emerald Queen*. The hall was empty when Moira opened the door and peered out. Retrieving her bag from beneath the bed, she quietly left her chamber and negotiated the front stairs without mishap. She had one anxious moment, when the front door gave a squeak of protest as she slipped outside.

Damp mist sent icy fingers along her spine, but she was grateful for the way it shrouded her tiny figure in concealing gray fog. Within seconds, she was no longer visible from the house. Due to the fog, it took Moira over thirty minutes to find a hackney, but she still arrived well before the ship unfurled its sails and inched down the Thames. Moira watched from the deck as dense fog swallowed the ship and obliterated the shore. When she glanced landward, she saw nothing but indistinct shapes looming through a soupy gray mist.

Force of habit made Moira reach up to grasp her locket, which always comforted her in trying times. A cry of dismay left her lips when she realized it was missing. The loss struck her forcefully. The locket had been more than a keepsake; it was a link with her past. Now she had nothing.

*   *   *

Jack returned home shortly before the dinner hour. When he inquired about Moira, he was told she was suffering from a headache and had been in her room all day. Immediately Jack felt a twinge of guilt. He shouldn't have been so hard on Moira last night, but he'd been so damn angry that he'd reverted back to his old self, a man he didn't like anymore. She had wounded his pride and hurt him deeply when she refused to marry him. He'd offered her his heart, his home, all his wealth, and she had turned her nose up at his offer.

Moira foolishly thought he'd sit back and let her leave him, but she hadn't counted on his possessiveness where she was concerned. She was his; no one else could have her. If she'd rather be his mistress, then so be it. Since last night, his temper had cooled somewhat, but he was still determined to install her in the house he had leased and see how she enjoyed being his mistress. Perhaps then she'd know what she had given up by spurning his legitimate proposal.

He'd never before told another woman he loved her— and he was unlikely to do so again, given the answer he'd received from Moira. Perhaps it wasn't love he felt for Moira; maybe it was lust. He couldn't keep his bloody hands off her. Damn Moira for being so damn stubborn and damn Lady Amelia for bringing them together.

Dinner was a dismal affair. Jack waited for Moira to join him, and when she didn't, he asked Matilda to hold dinner. He sat in silence, brooding over Moira's absence and his unquenchable need for the little vixen. Finally his temper snapped. He called Jilly from the kitchen.

"Jilly, please inform Miss Moira that I require her presence at the table."

Jilly bobbed a curtsey and hurried from the dining chamber. After a long interval, the maid returned. Her face was flushed, her expression pained. When she reached Jack's side, she threw her apron over her head and wailed.

Jack rose abruptly from his chair and threw down his napkin. "For God's sake, Jilly, what is it now? Is something wrong with Moira?"

"I can't find her, milord. I've looked everywhere."

Alarm bells went off in Jack's head. "What do you mean, you can't find her?"

"I fear she's gone, milord. Some of her clothing is missing."

"Get Pettibone." When Jilly failed to move fast enough, he shouted, "Now!" Hearing the ruckus, Matilda wandered in from the kitchen.

Pettibone came bustling into the dining room, Jilly hard on his heels. "Jilly told me, milord. I can't imagine where Miss Moira has gone."

"When did you see her last?"

"Yesterday, milord. Jilly brought her a headache powder early this morning, and Moira gave her leave to visit her ill mother. Then Matilda and I did the marketing. I thought Miss Moira was still in her room, but she could have left while we were all out."

"Do any of you have any idea where she might have gone?" His temper was near to exploding, but he kept it carefully under control. How could she do this to him?

"Not a clue. Except," Pettibone added with a pained look, "I found money missing from your strongbox today when I took some coins for the marketing. Do you think Moira could have stolen the money?" He sent Jack a searching glance. "Perhaps she had good reason."

Jack gave him a quelling look. "Are you in cahoots with Lady Amelia?"

"I beg your pardon?"

"Never mind." Jack turned to Matilda. "Well, did Moira mention anything to you about leaving?"

Matilda wrung her hands, plainly upset. "At one time, milord. After we left Sir Dashwood's estate, she said she was going to her brother's home near Kilkenny, in Ireland. She promised to take me with her."

Pettibone looked troubled. "That was before Lord Jack engaged me as his housekeeper," Matilda was quick to add when she saw the devastated look on Pettibone's face. "Perhaps she's gone to Ireland."

"Shall I book passage on the next packet to Ireland, milord?" Pettibone asked.

"No!" His outburst startled Pettibone. "Tomorrow, I'll inquire if anyone fitting Moira's description booked passage to Ireland on a ship sailing today."

"Will you follow, milord?" Pettibone wanted to know.

"I have no hold on Moira; she can do as she pleases. You may serve dinner now, Matilda."

Though his voice was cold and impassive, he felt as if he had just taken a blow to his gut. He couldn't believe Moira would go so far as to steal money from him in order to pay for passage to Ireland. Did she hate him so much? Had he gone too far by demanding that she become his mistress? If she hadn't refused his proposal, he would never have considered such an arrangement. Damn it, what did she want from him? When she refused his love, he'd withdrawn it in anger and offered something less respectable, wanting to hurt her as she'd hurt him. All he'd succeeded in doing was losing her. It would be a cold day in hell before he'd chase after her. His begging days were over.

"Milord." Suddenly Jack became aware that Matilda still stood quietly at his side.

"Is there something you wish to say, Matilda?"

"Aye, milord, just this." She dug in the pocket of her apron and produced a shiny gold object.

Jack held out his hand, and Matilda placed Moira's locket in his palm. He clasped it tightly, imagining it still held the warmth of Moira's flesh. "Where did you get this?" He could see at a glance that the fragile chain had broken.

Matilda looked him straight in the eye and said, "In your bed, milord. 'Tis Miss Moira's. She never took it off." Her voice held a wealth of censure.

Jack had the grace to flush. "I'm aware of that. Thank you. I'll take care of it. About dinner, Matilda—I find I'm no longer hungry. I'm going to my room. Pettibone can bring me a tray later."

"As you wish, milord."

Sitting in a wing chair before the hearth, Jack turned the locket over and over in his hands, recalling the countless times in the past months he'd seen Moira hanging on to the locket in stressful moments. It seemed to have an almost calming effect on her. Other than the fact that it had once belonged to her mother and grandmother, he knew little about the delicate piece of jewelry. Though not an expensive or valuable piece, it seemed to hold sentimental value for Moira.

Jack felt like an interloper as he carefully pried open the locket with his thumbnail. He had no idea what he'd find, but it certainly wasn't a faded miniature of a man in uniform. The image was so old that it had cracked in several places, but enough of it remained to reveal a pleasant-looking young man still in the bloom of youth. Taking a closer look, Jack was puzzled at the familiarity of the man in the picture. It was all very strange. Pettibone arrived a short time later with a tray of food, which Jack pushed aside with a curious lack of appetite.

"I'm going out, Pettibone," Jack informed his startled servant. "Get out my evening clothes and tell Colin to bring the Ailesbury coach around. I think I'll visit White's tonight and make the usual rounds."

"You're going out, milord?"

Jack's dark brows shot upward. "Do you have a problem with that, Pettibone?"

"No, milord. It's just that you haven't indulged in . . . er . . . excesses lately, and I thought . . ."

"Then I've been remiss, haven't I?"

Once Pettibone left, Jack aimed his boldly challenging gaze into the dark corners of the room. "If you can hear me, Lady Amelia, don't bother lecturing me. I've had enough of your interference. Your meddling has brought me nothing but heartache. I've gone soft-headed and look what it got me. Exactly nothing. I've inherited a dukedom I never wanted and lost a woman because of it."

If Lady Amelia heard, she chose neither to respond nor materialize. But Jack wasn't about to end his tirade. "I've decided to reacquaint myself with the Devil. Perdition has never looked more attractive than it does now." He strode purposefully to his liquor chest and poured a generous helping of whiskey into a glass. He lifted it in salute to the absent ghost and downed it in one gulp. His laughter reverberated in the room long after he left. He neither saw nor heard Lady Amelia, who hovered near the ceiling, gazing down upon him in pity.

Foolish man. 'Tis too late. You cannot return to your old ways.

A hush came over the crowd as Jack strolled into the game room at White's. It was his first foray into public since his prank was unmasked and he'd inherited the dukedom. He had no idea how his peers would accept him, and he cared even less. He felt more like Black Jack right now than he did Lord Jack, and Black Jack didn't give a fig what the macaroni dandies prancing around in high heels and satin breeches thought about him.

Jack tried to hide his surprise when Lord and Lady Crenshaw, respected leaders of London society, greeted him cordially. "Ailesbury, good to see you out and about again. Dreadful about your cousin, most dreadful indeed," Lord Crenshaw said.

"Yes, indeed," Lady Crenshaw echoed. "We're having a rout in honor of our daughter's eighteenth birthday next week. I'll send an invitation around. There aren't too many eligible bachelors of your standing left, and I'm sure you'll find many invitations coming your way."

The Crenshaws made way for the Gormans, and after that it was like a tidal wave of people coming forward to greet him. Most were the cream of society and had daughters of marriageable age. A few weeks ago, these same people saw fit to shield their innocent daughters from Black Jack Graystoke. It was amazing what a title could do for one.

"Jack, I didn't expect to see you here tonight. I've missed you, milord."

Jack smiled at Victoria. He no longer needed to marry money, but that didn't mean he couldn't dally with her.

"You're looking fetching tonight, milady. I'd forgotten how beautiful you were."

Victoria preened for his benefit and said archly, "They're playing the waltz, milord. Will you dance with me?"

Jack took her hand and led her into the next room, where dancers crowded the floor. "I thought you were angry with me, Victoria," Jack said as he whirled her around in a graceful circle.

"I was, but you're too intriguing a man to remain angry with for long. You were naughty to play a trick like that on me. I trust you sent your little whore packing."

Jack smiled through eyes as cold as ice. "Moira is no longer with me."

"I'm willing to take up where we left off with no hard feelings," Victoria cooed coyly.

"I'm no longer in the market for a wife," Jack drawled. "However, I'm open to other . . . suggestions."

Victoria gasped angrily, then quickly quelled her temper. She felt strongly that once she had Black Jack in her bed again, he'd change his mind. It had been far too long since she'd sampled his extraordinary brand of loving. She wished now she hadn't agreed to an assignation with Lord Renfrew later tonight. She could always beg off, but Renfrew wasn't a man to cross. "I'm not free tonight. Call on me tomorrow."

With a jolt of insight, Jack realized he felt nothing for Lady Victoria, not even passing interest. He wondered if the man she was sleeping with tonight knew she was already lining up her next lay. The old Black Jack wouldn't have cared who or how many men Victoria slept with as long as she gave him pleasure when it was his turn, but Lord Jack was somewhat more discerning. After making love to Moira, who had been pure and unsullied before he'd taken her virginity, Victoria held little appeal. Damn, he could wring Lady Amelia's neck for giving him a conscience.

"I'll call on you if I'm not busy," Jack temporized as the dance ended. "If you'll excuse me, milady, I think I'll try my hand at cards."

He made a quick getaway, counting himself lucky that Victoria wasn't his wife. On his way to the card room, he stopped off for liquid refreshment. With a large whiskey in his hand, he cut his way through the fog of cigar smoke, looking for a table with an empty chair. He spied Spence at one of the gaming tables and headed in that direction.

"Mind if I join you, gentlemen?"

"Jack! I'll be damned!" Spence crowed, jumping up and pulling out a chair for Jack. "Never expected to see you here. Just like old times, eh? Is that whiskey you're drinking? 'Bout time you saw the folly of your ways. I was beginning to think you'd reformed."

"Never say it," Jack said, sitting down and nodding to the other players.

Jack lost heavily. His mind wasn't on cards. His usual sharp card sense was blunted by the numerous whiskeys he was consuming. His mouth tasted like the inside of a trash bin, and a splitting headache began behind his eyes. He was beginning to think he was no longer capable of playing the debauched rake. Throwing in his hand, he rose somewhat unsteadily and announced that he'd had enough for one night.

"I'll go with you, Jack," Spence said. He sensed Jack's preoccupation and wondered what was bothering him. He was playing like a novice and drinking far too much, even for Black Jack.

"No need. I have my coach."

" 'Tis early yet. I'll accompany you home and we can have a good chat. It's been a while. Moira is well, I trust?"

At the mention of Moira, Jack's lips thinned into an angry line. "Come along, if you will, but I'm in no mood for foolish questions."

Jack lapsed into a brooding silence, which continued until he stepped down from the coach at Graystoke Manor. A grim-faced Pettibone opened the door.

"Brandy, Pettibone, in the study," Jack barked in passing.

"Milord, I don't think . . ."

"You're not paid to think, Pettibone."

When Jack entered the study, Spence held back to speak to Pettibone. "What in bloody hell was that all about? What's gotten into Jack?"

"Miss Moira left. His Grace is taking it badly."

"Why did she leave? Jack was crazy about her. He'd have given her the world if she'd but ask. He even wanted to marry her."

"I suspect he proposed but Miss Moira refused."

"The lady has good sense. It wouldn't have been proper. The Duke of Ailesbury has a standard to uphold. As much as I like Moira, marrying her would have been a mistake, one Jack would regret one day."

"Spence, are you coming or do you intend chatting all night with Pettibone?" Jack's voice held a plethora of impatience. Spence shrugged and followed him into the study. A few minutes later, Pettibone arrived with a full bottle of brandy and two glasses.

Connie Mason

"Close the door behind you, Pettibone, and go to bed. I won't require your services tonight."

"What's gotten into you, Jack?" Spence charged. "I've never heard you speak so sharply to Pettibone. The man worships you."

"I don't deserve his regard," Jack said plaintively. "I'm a black-hearted bastard; neither title nor wealth will change that. Even Lady Amelia has given up on me."

"Bloody hell, Jack, you're talking in riddles. What happened?"

"I'll tell you what happened. Moira left me. I'm almost certain she took ship for Ireland, but I won't know for sure until I inquire at the freight office tomorrow. I asked her to marry me, for God's sake, and she refused."

"She has more sense than you," Spence muttered. "Accept the fact that you need to marry someone of your own class. Hell, I like Moira, you know that, but I'm being practical."

"Practical be damned! I fancied myself in love with the girl, Spence. She was untouched until I took her virginity. She refused to marry me. I became enraged and demanded that she become my mistress. I even went out and leased a house for her. I planned to set her up in grand style. In my anger, I even convinced myself that I didn't really want a wife, that Moira would make a far better mistress."

"So what happened?"

"I should have known Moira couldn't accept my terms. She's too proud to live as a kept woman, so she left."

Digging into his pocket, he pulled out Moira's locket and turned it over and over in his fingers. It still held the warmth of her flesh. He sprung the lock and squinted at the miniature inside.

"What's that?" Spence asked curiously.

"Moira's locket. The chain broke, and Matilda found it after Moira left."

"May I see it?"

Jack tossed it to him with studied indifference. Spence caught it deftly and held it to the light. He gazed thoughtfully at the faded image of a young man, his brows furrowed in concentration. "I swear I've seen this very same picture before, only on a grander scale."

Jack shook his head to clear it. He regretted having taken that first drink tonight. Alcohol never solved a damn thing. It had taken him nearly thirty years to come to that conclusion.

"Are you sure? Think, man! I don't know what this will mean to Moira, but it has to be important or she wouldn't carry an image of the man. Take it and see what you can find out. The man is wearing an English army uniform; that should help."

Spence pocketed the locket and sent him an oblique look. "Damn it, Jack, you're head over heels for the girl, aren't you?"

"I might have been at one time. Now I don't know what I feel," Jack admitted bleakly. "I've never felt this way before—as if I've been chewed up and spit out. Bloody hell! I have this urge to lose myself in sweet-scented woman's flesh."

Spence grinned in perfect understanding. This was the Jack he knew and admired. "I know just the place. Madame Fifi has the best girls in town, but of course you know that."

"It won't work," Jack said regretfully. "Victoria was more than willing, but my mind utterly rejected the notion. Not to mention my flesh, which shriveled at the thought of bedding Victoria, or any other woman. My God, Spence, Moira has bloody well emasculated me! If I didn't know better, I'd think she put an Irish curse on me. You saw me at the gaming table tonight—I couldn't do anything right. Whiskey tastes like ashes, and fine brandy turns sour in my mouth.''

Spence shook his head in commiseration. ''You're in a bad way, mate. Go to bed. You'll feel more the thing after a good night's sleep. In the meantime, I'll try to find out what I can about the man in the miniature.''

Jack ignored Spence's advice. Instead of going to bed as his friend suggested, he sprawled in a chair before the dying fire and continued to swill brandy. Pettibone found him there shortly after dawn, his head slumped against his chest and a broken glass lying on the floor beside him. Pettibone sighed and shook his head. It was just like old times, he thought sadly, when Jack had returned home after a night of carousing too foxed to get himself to bed. Unfolding an afghan that lay on a nearby bench, he carefully covered Jack and tiptoed out of the study.

Closing the door quietly behind him, Pettibone looked around cautiously and whispered into the darkness, ''If you're watching over him, Lady Amelia, I implore you to do something. I had such hopes for His Grace.'' Breaking off abruptly and looking embarrassed at addressing someone or something that might or might not exist, he walked away with all the dignity he could muster. It wouldn't do to be found pleading with a ghost.

Moira felt ill the moment the *Emerald Queen* left London Pool. The days she spent in the tiny, airless cabin were among the most miserable she'd ever encountered. She couldn't understand why. She had thoroughly enjoyed the sea voyage from Ireland to England, so why was she sick now? Both the English Channel and the Irish Sea were calm and the air balmy for late summer, but she had vomited continually, mostly in the morning. By the time the packet docked at Rossiare Harbor, she was so weak she could barely stand.

Setting her feet on dry land helped somewhat, but not entirely. Lugging her single piece of baggage, Moira located the freight office and bought a ticket to Kilkenny on a public conveyance. It took all the meager coins left in her reticule, leaving Moira no money with which to purchase a bite of breakfast. Not that she was all that hungry. Her stomach still churned, and the green tinge around her lips attested to her early morning illness.

The public coach was crowded, and Moira squeezed in between an enormous woman carrying a basket of food and a priest whose thin lips moved in constant prayer. Moira couldn't remember the trip to Kilkenny being so long. Though the fat woman talked constantly, Moira heard little of what she said. When she kindly offered Moira a greasy sausage from her basket, the smell alone made her gag. Yet it was a food Moira had enjoyed enormously in the past. She could find no explanation for her delicate stomach and concentrated on holding further sickness at bay.

The coach rolled into Kilkenny in the waning hours of afternoon. Both the priest and the woman were going on to Carlow, and Moira bid them both good-bye and hurried off. Having spent her entire life in the area, Moira knew the village well, so she wasn't surprised when she was greeted by name by shopkeepers and townspeople.

"So yer back, are ye, lass?" the grocer called as she walked by his shop. "Yer brother will be glad of it."

"I hope so, Mr. Hurlehey," Moira called back, giving a little wave as she passed by. She still had five miles to walk before reaching her brother's farm, and her bag was getting heavier by the minute.

"Wait, lass, are ye goin' ta walk all the way?"

Moira stopped and looked back. "Aye. Kevin didn't know I was coming, so he won't be here to meet me."

"If ye wait until I've done up this order for Mrs. Bailey, I'll take ye in me wagon. Her place is near yours, and I can swing by and drop ye off when I deliver her order."

"That's very kind of you, Mr. Hurlehey."

A short time later, Moira was seated beside Mr. Hurlehey on the unsprung seat of his wagon, listening to his recitation of all that had transpired in her absence. "Too bad about Kayla McGuire," he lamented, shaking his gray head. "The fever took her not two weeks after ye left. Left her husband with two babes still in nappies."

"Oh, no," Moira said, aghast. "Poor Paddy. However is he managing?" Kayla and Paddy were the O'Tooles' closest neighbors. Somewhat older and more down-to-earth than Kayla, Paddy was a perfect foil for his spirited wife. Moira knew Paddy must be devastated by his wife's death.

"Paddy's mother is looking after the babes, but she's too old and sickly for it, and Paddy knows it. Rumor has it he's looking for a wife."

"I hope he finds one soon," Moira said with a hint of compassion. She was genuinely fond of Paddy and hated to see his two young children grow up motherless.

"We're nearly there," Mr. Hurlehey said as they drove down the rutted lane leading to the O'Toole farm. When the sturdy stone structure came into sight, Moira suddenly realized how much she had missed not just the place, but the people who lived there.

Kevin came from the barn when he heard the rattle of wheels and the clip-clop of hooves. The wagon had barely pulled to a stop when Kevin recognized Moira and started running. Jumping down from the seat, Moira rushed to meet him, falling into his arms with a sob of pure joy.

Chapter Eighteen

Once Kevin got over the shock of seeing Moira, he led her into the stone cottage that had been their home since their birth. Kevin's wife Katie was bending over the stove, her belly big with child. The children—Allie, Mary and Liam—were seated at the table doing their letters when Moira walked into the big cheerful kitchen.

"Moira!" the children cried in unison as they crowded around her.

Kissing each one in turn, Moira couldn't have asked for a grander welcome. Her homecoming was tempered only by the aching sadness of leaving the man she loved.

"Why didn't you write and tell me you were coming?" Kevin chided. "I would have met your ship. Are you home for good, then?"

Moira nodded, unable to speak past the lump in her throat.

"You look terrible," Katie exclaimed in dismay. "Sit down. I'll fix you a cup of tea."

"I'll be fine now that I'm on dry land again," Moira

said dismissively as she eyed Katie's protruding stomach. "Why didn't you tell me you were in the family way before I left?"

"I didn't want to worry you, dear," Katie said gently. She sent Kevin a tender look. "We're hoping for another boy."

"We missed you, Auntie Moira," Allie said, hugging Moira tightly. Red-haired and green-eyed, Allie was five and the demonstrative one of the family. Mary was seven, a shy, quiet beauty with dark auburn hair and golden brown eyes very much like Moira's. Liam was the oldest and took his responsibility seriously.

"And I missed you, love," Moira replied, giving the children another hug before dropping down into the nearest chair.

"You're exhausted," Katie said astutely. "Are you sure you're well?"

"Now that Katie's mentioned it, you *don't* look good," Kevin said worriedly. "What happened in England? You should have stayed home where we can take care of you. We may be poor, but we're not destitute."

"You worry too much, Kevin," Moira said, brushing aside his concern. "I'll be fine in a day or two."

"Go outside and play, children," Kevin said, sensing Moira's reticence to speak frankly before them. "Lessons are over for today."

Glad to escape the dreary world of letters and numbers, the children fled out the door. The moment they disappeared from sight, Kevin turned to Moira.

"Would you like to tell me about it, lass? Something is bothering you. What happened in England?"

"Give Moira a chance to catch her breath and rest," Katie said, sensing Moira's distress. "Questions can come later. Liam took over your old room, but he can move into the loft. Go on up, dear. I'll brew you a nice cup of tea and bring it to you later.''

''You're too good to me,'' Moira said, very close to tears. ''I wanted to help out so badly, but things didn't work out like I planned.''

''They never do,'' Kevin said astutely. ''Things will look brighter after a bit of a rest.''

Moira thought differently but held her tongue. Kevin had enough problems without taking hers on. The man she loved wasn't who she thought he was. Why couldn't Jack understand her refusal to marry him was for his own good? Why did he have to spoil everything by demanding that she become his mistress?

Moira rose unsteadily. ''You're right, brother, I do need a rest. We'll talk later.'' Her stomach was churning again, and this time there was no movement beneath her feet to explain it. Perhaps she *was* ill.

''What do you think happened?'' Kevin asked once Moira had left the room. ''I was against Moira leaving in the first place, but you know how stubborn the lass can be.'' His golden brown eyes turned dark with worry.

Katie stretched, placing her hands at the small of her back to ease her burden. ''I don't know, but I'll bet it involves a man.''

Kevin stared at her, aghast. ''A man? Our little Moira? She never expressed interest in any man before.''

''Our *little* Moira is a woman,'' Katie reminded him. ''Only time will tell what's troubling her.''

Jack tried his level best to maintain his reputation as a rakehell. He flirted outrageously, drank prodigiously and lost so much money at cards that Spence began to think his friend was possessed. Even Pettibone, long accustomed to his employer's decadent ways, became alarmed at Jack's accelerated journey to perdition. He and Matilda discussed it at length and came to the conclusion that Jack didn't give a tinker's damn what became of him. Obviously he was mourning Moira and too stubborn to do anything about it.

Jack couldn't muster the energy to care about his backslide to perdition. The only thing that truly angered him was his inability to raise sufficient interest in a woman to bed her. He flirted, stole kisses in dark corners and made appropriately suggestive remarks. But nothing stirred him. Consequently, he turned more and more to the soothing oblivion found at the bottom of a bottle. And cards. Drunk or sober, his losses at the gaming tables became the talk of the town. Since he now had plenty of money to gamble away, Jack paid little heed to the amount of his losses.

Spence had warned him that he'd soon fritter away the Ailesbury fortune, but even that failed to hinder his compulsive, irresponsible behavior. He was short with Pettibone, disagreeable to almost everyone and nearly consumed with self-loathing. During this time Lady Amelia's ghost, whether out of anger or disgust, failed to materialize. Jack assumed she had given up on him, and he thought it was about time.

Moira did her utmost to help out wherever she could but was aware that she wasn't the same girl who had left the farm several months ago. Easing Katie's burden was her main concern, and to that end she did most of the cooking and helped with the children. As the days passed and her strange illness persisted, Moira began looking seriously at her symptoms and didn't like what she discovered. It seemed she wasn't the only one concerned over her physical condition. After observing Moira for several days, noting her morning pallor and her general malaise, Katie came to a conclusion that both shocked and frightened her. One day when everyone was out of the house save for her and Moira, she broached the subject.

"Moira, dear, we haven't really talked about what happened in England. You've been so reticent about it since your return. Kevin and I both love you; you can tell us anything. There is a man involved, isn't there?"

"Aye," Moira admitted sadly. "It's worse than either you or Kevin could imagine. You'll be so disappointed in me."

"We love you, Moira. We're not going to judge you. Would you like to tell me what happened? Sometimes it helps to talk about it."

Moira bowed her head. "I can't."

Not one to mince words, Katie gave voice to her fears. "Are you in the family way?"

"Oh, God, how did you know? I wasn't aware of it myself until just recently."

"I've been pregnant four times," Katie reminded her.

"You must hate me," Moira said with a hint of despair.

Katie took Moira in her arms, rocking her against her ample bosom. "No, dear, we could never do that. Did he seduce you? Is he married? Did he abandon you after he ruined you?"

"Oh, no, it wasn't like that at all. I love him. He literally saved my life. He did propose, but I refused him. Of course, I didn't know at the time that I was expecting his child."

"You could go back and tell him. Surely he'd do the right thing by you. I don't understand why you refused him if you love him. What kind of man is he?''

"I can't marry him," Moira explained. "I love him too much to attach scandal to his name. He's a duke, Katie. I'm not his social equal. Imagine the uproar that marrying an Irish commoner would cause. When I turned him down, he became angry and demanded that I become his mistress." A sob left her throat. "I can't believe how hateful he acted."

"What man dared to ask my little sister to become his mistress?" Kevin thundered. Katie and Moira had been so engrossed in their conversation that they weren't aware Kevin had entered the kitchen in time to hear part of Moira's confession. His face was mottled with rage, and his huge hands were doubled into fists, just itching to pound his sister's tormentor into the ground. "Is that what's been troubling you, Moira? What has the bastard done to you?"

Her face as white as the apron she wore, Moira whirled to face her brother. "Oh, Kevin, I didn't want you to find out like this."

"Find out what? Tell me the name of the bastard who seduced my little sister."

Moira sighed in resignation. The fat was in the fire now. She had to tell Kevin that she was pregnant. He'd find out sooner or later anyway. According to her calculations, she'd become pregnant the first time she and Jack had made love. But nothing, absolutely nothing, would drag Jack's name from her.

"That's not the way it happened, Kevin. I was willing. Please don't hate me. I fell in love and couldn't help myself."

"You're young and inexperienced; I don't blame you. The bastard took advantage of you. Chalk it up as a bad experience. One day you'll meet a good Irishman and forget about the English whoreson.''

"It's not going to be that easy," Moira whispered, knowing what she was about to say would hurt Kevin deeply. "I . . . I'm pregnant."

Kevin exploded in rage. "Sweet Virgin! I'll kill him! I'll see that he marries you first, then I'll kill him."

"You don't understand, Kevin. He did offer to marry me. I refused."

Kevin looked at her blankly. "What in God's holy name is wrong with you? You said you loved the man— what more do you need?" Suddenly Kevin went still. "He's married, isn't he?"

"No, he isn't married. He's a duke; he can't marry an Irish commoner."

"Are you forgetting that your bloodlines may be every bit as good as his?"

"Neither of us can prove that, Kevin. We have only Mother's word."

"You have the locket. We've just never had the opportunity to pursue the identity of the man. 'Tis likely he's our grandfather."

"Perhaps," Moira allowed uncertainly. "Unfortunately, I no longer have the locket. I lost it."

Kevin groaned in dismay. "Are you determined then not to marry the father of your child?"

"Aye. I don't think he'd have me now. I hurt his pride. We both said some brutal things. But I want this baby," Moira said fiercely.

"Of course you do," Katie said compassionately. "We'll love it because it's yours."

"I'll find you a husband," Kevin said thoughtfully. "There has to be a good Irishman out there somewhere willing to take you and your child.''

''I don't want a husband,'' Moira insisted.

''You're not thinking clearly, lass. This is a small village. People here are no more forgiving than the nobility across the Irish Sea. I won't let you ruin your life. Think of your child if not yourself. He'll become an outcast. You'll marry, Moira, and thank me for making life easier for you and the child. I don't want to see my sister hurt. Will you allow me to find a good man for you?''

Tears gathered in the corners of Moira's eyes. Jack was lost to her. She didn't want to marry, but the thought of her child being hurt by cruel gossip made her physically ill.

''I don't know, Kevin, truly. What man would want a fallen woman? I know you mean well, but I can see no solution to my problem. If you want me to leave, I will.''

''You're being foolish, lass. This is your home. But you're wrong about no man wanting you. In fact, I already have a good man in mind. He'd take you, Moira, and willingly.''

Suddenly Katie clapped her hands. ''Of course! Paddy! The poor man is beside himself trying to care for his motherless children. Besides, he's always had a soft spot in his heart for Moira. He never fails to ask about her when we meet.''

''Paddy McGuire,'' Moira repeated thoughtfully. ''I heard Kayla died recently. What a terrible tragedy. He loved her dearly. I couldn't saddle him with a child that's not his.''

''Paddy will think no less of you for it. Granted he's somewhat older than you, but he's a wonderful father and a good provider. He'll be good to you, Moira, trust me in this.''

"I ... This is something that demands further thought," Moira said. "I can't just jump into marriage."

"You don't have a lot of time, dear," Katie reminded her.

"I don't know, I just don't know." Moira sobbed as she turned and fled.

"I didn't mean to upset her," Kevin said sheepishly. "Surely Moira knows I'd never do anything to hurt her. I wish I could get my hands on the man who put her in this predicament."

"Moira loves the man, Kevin. I don't know what happened between them, but she says he wanted to marry her. She's the one who refused him."

"He took advantage of her," Kevin said tightly. "I should have never let her leave home."

"You couldn't have stopped her. Give her time; she'll come around."

"Moira needs Paddy and Paddy needs Moira. As much as I hate interfering in my sister's life, I'm going to take the initiative and speak with Paddy."

Alone in her room, Kevin's words pierced the fog of Moira's despair. She knew how narrow-minded the villagers could be and what their prejudice would do to her child. He'd be called a bastard and ridiculed. Seeing her child treated as an outcast would destroy her. Moira drew a deep breath and exhaled slowly. Why must an innocent child pay for something that wasn't his fault? Moira didn't want to marry Paddy, but did she have a choice?

Two days later, Paddy McGuire came calling. Handsome in a rough kind of way, his dark eyes held nothing but kindness and respect for Moira. His voice was gentle despite his great size, and Moira thought his shyness rather endearing. Paddy wasn't Jack—no one could ever take his place—but something in his demeanor persuaded Moira that he'd never treat her or her child unkindly.

The first time Paddy came calling he stayed only a short while, spending scant time alone with Moira. But over the next week, Katie and Kevin saw fit to leave them alone for longer periods of time. By the end of the week, Paddy had mustered enough courage to speak frankly to Moira.

Hat in hand, he stood before her, a gentle giant almost too shy to speak his piece. "Would you care to go for a walk, lass? 'Tis a fine night."

More than a little apprehensive, Moira nodded agreement. "Just let me get my wrap."

The night was indeed fine, Moira thought as she and Paddy walked through the fields. After an interminable silence, Paddy said, "I know about your babe, Moira. Kevin told me. You need a husband and I need a wife. I promise to be a good husband if you'll promise to take care of my children. Kayla's death was a shock to all of us, 'twas so unexpected. I can't cope with two motherless children. I need you as surely as you need me. We've known one another for years. I remember when you were born. A wee little thing with beautiful eyes. You haven't changed, Moira. Will you marry me?"

Moira realized that this was probably the longest speech Paddy had ever made, and she was curiously touched. "You're kind, Paddy, and as good a man as I'll ever find, but . . ."

"I know I'm not the father of your babe, but Kevin said there's no chance he'll show up to marry you. I don't think any less of you for . . ." He gestured helplessly, at a loss for words. "Being in this predicament. God said that he who is without guilt should cast the first stone. I'll never cast stones at you, lass. Your babe will be treated the same as my own.''

"I know, Paddy. Kevin is right, you truly are a good man. I've always known it, just as I know you'll always love Kayla. It isn't right to saddle you with another man's child.''

"Wouldn't I be saddling you with two children who aren't yours?'' Paddy rebutted. '' 'Tis the same thing, to my thinking.''

"I need time to think, Paddy. I'll give you my answer in a day or two.''

Nothing convinced Moira more than Kevin's absolute certainty that marrying Paddy would be right for both her and Paddy. Since love wasn't involved, not even considered, she expected no emotional involvement. She refused to think about marital rights, which Paddy would doubtlessly expect. She knew she would have to endure it for her child's sake no matter how repugnant it was to her. For a brief moment, she entertained the notion of returning to England and becoming Jack's mistress. But what man would want a mistress large and ungainly with child?

Did Jack even want children? She vaguely recalled him mentioning that he wanted her for the mother of his children, but she didn't put any faith in words uttered when lust ruled his brain. Men often said things they didn't mean when thinking with their loins instead of their minds. God, she was confused. Jack had been so angry with her before she left, she could well imagine his rage when he found her gone without a word or message.

The very fact that Jack hadn't followed her to Ireland proved how little he cared for her. Stealing his money probably hadn't endeared her to him, but she'd had no choice. He would have forced her to become his mistress had she remained. A man's pride was his honor, and she had wounded Jack's pride by refusing to marry him. Perhaps she *should* have wed him, she reconsidered. That idea died as soon as it was born. She couldn't bear watching his love wither and die when his friends cut him off and he became an outcast in society.

Two days later, Moira agreed to marry Paddy. Kevin was overjoyed to see his sister's honor saved, but Katie had reservations. Paddy's rather sterile kiss sealed the bargain and afterward, recalling that passionless kiss, Moira imagined living out her life in joyless companionship. Of course the children would bring her a certain amount of happiness, but it wasn't the same as lying in the arms of a man she loved, responding to his caresses with nearly mindless ecstasy.

Jack paced the length of his room and back, his mind sluggish, his legs unsteady beneath him. Lord, how could he have fallen so low? He'd been drunk before, but never had he suffered guilt over his inebriated condition. Spence had lost patience with him, and Pettibone's staunch disapproval was the bane of his existence. The sorry state of the food Matilda placed before him when he took time to eat hardly passed for civilized fare. Jilly acted as if it were he who had turned Moira out of the house. He'd wanted to marry Moira—didn't they know that?

To make matters worse, Spence still hadn't discovered the identity of the man pictured in Moira's locket. Though vaguely familiar, Spence hadn't come up with a name. Jack couldn't understand why the man in the locket should be important, but something told him he was.

Planting himself in a wing chair, Jack stared into space, remembering the taste, the scent, the utter joy of possessing Moira. When he was with Moira, he felt so alive, so content and at peace with the world. Then he recalled how she had refused to marry him, and the joy he felt withered inside him. She had hurt him deeply, and he had retaliated by demanding that she become his mistress. Unfortunately, Moira had reacted in a manner he'd not expected. He wondered if she'd have left him if she'd known his old devils made him treat her in such a despicable manner. Now it was pride that was keeping him from following her to Ireland.

Hurry.

Jack raised his head and peered bleary-eyed into the dark corners of the room, seeing nothing but hazy shadows. But he didn't have to see her to know Lady Amelia was about to pay him another visit. He shot to his feet and poured himself a drink from the decanter sitting on the table next to his chair. He raised his glass in salute and said, "Here's to the Devil, milady." He drank deeply, nearly gagging at the vile taste. He raised the bottle to inspect the date and found it a very good year. With a curse, he threw the remainder of the brandy into the fire. He watched numbly as the fire flared and Lady Amelia materialized from the center of the flames.

Hurry.

"Go away, damn you! Can't you see I don't need you? You've brought me nothing but trouble. I was happy until you decided to reform me. I told you it was too late. The Devil's clutches are too deeply embedded in me."

He shan't have you.

Jack gave a bark of laughter. "You're too late, milady, he's already claimed me."

You must go to Moira. She needs you.

"She doesn't want me. She made that abundantly clear."

Men are such fools.

"What about pride? Aren't men allowed their pride?"

Lady Amelia bowed her head, and Jack swore he could see tears flowing down her cheeks. He knew he hadn't been mistaken when a drop of water splashed on the floor at her feet.

"What in bloody hell do you want from me? Go away, damn it, just go away!"

Lady Amelia pointed a finger at him, saying nothing, merely looking at him with the saddest expression Jack had ever seen. "Moira doesn't want me. She's gone. She played me for a fool, milady."

Your child needs you.

"I have no child," Jack scoffed. "Perhaps you've gotten me confused with some other Graystoke from another generation."

Your child . . . Your child . . . Your child . . .

Lady Amelia's words pounded against Jack's sodden brain until he thought it would burst. Clapping his hands over his ears, he tried to obliterate her words. Instead they grew louder and more insistent. Finally Jack could take no more. Grasping the brandy decanter by the neck, he flung it at the ghost. It passed through her and crashed harmlessly against the wall.

Remember my words. I won't be back.

"Good riddance," Jack snapped peevishly. "Find someone else to haunt."

"Lord Jack, are you all right?" Pettibone burst into the room, a candle held high to light his way, his nightshirt flapping around his bony legs. "I heard a crash, milord."

Jack glanced toward the fireplace and was relieved to

see that Lady Amelia had vanished. "Go back to bed, Pettibone," Jack said grumpily. "I dropped the decanter. You can clean up in the morning."

Pettibone glanced at the wall, saw rivulets of liquid trailing down to the floor and knew Jack's explanation was far too simple. "Very good, milord. Good night, then." He closed the door quietly behind him, fearing that his young master was losing his sanity.

Jack sat brooding long after Pettibone left, wondering if Lady Amelia would return or if she'd really meant what she'd said. The longer he brooded, the more puzzling her words became. She knew he had no children, so why did she insist his child needed him?

"Damn you," he muttered plaintively. "What did you mean?"

Lady Amelia chose not to answer. Nor did she reappear.

Suddenly Jack bolted upright in his chair, stone-cold sober for the first time in weeks. Could it be? Was Moira carrying his child? Had she left specifically to deprive him of his child? Rage seethed through him. The anger he felt before was nothing compared to what he felt now. Moira had no right, no right at all to keep something as important as his child from him. She may not want him for a husband, but the law was on his side. He still had the special license. If she was indeed pregnant, he would make her his wife no matter how fiercely she protested.

The following morning, Pettibone found Jack not only up at an ungodly early hour, but he appeared to be sober. "Ah, Pettibone, you've arrived in time to pack a bag for me."

"A bag, milord? Are you going somewhere?"

"To Ireland. Instruct the coachman to ready the coach

for a journey to the coast. Young Colin will accompany us. 'Tis faster than taking a packet from London. With any luck, I will be in Kilkenney inside a week.''

Pettibone's face lit up. "You're going after Miss Moira? Thank God you've finally come to your senses.''

"Aye, Pettibone, I've regained my wits. Moira has something of mine, and I want it.''

Pettibone blanched. "If you're referring to the money she stole, 'twas a paltry sum. Surely you don't intend pressing charges, do you?''

Jack sent him an oblique look. "Don't worry, Pettibone. Pressing charges is not my intention, though I can't promise not to wring her graceful little neck once I get my hands on her. Enough chitchat. Bring my bag down when it's packed. I'll leave directly after breakfast.''

Jack's departure was delayed by the arrival of Spence, who appeared in a high state of excitement. "Going somewhere, Jack? I saw a bag in the foyer. I'm glad I caught you before you left. I have information on the man pictured in Moira's locket. You'll never guess who he is.''

Somewhat distracted by Spence's unexpected appearance, Jack's attention sharpened when Spence blurted out his news. "Come into the study and tell me what you learned. I'm glad you caught me before I left for Ireland. It could be important or it could mean nothing, but either way, I want to be armed with the knowledge when I confront Moira.''

"You're going after Moira,'' Spence said, more or less resigned to the fact that Jack was head over heels in love with her. Despite his warning, Spence knew Jack intended to flout society and marry Moira. Perhaps the resulting scandal wouldn't be quite as bad as he assumed it would be, Spence reflected. But if it was, he imagined Black Jack

Graystoke would weather the storm in his own inimitable fashion.

"Aye," Jack admitted, "the moment you tell me what you learned."

"You'll never believe it, Jack. I certainly didn't. The man is highly respected and his name a legend of his time. He was a personal advisor to King George. He retired five years ago due to ill health. He now resides quietly in the country."

"Sweet Lord, you don't mean . . . No, it couldn't be. Why would Moira carry a picture of the Earl of Pembroke?"

"Aye, 'tis true. Herbert Montgomery, the Earl of Pembroke. The miniature looked vaguely familiar, but I couldn't quite place it. It wasn't until yesterday that I learned it might be the earl."

"Then you're not sure," Jack said, clearly disappointed.

"Not entirely certain. Only the earl himself can identify the picture. But he was once in the British army and quartered in Ireland."

"How did you come by the knowledge that it was the Earl of Pembroke's likeness in Moira's locket?"

"As a last resort, I showed the likeness to Father. He said he'd seen the very same picture hanging in Lord Herbert's gallery when he was invited to his country home for the hunt many years ago. He assumed it was Lord Herbert as a young man. So there you have it."

"You may be right, but I understand none of it. Moira said the locket belonged to her dead grandmother, handed down to Moira by her mother."

"What do you think it means?" Spence asked curiously.

"Damned if I know. Before I return to England, I'll have the answer. You've been a tremendous help, Spence. I owe you a debt of gratitude."

"Don't mention it. I just hope the information helps you in some way. I'm not sure we can ever get Lord Herbert to verify the fact that he is the man in the miniature, for he's a virtual recluse now. His only son died years ago, and he has no children or grandchildren to inherit the title."

"I'll contact you when I return. Moira isn't going to get away with keeping me in the dark about . . ." His sentence trailed off, unwilling to disclose information that may or may not be true. But true or not, Moira belonged to him, and willing or not, mistress or wife, she was going to remain his.

Chapter Nineteen

Moira stared at the pounding rain through the tiny window of her room. The day was as bleak as her heart. Bloated clouds turned the sky dark and forbidding. The air was heavy, thick and depressing; the wind was becoming brisker by the minute. The dismal day matched her mood. It was too late for tears, too late for second thoughts. Today was her wedding day.

The quiet ceremony was to take place that morning in the village church, witnessed by her family. It wasn't a match made in heaven but one of convenience. Moira was certain the whole village knew of the wedding, but not the reason for haste. She hoped they would assume it was because of Paddy's need for a mother for his children and not because she was swelling with another man's child.

A timid knock on the door brought Moira out of her reverie and back to the present. "'Tis Kevin, lass."

"Come in."

"We'll wait a while longer for the rain to let up before starting for the church," Kevin said, taking note of her paleness. "Are you all right, lass?"

"I'm fine, Kevin. Do you think this dress will do? 'Tis the best of the lot I brought with me from England." Moira pirouetted slowly before Kevin. Fashioned of violet brocade and lace, the gown fit her still-slim figure to perfection.

"You look lovely, lass. I've never seen you in anything so grand. Try not to fret. Everything will turn out fine. I promise."

"Nothing will ever be fine again, Kevin. I know Paddy is a good man, but he isn't Jack."

Kevin's attention sharpened. "Jack? Is that the name of the bastard who seduced you and left you with child?"

Realizing she said more than she intended, Moira sought to diffuse Kevin's curiosity. "The man's name is of little importance since you're unlikely to meet him. I'll not disappoint you again, Kevin. I'll be a good wife to Paddy."

"I'm not disappointed in you, lass. You're a special woman. Your Englishman doesn't know what he lost, and I'm not about to tell him. He doesn't deserve you and the babe. Now," he said, lifting her chin, "give me a smile."

Moira's lips wobbled into a parody of a smile, which seemed to satisfy Kevin. He left her then, to her dismal thoughts, until the rain let up enough to permit them to reach the church without getting soaked to the skin. An hour later, the rain had diminished to a fine mist. Kevin loaded the family into the farm wagon and set out for Kilkenny.

Jack debarked at Rossiare Harbor before dawn, the first person to step off the mail packet. He rented a horse at the livery and asked directions to Kilkenny. Suffering

through a long, tedious ride, Jack hoped Moira appreciated all the trouble he was going through to reach her.
Steady rain made a quagmire of the one-lane road and
chilled Jack to the bone. He reached Kilkenny wet, hungry
and feeling very much put upon.

The muddy, rutted lane through Kilkenny was nearly
deserted, due to the inclement weather. Since Jack had no
idea where the O'Toole farm was located, he decided to
find a room at an inn and ask for directions to the farm.
When the grocer stepped out of his shop to peer at him,
Jack reined in his horse. "Can you direct me to an inn,
sir?"

"Only one inn in town, mister. The Gull and Tern is
two blocks down on the right side of the street. You can't
miss it."

Jack found the inn with little trouble and paid in ad-
vance for the best room it had to offer. "Can you direct
me to the O'Toole farm?" he asked the innkeeper before
going up to inspect his room.

Strangers in Kilkenny were looked upon with suspicion, and Jack was no exception. "Are ye a friend of the
O'Tooles, mister? Don't recollect Kevin or the missus
knowing any Englishmen."

"I'm a friend of Miss Moira O'Toole."

A relieved look passed over the innkeeper's florid features. "Why didn't ye say so? Are ye here for the wedding?"

Jack went still. "The wedding?"

"Aye, Miss Moira and Paddy McGuire are tying the
knot."

Jack's heart beat like a trip-hammer. How dare Moira
marry another man?

"Aye, I'm here for the wedding. I'm not too late, am I?"

"The rain held up the ceremony. If ye hurry, ye might be in time to hear Father Sian pronounce them husband and wife."

Jack cursed beneath his breath. "For God's sake, man, direct me to the church!"

"Turn right at the corner; ye can't miss it. 'Tis the only building with a steeple."

Jack was out the door before the innkeeper finished speaking. The curious innkeeper walked to the doorway to watch Jack gallop off. He shook his head and muttered something about impatient Englishmen with no manners.

Jack located the church within minutes. He spied the farm wagon parked outside and feared he was too late. How could Moira wed another man when all she had to do was say the word and he'd have married her? He prayed he wasn't too late to stop this farce. If she carried his child, not even a religious ceremony would stop him from taking what was his.

Worked into a frenzy of fear and anger, Jack burst into the church. The murmur of voices drew him through the vestibule to the main part of the church. Shock rendered him mute for all of thirty seconds when he saw Moira standing before the altar beside a giant of a man, listening to the priest intone words that would join them irrevocably.

He found his tongue in a rush of words. "Stop! Stop the wedding!"

The priest looked up, bewildered. Moira turned slowly, recognizing Jack's voice instantly. In a single moment, Jack saw her paleness, her trembling lips, her pinched features, the thinness of her small frame, and knew intuitively that she carried his child.

"Jack." His name was a sigh on her lips.

"Who in the hell are you?" Kevin thundered.

For the first time, Jack noticed the other people in the church. The man who had spoken had to be Moira's brother. They had the same look about them. "I'm Jack Graystoke, Duke of Ailesbury."

"I don't care who you are! You have no right to barge in here and disrupt my sister's wedding."

Jack strode down the aisle, his volatile presence disrupting the ceremony. "I have every right in the world. Your sister is carrying my child."

Moira moaned in despair. "How did you know? I didn't even know myself until a short time ago."

Jack's silver gaze pinned her. "I don't suppose you were going to tell me I was going to be a father, were you?"

The priest looked distraught. "I don't know what this is all about, but I suggest we get on with the wedding."

"Aye," Moira whispered. "Please continue, Father Sian."

"Over my dead body," Jack roared.

Kevin stepped forward, facing Jack nose-to-nose. "That can be arranged, Your Lordship. My sister doesn't need you. You seduced her and left her with child."

"If that's what Moira claimed, I won't argue the point. However, no one but me is going to raise my child."

Father Sian raised his hand for quiet. "Is what this man claims true, lass?" he asked Moira. "Are you carrying his child?"

When Moira remained mute, Paddy sent her a compassionate smile and stepped forward. " 'Tis true, Father. I don't wish to deprive a father of his child. I'm still willing to marry Moira, but not until this matter is settled between them.''

''I agree,'' Father Sian said, sending Moira a censuring look. ''If Lord Graystoke is the father of your child, he should be consulted before you do anything rash. Perhaps His Grace wishes to right a wrong by marrying you.''

Moira glared at Jack. Did no one understand why she couldn't marry a lord of the realm? ''I'm going to marry Paddy McGuire.''

Jack returned her stare impassively. His opinion of the man Moira had chosen to wed rose the moment Paddy McGuire agreed to step out of the picture. ''I don't know you, Mr. McGuire, but you appear to be a reasonable man. I don't know what Moira told you, but as you can see, I'm not willing to give up my child to another man. I wish to speak to Moira alone.''

''Now see here, milord,'' Kevin blustered as he shielded his sister protectively. ''You seduced my sister. She was an innocent before she met you. I don't know what happened between you, but Moira wouldn't be willing to marry another man if she cared for you.''

Jack sent Kevin a chilling glare. ''Did Moira tell you she didn't care for me? Did she tell you I proposed marriage?''

Kevin looked at Moira uncertainly. ''Do you want to be alone with this man, lass? I'll abide by whatever you say.''

The lump in Moira's throat had reached monumental proportions. She swallowed convulsively before the ability to think returned. The shock of seeing Jack in Ireland had rendered her speechless. But learning that he was aware of her pregnancy when she had just come to that conclusion herself was frightening in the extreme. Not to mention profoundly confusing.

"I'll speak with Lord Jack alone," Moira said.

"Very wise," Jack said with quiet menace. He was certain she knew that if she refused he'd have carried her out bodily despite her brother's rather threatening attitude. "The rest of you can go along home. I'll bring Moira to you after our talk, if she still wants to go."

When Kevin seemed reluctant to leave, Katie nudged him in the ribs. "Moira knows what she's doing, Kevin. I'm sure His Grace won't hurt her."

"He'd better not," Kevin warned.

"If he does, he'll answer to me," Paddy said, adding his own threat to that of Kevin's.

"Fear not," Jack said, sending both men a look that would have melted iron. "I'm not a violent man. Do you think I'd harm the mother of my child?"

Somewhat mollified, Kevin left, followed in close order by Katie, the children, Paddy and Father Sian, who closed the door behind him. Alone at last with Moira, Jack pointed to a pew and said, "Sit down. You look ready to collapse."

Only too glad to take the weight off her quivering legs, Moira sank into the hard bench, never taking her eyes off Jack. "How did you know?" she whispered shakily. "Kevin, Katie and Paddy are the only ones I told."

Jack's brow lifted in surprise. "You told the man you were planning to marry that you carried another man's child?"

"It didn't matter to Paddy. He's a good man. His wife died recently, and he needs a wife to care for his two motherless children. We've known one another all our lives."

"He looks old enough to be your father."

Her chin rose fractionally. "He was willing to marry me and raise my child."

"*I* was willing to marry you," Jack reminded her. "Needless to say, you're *not* going to marry Paddy McGuire. If you marry anyone, it's going to be me."

Jack's arrogance tried Moira's Irish temper. He could demand all he liked, but she wasn't going to marry him. She was aware that stubbornness was largely responsible for her decision, but no man was going to dictate to her.

"I *won't* marry you."

"I see," Jack said with a calmness that belied his fury. "Raising a bastard won't be easy. Of course, I'll take care of you and the child, but think of the shame you'll bring to your family." Since Moira didn't react to reason, he decided to try another ploy. "The house I rented is still waiting for you should you decide to become my mistress."

Moira's eyes glowed angrily. "I'm going to marry Paddy."

"Over my dead body. Bloody hell, Moira, do you realize the anguish your leaving so abruptly caused me? My staff began to fear for my sanity. Pettibone treated me like a pariah, and Matilda set meals before me that weren't fit to eat. Jilly acted as if I'd committed murder. They all blamed me for chasing you away."

"You were going to set me up as your mistress," Moira charged.

"You pushed me into it. What I offered was an honorable proposal of marriage. A man can be driven only so far, and I'd reached my limit. I went as far as my pride would allow."

Jack's words rattled Moira's composure. Everything Jack said was true. He had saved her life, not once, but twice. He took her in and cared for her when she was injured. The prank he tried to pull on society backfired, but she could forgive him that. It had been a harebrained scheme from the very beginning. Falling in love with Jack hadn't been part of the plan, and making love with him had come as naturally as breathing. She had given him up because she loved him too much to marry him and cause a scandal.

Jack watched the play of emotion across Moira's lovely features. He saw determination, stubbornness, compassion, confusion and, yes, love. He smiled inwardly. No amount of denial could change the way she felt. Now he must convince her that he didn't give a bloody damn what society thought of their marriage. In Moira's absence, he had tried reverting back to the Black Jack of old and had failed miserably. What he wanted now was to be the best father and husband he knew how. No matter how big a scandal their marriage caused, some new scandal would replace it, and in time society would forgive his lapse. Not that he cared. Enough of the old Black Jack remained to make him oblivious to gossip. He'd flouted society before and probably would do so again.

Suddenly it occurred to Moira that Jack never did explain how he knew she was pregnant. She sought to remedy his omission. "How did you know I was going to have your child? Do you have the 'sight'?"

Jack grinned, recalling Lady Amelia's words and how puzzled they had left him. "Lady Amelia told me."

Moira frowned. "The ghost?"

"Aye. But I fear I offended her. She lost patience with me when I fell back into dissolute ways. I doubt she'll reappear any time soon."

"You talked to a ghost?" Moira repeated.

Jack paused thoughtfully, recalling his conversations with Lady Amelia. Though she'd spoken no words aloud, he knew exactly what she said. Call it telepathy, call it what you will, her words had penetrated his brain without sound.

"You might say that. Lady Amelia sent me to you that night I found you lying in the gutter. She told me you'd save me from perdition. Of course I didn't believe her. I didn't even want saving. I was content with my rakehell life. She must be quite pleased with herself by now. I almost married Victoria, and that frightens the hell out of me."

Moira found all this hard to believe. "How could I save you when I didn't even know you?"

"Damned if I know, but 'tis true I no longer find perdition attractive. I've never thought about becoming a father, and I find the anticipation quite pleasant. I knew Victoria didn't want children, and all I wanted from her was her fortune."

How could Moira argue with a ghost? Still, a doubt remained. When Lady Amelia directed Jack to her that fateful night, did the ghost know he'd become a duke? Moira didn't think so. And therein lay the problem.

"Lady Amelia's appearance doesn't change a thing," Moira declared, less certain now than she had been.

"I've engaged a room at the inn," Jack said abruptly. "Church is no place for a lengthy discussion, and I can tell it's going to take time to convince you that we belong together. Besides, I have something else to ask, something to do with the locket you always wore."

"I lost it."

"I know." Reaching into his pocket, Jack retrieved Moira's locket and placed it into her hand. Moira closed her fingers around it, overjoyed to have it back. "I found it in my bed. Now will you come with me?"

Moira flushed, recalling the night she spent in Jack's bed before she left. "It isn't proper for me to go with you to your room."

"We've already stretched the boundary of what is proper and what is not. You're carrying my child, Moira. You're mine; you've always been mine."

"Your possessiveness is appalling. How do I know you don't want me for the child I carry?"

"You are the most exasperating female I've ever had the misfortune to know! I had no idea you were pregnant when I proposed. Are you coming with me, or do I have to throw you over my shoulder and carry you out of here?"

Jack's logic defeated Moira. Besides, she knew he was capable of carrying out his threat. "Very well, though you know it will destroy my reputation."

"Not if I sneak you up the backstairs." Grasping her hand, he virtually dragged her through the church and out the door. A chilling rain greeted them. With an economy of motion, Jack lifted Moira onto his horse and mounted behind her. Though the ride was of short duration, they were nevertheless dripping wet by the time Jack left his mount at the stable behind the inn and instructed the stableboy as to its care.

Fortunately the back stairs of the inn lay only a few steps from the stable. They negotiated them without difficulty, and Jack located his room by the number painted on the door. He found it roomy, comfortable and reasonably clean. A bed covered with a colorful quilt took up a large portion of the room. A dresser, commode and desk completed the furnishings. Jack was gratified to see a fireplace and supply of wood and started a fire while Moira sat at the edge of the bed, shivering in her wet clothing.

"It will be cozy in here in a few minutes," he told her. "Take off your wet clothing and wrap yourself in a blanket. Your clothes can dry by the fire while we talk."

Moira didn't think taking off her clothes was a good idea. Just because she wouldn't marry Jack didn't mean she didn't want him. She'd always want him. She knew from experience how combustible they were together, and taking off her clothes would only complicate matters. When she made no move to comply, Jack lifted her to her feet, took the cloak from her shoulders and began unbuttoning her dress.

"I don't want you catching your death. Think of the babe if not yourself."

"I . . . I can do it myself." She grasped his hands to pull them away and felt a shock of awareness pass through her. She lifted her eyes to him, and he met her gaze, his lopsided grin telling her that he felt the same tingling sensation she did. He dropped his hands and stepped away.

Moira tore the quilt from the bed, drew it around her shoulders and undressed beneath it. Sending her an amused glance, Jack picked up her discarded garments and spread them out before the fire. When he started to remove his own clothing, Moira gasped and looked away.

"Isn't it rather late for shyness? You want me as badly as I want you. Deny it all you want, but your eyes tell me otherwise."

"You're conceited, arrogant and impossibly crude, Jack Graystoke. And nowhere near redemption. Not all women are enamored of you."

"Other women don't interest me. 'Tis you I care about. I'll admit to being arrogant. Even concede being conceited.'' He made a show of pondering. ''I'm rarely crude. At one time my vices were legend, but since meeting you I've foresworn perdition.''

Moira couldn't help but smile. His statements were so typically Black Jack that she wondered if he didn't still have one foot on the road to perdition.

''If you'll move from the bed for a moment, I'll remove a blanket and spare your dignity.''

Moira jumped up with alacrity, turning her back as Jack dropped his breeches and pulled a blanket from the bed. ''You can turn around now; I'm decent.''

Almost decent, Moira thought as she stared at his bare chest. He had wrapped himself in a blanket, all right, draping it loosely around his loins. So much for her dignity. ''You wanted to talk,'' she reminded him. ''What can you say here that you couldn't say at the church?''

He took her hand, pulling her down onto the bed beside her. ''I didn't want any interruptions. The church is too public a place for what I have to say.''

Moira found it difficult to think with Jack sitting next to her. He smelled delicious, a manly scent that was uniquely his. It reminded her of something dark, musky and irresistible. The urge to touch his lips, his shoulders, the thick thatch of hair covering his chest was so compelling that she had to curl her fingers into fists to keep from reaching out to him. When she realized what she felt must be reflected in her eyes, she quickly lowered her gaze.

''What is it you wanted to say?''

''It's not so much what I wanted to say as what I wanted to do,'' Jack said, grasping her chin and tilting it upward, forcing her to look into his eyes. What she saw sent liquid heat spilling into her loins. His silver eyes were glazed with passion, his face stark with hunger. "I want you, Moira. Let me love you."

"You're being unfair," Moira charged. "You know I can't resist you. I wouldn't be in this predicament if I could. I left you for your own good."

"How can you claim that leaving me was good for me?" Jack argued. "Don't you think I know my own mind?"

"Marrying me would cause a scandal."

"I've been involved in scandals before and survived."

"You've never been a duke before."

"Lord knows I never aspired to the title. Be honest, Moira. Would you have married me if I was plain Black Jack Graystoke?"

Moira paused for the space of a heartbeat. "Aye, but you're not just plain Black Jack. If you were, you'd be married to Lady Victoria. You couldn't have married an Irish commoner either way." Her logic defied him, so he adroitly changed the subject.

"Where is your locket?"

Moira looked askance at him. "In the pocket of my dress. Why?"

Jack rose, retrieved the locket and settled back down beside her. "Open it," he said, handing it to her.

With shaking hands, Moira sprung the clasp, revealing the picture inside. "There, are you satisfied?"

"Who is the man in the painting?"

Moira inhaled sharply and let her breath out slowly. "No one of importance to you."

"But someone of importance to you, I'll wager."

"Mother told me it was a painting of her father. Mind you there is no one alive to substantiate her claim, but she believed it to be so. It belonged to her own mother,

Connie Mason

who died giving birth to her.''

"Who gave your mother the locket and told her about it?''

"The nuns who raised her. According to Mother Superior, my grandmother's family disowned her when she became pregnant. Supposedly the father of her child was an English soldier of noble birth who was quartered in Ireland during a rebellion. Obviously my grandfather, if the story is true, abandoned my grandmother. But I can't see what difference any of this makes to our situation.''

"It makes all the difference in the world if the man in the painting is your grandfather.''

"You know who it is?'' Excitement colored her words and pinkened her cheeks.

"I think so. Have you ever heard of the powerful Earl of Pembroke?''

Moira shook her head. "Is my grandfather distantly related to this great earl?'' It didn't matter to Moira if her grandfather was a shirttail relative as long as the mystery of the locket was solved.

"Your grandfather *is* the earl. Your mother was the daughter of the future Earl of Pembroke. In time he inherited the title, married, had a son and lost him. He now lives in seclusion in the country.''

"How do you know all this?'' Moira asked suspiciously.

"Sleuthing, my love. I gave the locket to Spence and asked him to investigate, never suspecting its importance. His father was the one who finally identified the man in the miniature.''

"Are you sure? Absolutely, irrevocably sure?''

"Reasonably sure,'' Jack hedged. "The first thing we'll do upon our return to London is seek an audience with

340

Lord Pembroke. He's the only one who can verify the story."

Moira's face fell. "I'm not taking anything for granted."

"It's almost a certainty, love. Now will you marry me and give our child a name? The blood flowing through your veins is bluer even than mine."

"You're not making this up, are you?"

Jack shook his head, exasperated beyond endurance. What a contrary female. But that was but a part of her that made her so endearing. "Would I lie to you about something as important as one's lineage?"

Moira searched his face, seeking the truth. "No, I don't believe you would. I'll marry you after I've spoken with Lord Pembroke."

Jack grasped her shoulders and gave her a gentle shake. "Do you love me, Moira? At one time I believed you did. But your staunch resistance makes me wonder if I was mistaken."

The moment of truth had arrived. Moira knew it as surely as she knew the sun rose in the east and set in the west. She could deny it no longer. She joyously, happily, exuberantly loved Jack Graystoke. Even if Lord Pembroke turned out to be a case of mistaken identity, she could not deny her child its rightful father.

"I love you, Jack Graystoke. I love you beyond time or reason."

Jack blinked in surprise, unable to believe his ears. He'd always believed she loved him, but getting her to admit it had been more of a chore than he'd expected. And to think he'd almost given up on her. If not for a meddling ghost, he would have lost Moira forever. For that matter, he would never have found Moira in the beginning if not for Lady Amelia.

"I said I'd never ask you to marry me again, yet here I am, brought to my knees before you. I tried to tell myself I didn't love you, even tried bedding other women, but that didn't work, either. You've banished the old Black Jack Graystoke, and in his place you see a reformed man. Lady Amelia must be supremely satisfied.

"I love you, Moira O'Toole. I knew it the instant I realized I couldn't marry Victoria, even though it meant going to debtor's prison and watching Graystoke Manor fall down around my ears. You're the only woman I want, Moira. We'll be married before we leave Ireland. I can't wait to make you my duchess."

Moira opened her mouth to protest, then closed it. She'd put more obstacles in Jack's path than any man should have to hurdle in a lifetime. When he reached out and removed the blanket from around her shoulders, she had no desire to stop him. The room was warm, almost too warm, but Moira hardly noticed as Jack unwound the blanket from his loins. Never, she thought, gazing at him, had she seen a more beautifully made man. His size didn't worry her, for she'd adjusted quickly to the thickness of his sex that now swelled with his need for her. His strength and hunger for her both gratified and pleased her.

He took her into his arms, and she felt him against her hip, hard and solid and immense.

"I've waited a long time and come a long way to make you mine again," he whispered into her ear.

He took her mouth in a fiercely possessive kiss that healed her heart and fed her soul. Moira nearly swooned with delight. His kiss was everything she remembered, everything she could ever want, and more. Oh, God, so much more.

Chapter Twenty

Jack deepened the kiss, his mouth fierce and demanding. He was consuming her and at the same time creating a shattering hunger within her. His lips moved on hers, seeking a response that matched his own. Her lips parted beneath his, and he thrust his tongue into her mouth, exploring it with unleashed passion. The tantalizing taste and scent of him titillated her senses. She felt him stir restively against her hip and thrilled at her power to move him. Her tongue began a tentative dance with his as his large hand cupped one breast gently. Her nipple grew hard and throbbing as he took the swollen bud between his fingers and caressed it tenderly. Moira cried out in sweet surrender, wanting more of the sublime pleasure.

He bore her down onto the bed and buried his face between her breasts. She moaned and cradled the heat of his mouth to her flesh as he licked her nipples with the velvet roughness of his tongue. Then he drew her nipple into the wet, warm cavern of his mouth, suckling her with exquisite tenderness. The scrape of his stubbly chin against her smooth skin heightened her pleasure as his mouth blazed a path of fire across her sensitive skin. She became like quicksilver in his hands, hot and eager. Like warm liquid being poured over her, his mouth flowed sweetly over her flesh while his hands moved hot and insistent over her body.

As he slid slowly downward, tracing silky, wet patterns over her skin, Moira panted with anticipation of his next move. He gently nudged her knees apart and settled between them, pausing briefly to give her a small smile of stark sexual hunger before lowering his head into the damp, musky warmth of her loins. Moira stiffened and cried out as he parted the delicate pink folds with his tongue, seeking a greater intimacy.

Jack pressed a muffled groan into the juncture of her thighs as her sweetness flowed into his mouth, hot and sharp and arousing. Her body spasmed with pleasure. He could feel the tension building inside her as her fingers curled around his shoulders and her legs began to tremble. She arched violently into the sliding pressure of his finger inside her and the wet lash of his tongue, straining against their deft stroking as she melted around the slow deep caresses.

Her cries grew frantic as she clung to him, moving against the thrust of his fingers and the sweet exploration of his tongue. Jack pressed another groan into her musky warmth, his control slipping dangerously. The taste, the scent of her drove him wild to thrust himself into her and stroke himself to rapture. Suddenly her body stiffened and she writhed against him. Keeping his fingers buried deep inside her drenching heat, he raised up to watch her, to hold her as she climaxed violently. His mouth covered hers, swallowing her cries, his strokes continuing until her tremors subsided.

Then, with a mindlessness fueled by fierce need and long-denied hunger, he flexed his hips and thrust into the lush folds of her body. In all his life, Jack couldn't recall ever being so aroused. Pleasure had become pain, then unbearable agony as he stroked inside her, moving in and out deeply, frantically. His hands were on her buttocks, kneading, caressing, bringing her up to meet his bold penetration, arousing her anew. She arched upward, fever, madness and need driving her to an unbearable pitch, meeting his thrusts with frenzied, gasping cries.

He drove again and again, his face starkly beautiful in its intensity. Sheer, splendid glory washed over her as waves of sensation rolled through her body. Each jerk of her hips took him deeper and deeper into the core of her, fitting her as if he were made for her alone, throbbing against the walls of her sensitive interior. Tiny explosions burst inside her, thunderous and magnificent, like a tidal wave of pleasure sweeping through her.

"I love you, Moira," Jack cried as he drove into her one last time and shattered into a million brilliant pieces. "You're mine!"

Moira reacted with ancient feminine instinct, clasping him tightly and drawing him deeper and deeper until her body thrummed and vibrated with excruciating pleasure. Then, incredibly, she was launched into space, floating there weightless, immersed in perfect harmony as brilliant lights burst around her and her blood sang in her veins. A trembling sigh left her lips as the exquisite contractions tapered away.

Jack felt himself softening, but he was reluctant to leave the liquid warmth of her sheath. He wanted to stay this way forever, in her, over her, surrounding her. If he lived forever, he'd never have enough of her. When he slipped from her body, he rolled to his side, pulling her into his arms. He was numb and dazed and splendidly content.

"Now tell me we don't belong together," Jack said, daring her to deny what they had just experienced together. It had been a wild coming together—one billowing sensation after another, like thunderclouds swirling around them.

"It would be a lie," Moira whispered on a trembling sigh. "I could never deny you, Jack. I love you too much."

"Thank God," Jack replied happily. "I've come too far to be turned down again. I want our child to have his rightful name. We'll be married before we return to England. You deserve to have your family around you when we speak our vows. Lady Amelia must be absolutely gloating," he murmured as he turned her against him and pressed his lips to hers.

His lips abandoned hers to glide over the slope of her bare breast, capturing the peak of a flushed nipple. His hands ran the length of her body, seeking out each sensitive point, leaving her trembling with renewed passion. "I want you again, sweetheart, but only if you're not too exhausted." The scent of spent passion clinging to her was headier than fragrant perfume and a hundred times more arousing.

How could she ever be too exhausted for this magnificent man? Moira wondered. "You're wicked, Black Jack," she whispered as she pulled his lips down to hers, answering his need with a need of her own. "Don't ever change."

"Never, sweetheart. You're my passion, my life, my love."

Their loving was slow and leisurely, the rapture so intense Moira felt her soul leave her body. When Moira returned to herself, Jack was lying beside her, resting on his elbow and smiling down at her. "I want to keep that look on your face forever."

Moira blushed. "You're incorrigible."

"Aye. But I think I've worn you out. Sleep, love. I've arrangements to see to. I'll awaken you in plenty of time for our wedding."

Jack kissed her forehead and uncoiled his long length from the bed. Moira watched from beneath lowered lids as he pulled on his clothes. Her gaze charted the incredible width of his shoulders, his slim waist, his narrow hips, then continued down the supple length of his thighs, calves and ankles. When he bent to retrieve his trousers, she admired the taut, hard globes of his buttocks and rippling tendons of his muscular thighs. Sensing her scrutiny, Jack turned and gave her a cocky grin.

"Keep looking at me like that and we'll never leave this room."

Moira smiled sleepily. "I didn't realize I was staring. You're beautiful," she said shyly.

Jack flushed with pleasure. But when he tried to formulate a suitable reply, he wasn't surprised to find that Moira had dropped off to sleep. Dressing quietly, he left the room and spoke at length to the innkeeper. The man appeared more than a little surprised at Jack's request but consented without comment when Jack produced enough to pay for what he wanted.

Father Sian was agreeable to performing a wedding. More than willing, truth be known. His faith didn't condone premarital intimacy, and he was anxious to right a wrong. A child made it even more imperative that the mother and father be united in holy matrimony. Jack named four o'clock that afternoon as the hour for the ceremony, then asked directions to the O'Toole farm.

Jack cursed the infernal rain as he rode the muddy lane to the O'Toole farm. He was more than grateful when he spied smoke rising from a chimney and the outline of a house at the end of the lane. The cottage was in desperate need of a coat of whitewash and looked dingier than it really was in the misty grayness of the day. Jack reached the gate, bent to unlatch it and rode into the yard. He saw the curtains at the front window flutter as he dismounted, and then the door burst open before he reached it.

Kevin's jaw jutted out belligerently as he blocked the front door. ''Where is my sister, milord? What have you done with her?''

''Moira is safe and dry in my room at the inn. I'm sure you'll agree 'tis neither healthy nor wise to drag her out in this kind of weather, especially in her delicate condition. May I come in?''

Kevin wavered uncertainly. Katie glared at him and shoved him aside. ''Please come in, milord, where it's warm and dry. I'm sure we can sit and talk without animosity.''

Kevin moved aside with marked reluctance as Jack stepped through the door. He looked around curiously. Sparsely furnished but scrupulously clean and neat, the house was warm and inviting, telling Jack without words that the occupants were bound together by love. Jack smiled at the children as they crowded around him, their eyes wide with curiosity. They smiled back shyly before

Katie shooed them into the kitchen.

"Sit down, milord," Kate invited. "Kevin and I are both anxious to hear about Moira."

"Please, call me Jack. As I said before, Moira is fine. I left her sleeping. I'm here to invite you to a wedding."

Kevin bristled angrily. "What did you do to Moira to convince her to wed you?"

Jack faced him squarely. "Did you think I'd harm her? My God, man, I love Moira. It's taken me months to convince her to marry me."

"Your pardon, Lord Jack. 'Tis just that Moira was against marrying you," Katie intervened when she saw Kevin rousing himself for a nasty confrontation.

Jack grinned cheekily. "I'm a very convincing chap when I set my mind to something."

"Obviously," Kevin said dryly. "You seduced my innocent sister."

Jack did not deny it. "Someday I'll tell you how I met Moira. The danger she faced wasn't from me. But there isn't time now to go into details. Our wedding is set for four o'clock. Moira and I would be pleased to have you and Katie stand as witnesses."

It was apparent Kevin wasn't convinced that Jack was the right man for his sister. "What will your fancy friends say about you taking a Irish peasant to wife?"

"I don't give a damn. It's no one's business whom I marry. Besides, you can't be unaware that you and your sister may have noble blood flowing through your veins."

Kevin's attention sharpened. "What do you know of that? Such belief may be naught but the fancy of a woman who wished it were so. Our mother had no real proof that her father was a titled gentleman."

"She had the locket bearing her father's image."

"Moira lost the locket; we no longer have that as proof, if you could call such flimsy evidence proof."

"Moira left the locket in London. I found it. After some sleuthing, my friend's father identified the man in the miniature. Have you ever heard of Lord Pembroke?"

"No. Should I have?"

" 'Tis possible that Lord Pembroke, the Earl of Montgomery, is your grandfather. His title dates back to William the Conqueror. At one time he moved in high places. He has since retired to his country estate. He lost his only son before the son could produce an heir, and when his wife died several years later, he chose not to remarry. The earldom will die out for lack of an heir."

Kevin sent Jack a measuring look. "What makes you so sure this earl is our grandfather? Have you spoken with him?"

"I haven't contacted the earl yet. I intend to do so upon my return to England. Only Lord Pembroke can verify that he was ... er ... acquainted with your maternal grandmother. What was her name, by the way?"

"Sheila Malone. Our mother's name was Mary. Is that why you're so eager to marry Moira? Because she might be the granddaughter of an earl?"

"Bloody hell, O'Toole, I would marry Moira if she were a scullery maid. What will it take to convince you?"

Kevin muttered an apology of sorts, still not fully convinced of Lord Jack's tender feelings for his sister.

" 'Tis time I left to prepare for the wedding. Will you be there, O'Toole? It will mean a lot to Moira."

"Of course we'll be there," Katie interjected. "If Moira consented to the marriage, that's good enough for me."

"Four o'clock, at the church," Jack said, sending Katie a grateful look.

"Four o'clock," Kevin repeated with grudging respect.

Jack took his leave soon after that, pleased with his progress. He knew Moira's brother still didn't trust him, but he hoped one day to gain his full approval.

Moira was still sleeping when Jack let himself into the room. He hated to awaken her, but he didn't want to be late for their wedding. He shook her gently so as not to frighten her and watched with glittering interest as she stretched and smiled up at him. The blanket fell away as she lifted her arms, baring her breasts, and it took all Jack's willpower not to join her in bed.

"Get up, lazybones, 'tis time to ready ourselves for our wedding."

"So soon?" Moira's grin widened as she reached for him.

Jack recognized the invitation and groaned in dismay. "There is no time, love. Your brother and his family are already on the way to the church."

"You went to see Kevin, and he agreed to attend our wedding?" Jack nodded. "I love you, Jack Graystoke. If you join me in bed, I'll show you how much."

Jack's manhood stirred and he shifted uncomfortably. "I didn't know I was marrying such a brazen wench. Do you want to be late for your wedding?"

"We've waited this long, a little longer won't hurt."

It took little effort on Jack's part to relent. She looked so adorable, flushed from sleep and dewy-eyed that he couldn't deny her any more than he could deny his own clamoring need. He undressed quickly, his hot gaze fastened on her breasts, which seemed to swell with each breath she took. When she pushed the blanket aside so he could join her, his glittering gaze slid down to that part of her that gave him so much pleasure. But he didn't join her, not yet.

With slow purpose he walked to the washstand, poured water from the pitcher into a bowl and wet a clean cloth. When he returned, he spread Moira's legs and gently washed away all traces of their previous loving. When he finished, Moira rose from bed, took the cloth from his hands, rinsed it, and shyly performed the same service for him. Jack groaned, his passion ready to explode. Then they fell together on the bed, arms and legs entwined, bodies touching from breast to groin. When Jack slid over her, Moira gave him a mischievous grin and pushed him down on his back.

" 'Tis my turn to torment you, Lord Jack."

Sitting astride him, she kissed and nipped and teased, her hot mouth gliding over his face, his neck, his shoulders, devoting special attention to the hard nubs of his male breasts. Jack caught his breath and slowly let it out as her lips moved inexorably downward. He groaned and thrust upward into the soft nest of her palm as she curled her fingers around him, stroking his thick length to the root. But Moira was far from finished. Lowering her head, she tasted him delicately, with teasing little laps of her tongue.

"Enough!" Jack growled roughly as he seized her hips, lifted her high and thrust into her. She was open and wet and took him eagerly.

Arching her head sharply backward, Moira rode him shamelessly, her eyes glazed, her lips parted as tiny gasps of pleasure gurgled from her throat. Piercing her deeply, Jack could feel the tension quivering in his stomach and stroked her shallowly to regain control. When he felt he could carry on again, he took her breast into his mouth and began moving forcefully inside her, carefully bringing Moira to the point of no return.

By now Moira was wild to reach that elusive place where pleasure ruled. She wanted him deeper, faster, and she wanted it now. She was perilously close to the brink, and nothing short of sudden death would stop her from reaching it. Jack was more than willing to comply. With deep, probing thrusts, he brought her swiftly to climax. He continued stroking inside her until her explosive vibrations gained his own violent release.

"You'll make an old man of me before my time, love," Jack gasped as he lifted her from atop him and set her beside him on the bed.

" 'Tis rumored that Black Jack Graystoke is sexually insatiable," Moira countered saucily.

"Every man has his limits. But I readily admit that with you, my limits are severely strained. And before you get any more ideas, love, we really must get dressed. I'll wager the priest and your family are beginning to wonder if we're going to appear."

The wedding took place thirty minutes past the appointed hour. After one look at Moira's flushed face and Jack's contented grin, no one had the slightest doubt about the reason for their delay. Fortunately, all were too polite to mention it, though Katie's repressed smile said more than words.

The ceremony was blessedly brief and the children well-behaved. Jack's intent gaze never left Moira's face. He wouldn't, couldn't, relax until Father Sian pronounced them husband and wife. Then abruptly it was over, and at long last Moira belonged to him; no one could ever take her away from him.

Kevin's grudging congratulations pleased Jack, and he knew it meant a lot to Moira. Afterward he invited everyone, including Father Sian, to the inn for a wedding supper, which he had arranged with the innkeeper beforehand.

The meal was surprisingly good and well prepared on such short notice, and after seeing his sister's happiness, Kevin warmed up considerably. The children fell asleep over the meal and since the hour was late, Jack arranged for rooms for the entire O'Toole family. Moira slipped up to their room first, then Kate escorted the children to bed, leaving Jack and Kevin alone. Kevin raised his glass in salute.

"Here's to long life and happiness, and a healthy lad or lassie." He fixed Jack with a stalwart glance and said, "If you make my sister unhappy, you'll have me to answer to. England isn't so far away that I can't bring her back home if need be."

Jack returned the salute and drank deeply. "I'll never give you or Moira cause to regret this marriage. This marriage was ordained before Moira and I met. Lady Amelia must be the happiest ghost in that dark place where spirits dwell."

Kevin scratched his head. "Ghosts? Lady Amelia?"

Jack smiled. "Never mind, 'tis a long story. There is something I wish to discuss with you. I know your circumstances aren't the best, and that all Ireland is in the grip of poverty, and I want to help. You're my brother-in-law, and I have the means to make life easier for you."

Keven scowled. "I don't want your charity. Nor do I

want some old man to claim me as kin after he abandoned my grandmother.''

"It isn't charity I offer. I'd like you and your family to accompany Moira and me to England. Whether Lord Pembroke claims you and Moira as kin is not the issue. You could live at Ailesbury Hall and see to its upkeep. I prefer living at Graystoke Manor. It's in the process of being renovated in my absence. Think of the children, if not yourself. Ailesbury Hall sits amid countless acres. There are lakes, forests and gardens. I feel your family could be happy there.''

"Ireland is my home," Kevin said with wavering conviction.

"It would please Moira to have you in England. It was what she was working toward when I met her. You could either sell your farm or rent it out. At Ailesbury Hall, Katie would have all the help she needs with the children and servants to wait on her. She deserves it, Kevin. Katie strikes me as a loyal wife and loving mother.''

Kevin could not argue with Jack's logic. "I cannot pick up and leave on such short notice. You're right about one thing, Lord Jack. My Katie deserves the best, and whether 'tis true or not, I need to know for my own peace of mind if this Lord Pembroke is my grandfather.''

"Then you'll come with us to England?" Jack said, elated.

"Aye, as soon as I find the right tenant for the farm. I already have someone in mind. Young Peter Murphy is getting married and needs a place to live. He's a hard worker and a good lad. I'll lease the farm to him for nominal rent so long as he agrees to work the land. There is still some good left in the land, more than enough to feed him and his wife for a good long while.''

"Do you need more than two weeks to conclude your business and pack your belongings? You need take nothing but clothing and personal items you can't do without. I'll book passage if it's agreeable to you."

" 'Tis agreeable, Lord Jack. And I will take care of your property as if it were my own."

Before parting, they shook hands. Then Jack bounded up the stairs to join his bride.

Moira was waiting, propped up in bed looking like an angel with her dark red tresses spread about her naked shoulders. A tub of cooling water sat in the corner, and Jack decided to make use of it before joining Moira in bed.

"I'm sorry I had no time to buy you a wedding present," Jack said conversationally as he lathered his chest and shoulders. "But I accomplished one thing I hope you'll approve of."

Moira watched his soapy hands move over his body, imagining they were her own hands on his warm, pliant flesh. She smiled in lazy contentment, recalling their passionate coming together in this room earlier today. Finally his words worked through her satiated brain. "What did you accomplish, husband?"

Husband. The word rolled over him like sweet honey. "Kevin and his family are coming to England with us. They'll live at Ailesbury."

Moira's smile was dazzling. "That's the best wedding gift you could have given me. The only reason I took work in London was to help Kevin and his family, but all I did was get myself into trouble. If not for you, I might have become a victim of Roger Mayhew and the Hellfire Club."

"Your own resourcefulness saved you," Jack reminded

her. "When I attempted to rescue you, all I did was get myself shot. You and Matilda escaped the disciples of the Devil on your own. But I'm glad you're pleased about Kevin. We'll bide in Ireland until Kevin has made arrangements for the farm."

He lifted himself from the tub and walked dripping wet to the fireplace, where he shook himself like a shaggy dog. Moira watched as dancing flames burnished his flesh a deep gold, thinking him the handsomest man she'd ever seen. Her hands went to her stomach, where her child rested beneath her ribs, and she eagerly awaited the day she'd hold Jack's babe in her arms. Life had never been so good or so rewarding. With a smile on her lips, her eyes drifted shut and she fell asleep.

Jack climbed into bed carefully so as not to awaken Moira. Guilt rode him. Their vigorous lovemaking this afternoon had been too much for her, even though the last time had been at her instigation. Gathering her into his arms, he was content to hold her close to his heart and contemplate their future. For the first time in his life, he dared to dream about children of his own. He looked forward with relish to fatherhood.

A small smile lifted his lips. Who would have thought that Black Jack Graystoke would welcome fatherhood? Certainly not he. All Black Jack the rake had to look forward to was perdition. But thanks to Moira, he could thumb his nose at the Devil. He wondered if Lady Amelia knew that he'd married Moira. Of course she did, he decided, answering his own question. Everything he now held in his arms, his whole world, had been the result of Lady Amelia's meddling.

Chapter Twenty-One

Two weeks later Moira, Jack and the entire O'Toole family left Ireland aboard the *Bonny Prince*. The day was extra fine, the weather bright and sunny, the channel crossing uneventful. For the first time in her memory, Moira felt as if everything was right in her life. She had her family whom she loved and a husband she adored. And she had the baby growing inside her. Being so happy helped her to forget all the unpleasantness that had taken place in London. She was safe now, safe from Roger Mayhew and the Hellfire Club.

Once they debarked at London Pool, Jack hired coaches to carry the two families and all their baggage to Graystoke Manor. As Moira climbed into the carriage, she caught a glimpse of a man she thought she recognized and her breath froze in her throat. Her gasp alerted Jack to her distress.

"What is it, sweetheart? Are you ill? Is it the baby?"

Moira gave her head a vigorous shake. The man she thought she recognized had already disappeared into the milling crowd. " 'Tis nothing. For a moment I thought ... Never mind. I'm sure I was mistaken." Then the children climbed excitedly into the carriage and the moment was forgotten.

Moira was breathless with anticipation when their conveyance stopped before the stone facade of Graystoke Manor. She hadn't realized until now that she had missed the place. Already she could see improvements that Jack had ordered done in her absence and was anxious to see the inside all spruced up.

Pettibone met them at the door. "Welcome home, milord," Pettibone greeted enthusiastically. "And Miss Moira. We were all worried about you. I knew His Grace would find you." He eyed Kevin and his family curiously but was too polite to inquire.

" 'Tis good to be home, Pettibone. Damn good," Jack replied as he led the small entourage into the house. "Please greet your new mistress properly. Moira and I were married several weeks ago in Ireland."

Pettibone's face lit up. "Married you say?" He turned to Moira. "Felicitations, milady. You'll make a wonderful duchess. Wait until Matilda and Jilly hear."

"Have the upper floors been renovated yet, Pettibone?"

"Aye, milord. A hundred men worked virtually around the clock to finish before you returned."

Jack nodded. "Very good. Have the west wing prepared for Moira's brother and his family. Mr. and Mrs. O'Toole will stay with us for a time before moving on to Ailesbury Hall." He turned to Kevin and Katie. "This is Pettibone. As you come to know him, you'll learn why I cannot do without him."

Pettibone flushed with pleasure. "Lord Jack is generous with his praise. You must all be tired after your trip. I'll see that tea is served in the drawing room directly.''

Katie appeared to be in shock. The grandeur of Grays-toke Manor boggled her mind. Matilda and Jilly materi-alized from somewhere in the manor and introductions were made. Then Matilda bustled the children into the kitchen for cookies and milk. ''Your manor is magnifi-cent, Lord Jack,'' Katie said appreciatively.

''The downstairs isn't completely renovated yet, but soon it will be as grand as it once was. It's not as im-pressive as Ailesbury Hall, but this place is more like home to me. I will be taking Moira to Ailesbury Hall soon. She'll love the country.''

''What do you intend doing about Lord Pembroke?'' Kevin asked.

''I'll send a messenger to his estate tomorrow and ask when it will be convenient for him to receive us. I'll also send a note to the newspaper announcing my marriage to Moira.''

Moira shifted uncomfortably. ''Do you think that's wise?''

''Wise and necessary,'' Jack said crisply. ''Once people become accustomed to the idea, they will accept you as the Duchess of Ailesbury. For my part, society can go to the Devil, but I won't have them slighting my wife.''

Moira didn't argue despite her feeling that both she and Jack were likely to be treated as outcasts. She had tried talking him out of his folly, had even left him in hopes that he'd come to his senses. But Jack had been adamantly determined to marry her. She loved him so much that she hadn't the stamina to resist. For better or worse, they were husband and wife, and she prayed Jack would never regret his decision. The possibility that she was Lord Pembro-ke's granddaughter was too slim to set store by.

Later that night, ensconced in the master bedchamber, Jack endeavored to show Moira how much she meant to him. His loving was tender and excruciatingly intense as he skillfully teased and caressed her to gasping ecstasy. His gaze, dark and brilliant, rested on her in waiting silence as he brought her to shattering climax, then allowed himself to join her.

Lord Pembroke's return reply granted Jack a private audience two days hence. He expressed curiosity, since he'd never met the Duke of Ailesbury, but graciously granted the interview if it was kept short, due to his failing health.

Moira was nervous the day the meeting was scheduled to take place. She changed gowns at least three times and finally settled on a green satin morning dress with beige and green striped sleeves. Since Kevin had nothing decent to wear, Jack loaned him a suit of clothes, and once dressed, he looked every bit as elegant as his benefactor. Katie did not accompany them, preferring to remain home with the children.

Lord Pembroke's estate lay several hours west of London, so they left early in order to arrive at the appointed hour of two in the afternoon. "What if Lord Pembroke denies knowledge of my grandmother?" Moira asked anxiously.

" 'Tis no big thing, love. We're doing this for your sake, not mine. A farmer's daughter is good enough for me."

"Aye, and being a farmer is all I ever aspired to," Kevin agreed. "If this proves to be a wild-goose chase, I'll not be disappointed."

Lord Pembroke's ancestral home was a medieval manor

constructed on the grand scale of an ancient stone fortress with crenellated walls and several towers. They rode through the open gates to the main entrance, which was protected by a huge, wooden door richly carved and fitted with brass. They descended from the carriage the moment the steps were lowered and approached the portal. Jack gave Moira's cold hand a squeeze, then lifted the heavy knocker. A few moments later, the door was thrown open by an ancient footman dressed meticulously in black and silver.

"Lord Pembroke is waiting in the library," he intoned dryly. "Please follow me."

It was too late now to turn back, Moira thought as she drew in a deep, steadying breath. Either she was Lord Pembroke's granddaughter or she wasn't. For Jack's sake, she hoped she was. The butler opened the door, and she clutched her locket as Jack led her and Kevin inside a room that would have been depressing if not for the cheery fire burning in the grate.

Lord Pembroke rose from his chair before the fire and turned toward his visitors. Jack strode forward and took the man's hand. "Allow me to introduce myself, Your Grace. Jack Graystoke, Duke of Ailesbury. This is my wife Moira and her brother Kevin."

Though well into his seventies, the earl was still an impressive man in both manner and looks. Silver-haired and sharp-witted, he was slim and elegant still. Only his slightly bent shoulders and extreme thinness gave subtle hint to his age and state of health.

The earl stared hard at Moira for the space of a heartbeat, nodded in acknowledgment, then turned to Jack. "I must admit I'm curious to know why you wished an interview. Please sit down and join me. I was about to enjoy a brandy. I'll order tea for your lady, if that's agreeable.''

Moira flushed, certain that Lord Pembroke's sharp-eyed gaze had noted her pregnancy.

A servant entered directly with three glasses, a bottle and a pot of tea. The earl poured, took a sip of his own brandy, sat back and said, "Shall we get down to the reason for your visit?"

"Of course, Your Grace," Jack said. "I wish you to understand that we are not here to pry into your past but to clear up something very important to my wife and brother-in-law." Pembroke frowned but said nothing. "Somewhere in your past, were you ever acquainted with an Irish woman named Sheila Malone?"

Pembroke choked and the brandy spewed from his mouth. "My God, man, do you know how far back you're asking me to delve? Or the painful memories you're dredging up?"

"Then you did know her!" Kevin all but shouted.

Pembroke's eyes narrowed. "What do you know of Sheila? I never thought I'd hear that name again. Do you know how long I searched for her? No," he answered, shaking his head, "you couldn't possibly know. You're far too young."

With shaking hands, Moira removed the locket from around her neck and handed it to Lord Pembroke. "Open it, Your Grace, and tell me if you recognize the man in the miniature."

Releasing the latch, Pembroke stared at the miniature. His hands trembled and he paled, plainly shaken by what he saw. " 'Tis the miniature I had done for Sheila. How did you come by this?"

"My mother gave it to me. It belonged to her own mother. Sheila died giving birth to a daughter."

Pembroke stared at her, his keen perception sorting through the facts. "Did Sheila marry well?"

"She didn't marry at all. Her parents disowned her after they learned she carried a child out of wedlock. She ended up in a convent, where she died giving birth. The nuns raised her daughter to adulthood. Sheila died without ever mentioning the name of her child's father. The nuns later told my mother that her father abandoned them."

Pembroke came out of his chair. "My God! I looked everywhere for Sheila." He began pacing. "I was young and reckless when I joined the army and was sent to Ireland. I met Sheila, fell in love and intended to make her my wife. A bullet put an end to my hopes and dreams. I was wounded during an uprising and not expected to live. I was sent home to England to die. 'Tis a miracle that I lived. Months passed before I could return to Ireland and tell Sheila what happened.

"I was devastated when I couldn't find her. Her parents refused to talk about her. It was as if she didn't exist for them. Finally, I had to return to England. My father was ill and I could linger no longer. Years passed before I gave up on her and married a woman of my acquaintance." He stared at Moira and his expression softened. "You look like her, you know."

Moira smiled. "I'm glad. No one knew what my grandmother looked like."

"She was beautiful, just like you." Sighing heavily, Pembroke sank down into his chair and stared pensively at his tented fingers. "So I have a daughter. Tell me about her. Did she come to England with you?"

"Both our parents died of a fever," Kevin explained. "Mother's name was Mary. She was lovely. She died far too young."

Pembroke looked on the verge of weeping as he shifted his gaze to the window and stared at nothing in particular. "Had I known I had a daughter, I could have made life easier for her. Had I known . . . Had I only known . . ."

He looked so utterly lost, so utterly defeated that Moira rose and knelt before him. "Are you all right, Your Grace? We didn't mean to dredge up painful memories. I know your health isn't robust. Perhaps we should leave."

"Leave?" His gaze settled on Moira, then moved to Kevin. "I'm sorry if I seem shaken, but I can't allow you to leave. Not yet. I may have lost Sheila and Mary, but I still have Mary's children." He gestured toward Jack. "Do you realize, Ailesbury, that these two are my sole living heirs?"

Moira felt a surge of jubilation that went beyond mere happiness. Her father's family had always been dear to her, but it meant a great deal to know that she and Kevin also had roots elsewhere.

"That's not why we're here, Your Grace," Kevin said. His chin tilted at a stubborn angle, his pride too fierce to allow him to accept charity.

Pembroke smiled. "Do I detect a portion of Pembroke pride in your demeanor?"

"You'll not find Kevin lacking in pride," Jack allowed. "Nor his sister. Moira seems to have inherited pride and stubbornness in abundance. Thank God I finally convinced her to marry me."

"Thank God you cared enough to solve the mystery of her identity. I owe you a debt of gratitude, Ailesbury. As for Kevin and Moira, I'd like to get to know them better. As my sole male heir, Kevin will inherit the title one day. His children will be lords and ladies. And Moira will share equally in the bounty of my estate."

Kevin gave him an uncertain look. "I'm a farmer, Your Grace. I know nothing of lords and ladies."

"You'll learn. Are you married, my boy?"

Kevin sent him a genuine smile. "Aye. My Katie and I have three lively children and another on the way."

Pembroke shook his head, unable to believe he had gone from a lonely old man living in virtual seclusion to a man rich in heirs. If his judgment wasn't faulty, and he doubted it was, it looked as if Moira and Ailesbury would soon present him with another great-grandchild.

"You and your family must move to Pembroke Hall immediately. Children will liven up this old place, I warrant. And Ailesbury must promise to bring Moira regularly to visit. I'll send out an announcement to the newspapers immediately. I want the whole world to know that you and Moira are my heirs."

"That's not necessary, Your Grace," Kevin said. "I wanted to know about our maternal ancestors for my mother's sake. It would have meant a great deal to her to know that we have finally found our English roots."

"I insist. How soon can you move out here?"

Kevin looked thoroughly bewildered. Everything was moving too fast for him. "I promised Lord Jack that I'd move to Ailesbury Hall and keep an eye on the place for him. He prefers Graystoke Manor in London."

"Ailesbury Hall is available should you wish to live there," Jack said. "I can't blame Lord Pembroke for wanting to get to know his heir. The choice is yours, Kevin."

"And I will certainly visit often if . . . Grandfather wishes it," Moira said shyly.

The earl beamed, looking years younger than when they'd arrived. "You don't know how much that title

means to me. Thank you, granddaughter, for honoring me
in such a manner.'' He held out his arms, and Moira
moved unerringly into them.

They left a short time later, after the earl received Kevin's promise to bring his family to Pembroke Hall the
following week for an extended visit. Later, in the privacy
of his chapel, the old earl gave humble thanks to his
maker for granting him the joy of knowing his grandchildren and great-grandchildren in his declining years.
He felt years younger than he had even twenty years ago.

Moira felt the weight of loneliness after Kevin and his
family departed for Pembroke Hall. Kevin had asked her
to join them, but she was reluctant to leave Jack, even
though he spent long hours at his office with his man of
business. Taking over the reins of the dukedom was a
complicated affair, occupying a great deal of Jack's time.
Moira couldn't have borne it if she didn't know that when
Jack returned he'd devote all his attention upon her. At
night, they closed themselves in their bedchamber and forgot the world existed. Her growing girth did nothing to
dampen Jack's ardor, for which Moira was eternally grateful, as they delved more deeply into the realm of sensual
pleasure.

During those blissful days, Moira worried that she was
too content for it to last and feared something unforeseen
would interfere with her happiness. Fortunately, her
grandfather's notice in the newspaper had eased her entrance into society. Invitations were arriving daily, though
they had as yet to accept any of them, but still Moira was
troubled. She kept recalling the face in the crowd she'd
seen at the docks. She knew she was imagining things,
but Roger Mayhew's face had been so clearly defined that

she kept seeing his malevolent sneer everywhere she turned.

She deliberately refrained from confiding in Jack, realizing how foolish she'd appear when he proved her fears groundless. Instead, Moira tried to immerse herself in the renovation of Graystoke Manor and observing the growing affection between the dour Pettibone and Matilda.

"Would you like to visit Lord Pembroke again?" Jack asked one day before he left for another endless consultation with his man of business. "We can go out on Friday and spend a few days with him and Kevin. You must be missing the children something fierce."

"Oh, Jack, can we?" Moira enthused, throwing her arms around his neck. "Kate's time is drawing near. I'd like to be there when her child is born."

Jack kissed her soundly. "If I'd known you'd be so grateful, I would have suggested it while we were still abed. There's still time to . . ." His half-finished suggestion hung in the air like a fragrant spring day.

"Get on with you," Moira said, blushing prettily. "I knew I'd married a man with amazing stamina, but you're surpassing your own record."

"Few men are fortunate enough to encounter the pure temptation of a delicious little body like yours. And your face. God help me, Moira, for I can't help myself. Every day I want you more. I just wish I could thank Lady Amelia for throwing you into my path. Unfortunately, the lady hasn't reappeared."

Moira sent him a laughing glance. The Irish were known to believe in faeries and sprites and little people, but she'd always remained skeptical. "I'm sure your elusive ancestor knows everything that's occurred."

"Indeed," Jack replied, glancing over his shoulder as

if he expected the elusive lady to appear at his elbow. "If I can't entice you back to bed, I suppose I should leave." He kissed her with the fervor of a desperate man and reluctantly departed. Neither Jack nor Moira saw the man lurking in the shadow of the building, or his satisfied smirk when he saw Jack leaving.

It was a full two hours later when Pettibone answered the door and found a grubby urchin standing on the door-step.

"Beggars are fed at the back door," Pettibone said with a sniff.

"I ain't a beggar," the lad said, swiping his dripping nose against his dirty sleeve. "I got a message for Her Ladyship."

"A message? What kind of a message?"

"There's been an accident. His Lordship has been hurt," the lad repeated in a voice that hinted of coaching. "His friend is waitin' in the coach to take the duchess to His Lordship."

Moira walked into the foyer in time to hear the lad's words. "An accident! Dear Lord, how badly is Jack hurt? Where is he?"

"Don't know, milady. The nob in the coach paid me to give you the message. He's waitin' to take ya to his lordship."

"It must be Spence," Moira said, all reasoning leaving her as she hurried out the door toward the waiting coach.

"Milady, wait," Pettibone called after her. "I'll go with you."

"There's no time. Send for the doctor, Pettibone. You're needed here to handle things. I'll return with Jack as soon as I can."

"Milady, I don't think . . ."

Whatever Pettibone thought was left unsaid as Moira opened the door to the coach and was literally pulled inside. "Spence, whatever are you doing?" she cried as arms like bands of steel closed around her. "Let me go."

"Sorry to disappoint you, Moira, but you're not going to escape me again."

That voice! Turning her head sharply, Moira stared into the beady eyes of Roger Mayhew.

"Where is Lord Spencer? What are you doing in England? Let me go! I have to go to my husband."

"I'm afraid that's not possible. Your husband is dead."

A ragged cry left her throat, and Moira fainted for the first time in her life.

Chapter Twenty-Two

Jack left the office in a jovial mood. He had finished his business sooner than expected and looked forward with relish to spending the remainder of the day with Moira. Perhaps a ride in the park, he thought, or a matinee at Drury Lane Theater. For his part, he'd prefer spending the afternoon in bed with his delectable little wife, whose passion brought him untold joy.

His arousing thoughts were carrying him on such a delightful journey that he paid little heed to Colin, who waited patiently in the driver's box of the carriage parked at the curb. Jack paid little more than passing notice to Colin's bowed head and hunched shoulders as he ordered the lad to proceed directly to Graystoke Manor before climbing inside and settling against the leather squabs.

Jack's mind wandered along pleasant pathways as the carriage wended through London's crowded thoroughfares. Lost in thought, Jack didn't become alarmed until he happened to glance out the window and noted that they were traveling the outskirts of London.

Spitting out a curse, he pounded on the roof for Colin to stop and explain himself. A sudden spurt of speed tossed Jack onto the floor.

By the time Jack regained his balance, the carriage careened onto a deserted dirt lane that wound through hedgerows. Minutes later, it came to a screeching halt. He groped for the door, but it was flung open before he could reach it.

"What's the meaning of this, Colin?" Jack asked in his sternest voice. "Have you lost your mind?"

"Get out, Yer Lordship," a gruff voice answered.

Jack's head shot up. He saw at a glance that the man who spoke wasn't Colin. Nor was the man behind him Colin. Or the driver, who was stepping down from the driver's box to help his partners in crime. Jack had no choice but to climb out of the carriage. But before he did he reached behind the squabs, retrieved a primed pistol kept there for just such an emergency and thrust it into the waistband beneath his coat. At least he'd be able to get off one good shot before he was overpowered. If he was fortunate, it might even scare off the others.

"Who are you and what do you want?" Jack asked curtly. "I'm carrying few valuables on my person. I'll make it worth your while to let me go. Take me home and I'll reward you handsomely."

"Ye can be sure we'll take whatever yer carryin' on ye, but ye ain't goin' 'ome. We ain't fools. More than likely ya'll set yer men on us. Some bloke wants ya dead and paid us to do ya in."

Jack studied his adversaries, realizing he had little but his wits to get him out of this one. "I'll pay you more."

"Do ye have the blunt on ye?" one of the men asked hopefully.

"I told you, I'm carrying little of value. What have you done with my driver?"

"We weren't paid to kill him," the spokesman muttered. "We just roughed him up a bit and left him in an alley." He made a chopping motion with his hand. "Enough talkin'."

The men closed in and Jack moved out into the open, not wanting to be cornered with his back to the carriage.

The footpads were separating, each coming at Jack from a different angle, two brandishing knives and one a stout branch he'd picked up from the ground. Jack waited, knees bent, his body tense. The moment they rushed him, he pulled out the pistol, aimed and fired. One man fell. Momentarily stunned, the others halted to stare at their fallen comrade.

"Ye kilt old Henry!" the leader cried, his face mottled with rage. "Ye gone and done it now! Get him Dickey!"

Wishing he'd brought his short sword, Jack decided that flight was the better part of valor. He turned to flee and found his path blocked by Dickey, obviously a seasoned street fighter by the look of his bulging muscles. Glancing over his shoulder, Jack noted that the other man was quickly closing in on him from another direction. Finding no other option, he mentally prepared himself to fight.

Dickey threw himself at Jack, bringing him to the ground. "I got him, Robin," Dickey crowed as he pinned Jack down with pure brute force. Jack focused all his strength on keeping Dickey's knife from slashing him to ribbons. As soon as Robin joined the fray, Jack realized he was fighting a losing battle.

Jack sustained a nasty cut to his upper arm and another to his ribs. They were painful but not life threatening, but he realized it was only a matter of time before a mortal wound was delivered.

Suddenly shouts and the sound of creaking wheels reached Jack's fuzzy brain, nearly at the same time that Dickey and Robin heard them. With his knife poised at Jack's throat, Robin turned his head to stare at the carriage jolting down the dirt lane. He cursed violently and leaped to his feet. Jack wasted no time in throwing Dickey off and gaining his own feet.

"Ho, there, Jack! Can you use some help?"

The carriage ground to a halt and Spence leaped from it before it came to a full stop. Colin, his head dripping blood, followed close behind. They were joined by Spence's burly coachman, wielding a stout cudgel. When Robin and Dickey saw they were outnumbered, they turned tail and ran.

"Don't let them get away!" Jack yelled. Colin and the coachman caught them handily and dragged them back to where Jack and Spence were waiting.

"What should we do with them?" Spence asked, prodding Robin with the point of his short sword. "Who are they, and what did they want with you?"

"Obviously they're street thugs who were paid to do me in," Jack said, staggering weakly against the carriage.

"Bloody hell," Spence muttered darkly as he turned a ferocious glare on the man held captive by his sword. "Who paid you to kill Lord Jack?"

"I don't know his name," Robin said sullenly. "I think he's some high-born bloke, but I ain't sure. We was to collect the rest of our blunt at the Fatted Calf later tonight."

Jack frowned. "The Fatted Calf is the roughest dive on

the waterfront. What time were you supposed to meet him?''

"Ten o'clock."

"Someone will meet your benefactor, but it won't be you." He turned to Colin, wincing when he saw a lump crusted with blood blossoming on the lad's head. "There's rope in the boot, Colin. If you're up to it, help Spence's coachman tie them up and put them inside the carriage. I'll drop them off at Newgate and press charges."

"I'm up to it, milord," Colin said. "I'm sorry I failed you. They hit me in the head." He gave Jack a cocky grin. "'Tis the hardest part of me. They made the mistake of not tying me up. I staggered out of the alley just as they drove off. I assumed you were with them. The next person I saw was Lord Fenwick. He'd arrived at your place of business looking for you. I told him what happened and we gave chase. I should have been more vigilant."

"It's not your fault, Colin. No one was expecting something like this. I thank God you're not hurt and had the presence of mind to enlist Spence's help. Can you drive? I don't think I'm up to it."

"Christ, Jack, you're hurt!" Spence cried, noting the blood seeping through Jack's sleeve and vest where it covered his ribs. "Get inside the carriage before you fall down. You're pale as death."

"I've suffered worse," Jack said, though admittedly the pain from his wounds was making him light-headed.

"I'm taking you to the doctor."

"Not until these two are locked up. After I've pressed charges, you can take me home and send Colin for the doctor. I have this unaccountable urge to see Moira."

Spence grinned. "Matrimony must agree with you. Very well, as soon as my man loads up that dead fellow we'll be off. By the way, good shot. You always were accurate."

Jack limped into the house leaning on Spence's shoulder. Pettibone was beside himself with worry as he fussed over his master. Jack was surprised to see that the doctor had already arrived and was waiting. They bore him to his room and divested him of his coat, vest and shirt, laying bare his wounds. Very carefully, Dr. Dudley cleansed the lacerated flesh, clucking his tongue like a mother hen.

"These look like knife wounds," the good doctor said. "I thought you'd been injured in an accident."

"It's a long story, doctor. I assure you I'm not badly hurt. You must be a mind reader to have arrived so quickly."

"You'll need some stitching," Dr. Dudley said as he threaded his needle. "This shouldn't take long."

"Where is Lady Moira?" Pettibone asked as he suddenly realized Moira hadn't come in with Jack and Spence. "I must admit I was leery and more than a little worried when that grimy urchin told us some outlandish story about you being injured. Even though I knew Lady Moira would be all right with Lord Spencer, I greatly feared something was amiss."

The blood froze in Jack's veins, and he jerked spasmodically.

"Hold still," the doctor warned as he drove the needle into Jack's flesh.

Ignoring the pain, Jack tried to sit up. The doctor pushed him back down and glared at him. Mindless of the doctor, Jack grasped Pettibone's sleeve. "What are you saying, Pettibone? Isn't Moira home? As you can see, she isn't with Spence."

Pettibone's face turned gray with fear. "I thought . . . That is . . . The carriage . . . The lad said . . . Oh, my God!"

"Get hold of yourself, Pettibone," Jack said through clenched teeth. "Start at the beginning."

Pettibone swallowed convulsively. "Very good, milord. A ragged urchin appeared at the door this morning, bearing the news that you had been injured in an accident. He said your friend was waiting in the carriage at the curb for Lady Moira to join him. We all assumed it was Lord Spencer, and that he would take Her Ladyship to you. I wanted to go with her, but she bade me to remain here and send for the doctor."

Jack's expression grew grim. That explained the doctor's presence when he arrived home, he thought, but it still didn't explain Moira's disappearance, or with whom she had gone.

"No one could have known about my injury except . . ."

"The man who wanted you dead," Spence contended. "But why would he abduct Moira? It just doesn't make sense."

Jack felt as if his world had just come to an end. "Moira is carrying my child," he said tonelessly, addressing no one in particular. "If she or my child is harmed, I'll kill the bastard who took her."

Pettibone gave a visible shudder. Dr. Dudley took the last stitch, knotted the thread and said, "You're not going anywhere for a while. Your wounds aren't life threatening, but you've lost a considerable amount of blood. Bed rest is indicated for the next few days. I recommend that you contact the authorities and let them deal with this."

"Not bloody likely," Jack grit out.

"Listen, Jack," Spence urged, "the doctor knows best. Let me handle this for you."

"No! If some crazy bastard has my wife, I'm damn well going to be the one to get her back. And I strongly suspect that the man who took her is the same man who paid to have me done in. We won't know who or why until we have him in our possession."

"How do you intend to do that?" Spence wanted to know.

"I can see that you aren't going to follow my advice," Dr. Dudley said as he packed up his bag. "I have other patients to treat. If you need me, send someone around to my office. Good luck, milord. And congratulations on the forthcoming birth of your heir."

The moment the door closed behind the doctor, Jack eased into a sitting position, catching his breath when the stitches pulled against his lacerated flesh.

"What can I do, milord?" Pettibone asked as he hovered over Jack, wringing his hands in despair.

"Find me something to eat," Jack directed, more to get rid of him than because he was hungry. Pettibone left immediately.

"I know what you intend," Spence said, frowning. "You're going to go to the Fatted Calf and wait for the man who ordered your death. You're not up to it, old man. You don't even know the man's identity. Let me handle it. Or better yet, the police."

"No! If he sees the police, he'll likely be frightened off, and I'll never find Moira. Bloody hell, Spence, if only

I could find a reason in all this! Who would hate Moira or me enough to do this?''

Thoroughly stymied, Spence ran his fingers through his thick, blond hair. "I wish I knew. What can I do to help?''

"You can question the men we dropped off at Newgate earlier. I know they denied any knowledge of the abductor's identity, or his reason for wanting me dead, but it can't hurt to question them further. If you learn anything, I'll be here until it's time to leave for the Fatted Calf.''

Spence left, silently vowing to be at the Fatted Calf at ten o'clock with plenty of help no matter what Jack wanted. Jack was in no condition for a fight should he need to defend himself.

Jack stifled a groan, lay back against the pillows and closed his eyes. He didn't dare cave in to the pain with Spence and Pettibone looking on, but now that he was alone, he allowed himself the luxury of expressing his pain and anguish.

You must find her.

Jack's eyes flew open. She stood at the foot of the bed, shrouded in mist and shimmering light.

"Lady Amelia, thank God you've come back. Do you know who has abducted Moira? Can you help me?''

Lady Amelia shook her head.

You are the only one whose life can be changed by my intervention.

"God knows you've made a new man of me," Jack admitted, wincing as he levered himself up against the pillows.

She has redeemed you; now you must save her.

"I intend to. Are you certain I will succeed?''

You must succeed. The future of the dukedom lies within Moira's womb.

"I have no future without Moira," Jack said with slow emphasis. "Can you tell me nothing more?"

Beware the tides.

"What is that supposed to mean?"

Suddenly the door opened and Pettibone stepped in, balancing a tray in his hands. Jack spit out a curse as Lady Amelia receded into the shadows. "No, don't go! Come back, please."

Startled, Pettibone looked at Jack as if his employer had just lost his mind. Following Jack's gaze, Pettibone saw a flickering light in the corner of the room. He watched in stunned silence as it vanished before his very eyes.

"Bloody hell!" Jack said, sending Pettibone a disgruntled look. "You'd best set the tray down before you drop it, Pettibone. And close your mouth."

Pettibone carefully set the tray on the nightstand and looked askance at Jack. "Is aught amiss, milord?"

Jack swung his legs over the edge of the bed and waited until the pain subsided before speaking. "There's plenty amiss, Pettibone, as you well know. Set some clothes out for me while I eat. Nothing fancy, something dark and nondescript."

Pettibone cleared his throat. "Were my eyes deceiving me, or was there a strange light in the chamber when I entered?"

"You wouldn't believe me if I told you, Pettibone. I'm not sure I believe it myself."

"If you say so, milord," Pettibone sniffed. He wasn't stupid. He knew what was going on. Only one thing could have brought about Black Jack Graystoke's amazing transformation. From a rake well on his way to perdition, Black Jack had been transformed into the soul of respectability with a wife and a child on the way. He saw the fine hand of Lady Amelia in all this. And if he wasn't mistaken, Lady Amelia had just paid a visit to her reformed descendant.

Dressed in unrelenting black, his wounds bound tightly, Jack left the house at precisely nine o'clock that night. Colin drove the plain black carriage to the Fatted Calf, discharged his passenger and, following Jack's instructions, parked in the alley so as not to rouse suspicion. Jack entered into the raucous atmosphere of the crowded inn, deliberately selected a table in the farthest corner, sat down and waited for someone he recognized to show up.

Moira awoke to the inky blackness of fear and confusion. And a subtle rocking motion that sent panic racing through her. Rising gingerly, she tested her limbs and found them somewhat unstable but uninjured. She took a step forward and tripped over an object she soon discovered was a coil of rope. A pervading odor of rotting fish stung her senses, and when she combined everything she felt and smelled, she could only deduce that she was aboard a ship. And that Lord Roger Mayhew had brought her here.

Memory of the events that took place before she fainted emerged from her sluggish brain and she recoiled in horror. Jack was dead, not injured as she had assumed. Pain converged on her like rushing water, filling her with such anguish that her legs buckled beneath her. Choking sobs shook her body, sending scalding tears cascading down her cheeks. Did Lord Roger intend killing her, too?

Moira tensed when she heard a noise outside her dark prison. Suddenly the hatch above her opened and a man appeared in the opening, holding a lantern aloft. "So, you've finally awakened. Good.''

''Where am I? Why are you doing this to me? What have you done with my husband?''

Mayhew climbed down the ladder, closed the hatch behind him and hung the lantern from a hook on the ceiling. Hands on hips, he loomed over Moira, his eyes bright with anticipation. Or was it madness?

''You're the cause of all my problems. Because of you, my father disowned me and named my brother his heir. I was sent off to America in disgrace and told never to return. I'm an embarrassment to the family. All because of an Irish wench too good to spread her legs for the heir to an earldom. From now on, you'll spread your legs any time I order you to.''

''You're mad. What have you done to Jack?''

''His body will be discovered on a deserted road, or in an alley. The victim of footpads, no doubt.'' He laughed without mirth. ''A fitting end for a rogue.''

''I don't believe you. You're trying to frighten me. Where am I?''

''In the hold of a ship bound for China. I paid the captain a small fortune to take no other passengers and ask no questions of me. You'll find no help there. We sail on the midnight tide. I have a small piece of unfinished business to conduct at a nearby inn but will return in plenty of time. I suggest you rest while you can. When I return you'll be too busy catering to my needs to sleep. By the time we reach China, you'll know all the little tricks necessary to survive in a Chinese brothel.''

Moira inhaled sharply. This can't be happening to her! Lord Roger was supposed to be far away, where he could never hurt her again. She was Jack's wife and carried his child. She had found a grandfather she never knew she had, and her life was full to overflowing.

"What are you doing in England? Your father promised he would personally put you aboard a ship bound for America. You can't have returned already."

"My father is a stupid old man," Mayhew said irreverently. "He did put me aboard a ship. But I'm much smarter than those he paid to make sure I sailed with the ship. I jumped ashore moments before the ship pulled away from the pier, with no one the wiser. I've been living in London's underground, waiting for the opportunity to exact revenge. I made useful friends among the derelicts of the city. My friends would kill their own mother for enough blunt. Finding someone to do in Black Jack was easy."

Moira considered telling Roger that she carried Jack's child but decided against it. Obviously the man was mad; it was hard to tell what he'd do when he learned she was increasing. All she could do was hope and pray that Lord Roger had been lying about Jack. If he was truly dead, she'd feel it in her heart.

"Do you have proof that your friends killed Jack?"

Mayhew frowned. He'd sent three men—what could go wrong? "Not yet, but I will as soon as I meet my friends at the Fatted Calf and they verify his death. 'Tis almost time." He reached for the lantern and turned to leave.

"Wait! Leave the light. The dark frightens me." She wasn't really afraid of the dark; she needed light if she was to search for a way to escape. This time she didn't have Matilda to help her.

Mayhew considered her request, then nodded his head. "Very well. Just don't get any ideas about setting the place on fire, for it won't work. You'd probably die of smoke inhalation before rescue arrived."

Moira waited until Lord Roger climbed the ladder and secured the hatch before beginning a thorough search of the hold. If a means of escape existed, she'd find it.

The hour of ten arrived, and the Fatted Calf was nearly filled to capacity with boisterous, hard-drinking seamen and painted whores plying their trade. A fight broke out, which Jack watched with disinterest. A whore approached him and he quickly sent her packing. He shifted impatiently, his eyes never leaving the door, waiting, watching, wondering if he'd know the next man who walked through the portal. Pulling his hat down to shade his face, Jack tried to relax his tense body. It wasn't easy, for his thoughts kept straying to Moira, fretting over her safety.

When Lord Roger Mayhew skulked through the door of the Fatted Calf, Jack's shock was enormous. Tucking his chin into his chest, he watched Mayhew make a search of the room and saw him frown when he failed to locate who he was looking for. At length, Mayhew took a seat at an empty table facing the door.

Hunching his shoulders and pulling down his hat over his eyes, Jack rose and made his way slowly through the crowded common room, escaping Mayhew's notice as he came up behind him. Jack was fully armed. Besides a primed and loaded pistol, he carried a knife and a short sword beneath his coat. Palming the knife, Jack stopped behind Mayhew and pricked his neck with the weapon.

''Don't turn around, Mayhew. Get up slowly and walk out the door.''

Mayhew blanched when he recognized Jack's voice. ''You're supposed to be dead.''

''Your henchmen weren't as efficient as you'd hoped. As you can see, I'm very much alive. Move. You're going to take me to Moira. Make one false move and you're a dead man. I know where all the vital organs are.''

Mayhew did as he was told. No one seemed to notice anything amiss, for the revelry continued unabated. ''You don't dare kill me,'' Mayhew sneered. ''If you do, you'll never find your wife.''

''Try me,'' Jack challenged.

Mayhew decided to do just that. The moment he walked through the door, he bolted—and ran straight into the arms of Spence and the watch.

''Ah, just in time, I see,'' Spence said as the watch wrestled Mayhew into a pair of manacles.

''So much for following orders,'' Jack said dryly. ''All joking aside, I'm damned glad to see you.''

''I'm not alone. I've brought several of my retainers to aid us should Mayhew prove unmanageable.'' Several men materialized from the shadows, none of whom Jack would have cared to meet while alone on a dark street.

Jack turned to Mayhew, his face cold and unrelenting, his insides a seething cauldron of rage. ''Where is she, Mayhew? What have you done with Moira? I'd better find her unharmed, or your life is forfeit.''

Roger Mayhew was a coward. Unless backed by an army of men, he was all bravado and no courage. He cowered in fear when Spence's men made threatening moves in his direction, even pleading with the watch to protect him.

When the watch stepped away, leaving him to Jack's mercy, he started babbling incoherently. ''Pier ten, aboard the *Lady Jane*. She's locked in the hold.''

''Take him away and lock him up with his henchmen,'' Jack said, shoving Mayhew toward the watch. ''If he's hurt Moira, I'll make him sorry he was born.'' With his threat hanging in the air, Jack whirled on his heel and sprinted toward pier ten. Now he knew the meaning of Lady Amelia's warning. The ship was probably set to sail on the midnight tide. Spence and his retainers were hard on his heels.

Moira began to know true despair. She had searched the dark, dank hold thoroughly and found no visible means of escape. She had taken the lantern from the hook and searched every nook and cranny. She stumbled over crates and peered inside boxes containing cargo, food-stuffs and sundry other goods. On the verge of giving up, she found a crowbar lying atop a crate and crowed in delight. A weapon of any kind was a welcome gift.

Alerted by noise filtering through the hatch, Moira paused to listen. She heard muffled shouts, then running steps and indications of a scuffle. When the hatch opened suddenly, Moira blew out the lantern, grasped the crowbar and waited at the foot of the ladder. She had every inten-tion of bashing the first person to step foot into the hold.

Jack lifted the hatch leading down to the hold and stared into the darkness. He saw nothing, heard nothing. He was more than grateful that it hadn't taken much per-suasion to talk the unscrupulous captain and scurvy lot of seamen to tell him where Moira was being imprisoned. And he owed it all to Spence and his foresight in bringing help. He could have handled Mayhew alone, but defeating an entire ship's crew single-handedly went beyond his ca-pabilities. It never dawned on Jack that Moira's abductor would take her out of the country.

Fearing that Moira had been hurt, Jack stumbled down the ladder. When he reached the bottom, he heard a rus-tling noise and ducked instinctively. He felt the breeze from a heavy object ruffle his hair as it missed him by scant inches. Had it hit him, it would have fractured his skull. He cursed roundly. He'd been so intent on finding Moira that he'd thrown caution to the wind.

Moira froze, the crowbar slipping from her nerveless fingers. "Jack?" She'd recognize his voice anywhere. It was as familiar to her as her own, and dearer. The crowbar hit the deck with a resounding thunk.

Jack whirled on his heel when he heard her voice. "Moira? Is that you? Dear God, please let it be you." He opened his arms and Moira unerringly found her way into them, guided by the light of his unquenchable love.

Sobbing quietly into his chest, Moira clung to Jack with a desperation that was as great as his own. "I thought you were dead," she said. "Lord Roger said his henchmen killed you."

"I'm very much alive, sweetheart," Jack said soothingly, brushing her hair with his lips. "This time I'm going to make damn sure Mayhew never bothers us again. I've enough evidence against him to have him transported to the penal colony in Australia." He lifted her chin with his finger and found her lips with his.

"Is everything all right down there?"

Jack sighed and broke off the kiss. "We'd better leave before Spence and his men come charging down here to save us. Are you and the babe all right? Mayhew didn't hurt you, did he?"

"He never laid a finger on me," Moira said. "But if you hadn't come when you did . . ." Her sentence trailed off and she shuddered.

"You would have bashed Mayhew over the head and escaped," Jack said with a laugh. "Your ingenuity and courage never cease to amaze me. Let's go home, sweetheart."

Epilogue

Moira curled up against Jack, safe and content in their own bed. "Every time I think of how close I came to losing you, I get chills," Jack admitted, hugging her tightly. He placed a hand on the small mound of her stomach, cherishing the child that grew beneath her heart.

"You didn't lose me, Jack. I'm very much alive. I'm going to be here when Pettibone finally finds the nerve to ask Matilda to marry him and when Jilly and Colin decide to tie the knot. And I'm going to give you a healthy child. But right now, I want to think of us and no one else. I wanted to die when Lord Roger told me you were dead. I need you, Jack. Make love to me. Replace Lord Roger's vileness with your sweetness."

"I don't think it's wise, sweetheart. You've been through a lot and . . ."

Rising on her elbow, Moira shushed him with a kiss that sucked the breath from him. "Witch," he growled as he pulled her atop him. "Are you sure?"

"Very sure."

He roused her slowly, tenderly, with a thoroughness that brought tears to her eyes. Her breasts swelled against his mouth as he licked and sucked her nipples into erect buds, so sensitive she was inundated with waves of exquisite pleasure. The effect on Jack was profound, rendering him instantly hard, violently aroused. Everywhere Moira touched Jack was hard and tense and straining. Flipping her on her back, his lips blazed a trail down her body, lavishing careful attention on the hollow of her waist, the turn of her hip, the slightly convex roundness of her stomach, the satiny smoothness of her inner thigh.

Moira sighed and felt herself go liquid with need. Then he lowered his head and tasted her, his breath a scorching flame that licked erotically against her damp and dewy flesh. He groaned. She tasted tangy-sweet, and hot enough to scald him. She thrashed wildly as again and again he teased sleek, swollen recesses, passion-slick and wet. She whimpered, her hips unconsciously seeking a deeper union as his tongue sought her swollen core. A convulsive shudder wracked her as he brought her to the pinnacle of sensation.

Feeling himself losing control, he brought himself over her and, with a groan, plunged deep, embedded tight within her scorching heat. Again and again he came inside her, pumping with mounting frenzy. He felt his seed rising, felt his blood thickening, burning him from within, yet he held back, waiting for Moira. He was but a moment away from spilling himself when he felt her nails sink into his shoulders and heard her cry out.

Her cry echoed in his throat as he claimed her mouth in a kiss that gave full vent to his hunger, his love, his total commitment to his wife. He thrust harder, deeper, faster, until he felt the explosive force of her contractions.

His control shattered. With a cry of surrender, Jack joined his wife in a prolonged outpouring of bliss.

"I love you, Moira," Jack whispered moments before she slipped into peaceful slumber.

Sighing in perfect contentment, Jack held Moira against his chest and smiled when he thought about the son or daughter she would give him. Either would be welcome, he decided, imagining a child who looked like Moira.

The child is a boy.

Jack jerked his head from the pillow and searched the dark recesses of the chamber for Lady Amelia. She was standing by the door, clothed in light and mist, her face radiant.

"You manage to show up at the oddest times," he whispered so as not to awaken Moira. For the first time in his life he blushed, wondering if Lady Amelia had been present when he made love to Moira. "Are you positive Moira is going to give me a son?"

The child is a boy. But fear not, there will also be daughters.

"What? What did you say?"

You will have a son.

Lady Amelia folded her hands and smiled a secret smile. Jack watched in awe as her image flared with luminous intensity, forcing him to close his eyes. When he opened them again, she was gone, leaving naught but a pale flicker of light in her wake. Jack experienced an unaccountable sadness. He knew intuitively that his meddling ancestor had made her final visit. Hugging Moira tightly, he smiled wistfully. He was going to miss Lady Amelia.

Author's Note

Dear Readers,

This book is somewhat of a departure for me, but I hope you enjoyed it. Creating Lady Amelia was a delight. For my next book, I'm going back to the American West. I still depend on your letters to let me know what you enjoy. For a prompt reply, newsletter and bookmark, please enclose a self-addressed, stamped envelope. I regret that I cannot reply unless a stamped envelope is enclosed. I hope my readers will understand. Sometimes the letters become separated from their SASE, and unless your address is placed on the letter itself, I am unable to reply. I hate disappointing any of my readers. Write to me in care of Leisure Books at the address listed at the front of this book.

All my romantic best,
Connie Mason

SIERRA
Connie Mason

Bestselling Author Of *Wind Rider*

Fresh from finishing school, Sierra Alden is the toast of the Barbary Coast. And everybody knows a proper lady doesn't go traipsing through untamed lands with a perfect stranger, especially one as devilishly handsome as Ramsey Hunter. But Sierra believes the rumors that say that her long-lost brother and sister are living in Denver, and she will imperil her reputation and her heart to find them.

Ram isn't the type of man to let a woman boss him around. Yet from the instant he spies Sierra on the muddy streets of San Francisco, she turns his life upside down. Before long, he is her unwilling guide across the wilderness and her more-than-willing tutor in the ways of love. But sweet words and gentle kisses aren't enough to claim the love of the delicious temptation called Sierra.

_3815-3 $5.99 US/$6.99 CAN

Sheik's Glory

CAROLE HOWEY

Bestselling Author Of *Touched By Moonlight*

Missy Cannon is a woman who doesn't have time for fancy dresses or sweet talk. The no-nonsense horse trainer is looking for a brood mare, and she is bound and determined to get the best money can buy. Then a run-in with a riled filly leaves the untouched hellion as skittish as the animal itself—especially after a charming rogue rescues her and stirs a longing she cannot deny.

But Flynn Muldaur isn't after Missy's heart: He wants her South Dakota ranch. Gambling has won him half the spread, and she fears he will use any conniving trick or seductive strategy to get the rest. Yet the harder Missy fights Flynn, the more she realizes she wants him, needs him, and will risk all she possesses to have him.

_3903-6 $5.50 US/$7.50 CAN

SWEET CHANCE

CAROLE HOWEY

Bestselling Author Of *Sheik's Promise*

Paris Delany is out to make his fortune, and he figures cattle ranching is as good a way as any. But the former Texas Ranger hasn't even set foot in Chance, Wyoming, before his partner becomes smitten with the local schoolmarm. Determined to discourage the match, he enlists the help of a sharp-tongued widow—and finds himself her reluctant suitor.

Pretty, reserved, and thoroughly independent, Cressida Harding has loved and lost one husband, and that is enough for her. She doesn't need a man to stand up for her rights or protect her from harm, even if dumb luck has brought virile Paris Delany to her doorstep. But the longer he is in town, the more Cress finds herself savoring the joys of sweet chance.

_3733-5 $4.99 US/$5.99 CAN

Sheik's Promise

Carole Howey
Bestselling Author Of *Sweet Chance*

Allyn Cameron has never been accused of being a Southern belle. Whether running her own saloon or competing in the Rapids City steeplechase, the brazen beauty knows the thrill of victory and banks on winning. No man will take anything she possesses—not her business, not her horse, and especially not her virtue—without the fight of his life.

An expert on horseflesh and women, Joshua Manners desires only the best in both. Sent to buy Allyn's one-of-a-kind colt, he makes it his mission to tame the thoroughbred's owner. But his efforts to win Allyn for his personal stable fail miserably when she ropes, corrals, and brands him with her scorching passion.

_51938-0 $4.99 US/$5.99 CAN

Touched By Moonlight

CAROLE HOWEY

Bestselling Author Of *Sweet Chance*

Terence Gavilan can turn a sleepy little turn-of-the-century village into a booming seaside resort overnight. But the real passion of his life is searching for Emma Hunt, the mysterious and elusive creator of the tantalizing romances he admires. When he finds her, he plans to prove that real life can be so much more exciting than fiction.

To the proper folk of Braedon's Beach, Philipa Braedon is the prim daughter of their community's founding father. Yet secretly, she enjoys swimming naked in the ocean and writing steamy novels. Philipa has no intention of revealing her double life to anyone, especially not to a man as arrogant and overbearing as Terence Gavilan. But she doesn't count on being touched by moonlight and ending up happier than any of her heroines.

_3824-2 $5.50 US/$7.50 CAN

Dorchester Publishing Co., Inc.
65 Commerce Road
Stamford, CT 06902

Please add $1.75 for shipping and handling for the first book and $.50 for each book thereafter. NY, NYC, PA and CT residents, please add appropriate sales tax. No cash, stamps, or C.O.D.s. All orders shipped within 6 weeks via postal service book rate. Canadian orders require $2.00 extra postage and must be paid in U.S. dollars through a U.S. banking facility.

Name _____

Address _____

City _____ State _____ Zip _____

I have enclosed $_____in payment for the checked book(s).

Payment <u>must</u> accompany all orders.☐ Please send a free catalog.

Scoundrel
Debra Dier

"A sparkling jewel in the romantic adventure world of books!"
—*Affaire de Coeur*

Emily Maitland doesn't wish to rush into a match with one of the insipid fops she has met in London. But since her parents insist she choose a suitor immediately, she gives her hand to Major Sheridan Blake. The gallant officer is everything Emily desires in a man: He is charming, dashing—and completely imaginary. Happy to be married to a fictitious husband, Emily certainly never expects a counterfeit Major Blake to appear in the flesh and claim her as his bride. Determined to expose the handsome rogue without revealing her own masquerade, Emily doesn't count on being swept up in the most fascinating intrigue of all: passionate love.

_3894-3 $5.50 US/$7.50 CAN

DECEPTIONS & DREAMS
DEBRA DIER
Bestselling Author Of *A Quest Of Dreams*

"With her bright talent, intelligent voice, and elegant prose, Debra Dier creates characters we can believe in and stories we can experience."
—Connie Rinehold, author of *More Than Just A Night*

Sarah Van Horne can outwit any scoundrel who tries to cheat her in business. But she is no match for the dangerously handsome burglar she catches in her New York City town house. Although she knows she ought to send the suave rogue to the rock pile for life, she can't help being disappointed that he is after a golden trinket—and not her virtue.

Confident, crafty, and devilishly charming, Lord Austin Sinclair always gets what he wants. He won't let a locked door prevent him from obtaining the medallion he has long sought, nor the pistol Sarah aims at his head. But the master seducer never expects to be tempted by an untouched beauty. If he isn't careful, he'll lose a lot more than his heart before Sarah is done with him.

_3674-6 $4.99 US/$5.99 CAN

Dorchester Publishing Co., Inc.
65 Commerce Road
Stamford, CT 06902

Please add $1.75 for shipping and handling for the first book and $.50 for each book thereafter. NY, NYC, PA and CT residents, please add appropriate sales tax. No cash, stamps, or C.O.D.s. All orders shipped within 6 weeks via postal service book rate. Canadian orders require $2.00 extra postage and must be paid in U.S. dollars through a U.S. banking facility.

Name _____
Address _____
City _____ State _____ Zip _____
I have enclosed $_____ in payment for the checked book(s).
Payment <u>must</u> accompany all orders.☐ Please send a free catalog.